Susan Duncan took up a cadetship on the Melbourne *Sun* which led to a 25-year career spanning radio, newspapers and magazines. She quit journalism after her brother and husband died within three days of each other and eventually wrote the best-selling memoir *Salvation Creek*. Later branching into fiction, she wrote about good communities creating a sense of belonging and leading to contentment.

Susan now alternates between boats on Pittwater and raising cattle at Wherrol Flat with her second husband Bob, writing occasionally for *The Australian Women's Weekly*.

SUSAN DUNCAN

SLEEPLESS IN STRINGYBARK BAY

ALLEN&UNWIN
SYDNEY · MELBOURNE · AUCKLAND · LONDON

First published in 2023

Allen & Unwin
Cammeraygal Country
83 Alexander Street
Crows Nest NSW 2065
Australia
Phone: (61 2) 8425 0100
Email: info@allenandunwin.com
Web: www.allenandunwin.com

Allen & Unwin acknowledges the Traditional Owners of the Country on which we live and work. We pay our respects to all Aboriginal and Torres Strait Islander Elders, past and present.

A catalogue record for this book is available from the National Library of Australia

ISBN 978 1 76106 796 9

Set in 12.5/18 pt Adobe Garamond Pro by Bookhouse, Sydney
Printed and bound in Australia by the Opus Group

10 9 8 7 6 5 4 3 2

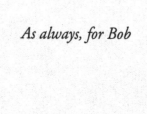

As always, for Bob

CHAPTER ONE

WALKING IN THE SHALLOWS OF the bay, Ettie Brookbank wriggled her toes in the cool sand, sidestepped a starfish and raised her eyes to delight in the sight of frothy pink clouds skittering along the horizon. Blessed, she thought, smiling inwardly. I am blessed. To be sure her joy didn't inflame those capricious gods who hid around corners, determined to pounce on a person's good fortune and send it crashing to the ground, she reached to touch the timber piles supporting the Briny Café. The haphazard construction of planks silvered by the sea and sun, perched on oyster-encrusted pylons, had a slightly cartoonish lean towards the east, courtesy of the August westerlies which, in a big blow, could reduce the lot to toothpicks. 'Touch wood,' she said aloud. Then she laughed. Science trumped superstition. Hadn't she heard it repeated like a mantra for the current age? Time to move into the twenty-first century, Ettie, she told herself.

It was an hour before opening. Time to mise en place, as her beloved Marcus, a retired chef, would say. Get everything in

order before unlocking the doors for the first hordes of hungover
tradies to stampede inside for a caffeine fix. Youth, she thought, without envy. She wouldn't swap places with them for a small fortune. Or
even a large one. At fifty-five, she had never been happier in her life.
A good man to lie alongside at night. A clever and committed business partner, Kate Jackson, to steer the Briny Café from loss to profit.
A community of like-minded eccentrics with an unshakeable belief
that kindness had the power to pummel evil into oblivion. Replete,
she thought, that's how she felt. She gathered her voluminous tie-
dyed skirts, stepped from the shallows and clambered up the slippery
seawall to the Square, the shabby offshore community hub and drop-
off point for the local ferry where celebrations, funerals, protests,
environmental campaigns and business deals sealed with a handshake took place at scarred picnic tables shaded by tired casuarinas.

'Did you see what Glenn's up to, Ettie?'

'Sam! Lord, you gave me a fright.'

'Well, if you weren't so caught up in those dreams that are makin''
your face all mushy and rosy, you would have seen Glenn's punt
weighed down with goods and chattels headed for the resurrected
sandstone shack at the end of Stringybark Bay with the most
expensive jetty in Cook's Basin—four hundred thousand dollars
according to the grapevine that's more reliable than a newspaper.
Reckon the new owners will live like kings until they check out
for the next destination, wherever that might be since not even
Kate—brilliant journalist that she was before switching from print
to pies—has interviewed anyone who's made the return trip.'

'Speaking of pies, I'd best get to work or I'll never catch up.'

'Kate's ahead of you. Said she might as well get started instead of lyin' awake thinkin' about it while the bub played World Cup soccer against her ribs.'

'Not long to go now. You and Kate will make wonderful parents. And I'll enjoy having a baby around the café,' Ettie said.

Sam shook his head: 'While I'm fully aware of the importance of a decent meal and a sublime cup of coffee, this little sailor is destined for the gleaming deck of the *Mary Kay*. Rocked by the gentle pulse of the sea under the hull and eyes open to the glory of nature from day one.'

Ettie sighed with a hint of resignation. 'Ah, Sam, you and your dreams . . .'

He raised his eyebrows at her. 'And aren't we both living proof that after the storm there's always another sunrise, heralding a day filled with glorious potential?'

Ettie laughed and made a gagging gesture.

A voice rang out from the deck of the Briny Café: 'You two going to chat all day? There's work to be done. And Sam, Jimmy just called to say he can see you wasting time from the jetty while he and Longfellow are waiting to be picked up.'

Sam turned to salute the rounded figure of Kate, standing in a shaft of golden sunshine. 'Gettin' bossier and bossier, like she's practising her moves for motherhood.'

'Here's your coffee,' Kate said, coming over to hand him a giant reusable mug. Standing on tiptoes—Sam was a shade over six foot two—she planted a kiss on his cheek.

He smiled his thanks. 'See you for brekkie in a couple of hours,' he said. He was a man overloaded with good fortune, he knew, and he had the good sense to recognise the fact.

⁓

Sam strolled the short distance along the seafront from the Square to Cargo Wharf, where his cherished, canary-yellow working barge, the *Mary Kay*, was securely tied to bollards. He checked the landscaping material lined up on the deck in massive white bulka bags, ready for delivery to the new house in Stringybark Bay, kicking the sides to test their stability. Even on a dead calm morning, the wake of a passing stink boat could shift the balance, placing man and vessel in jeopardy. Satisfied, he untied, stepped on board, made his way to the wheelhouse and turned the key. The engine thrummed, deep-throated and guttural. He spun the helm with a single finger and headed east at a steady pace, towards Cutter Island, a mound of earth, rock and towering spotted gums rising out of the sea and dotted with a chaotic collection of boatsheds and houses of every conceivable architectural style, depending on the often fluctuating financial circumstances of the owners.

On the far shore, Sam could see young Jimmy, his first mate, pacing restlessly, his ever-patient black-and-white border collie, Longfellow, by his side. Around him, the residents of Cook's Basin were clambering into their tinnies for the commute from their island homes to the mainland and the end of the working week. A challenge on days when the wind whipped the sea into a bucking roil or the rain came down in iron sheets, but even a veiled hint that a bridge to the mainland might be handy someday would see locals lining up to pack your bags and boot you in the direction of suburbia.

A few early starters waved sleepily as they passed. Sam raised a hand in response, slowed his speed. Some days were too perfect to rush, he thought, as the sun flecked the bay with shards like broken glass, dusting treetops with gold. He breathed deeply, the tang of salt air touching his lips like wine and travelling deep into his lungs. Although his preferred beverage, if he were asked to name it, was a frigidly cold ale.

'Where ya bin, Sam?' shouted Jimmy as soon as the *Mary Kay* glided into earshot. His purple shorts and magenta T-shirt surpassed the sunlight for brilliance.

The barge drifted alongside the weathered pontoon at the foot of the forty-two steps leading to the house where Sam had lived before he and Kate hooked up permanently and he shifted into her newly renovated home in Oyster Bay.

Jimmy, bending to check Sam's docking skills, gave a low whistle. 'Couldn't even fit me finger in the gap without riskin' losing it.'

'I'm a genius, mate,' Sam agreed, 'no doubt about it. Now you and the mutt get on board quick smart so we can offload and be back in time for a slap-up feed at the Briny.'

'Ya shoulda told me earlier. Me mum's just made me eat me Weet-Bix.'

'How many this morning? The usual twenty-two?'

Jimmy, laughing, jumped aboard, followed by his furry companion. 'You're a card, Sam. Ya know it's always twenty.'

'That's okay then,' Sam said, steering the barge in a tight circle, checking her matronly beam was clear of the pontoon before deftly dodging a flotilla of yachts rarely freed from their moorings. 'Plenty of room left for a mushroom omelette and one of Ettie's famous raspberry muffins.'

Jimmy frowned, absent-mindedly rubbed Longfellow's silky black ear as he considered the options. Eventually, he said: 'Skip the mushrooms; I'll have eggs and bacon, and if I can't cop the lot, Longfella'll help me out.'

'Done deal!' Sam said, ruffling the boy's carrot hair, instantly regretting the gesture. He wiped a glug of gel on the sides of his navy shorts.

In the wheelhouse, the man and the boy were silent. They passed sleepy bays, large bites out of the shoreline: Oyster, Blue Swimmer, Kingfish, all stirring under the first fingers of sunlight. 'Stringybark's next,' Jimmy announced, as if Sam might need reminding.

The barge, handcrafted from seasoned spotted gum, cypress pine, huon and jarrah as tough as iron, slipped smoothly towards its destination. Sam checked his watch and the anxiety that conjoined with Jimmy's restless feet rocketed to the surface. 'Are we late, Sam? We gunna have to pay hell?'

Sam gave the boy a reassuring smile. 'All good, Jimmy. Why wouldn't we be with a first-class first mate like you on board?'

The boy's frown eased.

Sam remembered the day Jimmy's mother told him a doctor had insisted her only child would need medication to tie down his feet and focus his thoughts if he were to function satisfactorily in the wider world. Sam had disagreed; pinning down a golden spirit like Jimmy's would be an act of ignorant savagery, he told her. Time had proved him right, although there'd been some stellar bumps along the way. In any other environment, they might have damaged the kid beyond repair, but in Cook's Basin, people took care of each other in ways so subtle they were mostly unseen and therefore bypassed debts of gratitude, which in turn left everyone on an equal footing. Mind you, he thought, Amelia's prison sentence—her quest to build a nest egg for Jimmy having led her to rort social service payments—had left the kid vulnerable. Sam had moved Jimmy into his house and employed him as a deckhand to keep him out of trouble till his mum was released. Now he thought the *Mary Kay* would be a dull and dreary old girl without energetic Jimmy in his equally energetic clothes, and the gentle mutt curled in his basket in the wheelhouse.

'Destination in sight. Jimmy, standby to tie up at that spiffy new jetty,' Sam ordered. 'Wait—show me your hands first.'

Jimmy held them out obediently.

'Right, well if the new owner offers to shake your mitt, you're good to go. Okay, hop to it.'

The kid bolted from the wheelhouse, spindly legs and arms wheeling, and grabbed a stern line. He stood straight-backed, chin thrust forward, a sailor ready for royal inspection—aside from some muted toe-tapping.

Ahead, a silvery tangle of mangroves hovered over a turquoise lagoon embraced by a haphazard ring of boulders, a sandy beach. 'Bloody magic,' Sam whispered, trying and failing to suppress a twinge of envy. It was an unfamiliar emotion for a man who cherished simple pleasures. He chewed his bottom lip thoughtfully, trying to work out the source of his sudden desire for more than he'd ever need. Kate and the bub, he thought. He'd give them the world, if he could find a way to gift-wrap it.

By the time he throttled back to come alongside the jetty, he'd consoled himself with the knowledge that love trumped bricks and mortar, and too much of a good thing could do more harm than good. He leaned out of the wheelhouse and yelled: 'Tie us on, Jimmy. Tight as a . . .' He bit his tongue. He'd have to watch his language once the baby was born. 'Yeah, good and tight, Jimmy,' he added, almost demurely.

'Gotcha, Sam. Tight as a cat's—'

'No need to spell it out. Now look tall. Here comes the new owner.' A man was striding briskly down the jetty, immaculate in pressed khaki chinos, polished tan boat shoes and navy polo shirt. Sam glanced curiously at the ramp designed to accommodate physical frailty. For his wife, perhaps? A grandchild? With his own progeny so close to entering the world, he shied away from the thought of a child in a wheelchair.

'Sam Scully,' he said, stepping off the barge, a grin on his face and his powerful, work-callused hand thrust out in greeting. 'And this here is Jimmy. First mate.'

The kid puffed a chicken chest and followed Sam's lead, offering his hand. The left one.

'A southpaw, eh? Supposed to mean a creative mind. Good to meet you, son.' Without missing a beat, Cook's Basin's newest arrival shook Jimmy's hand, left to left. Then he turned to Sam. 'Mike Melrose. Welcome to GeriEcstasy.' A traditional handshake this time, strong and firm, but the hand looked about twenty years older than the face.

'Helluva a name for a house,' Sam said, deciding it wasn't his business if a bloke fancied a few nips and tucks to boost his morale.

Melrose looked at the word scorched onto a large square of timber hanging by chains from the handrails at the end of the jetty. 'You don't approve?'

'Didn't say that, mate. Live and let live, the Cook's Basin motto.'

Melrose grinned, revealing a perfect set of blindingly white teeth. 'Good to hear. Now, follow me and I'll show you the spot to unload. Things are a little chaotic up at the house. It's taken longer than we thought to move in our belongings.'

'Standby, Jimmy. I'll be back in a sec.'

The two men set off along a jetty as long as a country train platform. 'Saw Glenn heading your way earlier. Everything go okay?'

'Couldn't have managed without him.'

Sam hid his relief. Glenn's removals were legendary, mostly for the wrong reasons.

'Five truckloads of furniture were delivered yesterday on the garbage truck barge. Took six hours. No one mentioned the fact that the barge could only handle two trucks at a time. Glenn handled the leftovers with care and caution. Er, that punt of his ever sink?'

'Five trucks!' Sam exclaimed, sidestepping the issue of Glenn's punt's seaworthiness.

'Five households,' Melrose said. 'Even reduced to a bare minimum, it added up to enough stuff to fill a department store.'

Sam shook his head. 'Well, mate, if you don't mind me saying, I hope you folks all get along, 'cause if someone has a tantrum, the closest five-star billet is a three-day hike. Quicker by boat, of course, if you're planning to invest in a runabout one day.'

Melrose laughed. The sun caught his teeth. Sam almost had to close his eyes against the glare. 'Fair point,' Melrose said. 'It's a risk but a calculated one. Most of us have known each other since university, and even married within the group. Drifted in different directions after kids and grandkids, but we made it a mission to get together for every birthday. Kept the connections strong. GeriEcstasy is our last-ditch adventure.'

'Your idea, all this?' Sam asked, waving his hand in the direction of the glamorous house, the sparkling water and the forest of mangroves, deciding it wasn't his place to mention the unrelenting isolation of offshore living.

Melrose, settling into the role of lord of the manor, continued in the warm tones of a born storyteller. 'About ten years ago—it was a birthday, can't remember whose—we were sitting around a dinner table with a couple of bottles of good red wine and the talk turned to old age and the amount of money we'd need to live well until the end. None of us had quite enough. I came up with the idea to pool our resources and see if we could raise a decent enough sum to buy our way into geriatric nirvana.'

'Ten years, eh? Long time between drinks.'

'Yeah. Seemed like a pipe dream until I went on a bushwalk in the national park and got hopelessly lost. I struck out in the direction of what I hoped was the coast and found a dump of a house with a derelict jetty. I spotted the mangroves and, beyond them, water spun with blue and gold.' Melrose gestured expansively, taking in the jetty, the mangroves. 'It was like an epiphany. Saw all our futures unrolling in peace and beauty, with enough challenges to keep us stimulated.'

'You know much about boats?'

Melrose laughed, continued along the jetty. 'Not a thing. That's the beauty of our sea change. Always new skills to be learned and mastered. Essential at this stage of our lives, to avoid feeling redundant.'

They reached the shore and Melrose pointed at a seawall. A few sandstone blocks had broken loose and tumbled onto the sandy beach, and more were on the verge of following. 'That's where we need the fill, Sam. Next big storm we'll lose the lot if we don't reinforce the bank. Reckon you can nose in close enough to dump the soil in all the damaged spots?'

Sam scratched his chin. 'Need a king tide to do it right, do it once.' He fished in his hip pocket for his mobile phone, hit a few buttons, squinted at the screen. 'Nothing suitable for a week, and then it's a midnight job.'

Melrose's face showed his disappointment. 'I should know by now that nothing is ever going to be straightforward when you're working with boats and tides. Should've checked with you first. My mistake.'

'Feel for you, mate. Best we can do is offload on the jetty and come back to finish off next week. It's a bugger, but a better option than barrowing dirt from the drop-off.'

'Yeah. Makes sense. So, what's the bottom line?'

'It'll take more time at night. Might want to factor in an extra hour or two, tops. Same hourly rate, though.'

Melrose held out his hand to shake on the deal, his expression easing. 'It's not easy being chancellor of the exchequer for the group. There's a strict budget and no provision for blowouts barring a tsunami—and every extra cost means one less bottle of vintage red.' He grinned. A joke.

Sam missed the irony. 'Look after the pennies and the pounds'll take care of themselves, eh? My partner Kate—she's co-owner of the Briny Café—swears by that approach. Seems to work.'

'Kate? She's the one who's pregnant?'

Sam stared at the steel-capped toes of his work boots, a shy but proud smile lifting the corners of his mouth. 'Yeah. Our first kid.'

'Congratulations! Make sure you drop by for a glass of champagne to celebrate the birth. Our wives are baby mad, and with grandchildren scattered from one end of the continent to the other, they're missing them like mad. Soon as I tell them, they'll start knitting. Boy or girl?'

'Still a mystery. I'm betting a boy. Kate's sure it's a girl.'

'Long as it's healthy, right?'

Sam nodded, suppressing a sudden surge of queasiness. 'Might as well start unloading,' he said, to shake loose his fear. 'Jimmy!' he shouted. 'Roll up your sleeves, mate. We've got work to do.' Sam turned back to Melrose. 'When's the rest of the group arriving?' he asked.

'Tomorrow morning. We're meeting at the Square, pausing for coffee and cake at the Briny Café, then we've booked a water taxi— Freddy, is that his name?—to ferry us to our new home.' He paused, the expression on his face switching from anticipation to something more solemn. 'Beginning of the end, I suppose.'

'May that end be decades away,' Sam said magnanimously. 'Give me a hoy when you're all seated at the Briny. I'll drop by and introduce you to the magnificent women who keep the louts, layabouts and hard sloggers of Cook's Basin fed and watered.'

'Very kind of you, Sam. We're looking forward to meeting the locals and settling in as quickly as possible. Does the café do deliveries?'

Sam, about to say no, instead did a quick calculation in his head. Five households equalled five couples, which equalled ten orders at a time. A worthwhile sale for the café and the delivery could turn into an extra little earner for young Jimmy. 'Anything's possible, mate, weather permitting. I'll run the request past the bosses.'

He set off, felt a pang at the thought of his dirty work boots leaving marks, then shrugged. That's what rain was for. The great floating cosmos always had a solution if you looked and listened hard enough.

CHAPTER TWO

IN THE WAKE OF THE tradie breakfast rush and before the shuffling arrival of grey-haired lunchtime swanners with time on their hands, Sam and Jimmy tied the barge alongside the rear deck of the café. 'Stay where you are, mate, and I'll order for you,' Sam said.

The kid pouted. 'Aw, Sam, I know you're just tryin' to sneak a few more greens on me plate but it won't do you no good. Me stomach's not programmed for them.'

Sam sighed and relented. 'Okay. Take a seat at a table and I'll be back in a minute.'

He weaved his way through the assortment of chairs painted in rainbow colours and scratched tables, each adorned with a cactus in a small pot. Two cumquat trees, golden fruit hanging like Christmas baubles, claimed the sunniest corners. At the front counter, where Ettie's baked goods sat temptingly on white plates, Sam placed an order for bacon and eggs, a mushroom omelette, coffee and a green smoothie, then he informed Ettie of the GeriEcstasy crew's plan to visit the café the following morning.

Ettie, her blonde hair frizzing in the heat from the oven as she checked the doneness of a cake, turned to face Sam, her face pink and shiny with perspiration. 'This about the barge business this morning?' she asked.

Sam nodded. 'The population of Stringybark Bay has increased by ten.'

'Kate!' Ettie called to the kitchen, 'I'm on a break. Jenny, pull the cake out of the oven in three minutes.'

She followed Sam outside. Jimmy was sitting at a table on the deck within touching distance of the barge, holding his knife and fork in readiness.

'Tell me everything,' she said, eyebrows raised in anticipation of juicy details.

Sam, as if oblivious to her eagerness, addressed his first mate. 'I ordered you eggs and bacon, and a fancy new drink for you, Jimmy,' he said. 'Not going to tell you what's in it, though—you'll have to guess. But trust me, you're going to love it.'

Jimmy eyed him suspiciously. 'I can see you're crossin' your fingers, Sam, so you're tellin' me a porky pie.'

'Well, there might be a hint of spinach . . .'

'Argh!'

'But there's lots of other stuff. All good.' He pulled out a chair and, sitting down next to Ettie, opened a newspaper he'd grabbed from the counter, spinning out the suspense until the kid couldn't take Ettie's agony a moment longer.

'Five couples, Ettie,' Jimmy said. 'All movin' in together till they cark it.'

'Thanks for stealing my thunder and you just earned a double dose of spinach,' Sam said.

'Aw, Sam, Ettie was fit to bust.'

The screen door burst open with ear-splitting reluctance. Jenny appeared and placed two overloaded plates on the table. Jimmy checked the ingredients and failed to find a hint of green. Grinning, he plucked a couple of bits of bacon from his plate and wrapped them in a serviette. Catching Ettie's querying look, he said: 'For Longfella, who's waitin' in the wheelhouse of the *Mary Kay*.'

Ettie smiled. 'Good boy. Kindness never goes astray.' She turned narrowed eyes on Sam. 'Spill the beans.'

Sam attacked his omelette with a vengeance. Jenny returned with the drinks. At the sight of a tall glass filled with green foam, Jimmy's eyes popped with alarm. 'Ah, Sam, jeez . . .'

'Give it a go, mate. You might even like it!'

'If you don't dish the dirt right now, Sam Scully, you'll be hit with a lifetime ban from the Briny,' Ettie threatened.

Sam laid down his knife and fork. 'Can't tell you much more than Jimmy did, Ettie. Five couples who've been friends for decades have pooled their resources to spend their twilight years in the paradise of Cook's Basin. The house restoration looks a treat. Not that I set foot inside, but even from the outside it's pretty impressive. All sandstone and white timber trim. The jetty is an engineering marvel, and the bloke who calls himself chancellor of the exchequer looks like he might have been a TV or film star in his youth.' He paused, a frown on his face. 'Can't say why, but I thought of an Agatha Christie novel where people gather for a house party and one by one they drop off the perch. Maybe 'cause they're all pretty old—wasn't thinking murder or anything like that. I reckon what they're doing takes guts. Least they didn't go for the closest location to a hospital.'

Jimmy, meanwhile, had bolted his food. Arranging his knife and fork together on his empty plate the way his mother had drilled into him, he asked to be excused to give Longfellow his treat. The smoothie was untouched. 'Sorry, Sam. Just can't go there. Me stomach's doin' cartwheels at the thought of it.'

Ettie took pity on the kid: 'Carry your plate inside and you're free to go.'

Jimmy did as instructed, then leaped aboard the *Mary Kay*. Longfellow greeted him as though they'd been separated for an age. Ettie and Sam smiled at the sight of Jimmy doling out the bacon in tiny morsels that the dog plucked delicately from his fingers, then turned their attention back to the subject of GeriEcstasy.

'They're arriving tomorrow,' Sam said. 'Planning on stopping here for coffee and cake on the way to their new life.'

'Ten people, all elderly, opting for a tough offshore life,' Ettie mused. 'Even Marcus and I have late-night discussions about what we'll do when commuting by boat becomes an unacceptable risk instead of an exhilarating and life-affirming challenge.' She sighed and pushed back her chair. 'Can't wait to meet them. They're either fools or incredibly brave. I'll set up a long table on the deck close to the kitchen. I don't want to miss a word.'

'Ettie!' Sam said, feigning shock. 'Never picked you for an eavesdropper.'

'Information is important in a community where we all depend on each other,' she said defensively, a warm blush rising from her chest to her cheeks.

Sam held up his hands. 'You don't have to explain. I'm with you all the way. Er, how's Kate managing?'

'She's fine, Sam. There's at least three whole months to wait and first babies are usually late. If anything happens, I'll call you. Now shift your barge from the end of the deck so my lunchtime customers can enjoy an uninterrupted view of sparkling blue water and yachts swinging on their moorings, all of which is built into the price of their food.'

'You're not suggesting the *Mary Kay* isn't a wonder to behold, are you?' he asked, twisting in his seat to gaze at the sturdy lines of his cherished vessel.

'Wouldn't dare. But not everyone appreciates a working boat tied so close to their table that if the wind suddenly whips up, they might get knocked out by the giant hook swinging from the end of the crane.'

'No accounting for taste, is there?' Sam said.

Ettie punched him lightly on the arm, then rose and gathered the dirty dishes in her arms. With a wink over her shoulder, she kicked open the flywire door and disappeared inside. In her wake, Sam caught the sound of humming: a song he remembered about a new world somewhere in a promised land. He hoped it turned out to be true for the new arrivals in Cook's Basin. No matter how you looked at it, what they were doing took courage. And courage, he told himself, should always be rewarded. If necessary, he'd rally the community to provide support. Communities looked after each other. And Cook's Basin did it better than most.

He sat a while longer, savouring the last drops of his coffee, fighting the urge to seek out Kate and place his two great hands on her belly. He'd give up breathing if it secured health and happiness for her and the baby. Who knew love came with such a heavy price tag? Not that he'd swap his current status for a second. He just wasn't used to carrying around a deep-gutted fear that refused to shift no matter how many times he reminded himself that worrying never solved anything.

He scanned the deck of the *Mary Kay*, looking for Jimmy. The boy and his mutt were seated side by side at the stern. For some reason, the sight made him feel as though his heart might break. 'Ah, jeez, Sam,' he muttered, 'have a cup of concrete and harden up or you'll be no good to man nor beast.'

He had three moorings to service and a stack of timber to pick up from Cargo Wharf for delivery to the south side of Cutter Island. Spring had sprung, and every man and his dog suddenly had a new project on the go. The deadline—as per usual—was Christmas. Christmas, he thought, his stomach heaving with sudden nerves. More than twenty years of rocking up as one of the waifs and strays that gathered at Ettie's celebration table and now he would have his own clan. How did he get so bloody lucky? He dabbed at a drop of moisture in the corner of his eye. And how come love made you so bloody vulnerable?

Sam stood and, giving himself a mental shake, jumped aboard the *Mary Kay*, landing so lightly the vessel barely rocked.

'Runnin' late again, Sam,' Jimmy said accusingly. 'Me mum says it's baby brain. Says I shouldn't pressure you 'cause there's no help for it. Says you'll be back on track once Kate sprogs.'

'Thanks for the diagnosis, Jimmy. Now you going to stand there pontificating, or you gonna untie so we can earn a dollar or two before it's too dark to see where we're going?'

'Just sayin', Sam . . . No point shootin' the messenger—though me mum says that's normal, too.' He scurried away, laughing to himself. Longfellow, sensing they were about to cast off, trotted to his basket in the wheelhouse.

Sam started the engine and slipped into gear, sliding away from the Briny Café with hardly a ripple in the clear blue water. With the helm in his hands, the gentle sun warm on his neck, he was a man at one with the sea, his feet so exquisitely tuned to the rise and fall of the living water he struggled to find his balance on land.

CHAPTER THREE

THE FOLLOWING MORNING, SAM WOKE at first light and crept from the bedroom where Kate lay sleeping, her dark hair falling across her face untidily, her fists clenched tightly. Wearing boxer shorts and a T-shirt, he tiptoed along the hallway to the kitchen, where he filled the kettle. While he waited for the water to boil, he stepped onto the verandah. Overnight, a light wind had kicked in from the nor'east, bringing low-lying cloud and drizzly rain that landed like delicate dewdrops but quickly soaked to the skin. The morning was chilly and damp, thick with the fishy smell of low tide. Seagrass lay bowed in dark patches; the sandflats were smooth as a ballroom floor. A soft day, flat and windless, but it would be slippery as hell on a boat. He rubbed his arms and went inside.

Despite his care not to disturb her, he heard Kate's bare feet padding across the bedroom floor and down the hallway. She appeared by his side in loose, pale blue pyjamas, sleep-tousled and bleary-eyed. He slipped an arm around her waist, but she quickly slid away from him. 'Green tea for me, please.'

'Coming up,' he said, ignoring the rebuff, aware that the woman he loved would always be complicated, with deep undercurrents. 'How are you feeling?'

'Great.'

She sat at the kitchen table, dropping the last few inches in a rush and landing with an uncomfortable thud. She squeezed her eyes shut, her face scrunched tightly for a second or two.

'You okay?' he asked, looking at her closely, attempting to gauge her mood.

'Great,' she repeated, her tone flat.

He made the tea, placed the steaming mug in front of her. 'Toast?'

She nodded, sniffing, then wiped her nose on her wrist. The gesture set a siren blaring in Sam's head; Kate was meticulous in all things. He passed her a tissue. She took it without a word.

'Jam, Vegemite or marmalade?' he asked.

'Just butter.'

'More tissues?'

She shook her head.

He poured his own tea, strong and dark, and sipped while the bread toasted. He placed a butter dish, knife, plate and napkin in front of her. Delivered the toast in a fancy silver rack, fumbling just a little as he lined up the slices. Rituals, he understood, gave her comfort, a sense of control. He gulped more tea, swallowing silently. The sound of a drink being noisily consumed made her cringe, she'd told him once. He waited silently, patiently, the way he had learned since he'd begun to leave his work boots at her back door and occupy one side of her bed.

'Are you sure I won't be a terrible mother like my mother?' she whispered. 'Are you certain I will be kind and caring instead of mean and jealous? Can I trust you when you say I won't bend this baby into someone bruised and broken, because that's how I've been programmed?' Tears slid down her face. Her lower lip trembled. She ignored the food, the tea, both hands resting on her stomach.

Sam took his time replying. Kate's mind and journalistic training were tuned to pounce on false words and gnaw away at them until she exposed the truth. His response had to be bare-bones honest. For Kate, lies—even those told with the utmost skill and even sincerity—sounded louder than a claxon. He settled for the simple facts as he saw them. 'You'll be a good mother, Kate.'

'Why?' she asked, testing him.

Again, Sam chose his words with the care honed by the experience of loving an emotionally damaged woman. 'Emily may have bruised you, but she didn't come anywhere near breaking you. You're tough, Kate, but you're also fair and deeply compassionate—although you try to hide it. And there's not a mean bone in your body.'

She brushed a strand of dark hair out of her eyes, tucked it behind an ear and smiled up at him tearily. 'Pass me the butter, please. And the jam. I could eat a horse.'

In quiet moments alone, Kate's history worried at him: her habit of bolting when she felt overwhelmed by curiosity, the pursuit of justice, anger. And bugger the consequences. Pregnancy had seemed to settle her, but recently he'd seen signs she was fighting to stay grounded in the café and Cook's Basin. Struggling not to feel trapped by the daily round of chores that anchored most of humanity. The time between her episodes of self-doubt seemed to be compressing and, despite her best intentions, it felt to him as though she had one foot out the door and the slightest trigger would send her rocketing into the blue beyond. Families, he thought, thinking of Kate's mother,

Emily, a rage-fuelled virago who'd made a lifelong habit of chiselling into her daughter's self-esteem—out of . . . what? Jealousy? Envy? Or the simple desire to destroy? He'd need a degree in psychiatry to figure that one out, he thought. Despite Emily's cruelty, under her cool aloofness, Kate was a kind and generous woman, but she was nobody's fool, and he admired that.

Since the pregnancy, though, he'd found it increasingly difficult to get her measure, judge her mood. Once, in a voice hushed with what he now understood was shame but which he'd initially mistaken as offhand, she'd told him that children terrified her. He'd responded laughingly that all prospective parents were filled with doubts and pointed out that babies were blissfully non-judgemental. She'd responded with a look that could have melted metal. He'd watched her carefully since then, been more careful with his choice of words, but no amount of reassurance seemed to help for long.

In a way, he realised, she was following the same path as Emily; Kate's pregnancy was unplanned and there was no ring on her finger. But the similarities ended there. This baby, unlike Kate's half-brother, would never be put up for adoption, taken to a home on the other side of the world to hide his existence. If Sam had his way, he would never let their child out of his sight.

He walked to the window and looked outside. The weather showed no signs of clearing. He considered postponing the delivery of Fast Freddy's new hot water tank until the sun came out, wondered at the same time if signing a marriage certificate might give Kate stability, signal his deep and abiding commitment. He briefly considered dropping to his knees and asking the big question, but without a ring to slip on her finger, the act could ring hollower than an old log. Instead, he said casually: 'You think we should tie the knot someday?'

Kate looked at him, astonished. 'Whatever for?'

'Thought you might want a fancy diamond ring and a gold band . . . or something.'

'We live together, Sam. I'm already entitled to half your worldly goods.' She mistook his look of hurt for one of alarm and added: 'You are also entitled to half of mine, so let's not worry about bureaucratic details, okay?'

He gave a wry grin. 'Whatever happened to romance?'

Kate shrugged, avoided his eyes.

'Word for the day,' he said, leaning against the sill, folding his arms, and attempting to ease a suddenly soured atmosphere.

She looked at him with raised eyebrows.

'Bumfle.'

'You made that up.'

'Nope. True as the day. Bumfle,' he repeated, smiling widely now.

She shrugged. 'Okay, I give up.'

'It means wrinkles in a fabric.'

'You're having me on.' She went to fetch the dictionary from her study. 'Can't find it anywhere,' she said, after a quick search. 'It's so good, though, I want it to be true. Bumfle. Imagine telling a bloke his shorts are bumfled.' She grinned. 'It's a classic. You sure it's correct?'

'Yep.' He nodded. Smug.

'Who told you?'

'Simon. On the island.'

'Ah.' She picked up a knife and added more butter to a dry corner of toast. 'Well, he'd know. English professors never really retire.'

'Anything else I can get you?' he asked when she'd finished eating.

She shook her head and he cleared away her plate, the delicate hand-painted Meissen porcelain cup and saucer she told him she'd picked up in a Marrakech market for next to nothing, placing them carefully in the sink.

'I'll wash up,' she said, pushing to her feet. She turned on the tap and reached under the sink for the detergent.

'I'll head for the shower then.'

The weather would lift, he figured, and it would take less than an hour to deliver the tank and Freddy probably had the electrician on standby anyway. Afterwards, he'd drop by the café and introduce the new residents of Stringybark Bay to the hub of the community.

He left the house whistling.

⁓

Saturday morning business was slow at the Briny. Although the drizzle had drifted out to sea where it wouldn't water gardens or fill tanks, the gloomy cloud cover kept the less stout-hearted punters indoors. Only the cyclists—resplendent in flaming fluoro colours that would make a rainbow lorikeet reach for sunglasses and emitting the strong meaty scent of eau de bicyclette—were out in packs. A few tucked into bacon-and-egg rolls slathered with Ettie's famous tomato relish, tickled with a hint of chilli or curry or both (no one was quite able to pinpoint the mix of spices and Ettie refused to divulge her secret recipe). Jenny had an equally loyal following for her blueberry pikelets. Having stepped in to help with the cooking (when Kate disappeared abruptly on a private mission to research her family history after her mother revealed the existence of a half-brother),

Jenny was now an indispensable member of the Briny crew. 'It's the orange zest that lifts them,' Jenny willingly divulged to devotees who waxed lyrical over the taste and lightness. She failed to mention the critical inclusion of buttermilk in the recipe. All good cooks, no matter how generous of spirit, had their limits.

By mid-morning, with the café tidied and ready for lunch and the drizzle once again drifting in from the sea, Kate was seated at her desk in the Briny's office. She checked invoices and filed accounts. Every so often, she swore softly and swapped one piece of paper for another until each landed in the right folder. She fought off drowsiness, determined to remain professional, but the desire to lay her head on the desk and surrender to sleep was almost overwhelming.

Ettie, concerned the damp weather might deter the newcomers to Stringybark Bay from calling in for morning tea and thus depriving her of firsthand knowledge of the group, directed Sam and Jimmy to reorganise the upstairs attic that Kate had transformed into a 'penthouse' to save Ettie the back-breaking trek up two hundred steps from the ferry stop at Triangle Wharf to her tiny cottage at the peak of Cutter Island. She'd lived happily above the café until she'd found the love of a good man at an age when she thought her best years were well and truly behind her.

'You're going to a lot of trouble, Ettie,' Sam said, turning tables and chairs towards the spectacular view, directing Jimmy to brush away cobwebs and dust the furniture.

'Newcomers need to know they're part of the community,' she replied airily. 'In the old days I would have cooked them a welcome dinner, but there's no time for that with the café to run so this is the best I can do.' She rummaged in a cupboard, emerged with a sea-green tablecloth, a few cushions and a vase. Returned the vase to a shelf and opted for a couple of old hurricane lanterns with candles inside. She stood back and checked her handiwork. 'It'll do. Now we wait. What time did you say they were arriving?'

'Sometime this morning is all I know. Melrose mentioned something about occasional takeaway orders, too. I know you draw the line at deliveries, Ettie, but remember it would be ten meals at a time, and if Jimmy wants to add another sideline to his worm enterprise, it could add up to a few windfalls here and there for you both.' Jimmy, showing hitherto unsuspected entrepreneurial instincts, had set up a lucrative business recycling the café's scraps and supplying islanders with rich compost for their vegetable plots.

The kid nodded enthusiastically. 'I could do it, Ettie! Rain or shine. And they're gunna be anchored and starving to death if they're short of food after a run of bad weather.'

'I'll think about it. I can see a couple of webs hanging from the balcony railing. Sweep them off, will you, Jimmy? Ruins the view.'

She went down the stairs, humming. Sam didn't recognise the tune this time.

～～

At 11 am, two low-slung, black stretch limousines surfed the sandy track from the sealed road to the Square and fishtailed to a standstill as the aged red-and-blue *Seagull* loomed out of the fog to thump hard against the ferry wharf, forcing passengers on the rear deck to brace themselves. 'You get out of the wrong side of bed this morning, Chris?' shouted one cheeky kid.

Chris Black, the ferry driver, a short-tempered man with a ruddy face and scaly hands, and on the edge of retirement, stepped ashore to wind a thick rope around a cleat, giving an extra tug. He straightened, hands on the small of his back as though to contain a twinge before it switched to a full-blown spasm. Gave the kid a filthy look.

Myrtle Skettle and her sister Violet, whom Chris regularly collected from their private jetty after a community vote endorsed the illegal practice when the twins turned eighty, as an incentive to prevent them using their boat, swept ashore, their string shopping bags over their arms. The community had also decreed free travel.

The rest of the passengers disembarked behind them, ambling towards the Square, where the sight of two shiny, sleek limos stopped them in their tracks. They looked at each other, confused. There'd been no talk of a wedding or a funeral. Clutching shopping bags, empty gas bottles, dragging dogs on leashes, they stampeded towards the café. Ettie would know the score.

Before they could breach the entrance, Sam appeared in the doorway and strode purposefully towards the cars. The crowd skidded to a halt. Watched. Waited.

Maybe, someone whispered, they were scouts searching for movie locations. Or celebrities who'd heard about Ettie's cooking. Or . . . well, as long as they weren't a bunch of property developers. The community had had enough of ratbags intent on wrecking the natural beauty of Cook's Basin with resorts and high-rise apartments.

The chauffeur emerged first from the nearest limo, but Sam beat him to the passenger door, which he opened with the flourish of a maritime Sir Galahad who'd swapped his armour for shorts, a T-shirt, boat shoes and a battered hat.

A skinny, tanned arm emerged, its wrist decorated with gold bracelets, followed by two slim legs encased in blue jeans, feet tucked into white tasselled loafers, then shining, silver hair, severely cropped, above a face nearly everyone in the Square felt was vaguely familiar, although they couldn't say why, even after she smiled enigmatically over their heads and then turned her back as though she'd given them more than their due.

Mike Melrose emerged next. Casually dressed in a sky-blue shirt and chinos so crisp they had to be new, he shook Sam's hand enthusiastically. 'Today's the day!' he said. 'The deed is done, for better or worse.'

'Cook's Basin is always for the better, mate,' Sam said.

Two men, deep in conversation, spilled out next. Again, their clothing was smarter than anything the average Cook's Basin resident would find in their wardrobe. One bloke, his hair neatly cut and peppered with a few strategically placed blond streaks, wore a pink-checked shirt and watermelon jeans. The other, more dishevelled but equally splendid, was dressed in pale lemon trousers topped with a flowing baby-blue linen shirt that didn't quite disguise an ample paunch.

Another couple exited the car on the far side. The woman, encased in a hot pink cotton dress that matched a racy pink streak down the middle of auburn, shoulder-length hair, had a smiling face and unflappable demeanour. Her husband was thin and spidery with spindly legs in tight blue jeans and a cowboy shirt.

A flaming head of fire-engine red hair appeared next, followed by a bald man whose face was anchored by a large nose. The redhead stumbled in the sand. 'Bugger!' she said. The bald head responded calmly: 'Told you not to wear stilettos.' The woman's red lips stretched so thin they became a single line. Definitely high maintenance, Sam decided.

Hardly anyone noticed a wheelchair materialise from the trunk of the second limousine and the chauffeur, a bruiser of a bloke in a dark suit stretched too tightly across his shoulders, gently lift a tiny, frail woman from the car with a concentrated tenderness mostly reserved for newborns. He settled her into the chair with a broad smile, as though it had been his privilege. A stooped, refreshingly understated man with grey hair and a ruddy complexion, wearing plain navy trousers and a white shirt with a navy sweater draped across his shoulders, appeared at her side and fussed with her cardigan, draped a light blanket over her knees. He tried to push the chair, bogged in the sand, towards the hard surface of the Square.

Sam leaped forward to help.

'Thank you, thank you. Not as strong as I used to be, but we manage, don't we, darling? I'm Rob James. My wife, Daisy.'

Daisy inclined her head, a small bird.

'Sam Scully,' Sam said.

One puff of wind, Sam thought, and Daisy James would be blown out to sea forever. Ettie was right. He was looking at a bunch of dreamers in denial. The grand plan would end in disaster. He was sure of it.

At that point, the crowd, still deeply interested, checked their watches, yelped as one, and took off in all directions. The grape-vine, while not always infallible, was at least as reliable as daybreak, and by early evening the story behind the two slick cars and their intriguing occupants would be recounted around every dinner table.

'It's raining, Mike. How long are were going to stand here drowning?' demanded the hauntingly familiar silver-haired woman.

Sam stepped forward. 'Mist, mostly,' he said, trying to be helpful. 'Not enough wet in it to curl your hair.'

'Right. Let's get going, shall we?' Melrose said quickly.

The fellow in blue linen produced a stick from under his arm that clicked into full length. The redhead limped along with a broken shoe in one hand, ignored by her husband, who refused to slow down to support her. The woman with the spiky silver hair seemed to have trouble with her balance, gripping Melrose's arm every so often as if to prevent falling. Daisy looked secure in her wheelchair. Pushing it, Rob radiated noble purpose. Spider man and his wife almost skipped along, holding hands, their heads bent in a private conversation that erupted occasionally in barely controlled giggles. In the rear, the man in watermelon trousers produced a colourful handkerchief and mopped his face repeatedly, even though the temperature was on the cool side of average. As they crossed the wonky paving of the Square, dodging the spindly leaves of a scrappy casuarina, they could have been a procession of aged tourists off a bus for a rest stop.

Sam shook his head. As far as he could judge, there were three people fit enough to survive a couple of years of boats, storms and offshore living. The others were casualties waiting to happen. An image of a queue of the recently condemned waiting their turn at the guillotine during the French Revolution popped into his mind. He shook his head to shake it loose, rushed to hold open the café door. 'Ettie,' he shouted, 'the GeriEcstasy mob has arrived!'

The group splintered to allow the spiky-haired woman to enter first.

Ettie looked up from stirring the batter for an orange and almond cake and then wobbled on her feet as alarmingly as the redhead wearing one high heel. 'Donna Harris,' she whispered, her eyes wide. 'Oh, my goodness. Donna Harris.'

Flustered, she thrust the mixing bowl at a bewildered Jenny, who was midway through preparing lunchtime sandwiches. 'Finish this, would you, love? I'll see to this customer myself.' She untied her floral apron, screwed it into a ball and shoved it under the counter, patted her fluffy hair into submission and sashayed from behind the counter with her shoulders back and her best meet-and-greet smile firmly in place. Her eyes were fixed on the woman she'd called Donna. Ignoring or completely oblivious to the rest of the group, including Daisy in her wheelchair, she said in a hushed tone implying a complicit understanding: 'I've given you a private table upstairs.'

She grabbed a stack of menus and proceeded to climb the stairs with the regal bearing of a maître d' at a five-star Parisian establishment.

The rest of the party lurched after her to the best of their ability until only Daisy, moored by her wheelchair, remained.

'Rob's gone to the loo and it seems like I've been abandoned by everyone else,' she said to Sam, giving a slight shrug as though it was of no consequence and she was used to being left behind.

'Not sure Ettie knew you were part of the group or she'd have come up with a plan B,' Sam said loyally.

'Don't worry. We're all used to being eclipsed by Donna,' Daisy assured him without rancour.

Sam, determined to preserve the honour of the offshore community, said: 'Fear not, Mrs James, I'll deliver you upstairs in one piece. All part of the service. What would you prefer—over the shoulder fireman-style, or bride in arms over the threshold?'

The woman's face lit up, her blue eyes sparkling in anticipation. 'Please, call me Daisy. And I must say, that's the most tempting offer I've had in a very long time.' She tapped her index finger on her bottom lip thoughtfully. 'Fireman-style. Yes. That will make a better story. We should wait until my husband returns, though. He'll think I've been abducted if he finds an empty wheelchair.'

Sam laughed, snared Kate's hand as she tried to squeeze past to help behind the counter. 'Kate, this is Daisy. She's moving into Stringybark Bay.'

'Hi,' Kate said, her eyes sliding over the wheelchair doubtfully.

'Crazy, isn't it?' Daisy said, as if sensing Kate's misgivings. 'But I already feel a new energy, and not many women of my age have the opportunity to be carried over the shoulder of a handsome man.'

'I'm not sure this is a great idea . . .' Kate began, thinking about liability and insurance coverage.

Rob appeared, beaming at his wife: 'There's tables out the back on the deck. Umbrellas, too. You and I can have our coffee and cake there.'

'No way.' Daisy shook her head. 'I've been offered a fireman's lift upstairs, darling. Be criminal to miss an opportunity to steal Donna's thunder for a minute or two.'

'Eh?' was all Rob managed to say, before Sam kneeled in front of the wheelchair, one shoulder angled for Daisy to drape herself over.

Kate closed her eyes. Rob looked terrified.

Sam rose to his feet without stumbling and patted Daisy's back, feeling a tremor of compassion at the brittle bones: 'Ready?' he asked quietly.

She grinned. 'Ride 'em, cowboy.'

When Sam appeared at the top of the stairs with a woman slung over his shoulder, there were cries of delight, a cheer.

Ettie rushed to make room at the head of the table. Sam strode across the floor and gently lowered Daisy safely onto the only chair with armrests. A cheer of appreciation erupted for a job well done.

'Thank you, Sam,' Daisy said. 'If I die tomorrow, it will be as a happy woman.' She tucked her hair behind her ears, gazed serenely around the table.

Rob pulled a chair close to his wife and found her hand, holding it tightly.

'Let me make the formal introductions,' Mike Melrose said. 'You've met Rob and Daisy James, of course. Former cattle farmers from central New South Wales. Survived droughts, floods, heatwaves and a six-week stretch of black frosts unscathed, until a cow thought Daisy was getting too close to her calf and took offence. The rest of this motley crew includes Brian Callaghan, whose colour sense is debatable, and his partner, Cameron Smith, known for his flaw-less taste. Formerly Melbourne antique dealers. Sheila and Gavin Flowerdale, also from Melbourne, were in the retail shoe business before retirement.'

Sheila waved her broken stiletto in acknowledgement. 'Six hundred bucks and busted beyond repair. Oh, and thanks for all your help, Gavin. Could've broken a leg for all you cared.'

'I warned you about wearing the shoes,' he replied mildly.

'Sally and David Kinane are from a small country town on the south coast of New South Wales, where they were hailed as the greatest cheesemakers outside south-west France. Now their kids run the business.' He paused, took a deep breath and made a small bow towards the silver-haired woman. 'Last, but certainly never least, my partner in all things, Donna. In her day, a household name, and to this day the light of my life.'

Donna looked as though she were about to say something but then changed her mind.

Ettie let go of a breath she didn't know she'd been holding. 'I knew it!' she whispered in Sam's ear. 'I'd know that face anywhere.'

Mike Melrose continued: 'As the lunatic who agreed with the crazy idea of setting up a communal home for a group of old friends in an environment that we hope will inspire a golden old age, I think a bottle of champagne is called for.'

The group—apart from a bored-looking Donna—cheered. 'Better to go out with a bang than a fizzle. All for one and one for all. Hooray!'

'The sun is over the yardarm somewhere in the world and it's my shout,' Melrose said.

'Mate, the café's not licensed . . .' Sam began.

Ettie interrupted, sounding a little panicky: 'I happen to have a bottle of bubbles in my private fridge that has been waiting for the right occasion. Think of it as a personal welcome to Cook's Basin, with the compliments of the Briny Café.'

Brian and Cameron grinned. Rob, adjusting the hearing aid tucked neatly behind his ear, struggled to pick up the gist of the conversation. Sally and David murmured their thanks. But Daisy James protested politely. 'No, no, that's far too generous . . .'

Donna Harris cut her off bluntly: 'Oh, let the woman get on with it, Daisy. Then we can all get out of this dump.'

The words struck Ettie like the blow from a hammer. She staggered backwards. Sam put out an arm to steady her. The table went silent.

Sally and David cut through the tension with what Ettie later thought of as the ease of experience: 'Look at the paintings on the walls, everyone—aren't they great? Especially the seagulls. Who's the artist?'

Ettie, still reeling from the unprovoked cruelty of a woman she'd once worshipped, whispered: 'I am!'

There were murmurs of appreciation. 'A talented artist as well as a great cook,' Daisy said warmly, reaching out a hand to Ettie.

'Is there no end to the talents of the people around here?' Donna muttered. She curled her fingers, inspected her bright red nails, avoided looking anyone in the eye.

Ettie, to cover her embarrassment, busied herself with finding an ice bucket, removing the champagne from the fridge, collecting glasses. She popped the cork, poured the drinks. Served Donna first and politely. She couldn't explain why, but she was absolutely certain that for her to succumb to cheap rudeness would lead not to a sense of victory but to a poverty of spirit she might never dislodge.

The atmosphere had curdled, though, and no one seemed to have the energy or inclination to make the effort to restore it to sweet equanimity. As soon as it was decently possible, Mike Melrose reminded the group that Fast Freddy, the man with the only water taxi big enough to seat the group, was due at the ferry wharf in a few minutes. The final leg of their journey to new beginnings awaited.

The champagne was sculled with relief.

'We'll leave the coffee and cake for another day,' Melrose said by way of an apology.

Ettie shrugged. She didn't trust herself to speak.

How, she wondered, did a woman who'd been the toast of an entire country turn into such a mean-minded narcissist? Or was that what it took to become the toast of a nation? Whatever the truth, the spell had been broken. From this moment forward, Ettie vowed silently, Donna was just another punter. If she wanted coffee or muffins from the Briny Café, she could queue up like everyone else. Reaching for the moral high ground, she made a point of looking into Donna's famous green eyes and warned her about the danger of slippery surfaces after the recent drizzle. Noticed, as though a curtain had been drawn aside, puffiness under the eyes and small broken veins inadequately camouflaged by the thick layer of make-up trowelled onto the once-flawless alabaster skin. Ettie's disdain melted into sympathy. For a woman worshipped for her incandescent beauty, old age had to be brutally offensive, pitiless.

'Do I look like a moron?' Donna hissed, pushing past Ettie to be first down the stairs.

'Takes all kinds,' Ettie said under her breath, ditching the moral high ground with relief.

Leaving her now-unwelcome guests to see themselves out, she retreated to the upstairs kitchen. There she filled the sink with hot soapy water and washed the glasses, then she whipped the table-cloth from the table and threw it in a laundry basket, straightened the chairs. She paused to take a deep breath, surveyed the space that had been a blessed refuge until Marcus arrived like a knight in shining armour to carry her off to his castle in Kingfish Bay, where he promised to rub her aching cook's feet for the term of his natural life. She felt a wave of nostalgia. Recalled the adrenaline rush of buying the Briny Café at an age when most people were planning their retirement, dreaming of how she would transform a crumbling wreck best known for toxic coffee, life-threatening egg-and-bacon rolls and deadly hamburgers. The thrill of her first night in a single bed in her 'penthouse'. Most of all, the joy of understanding she had a future in a place where she knew she belonged.

She heard the unmistakable thrum of Fast Freddy's water taxi and moved to the balcony to watch the GeriAncients—as she now thought of them—depart. The boat was painted a glowing apple green. Fast Freddy, resplendent in a daffodil-yellow waterproof jacket, tomato-red trousers and purple beanie, cruised towards the café like a bird of paradise. Colour, he believed, restored a tired spirit. A fond smile lifted the corners of her mouth at the same time as she wondered what the shy little Buddhist would make of his passengers. She would ask his opinion, fully aware that if he had nothing good to say, he would remain silent.

Ettie wasn't a betting woman, but she didn't like the odds of the group from Stringybark Bay making a go of their ambitious experiment. All for one and one for all? If today's little social gathering was anything to go by, a group of strong-minded individuals living in close proximity was a recipe for disaster, especially in an environment that could test even the toughest men and women.

Ettie made her way downstairs, a spring in her step as she inhaled the sharp citrus scent of an orange and almond cake fresh out of the oven, heard the satisfying clatter of industry. Once she'd envied Donna Harris. Now she pitied her.

❦

At home that evening, Sam gave Kate an account of the disastrous scene in the penthouse, Donna's cruel dismissal of Ettie's efforts. 'Turns out, she was once a famous actress. Appeared in all sorts of hit television series but hasn't been seen in public for forty years. Dropped off the radar after a rumour about an addiction to prescription drugs and time spent in rehab. Ettie recognised her in an instant and fell under a weird kind of spell. I've never seen her like that before—the way she was grovelling to that woman. Afterwards she made me swear I wouldn't tell anyone how she lost the plot for a few minutes and made an idiot of herself.'

They were talking in Kate's study, where she had her head bent over the café accounts, which she'd failed to finish earlier. 'Should you be telling me all this?'

Sam waved away the question. 'I'm sure she didn't mean you, Kate. Just the rest of the nosy buggers around here.'

'What did you think of the others?' Kate swivelled around in her chair and gave Sam her full attention.

He hesitated. 'They seem okay. Ordinary enough. Except for Melrose. There's something a little off about him.'

'What did you make of Daisy?' Kate asked. 'And by the way, hoisting her over your shoulder was a nice touch but it's never to be repeated. I checked our insurance policy, and it doesn't cover dropping people from a great height.'

'She's got more courage than the rest of them thrown together. That husband of hers, though, he's going to have a heart attack if he doesn't stop mollycoddling her.'

'He's afraid,' Kate said, swivelling back to her accounts.

'Afraid? Of what?'

'Being too old and frail to save her if she finds herself in jeopardy.' Kate winced suddenly and gripped the edge of her desk.

Sam was at her side in an instant. 'You okay, love?' He hovered, unsure what to do. What it meant.

The spasm passed. Kate relaxed her grip and took a deep breath. She stood and stretched her arms above her head, bent from side to side. Sam thought she looked tired and fed up.

'Busy day at the café?'

'Not too bad. Might lie down on the couch until dinner. What's on the menu?'

'Your wish is my command,' Sam said lightly.

'Spag bol again, huh?' She rubbed her neck. 'Maybe being pregnant is making me a bit odd, but I have the strangest feeling about the whole Stringybark Bay experiment.'

Sam, as superstitious as any man who earned a living on a sea, took her seriously. 'Strange in what way?'

'Not a good way. No. Definitely not a good way.'

'Ah, they'll be right. We're more familiar with old folk leaving the bays, instead of moving in, that's all. Go and put your feet up, and I'll bring a cuppa. Would you like to eat dinner on your lap or at the table?'

Kate rolled her eyes. 'Not even I could get a forkful of spaghetti across my stomach without losing most of it on the way. The table, please. And don't forget the napkins.'

Sam went into the kitchen, thinking about the great cultural divide signified by a harmless word such as *napkin*. In his world, the term for a piece of fabric or paper to wipe your mouth was *serviette*, and battling families were bloody lucky to have any on the table at a given time. Kate had corrected him in the early days of their relationship. Noted his embarrassment and covered the moment by laughingly referring to the difference between people raised in Victoria and those from New South Wales. Victorians were much more formal, apparently.

Maybe, he thought, that bloody incomprehensible morass of rules that centred around whether you said *serviette* or *napkin* was at the core of their differences. Whether you pushed in a chair when you left the table. Whether you tipped your cereal bowl forward or backwards to scrape the last bits. Whether you instinctively reached for the proper wineglass for red or white, whether you faced the blades of knives inwards or outwards when you set the table. Then there was the day he was eating an orange and he spat orange pips from the deck. Her face went white. Make a fist, direct the pips into the resulting tunnel, open your fist and drop the pips discreetly, she explained as though the information was gold and world peace depended on getting it right. The pips had stuck to his skin. He'd laughed and waved his hand around, joking. She'd gone inside, thin lipped. So many rules and regulations. A quagmire of niceties that amounted to *breeding*, as Kate would say, when all his life he'd believed kindness and compassion outranked etiquette every time. And that good manners were a thousand miles from etiquette. He'd bend over backwards to make her happy, though, even if he ended up bent out of shape for the rest of his life.

He opened the freezer and checked the plastic containers labelled in Ettie's flamboyant script. 'No spag bol. Chicken curry or beef bourg . . . stew?'

Kate came to stand beside him. 'Beef bourguignon,' she said.

'Yeah. French for stew.'

She sighed. 'I'd kill for a glass of wine and some mouldy cheese.'

'How about the curry? Good weather for it.'

She nodded. 'And green tea, please.' She leaned against him briefly, slipped an arm around his waist, and just like that every little niggle dissolved.

CHAPTER FOUR

A WEEK LATER, SAM RESTLESSLY paced the spartan rooms of his former home on Cutter Island. He'd suggested spending the night away from Kate so he wouldn't disturb her when he returned from the Stringybark Bay delivery. 'Won't finish till sometime after midnight,' he'd said.

She'd looked at him steadily, her blue-green eyes dark and questioning.

'You need rest, Kate,' he'd explained. 'You don't want me coming in stinking of sand and sea and turning the bathroom into a slurry of mud and grass.'

She'd just nodded before silently returning to the accounts for the café.

Now, as he opened musty cupboards, lifted cushions and looked under beds to check no free-loading antechinuses, diamond pythons or goannas had taken up residence in his absence, he wondered if he'd misjudged the situation; if her dislike of dirt was less rigorous than he'd thought. He'd reached for his phone umpteen times.

Punched in her numbers but hit the kill button. She might be asleep and he'd wake her for no reason. She might be in the bath, hear the phone and slip while rushing to catch the call. She might be enjoying her solitude and resent his intrusion. Truthfully, he had no idea what to do and it was driving him quietly dingbats. He wondered if all relationships fluctuated wildly between mutual understanding and complete confusion. Or were he and Kate terribly mismatched? He was a barge man. She'd worked at the top end of town. He left school at sixteen. She did a journalism and business degree. He'd never travelled further from Cook's Basin than half a day's drive. She'd travelled the world.

There were days—probably not enough, now that he thought about it—when he felt they were comrades joined in a single magnificent cause: their love for each other and their baby. Then, out of the blue, he'd reach for cheese and crackers at a dinner with Ettie and the chef, and for no reason he could fathom she'd let her silky black hair fall forward so he couldn't read her face and she'd go still and silent and he'd feel slaughtered by inadequacies he was unable to name. 'Have I done something wrong?' he'd ask her. She'd shake her head in the negative, but to him those silent emotional withdrawals sounded louder than chain running out after an anchor. In the early days, when Kate had struggled to learn and understand the basic etiquette (that bloody word again) of boats and offshore living, he'd worn his superiority like a crown, pointing out her shortfalls for her own safety but also—if he was being strictly honest with himself— with impatient arrogance. Now she was a gifted boatwoman and the tables had turned. Jimmy would call it karma. There were moments when it felt more like payback.

He finished his house inspection, which was blessedly devoid of wildlife, made up the bed with threadbare sheets he knew Kate would burn on sight, and then punched in Jimmy's phone number.

'Sam?'

'Jimmy! Time to get rolling. You ready, mate?'

'Aye, aye, Cap'n. Me 'n Longfella.'

'See you on the dock then.'

Outside in the cool night air, the yellow glow of a full moon reflecting off the water's ruffled surface, Sam felt his mood settle. He imagined Kate at home in bed—sleeping, maybe, or with a book propped on her stomach, enjoying her solitude. In the morning, he'd call Simon for a word that would bamboozle her but bring a smile to her face. Something really, really wicked.

The king tide, half a metre higher than a normal high tide at this time of the year, had redrawn the coastline. Only a few large rocks of the goat track that passed as a pathway for Cutter Island residents to reach Triangle Wharf remained visible. His own jetty, forty-two steps below his weatherboard home, was six inches underwater. With a grunt he feared might signal that his greatest physical years were behind him, he bent to remove his boots and sloshed barefoot along the dock towards the *Mary Kay*. There was a flash of torchlight, and the dog and the boy waded towards him like a psychedelic tsunami.

'I've got me new life jacket on, Sam—the one me mum bought so you could find me in the dark,' Jimmy said, aiming the light at his chest to reveal a vest in a colour that drifted between lime green and daffodil yellow. He swung the beam on his dog: 'And Longfella's sorted, too.'

Longfellow's head hung uncharacteristically low, a hint of doleful shame in his eyes. Around his torso, clipped tight, he wore a fluoro pink buoyancy pet vest.

The kid whipped an arm from behind his back and held up a similarly lurid vest. 'For you, Sam, from me mum. She reckons when you're workin' in the dark every little bit helps.'

'Er, thanks, mate. Very thoughtful of her. Now let's get this show on the road.'

The *Mary Kay* slid past the mouths of the bays from Cutter Island to Stringybark, barely disturbing the surface of the open waters. The man, the boy, the dog—resigned to his clingy new clobber— were silently intent, content.

Only a few lights shone from Cutter Island, but even in the dead of night Sam could place every home.

'Seaweed's up late,' Jimmy said, as if reading Sam's mind.

'Nah, fallen asleep with his light on,' Sam replied.

'Me mum reckons electricity costs too much to waste,' Jimmy said, the thought of the energy bill triggering a little soft-shoe shuffle of nerves.

Sam laid a reassuring hand on the boy's shoulder. 'Your mum's a wise woman and you can bet she's got everything sorted.'

In the light of the control panel, Jimmy's innocent face beamed. 'She's alright, me mum.'

At the approach to Stringybark Bay, Sam gently spun the helm with his index finger and narrowed his eyes, straining to see ahead. Towering escarpments blocked the moon's glow, making a dark canyon of the waterway. He did a mental tally of the number of cashed-up comparatively young retirees who'd downsized from their expensive inner-city homes to buy affordable waterfront real estate. Maybe, he thought, Stringybark Bay should be renamed Retirement Cove. His thoughts wandered towards the feisty, much-loved Misses Skettle, who'd been born and still lived in an antiquated shack on the shore of Rocky Point, where they dressed formally in long skirts and frilled shirts each evening for dinner and kept a vigilant eye out for boats in distress. After a lifetime of generosity and commitment to upholding the rites, traditions and core values of Cook's Basin, they'd earned the right to be carried out in a body bag if that was their choice. But blow-ins, such as the eclectic group who now resided at GeriEcstasy, had no real links to the community and seemed to lack the desire or energy to build them— although it was early days, and Daisy had good instincts. Sam smiled, remembering the laughter shaking her frail body as he'd hoisted her over his shoulder.

'Gunna share that joke?' Jimmy asked, noticing the shift in Sam's expression.

'Later, mate, later.'

In silence, Sam steered the *Mary Kay* at a stately speed through yachts hanging off their moorings like ghostly ships abandoned in the night. A yellow moon hung above the escarpment, flooding the bay with light. In the distance, the silver trunks of mangroves came alive and writhed like spirit people. 'Bloody spooky, in't?' Jimmy said, instinctively shifting closer to Sam.

There was a low growl, and like a bolt of lightning, Longfellow shot out of the wheelhouse.

Jimmy jumped, grabbing Sam's arm. Sam throttled back instantly, reversed until the barge came to a standstill.

On the bow, the dog yipped and spun frantically. Sam locked eyes with the boy, reached for Jimmy's hands and placed them on the helm. 'Keep the boat in neutral but be ready to reverse if I give the order. I'll take a look. It's probably nothing.'

Jimmy nodded and stared at Sam with wide eyes. 'Longfella's upset. I reckon somethin's up. Somethin' big.'

Sam kept his voice calm. 'Remember, Jimmy, steady does it. I'm relying on you, mate.'

He grabbed a torch from the dashboard, stepped outside the wheelhouse, glanced up at the night sky. The moon, rising higher by the second, now illuminated the scene.

Longfellow gave a short bark.

'Good dog. Let's see what's got you going.'

As Sam made his way along the length of the deck, a light came on in one of the houses. Georgie, if he had his bearings right. A thin-lipped woman as vigilant as the Misses Skettle but without their underlying benevolence.

The dog barked again, high-pitched.

'You're waking the neighbourhood,' Sam called out softly. 'Settle. I'm coming.'

He reached the bow and leaned forward, directing the beam of the torch into the water.

'Ah, jeez.' He closed his eyes and reopened them, hoping the sight of billowing fabric was a trick of the light. 'Ah, jeez,' he repeated, dropping his head.

One of the antique dealers from Melbourne—Brian or Cameron. He couldn't remember which of the men had favoured flowing shirts in pale colours. Face down, splayed as if in supplication, his body rocked by the sea, he was way beyond help.

Sam leaned back on his heels and scrabbled in his pocket for his mobile phone. Dialled triple zero.

He answered a few questions and gave his phone number. The Water Police would be contacted and would call him directly. Midnight calls were always emergencies, and his phone rang almost instantly. He reported the body and the location, was ordered to stay where he was until the police boat arrived.

In the wheelhouse, the kid's face, yellow-green in the overhead light, was wreathed with anxiety. 'Dead fella, eh?' Jimmy said, before Sam could say a word.

Sam nodded. 'Nothing to be done for him, mate.'

Jimmy nodded silently, tears welling. He reached for Longfellow's ear and began rubbing. The mutt leaned hard against the boy.

'I need you to drop anchor and keep the *Mary Kay* steady. I'm going to go over the side with a sling. I'll call if I need a hand. You got all that?'

Jimmy nodded. A single fat tear rolled down his cheek. 'He's a good dog, isn't he, Sam?' he whispered.

'None better, mate.'

Sam grabbed a sling from among a pile of chains in the hold, stripped to his underwear, and slipped over the side into dark water still holding tight to the chill of winter. Even though he barely knew the man, he felt overwhelmed by the sadness of a life unfinished. Were lives ever finished? He couldn't say. He reached for the body and brushed away the indignity of a few dead leaves caught in the shirt collar. Slipped the sling under the arms with an unspoken apology if he was being a bit rough. Then he trod water until the police launch arrived, knowing there was no more he could do but unwilling to do nothing at all.

∽

The police launch, a sturdy aluminium Naiad, nine and a half metres in length with engines that could top a speed of forty knots if called upon, approached, red and blue lights flashing, an infrared spotlight scanning the water. It glided within close range of the barge. Richard Baines, the younger of the two cops, swung his torch over the water until he picked up Sam and the body on the port side of the *Mary Kay*, then used hand signals to direct his boss, Abe Smith, to come alongside on starboard.

Jimmy, worried the launch might mar the *Mary Kay*'s glossy paintwork, rushed to throw over fenders then sprinted back to the wheelhouse. Stuck out his head: 'I'd help ya more but Sam told me not leave me station. Can ya manage on your own?'

Baines smiled inwardly. 'Had a few goes at this in my time, Jimmy.'

He vaulted over the gunnel of the barge and landed lightly on the deck of the *Mary Kay*. Jimmy chucked him a salute. Surprised, Baines almost lifted a hand in response but settled for a nod. The chief, Abe Smith, tossed a stern line; Baines caught it with one hand and wrapped it around one of the barge's cleats, ending with a tug to make sure the half-hitch would hold. He moved forward to do the same with the bowline. When the launch was secure, he crossed the barge to port side and shone his torch into the water.

Sam threw up a hand to shield his eyes. 'Jeez, mate. Have a heart.'

'Sorry,' Baines replied, hastily dimming the beam with the press of a button.

By now, the bay was sepulchral, the light of the moon lost behind banks of rainclouds. Sam swam towards Baines and held up the rope attached to the sling. Baines grabbed it and wound it around a cleat. Inside the cruiser's cabin, Abe Smith talked softly into his phone. Baines leaned over the gunnel, offering a hand to hoist Sam on board.

'Doesn't seem right, leaving him alone,' Sam said, looking at the body lying face down, rocked by the ebb and flow of a tide indifferent to life and death.

'Nothing much can happen to him now.' With a silent apology to the dead man for abandoning him, Sam ignored the proffered hand and grabbed the gunnel with both hands, hoisting his solid body as though propelled by an unseen force. On board, half-naked and dripping wet, blue with cold, he stamped his feet and gave a light whack to each ear. Jimmy ran to his side and shoved a towel at him then rushed back to the wheelhouse. Sam rubbed himself down.

'Do you know who he is, mate?' Baines asked, staring over the side.

'Was,' Sam said. 'Who he was.' He looked around for his clothes, found them lying in a mound on the bow where he'd left them. Pulled off his wet jocks and reached for his jeans. Dragged them on, hopping first on one leg and then the other, his damp skin making it awkward.

'Yeah. Any idea?'

'Lived in the house next to the mangroves.' Sam shook his flannel shirt and slipped his arms into the sleeves, fumbled with the buttons. 'Moved in a week ago.' He picked up the life vest. Let it drop.

Richard spun to face him. 'What? The house with the bloody great jetty that shoots halfway into the bay?'

Sam nodded. 'Five couples. Four and a half now.'

'Christ,' Richard breathed, shaking his head. 'What a bloody mess.' He looked beseechingly at Sam. 'Mate, since you've already met them, reckon you could stand beside me when I knock on the door? Might help ease the shock if they see a familiar face.'

'Headed there anyway. Due to shift a load of soil on the king tide.' Sam bent down and picked up the vest again. 'Give me a minute to check in with Jimmy. Long as he knows what's going on, he's okay. It's the not knowing that sends him into a spin.'

'Take your time. No reason to rush.'

In the wheelhouse, Sam explained to Jimmy what would happen next. 'I'm going to go ashore with Richard to let the folks in the house know what's happened. You okay if I leave you here with Longfellow?'

Jimmy, the dog at his feet, looked uncertain. Drummed fingers on the console. Rubbed his chin with his hand. Shuffled.

Sam said, 'I can stay here if you'd rather. Richard can manage on his own.'

'It's gunna be hard on ya, Sam, tellin' them the news.'

'No easy way, that's for sure.'

'Longfella, he could go with ya. For support.' The boy's face was wrinkled with concern.

Sam said, 'Thanks for the offer, mate, but as you'll be captain in my absence, I reckon that makes Longfellow first mate. His place is beside you.'

Jimmy nodded. 'Ya better get goin',' then,' he said.

Sam gave the kid a pat on the back. Onshore, lights had begun to flare like small explosions. Only GeriEcstasy, hunkered deep at the end of the bay, remained in darkness. Sam, a man who prided himself on facing down the hard stuff whenever it was thrown his way, fought the urge to bolt.

CHAPTER FIVE

ABE SMITH, GREY-STUBBLED WITH BLOODSHOT eyes and a downturned mouth, dropped Sam and Richard Baines at the GeriEcstasy jetty. The two men waited while Abe pulled away to join the police divers, who'd paint a picture for the coroner with photos, measurements and the smallest details to establish the cause of death, expose anything that didn't look quite right.

Richard Baines, thirty years Abe's junior, thrust his hands into his pockets. 'How do you want to handle this?' he asked.

'I dunno,' said Sam. 'Are there any rules?'

'Yeah. Nah. Different every time. Let's play it by ear.' He didn't move.

'Might as well get it over and done, eh?' Sam said.

They began the long, wordless journey to the house. Halfway, Richard stopped to look towards the forest of mangroves, spooky in the night light. 'Never had much good feeling for this bay.'

Sam followed his gaze. 'Any reason?'

'Can't explain it. A copper's instinct.'

Sam couldn't think of anything to add to that. They continued up the jetty to the shore.

At the door of the house, they paused for a few seconds. Then, taking a deep breath, Sam knocked lightly.

Brian Callaghan, wearing purple silk pyjamas, red velvet slippers and an embroidered sleeping mask dragged up to his forehead, opened the door so quickly he must have been standing next to it. 'Cam . . .' he began, sounding relieved. But at the sight of the two men his face collapsed in disappointment, which was replaced quickly by confusion. Frowning, he looked past Sam and Baines to the jetty.

'Mate,' Sam said. 'Can we come in?'

Slightly disorientated, Brian hesitated then stood aside. 'Excuse the déshabillé,' he murmured, indicating his clothes. 'I wasn't expecting guests at this hour.' There was a hint of disapproval in his tone, as though decency had been breached but he was too polite to point it out.

Richard stepped inside, removing his cap. He scratched his head and looked at Sam with raised eyebrows.

'How about the kitchen?' Sam suggested. 'Could you lead the way?'

Brian held a forefinger to his lips, signalling for quiet. He removed his sleeping mask and stuffed it in his pyjama pocket. 'The household's slumbering. Best we don't wake them. Interrupted sleep makes one or two of the camp cranky,' he whispered, rolling his eyes.

Without waiting for a response, he tiptoed down a narrow hall towards the rear of the house. 'The work all done then?' he said over his shoulder. 'Dropping off the invoice, are you? Mike's asleep, of course. I don't think he realised you'd be calling in. I expect you'd like a cup of tea or something.' He opened a door and fumbled for a light switch.

A gleaming, state-of-the-art kitchen, as clinical as an operating theatre, was revealed. Brian pointed the two men towards a granite-topped island bench. 'It's a local custom, is it? To knock on the door when a job is finished, no matter what time of the day . . . or night? Quaint. Mm. Yes. Quaint.'

Brian reached for the kettle. Then he turned abruptly to the policeman. 'It's Cam, isn't it? He went out to see the moon come up. That was hours ago. I've been calling him, but the phone goes straight to voicemail.'

'Yeah, mate, it's Cam,' Sam said softly. 'I'm sorry. Really sorry.'

Brian's eyes slid around the four corners of the kitchen. 'The silly bugger's gone and hurt himself, hasn't he? I told him to be careful. So what's he done? Broken a leg, sprained his ankle?'

Sam and the cop exchanged a look.

'Mate . . .'

'He's had a fall, has he? Silly bugger. Told him not to go out. That moonlight wasn't like streetlight.'

'No, mate. It's not that.'

Brian held his hands over his ears and squeezed his eyes shut. 'He will walk through that door in a minute. He will.'

'No. He's . . .' Sam struggled to find a word to soften the blow. Passed? As if he were on his way somewhere? 'I'm sorry. He's dead.'

Brian flinched. 'But . . .'

'He's dead, Brian. I wish I could offer some hope but there's none to be had.'

The big man let out a groan that started in his gut and erupted in a roar. He sank to the floor, his back against the wall, and laid his head on his knees. 'No,' he sobbed. 'No.'

Baines, awkward, opened cupboards looking for mugs, alcohol, anything. Around them, the household began to stir.

⌒

Daisy, a tiny, wide-awake sparrow in plain cotton pyjamas with a pink chenille dressing-gown draped across her knees, appeared in her wheelchair, pushed by her sleepy-eyed husband. She surveyed the room from the doorway, her eyes lingering on the policeman. 'Has there been an accident?' she asked. 'The boy?'

Sam went to her side and kneeled, reached for her hand. 'Not the boy. Not Jimmy.'

'Thank God for that.'

Behind her, Gavin Flowerdale demanded: 'What the hell is going on? It's two o'clock in the morning, for God's sake.'

His wife, Sheila, pushed him aside and squeezed past the wheelchair into the kitchen. She took in the stunned faces, Brian slumped on the floor, and then turned back to look at Daisy.

'What's going on?' Her hands clutched the collar of her floral nightie.

'It's Cameron,' Sam said. 'I'm so sorry. He's dead.'

Brian struggled to his feet. He looked like he might vomit. Sheila looked at Gavin, unsure.

Sally and David Kinane appeared, carrying their slippers and struggling into dressing-gowns. 'Is someone ill?' Sally asked. She threw her slippers on the floor and slipped her feet into them. David rubbed his head, confused. He placed a hand on his wife's shoulder for balance and dragged on his footwear.

'Put on the kettle please, Rob,' Daisy said. 'Gavin, there's a bottle of cognac in the drinks cabinet in the sitting room. Do you think you could lay your hands on it? Sally, the mugs and milk, please. Does anyone take sugar? Perhaps you could find it, Sheila. And a glass for the brandy.'

Sam crossed the room to help Brian into a chair at the table.

'It's my fault,' Brian said. Tears rolled down his cheeks.

Rob, struggling to hold up his pyjama bottoms, passed him a handkerchief from his pocket. 'It's clean,' he murmured before retying the cord securely.

Richard Baines stood in a corner near a window that drew the bush into the house during the day but was blank and ominous at night. He watched the scene before him like a member of an audience. After a minute or two, Sam joined him.

With the tea made, Sally and Sheila took seats. Gavin appeared with the brandy and held it up in question. Daisy nodded towards Brian. 'A large one,' she said.

Rob pushed her wheelchair to the empty space at the head of the table and then stood back. Gavin and David sat down beside their wives and reached to hold their hands.

'We need to wake Mike and Donna,' Daisy stated. 'Sheila?'

'Not me. Someone else can brave the lion's den.'

Daisy gave her a stony look. 'Just do it, Sheila,' she ordered, fussing with the dressing-gown covering her legs to cut off any debate.

Brian, his face grey with shock, closed his eyes, said: 'It was my idea. To see the moon rise. I should have gone with him. I meant to. But I knew Cam would never go near the water. Country boy.

Ordered to stay away from dams because of snakes. He never learned to swim. It's just . . . I didn't want to get sand and salt water on my new pyjamas.' He straightened, sculled the brandy, pulled himself together. 'Excuse me,' he said, with a formal little bow of apology. 'I need to go and change into something more suitable. Yes. Excuse me.' He pushed back his chair, spun on his heel and left the room.

Daisy beckoned Rob with her little finger. He leaned down to hear her instructions: 'Go with him, darling, would you? Not the right time for him to be alone.'

Rob squeezed his wife's shoulder in agreement and followed Brian's hunched figure from the kitchen. Daisy continued to fuss with her dressing-gown. Nerves, thought Sam.

Sheila returned, rolling her eyes. 'I deserve a medal,' she said. An awkward silence descended on the room.

'Sam, would you mind making me a cup of coffee?' Daisy asked. 'Instant is fine.' She pointed at a cupboard. 'It's going to be a long night.'

'Make mine a mug of brandy, and could someone tell me what the bejesus is going on?' Donna Harris, in red baby-doll pyjamas with white polka dots, fluffy red slippers on her feet, clutched the doorframe. Her cropped silver hair stood on end. Her face, without make-up, was a network of fine red lines. Behind her, Mike Melrose held a diaphanous robe, raised high to slip over her shoulders. She shoved him away with such force, she almost fell.

'Come in and sit down, Donna,' Daisy said calmly. 'There's been an accident. A rather terrible one.'

The actress entered the kitchen, wincing under the glare of the lights. 'Jesus, turn down the spotlights, will you?'

Melrose, still carrying his wife's robe over his forearm, followed. He wore navy cotton pyjamas and soft tan slippers; the lack of dressing-gown made him look vaguely under-dressed. He studied the tableau of worried faces, singled out Sam: 'A problem with the job?' he asked. 'The boy? He's okay?'

'He's fine, mate. It's Cameron . . .' Sam looked towards Daisy.

Donna seemed to notice her semi-dressed state for the first time. 'Where's my bloody robe, Mike?'

He passed it to her without a word, watched her struggle for a minute before helping her to shrug into the sleeves. Donna grunted, fumbling almost drunkenly with ribbons at her wrists. Gave up in frustration and wriggled onto a stool at the counter, giving those assembled a clear view of her crotch. She adjusted the fabric clumsily, smiling demurely. The effect was quietly, stunningly, tragic.

Melrose said, 'Daisy? What about Cameron?'

'He's dead, Mike. Stepped out to see the moon rise, must have fallen in the water and drowned. The police are—'

'Does Brian know?' Melrose interrupted.

Daisy nodded. 'He's gone to get dressed. Rob's with him.'

'Sorry, what?' Donna asked, frowning. 'What's happened?'

'Why don't you go back to bed, Donna?' Melrose said soothingly. 'Let's tuck you in again.' He sounded as though he were dealing with a child. 'What do we always say? Things will be better in the morning.'

Donna Harris tipped her head to the side, like an indecisive bird.

'C'mon, darling,' Melrose cajoled. 'A gorgeous girl needs her beauty sleep.' He slipped his hand under her elbow and gently guided her out of the room, looking back over his shoulder and mouthing a single word: 'Wait!'

Sam passed Daisy a steaming mug. The group stared at their hands in silence. The policeman remained in the corner near the window, propped against the wall with his arms folded. Time felt suspended.

Eventually Melrose returned to the room, and Baines took him aside to explain what had happened. Rob followed soon after, reporting that Brian had told him to go away or he might get violent.

A boat engine could be heard outside. Shortly afterwards, there was a knock on the door. 'I'll go,' Gavin said, pushing back his chair.

He returned with the senior policeman.

Abe, looking wiped out, refused any refreshments. Holding his cap in both hands, he said, 'We've established a crime scene, which is routine procedure. Based on data from the divers, forensics will sketch out a timeline of what they believe occurred. If anything untoward surfaces, we'll pass the case on to homicide. Right now, it looks like misadventure.'

Daisy was the first to respond. 'What happened to him?'

'We won't really know until after the autopsy, but we're not expecting any surprises. Richard here will be the investigating officer. He'll take statements from everyone tomorrow. A formality, nothing more. Now if you'll excuse me . . .' He turned to speak quietly to Richard Baines. 'I'll wait on the boat. Soon as you're finished, eh?' He paused in the doorway to address the group. 'There'll be a media statement issued with the name and details of the deceased, a brief description of the scene.'

'Is that necessary?' Melrose asked sharply.

'Part of the procedure.'

'We'd prefer the matter remain private, if you don't mind.'

'Sorry, mate, that's the way it's done,' Abe said flatly.

After Abe Smith had gone, Melrose wrote out his phone number on a piece of paper and handed it to Richard Baines. 'I'll handle all enquiries from now on,' he said.

Baines looked nonplussed. 'Ah. Right. We'll still need to take statements from everyone. Like the boss said, it's procedure, that's all. Won't take long.'

Melrose nodded. 'You know where to find us.'

⸎

Sam and Richard Baines stepped onto a jetty slick with damp. The tide, much lower now, lapped at smooth pylons. The muddy smell of mangroves was thick enough to chew. The GeriEcstasy sign hung forlornly in the sea mist. Sam took a deep breath and looked away. Not much ecstasy ahead as far as he could see.

'They're never going to recover from this,' Sam said. 'It's the end of the dream. One bloody week. That's all it took for the whole damn enterprise to go up in smoke. Poor bastards.'

He turned his eyes skywards, where a grey loom eased above the escarpment, beginning to cancel out the night, making way for the sun. He felt a pang of deep compassion for the naive group he'd left in the kitchen, struggling to make sense of a stupid, freak accident caused by what could only have been a moment's lapse in concentration. Bad stuff happens fast—wisdom from the Misses Skettle, who'd seen their fair share of bad stuff. That poor bloke, Cameron. Died trying to catch the rise of the moon. You couldn't fault him for that. Bloody terrible luck, though, whichever way you looked at it.

Both men stepped aboard the launch and Abe started the engine with a turn of the key. Over the roar of the engines, they heard a shout from the house. Richard went to the bow, unsure.

'Wait for me!' Brian ran towards them, waving an arm, carrying a leather overnight bag. 'Wait! I'm coming with you.' He panted up to the launch, his face puffy from crying. 'Take me anywhere,' he pleaded.

In the cabin, Abe, his eyebrows raised in a question, threw up his hands.

'Mate,' Sam said, 'I understand completely where you're coming from, but you'd be better off stayin' with your friends right now. You need support . . .'

'If you won't take me, I'll jump in the water and start swimming,' Brian threatened, almost hysterical.

'Ah, jeez,' Sam said. While Baines went to tell Abe what was happening, Sam took the overnight bag and then gave Brian a hand to board. 'Do you have any idea where you're headed?' he asked.

'As if I care,' Brian replied. 'As if I bloody well care.'

Abe emerged from the cabin and took Sam aside with a hand on his shoulder. 'Just so we're all clear, he's your problem. I'll unload you both on the *Mary Kay*. End of story.'

Back in the cabin, he reversed into the waterway and pointed the launch towards the barge, now alone in the bay. He stuck his head out for a final word. 'By the way, the kid's sound asleep. So is the dog.'

Brian stayed perched on the gunnel, his overnight bag on his knees. Held tightly with both hands, like a man waiting at a train station.

Baines and Sam went to the bow where they stood side by side, legs apart for balance.

'Donna,' Baines said softly. 'She the full quid?'

'Floats in a parallel universe. Pills, they say.'

'Ah.'

'Reckon Georgie is still up,' Sam said, pointing at a single light burning onshore.

'Abe said the bloody woman came alongside the police boat in her tinnie. Held up a thermos and a container of sandwiches. He thought her neck would snap she stretched it so hard to get a squiz at the goings-on. Refused to leave until he threatened to itemise all the safety infringements on her boat and arrest her. Took off like he'd lit a fire under her backside. Good sandwiches, apparently. Boiled egg and lettuce. I'm a ham, cheese and tomato man myself.'

꩜

On board the *Mary Kay*, Sam gently shook Jimmy awake. 'All hands on deck and make room for a guest.'

The kid rubbed his eyes sleepily, reached blindly for the feel of fur under his hands. The mutt, tucked into the curve of his master's body on the red banquette in the wheelhouse, shifted his head so it fitted under Jimmy's hand. Reassured, the kid threw off his blanket, swung his feet to the deck. Stretched his arms above his head.

Brian stood in the doorway like a lost soul.

'This is Brian, Jimmy.' Sam tried and failed to think of something to explain the man's presence. At a loss, he steered Brian to the banquette, wrapped the discarded blanket around his shoulders. The dog sat at his feet, dropped his head on Brian's knee and stared at him with sad brown eyes.

Jimmy, watching closely, said, 'Longfella reckons ya need a bit o' lookin' after. He's a good dog.'

Brian's face crumpled. Sam quickly sent the kid to raise the anchor, dug out his mobile phone and called Ettie without bothering to apologise for the early hour.

'No, love, Kate and I haven't had a barney and the baby's still takin' his time. There's been a bad accident. One of the GeriEcstasies. Cameron is dead. His partner, Brian—remember Brian?—he needs a place to stay for a while, just till he gets his bearings. The spare café key still in its usual spot?'

A minute later, Sam ended the call. He started the engine and slipped into reverse. The sky, lemon with first light, gave hints of a thumping great sunrise. Sam gave silent thanks for his own blessings and the good fortune of living among people who were willing to give without needing to ask why. Most of them, anyway.

'It's all set,' he explained to Brian without turning around, giving grief its privacy. 'Ettie says you're welcome to her penthouse for as long as you like.'

'That awful morning tea,' Brian whispered. 'Donna behaving badly. Donna always behaving badly. I told her off that day, you know. I'm the only one who has the guts to stand up to her. Told her she'd made us all look like entitled morons. She laughed. Not that it matters now. Not a damn thing matters anymore.'

Sam turned the helm. The kid sprinted to the stern to check behind. Slowly, fluidly, the barge came about. Sam pointed towards the mouth of Stringybark Bay and set off at a steady eight knots.

'I'll never go back,' Brian continued, almost to himself. 'A pair of pyjamas for a life. I will never, ever forgive myself.'

Sam stuck his head out of the wheelhouse door and called to Jimmy: 'We're headed to the Briny, Jimmy. Get ready to tie up.'

Onshore, he saw that Georgie's light had finally gone out. Excitement over. He wondered what spin she'd put on the story, whether she'd disparage the dead man for his stupidity or put his death down to a shocking tragedy. Either way, she was guaranteed to make herself the centre of attention.

❧

They docked at the Briny's deck as a great golden ball breached the horizon, igniting sparks across land and sea, setting a new day in motion. Life goes on, Sam thought, and despite the horrors of the night, he felt his spirits lift. As soon as he decently could, he'd call Kate.

A figure in a floaty kaftan waved from the deck of the penthouse. He smiled. He should have known Ettie would beat him to the café.

She disappeared and re-emerged through the flywire door, crossed the deck, dodging tables and chairs, and kept on towards the barge with a steady step.

On board, she found a space to sit beside Brian and reached for his hand. 'Oh, my love,' she murmured.

'Cameron. He went outside to watch the moonrise and fell in the water. Couldn't swim,' Sam explained in a low voice.

Ettie put a hand to her chest in horror, then together she and Sam supported a staggering Brian off the barge. Jimmy followed with the bag.

At the door of the café, Ettie turned to Sam and Jimmy. Taking Brian's bag from the boy, she said, 'Off you go. He's on my watch now.'

Sam checked the time. It was 6 am. Still too early to call Kate. He ordered Jimmy back on board the *Mary Kay* and cast off for Cutter Island. He'd send Jimmy home to catch up on his sleep and grab an hour's rest himself before he began setting up for the day.

The first tinnies were already chugging about the waterways: commuters probably. Barge work was dirty work, some said. Sam never bothered to argue. To him, sitting in peak hour traffic, being chained to a desk in an airless room with closed windows—or no windows at all—well, there was still plenty of dirt around, it was just invisible. At least he could rub off the grime with a bar of soap. There wasn't a cleanser invented yet that could scrub a dusty lung.

'Sam,' Jimmy said, 'we gunna finish that job in Stringybark later?'

'We'll leave it for a while. Those folks have got a lot to sort out right now. We're on standby until we get the word to go ahead.'

Jimmy sighed, shaking his head like a tired old man. 'It's a bloody sad day 'n' all. You wouldn't wish it on a peanut.'

CHAPTER SIX

THE NEWS OF CAMERON'S DEATH quickly circulated amongst the offshorers and Freddy, ditching his parrot-coloured clothing out of respect for the recently dead, had dressed in sombre blue. Late in the afternoon he picked up the shell-shocked GeriEcstasy crowd from their home and sped his apple-green water taxi towards the Square over calm seas and into a breeze that carried the floral scent of spring. With a gentle flourish he swung alongside the ferry wharf and grabbed a rope, tying the bowline quickly. 'Stay seated, if you don't mind, until the wash passes,' he said. 'Safer that way.'

The women, who had half-risen, sank back.

A few seconds later, the boat rocked violently as the wash hit. When it was over, Freddy tied on at the stern and stood ready.

'Right, men first,' Freddy said, offering his hand.

Rob began to disembark with the wobbly uncertainty of age. For an agonising moment, he teetered, one foot on the pontoon, the other in the boat. As he began to fall backwards, Freddy gave his backside a hefty shove. Rob stumbled but landed upright. 'Not too rough on you, I hope,' Freddy said apologetically.

Rob, embarrassed, said: 'Weak knees. Been kicked by too many cows. And their calves.'

The other men were stronger in the legs.

The women stood. Two hefty island kids emerged from the passenger shelter. The men, relieved, took a step backwards.

Strong arms reached out and lifted Sheila and Sally ashore with the effortlessness of youth. Freddy passed across the wheelchair. 'Daisy is going to need a bit more help,' he said with an apologetic look at the woman in question, worried his allusion to her infirmity might have upset her.

'No worries, Freddy. Easy as.' Exchanging grins, the boys stepped into the water taxi and locked their hands in a seat. 'Here you go. A throne fit for a queen.'

With Daisy's arms around their shoulders and a nod to each other, they stepped up from the boat and onto the pontoon to a round of applause. 'Light as a feather,' one of the boys proclaimed as Rob hurried forward with the wheelchair.

Fast Freddy, a sheen of nervous sweat on his face, made a note to include a ramp as part of his equipment in the future.

Melrose paid. Freddy took the opportunity to discreetly mention that tossing rubbish overboard was an offence. Melrose replied that he'd found a half-eaten sandwich on the seat. Freddy, who checked his boat after every ride, knew the man was lying but left it alone. Difficult circumstances called for leniency.

The group set off towards the café, having shaken off a little of their distress and tiredness.

Inside the Briny, Melrose asked for Ettie.

Marcus, helping with the cooking on an emotionally harrowing day, explained: 'She is upstairs with your friend. She was afraid to take her eyes from him in case he lost, for a moment, his good sense and attempted to make a decision that was ill-considered and unwise.'

Jenny, tall, skinny and brutally efficient, slid alongside the chef and, wiping her hands on her apron, offered her condolences. She'd come up shortly with refreshments, she promised, adding: 'Ettie said you might be here for a while. Said to tell you Brian's hell-bent on discussing his future now or never—his words, not Ettie's. Said to make that very clear. Ettie tried to persuade him to slow down, not to make any hasty decisions, but she said she couldn't get through to him. She said I should warn you before you went upstairs that there's a'—she hesitated and consulted a handwritten note she dragged from her apron pocket—'a maelstrom waiting for you.' She looked up. 'It means a shitstorm, in case you're wondering.' Having fulfilled her duty, she threw the note in the bin, picked up a palette knife and began applying a thick layer of cream cheese topping to a dense carrot cake with the intensity of someone who didn't wish to be disturbed.

Behind the counter, Marcus twisted sideways to squeeze past Jenny and break through the GeriEcstasy throng to place himself at the foot of the stairs. 'Come, this is the way to Brian.'

The group lingered, unsure, looking around a little desperately.

'This is ridiculous,' Melrose said impatiently. 'We can talk on the back deck. Daisy . . .'

'Ah yes,' Marcus said, slapping his forehead. 'Miss Daisy. For this I will find a remedy.'

Melrose put out a restraining hand. 'Brian can come downstairs.'

'Yes, of course, this must be the way if the remedy cannot be found. But I am a man who finds solutions. Am I not here returning to the mixing bowl and hot stove while my love offers warmth and comfort to a man whose heart is broken?'

Melrose, not sure he was entirely following the gist of the chef's unusual use of language, looked like a rabbit caught in headlights. Sheila and Sally shrugged and headed upstairs.

Marcus stuck his head out the door and scanned the Square. His eyes fastened on the two strapping young lads still waiting for the bus. He called them over and they cheerfully agreed to lend their arms to Daisy's cause once more.

Melrose shook his head. 'What's wrong with the deck? Why is everything around here always so bloody complicated?'

∾

The GeriEcstasies stood in an awkward group near where French doors opened onto Ettie's penthouse deck. No one spoke. A barely touched plate of food sat in the middle of a brightly painted dining table, where Brian was hunched low in a wicker chair, his face splotched with dried tears, his shaky hands wrapped around a herbal tea. Ettie had refused him coffee. 'It'll rattle your head and insides even more,' she'd said firmly. A cloud of grief and fury hovered over him. His overnight bag lay on a chair like a statement.

Mike Melrose stepped forward. 'We're all gutted,' he said. 'We can't even imagine how you must be feeling.' He briefly laid a hand on Brian's shoulder, moved to stand behind the wicker chair.

Brian nodded, unable to speak. One by one, the others came forward to offer wordless sympathy with a small touch to a cheek, a hand, an arm. Daisy turned the wheels of her chair with her sparrow hands and, when she was close enough, reached out. 'My dear boy,' she whispered, 'nothing we can say will ease the pain. We can only give you our love.'

Brian straightened visibly, took a deep breath. 'I have a plan, Daisy. You're all going to hate it, so let me apologise in advance. But please, please don't try to dissuade me. I have made up my mind.'

As Ettie indicated the chairs around the table, Jenny came up the stairs with a tray of sandwiches and slices of carrot cake. She placed the tray in the centre of table, said she'd be back with plates and serviettes. 'Would you like tea? Coffee?'

'Hot chocolate and chamomile tea,' Ettie said, in a tone that brooked no dissent. She gave Brian's shoulder a consoling pat. He placed his hand on hers, then let it drop. 'Well, I'll leave you all to it. Just remember, everyone is here to help.'

There were nods of thanks. Ettie floated down the stairs in her kaftan, wishing she'd taken an extra moment to put on her work clothes when she'd rushed out after Sam's dawn call. One look at her odd clobber and she'd be bombarded with questions from the community that she didn't feel she had the right to answer.

Melrose was the last to sit down at the far end of the table. Brian looked at the empty space. 'Donna too ill to come?' he asked, unable to keep the sarcasm from his voice. He held up a hand: 'No need to explain, Mike. We all understand Donna's . . . frailties.'

Melrose shook his head. 'She loved him more than any of us. She is devastated. Inconsolable. It would have been an act of cruelty to include her here.'

Brian raised an eyebrow but said nothing more.

'So what's this plan?' Melrose asked, folding his hands and placing them neatly on the table.

'I will sell my share of the house.'

For a full minute, no one moved. Then everyone spoke at once. 'Too soon . . . time to think . . . hasty decisions end in regret.'

Brian, his eyes downcast, waited as one by one the voices petered out.

'I can never go back to the place where Cameron died. I cannot be reminded, every time I step outside, that I let him go out alone, that I contributed to his death. I'm sorry. I know I'm breaking some sort of weird pact between you all that, frankly, I have never quite understood, but my mind is made up. I'm sorry.' He looked up, laid his hands flat on the table. 'Ettie has kindly offered me the penthouse for the time being. I'll make further plans once'—he cleared his throat—'once the details of death have been dealt with.' His eyes filled with tears. He pulled a handkerchief from his pocket and blew his nose loudly.

'Are you sure you want to leave the people who will support you most?' Daisy asked.

Brian's demeanour changed instantly. His tone switched from emotionally fragile to flat and hard. 'I will never set foot on that bloody long plank of a jetty or walk through the door of that overdesigned house again. Never!'

A chair scraped against the floorboards. Standing, Melrose leaned on the table with his fists clenched, his face white. 'You've had a terrible shock. You're rushing into decisions you may regret.'

Brian straightened, suddenly clear-eyed. In a cold brutal voice, he said: 'I want my share of the investment. If you can't manage it, then I'm afraid the house will have to be sold.'

Just then, Ettie appeared at the top of the stairs with the beverages on a round tray. Noting the stunned silence and stricken faces, she hesitated, then quickly placed the tray on the bench near the kitchen sink. Without a word, she turned and went slowly downstairs.

Melrose spoke first. 'Impossible, I'm afraid.'

Brian thumped the table with a tightly clenched fist. 'Oh, it's possible alright. Or I'll make your life hell, Mike—and take Donna down in the process.'

There was a collective gasp. Gavin was about to speak but Melrose held up a hand to cut him off. 'Be careful, Brian. Threats can rebound. We'll leave before any more is said. Call us when you can think straight. Right now, you sound like a madman. We'll call it grief, okay? The madness of grief. But I really would advise against threatening us again. And remember: Cameron was our friend, too. We are also grieving.'

All the GeriEcstasies except Rob and Daisy rose and filed wordlessly down the stairs.

'Better go and see if those young men are still hanging around,' Daisy said to her husband.

Rob nodded and bent to kiss Daisy on the top of her head. She patted his hand. When she heard him reach the foot of the stairs, she fixed her gaze on Brian. 'I will forgive this, because you are not in your right mind, but I will never forget. Neither will the others. If you insist on going ahead with a plan that you must understand will cause us deep distress, you will be dead to all of us.'

Brian stared into his cup and saucer, unable to meet Daisy's eyes. 'Without Cam, I might as well be dead.'

'That's poppycock and you know it,' Daisy said coldly.

Brian's head shot up.

'Who do you think Cam confided in when you disappeared for a few days, a week, even a month once, wasn't it?'

'Get out,' he whispered.

'The house in Stringybark Bay was meant to be a clean start, the beginning of a golden age . . .'

Before she could finish, the youths thundered up the stairs, followed closely by a worried-looking Rob. 'Please be careful,' he begged. 'It's harder going down than coming up. More treacherous . . .'

'I'll be fine, darling,' Daisy said soothingly. 'C'mon, boys. One more heave-ho and you'll have done all your good deeds for the week.' She locked eyes with Brian. 'We'll leave you to your grief, Brian.'

The boys delivered Daisy safely into the care of her husband and made a mad dash for the bus. Daisy and Rob went to join their friends who were clambering into Fast Freddy's water taxi.

Ettie watched them go. Seated at Kate's desk under the stairs, she had heard every word uttered by the GeriEcstasies—including the last uncomfortable exchange between Brian and Daisy.

ல

In the early evening, Ettie and Marcus sipped a cold glass of wine at the end of their jetty. 'I am not in training for this kind of café work anymore,' Marcus said, wriggling his hot and hurting toes in the cold water of the bay. 'My hoofers are kaput. It is unthinkable, of course, that I may be ageing.'

Ettie laughed: 'Nothing to do with age. It was a shocker of a day. Right up there with the worst. Dealing with a death knocks the stuffing out of you.'

Marcus reached for the wine bucket, held up a bottle of riesling dripping with icy condensation: 'Refill?'

Ettie sighed. 'No. I'll wait. Have a glass with dinner.' Once, she thought, she would have toppled a whole bottle before dinner. Those lonely days were over, but the memory made her wonder what strange and random series of conjunctions had spun her chaotic life into contentment and seen the GeriEcstasies' carefully planned future descend into chaos.

They were silent for a while, each lost in their thoughts, watching the light fade and birds find shelter for the night.

'It will be a sad house near the mangroves tonight,' Marcus murmured. 'To start again, well, they are not young. This was, for them, the big throw of the dice. But the money was on the wrong horse.'

'Such bad luck,' Ettie said. 'I must confess . . .'

'Yes, my love?'

'I left them to their privacy, of course . . .'

'Of course. This goes without saying,' Marcus assured her, smiling to himself.

'But I couldn't help overhearing. It seems Brian wants to leave. He said either the others must buy him out or the house will have to be sold. The others are against it—or maybe there isn't enough cash.'

'This is none of our business, Ettie.'

'To have the whole venture fail after a single week, well, they can't give in so easily.'

Ettie twisted towards Marcus. 'There must be some way to compromise.'

Marcus took a deep breath. 'My love . . . This man, Mike Melrose, he does not strike me as a man who can comprehend the concept of "compromise" unless it is in his best interests. And to engage the services of lawyers would benefit only the lawyers. In the end, if they are not careful and wise, perhaps there will be nothing left for any of them.'

'That's why we've got to help them to find a solution,' Ettie said firmly.

'Ah, my love, you cannot save the world. Although, of course, you have done this many times, I am sure . . .'

Ettie jumped to her feet. A tinnie was chugging towards them. She waved. 'Here they come.'

She bent, extending a hand to Marcus and yanking him to his feet.

'We are so lucky, you and me,' she said, touching the timber railing to ward off bad luck. 'Every day, I ask myself how I got so lucky.'

'For me,' Marcus said, planting a kiss on the side of her head, 'it is the same.'

A flock of noisy, glossy black cockatoos flew past in V-formation, the underside of their tails deep red. 'Sure sign rain's coming,' Ettie said.

'Or they are on their way home to their chosen beds,' Marcus replied. 'Because they must, of course, sleep somewhere.'

Together, Ettie and Marcus helped Kate from the tinnie while Sam held the boat steady and tight against the jetty. On solid foundations, Kate stretched her body sideways, backwards. 'Bumpier than a country road out past Rocky Point,' she said. 'Thought the baby might be shaken out at any moment.'

'Everything alright, Kate?' Sam asked anxiously.

Ettie linked her arm through Kate's with a roll of her eyes. They set off towards the house, a low-slung 1950s timber home restored to perfection under the eagle eye of the chef. 'You'd think no one had ever had a baby before,' she called over her shoulder.

'Well, I know for sure Kate never has,' Sam yelled after them.

Marcus secured the stern line. 'Come, it has been a hard night and day for you, yes?'

'Yeah. But harder for Jimmy. The sight of a dead man floating in the water. A horror he'll carry with him maybe forever. And his mental balance is so delicate . . .'

'Ah, my friend, you do the boy an injustice. He has his own beautiful way of making sense of the world. He will accept—with more equanimity than we who are much closer to our last breath—that death is the inevitable result of life and that it is the small, everyday kindnesses you show along the way that bring purpose and joy.'

For a whole minute, Sam didn't move. His eyes followed the two women onto the deck and through the front door. In an anguished voice, he said, 'Some days I am so paralysed with fear, Chef, I can't move or even think straight. What if I fail Kate and the baby at a crucial moment? What if I let her down when it counts the most?'

Marcus pressed his forefinger into the small of Sam's back to nudge him along. 'Let's eat, my good and capable friend who has never failed a soul in his entire life. Food is fuel but, even more, it comforts, yes?'

Sam forced himself to relax. 'What fabulous feast have you prepared for us tonight, Chef?' he asked.

Marcus shook his head, smiling. 'You will find tonight's meal far from fabulous, alas, because today I have been working in the café while Ettie cared for the man whose partner died. We will eat café leftovers. A travesty, is it not, for a chef to rummage for scraps to feed his guests?'

'Your scraps will be five-star, I can guarantee it,' Sam said.

'Of course, you are right,' Marcus replied, without a hint of irony.

❧

Ettie and Kate set the table on the deck. The balmy spring evening, they agreed, was too glorious to waste by eating indoors. If the air turned chill, blankets could be fetched.

Sam heaved a sigh of relief. The chef's cosy dining room, located at the rear of the house, was deeply formal, with antique chairs so fragile Sam feared for their safety under his bulk. The chef had told him often enough that food was all about performance, and a beautiful setting was part of the show, but Sam had to beat back the feeling that there wasn't enough oxygen in the room. Raised in a boatshed, with Vegemite jars for glasses and plates bought at Vinnie's, precious bits and pieces scared him rigid. The thoughtless wave of an arm to make a point and he might strike the chandelier; replacing a wineglass too heavily could snap the stem; clattering cutlery on antique porcelain plates might chip the gilt edges beyond repair. Every meal inside was slow torture, Sam fearing he might accidentally destroy the family heirlooms and break the chef's generous heart.

Despite tonight's more casual approach, by the time Ettie had finished with the table it could have been photographed for a magazine. Candles flickered in large lanterns, carnival-coloured napkins rested on deep yellow side plates, a rustic pottery jug filled with sunflowers (fake but fabulous) stood in the centre. 'Perfect,' she breathed, her face shining with pleasure.

'You are a true artist, my love,' said the chef, slipping an arm around her waist. Ettie turned in his arms and kissed his cheek.

It was a moment of such intimacy Sam had to look away, knowing the knot in his stomach wouldn't have been there if he and Kate shared a similar devotion. To cover his unease, he pulled out a chair, held it steady while Kate negotiated her bulk into position. She gave him a soft smile, whispered thank you, and the knot released. You're picking at sores that don't exist, he told himself, mentally vowing he'd do well to focus on the strengths in his relationship instead of the weaknesses. A bloke could breathe life into dark fantasy if he wasn't careful and live to regret it forever.

Ettie and Marcus disappeared into the kitchen and returned holding exquisitely arranged platters of salami, cold chicken, roasted vegetables dripping in olive oil, a slab of pecorino and two warmed loaves of bread with a yeasty scent that made Sam's nostrils twitch and his mouth water.

'We start without formality,' Marcus announced. 'Hands to break the bread that we will use to mop up the juices when the time is right. This is our full repast for the night.' He paused dramatically. 'Except, naturally, for dessert, which will remain a mystery until it is served.' He put two fingers to his lips and made a kissing sound, as though nothing short of ecstasy lay in wait.

'Thanks, Ettie, Marcus,' Sam said. 'What a wonderful gesture to take the edge off a rough day.'

He offered the platter to Kate, who used a spoon and fork to take a small piece of chicken, a few chargrilled vegetables. She ignored the salami but tore a piece of bread from a loaf, brushing crumbs from where they'd fallen on the tablecloth.

Ettie shot a guilty look at Marcus and her face turned pink. Sam was oblivious to the undercurrent, but Kate picked up the vibe instantly. 'So there's more to tonight than a casual dinner to . . . how did you word it? Put aside the horror of Stringybark Bay and celebrate the arrival of spring?' She leaned forward a little, her dark hair falling across her face. 'What else is on the agenda, Ettie?' she asked sweetly.

'Eh?' Sam paused in the act of loading his plate. 'This chicken, Chef, it smells like a culinary miracle. What did you do to it?'

Marcus managed to utter 'Brine,' before Ettie, who found duplicity exhausting, cut him off in a rush to confess the true purpose of their seemingly impromptu gathering.

'There was a meeting of the GeriAncients at the café this afternoon,' she began. 'I thought they were getting together to comfort Brian, plan the funeral, shed some tears, tell lovely stories about their friend who had just died. But Brian hit them with a bombshell before they could say a word.'

'Bombshell? After someone drowned? Hard to think what could be worse,' Sam said.

'Brian wants—no, he demanded—that his investment in the house be returned immediately. He plans never to set foot there again.'

'Brian's in shock,' Sam said dismissively. 'He'll come right once the funeral is over.' He ripped into a chicken thigh with his teeth and caught Kate's raised eyebrows. He'd thought tonight's dinner was merely a small step up from a picnic and just as casual, but clearly he'd been mistaken. About to wipe his greasy hands on the napkin, he dabbed the corners of his mouth instead. He saw the tension ease from Kate's shoulders at the same time as a knot formed in the back of his neck.

'Apparently, it was Cam's idea to move here,' Ettie explained. 'Brian was against it. He had a bad feeling from the beginning, he told me. No sane person, he said, could tolerate Donna for more than a minute at a time. It should have been her who drowned, he said. Her death would have done everyone a favour.' Ettie's face reflected mild despair at the thought of wishing anyone harm. 'He didn't mean it, of course.'

Sam attempted humour. 'Well, if we find her dead, we'll know who did it.'

Nobody even smiled.

'Sorry. It's the Irish in me. You know—laugh in the face of adversity?' He shrugged. 'Well, it works some of the time.'

Kate broke off another hunk of bread. 'It's about money, isn't it? Brian wants to reclaim his stash and bolt.'

Ettie nodded. 'And when Mike told him that would be imposs- ible, Brian insisted the house would have to be sold.'

Kate chewed and swallowed then said, 'I don't mean to be rude, Ettie, but how do you know all this?'

Ettie fumbled with her napkin, adjusted the position of a sunflower, hummed under her breath.

Marcus came to her rescue. 'The voices, they were raised, and Ettie, who was sitting at your desk under the stairs while you were attending to the condiments on the deck tables . . .'

Kate cut in: 'Yeah, I get it. You couldn't help overhearing, right?'

Ettie nodded.

'I can't help wondering, though,' said Kate. 'Surely, no one, no matter how trusting, would invest in a very expensive scheme without a water-tight legal agreement that covered every foreseeable circumstance, which—given their ages—would have to include death?'

Marcus immediately saw where she was coming from. 'Ah,' he said. 'Yes. I see.'

'Well, I don't!' Ettie responded with a hint of petulance.

'If none of the other residents wants to sell the property, it stands to reason there's a piece of paper in some lawyer's office that says Brian will either have to return to the house or kiss his investment goodbye,' Kate said, pushing her empty plate away and leaning back with her hands held protectively over her stomach. 'Unless he has something to use as leverage over the group.'

'Oh. He did say . . . well, he probably didn't mean it—just the heat of the moment, of course,' Ettie mumbled.

'What did he say?' Kate asked.

'It's just . . . well, I heard Brian threaten—well, almost blackmail—Mike. Said he'd bring the whole house down if he had to.' Ettie looked uncomfortable. 'It made the hairs on the back of my neck stand up. I mean, they're all meant to be close friends: close enough to live side by side for the rest of their lives.'

Marcus, shocked, reached for Ettie's hand. Sam tilted his chair backwards, rocking on two legs. Kate frowned, puzzled. 'Strange thing to say,' she said, reaching for yet another piece of bread, chewing thoughtfully. 'I have no idea what caveats have been put in place to protect the original investors, but if he's determined to leave, his best and least destructive option might be to find a buyer the household will accept,' Kate said.

Sam butted in: 'But, love, it's such a tight-knit group. Not sure an outsider, even one with the instincts of Mother Teresa, would be welcome.'

'Which, of course, brings us to another question,' Marcus said, reaching for the empty plates. 'These people are not in the first or even the second flush of youth, yes? Some, Ettie says, are perhaps not in the best of health. One by one, death takes its due, until . . .'

'There's one poor old sod left standing?' Sam finished.

Marcus stood, holding the plates in front of him, the knives and forks balanced expertly on top. 'Yes, my friend. What then?' He looked at Kate for an answer.

'Depends on how they've structured a succession plan, but you'd have to assume that the sole survivor would have the right to stay until he or she chooses to leave or dies. Correct me if I'm wrong, but it sounds like the group had fairly successful businesses before retiring.'

'Hard to know,' Sam said. 'Although it must have taken a fortune to set up the Stringybark Bay house. Offshore renovations—well, add an extra thirty to fifty per cent to costs. Maybe there wasn't a lot of cash left over. Anyway, what would be the point of ending up with a fortune if you were too old to enjoy it? Nah. Nothing shonky going on there. I'd stake my life on it.'

Kate murmured agreement.

Ettie cleared the rest of the table, insisting Kate and Sam stay seated. 'A few finishing touches to the dessert and we will return.'

She bent to whisper in Sam's ear: 'Trumpet fanfare is mandatory.'
Using her hip to hold the flywire door open, she retreated backwards.

'Might stretch my legs for a minute, ease my back,' Kate said.

Sam leaped up to pull out her chair. 'Do you want to go home?
Ettie will understand.'

'And miss dessert? Never!'

'Might grab another beer, then,' he said.

In the kitchen, he caught Ettie swaying to Norah Jones while
she stirred what smelled like a vanilla-based sauce. The chef was
building a pyramid of singed pears encrusted with thin strips of
roasted ginger and orange peel on a chocolate tart. 'You guys are
stars,' Sam said appreciatively, leaning over the tart, inhaling deeply.

'Out!' ordered Marcus furiously. 'Now! You will breathe on my
creation and bring it undone to collapsisation.'

Sam saluted with a grin, grabbed a beer from the fridge and fled.

At the end of the jetty, Kate's rounded body was etched in
exquisite detail by the dock light, gold-tipped water rippling at her
feet. He thought she looked unutterably beautiful, and even though
he was a man who considered nature to be the only rational religion,
the word 'madonna' sprang to his mind. Unwilling to disturb her,
he squatted at the edge of the deck, leaning forward to rinse his
hands in sea water. An orange jellyfish with finger-thick tentacles
parachuted to the surface and slowly sank back into dark anonymity.

Hearing the approach of dessert, he moved forward to help Kate
to her feet. She smiled her thanks and didn't let go of his hand until
they reached the table.

Ettie held open the door for the chef. Sam curled his hand into
a loose fist and blew air through it. The result was less trumpet
fanfare than rude noises. Kate laughed, put her hands over her ears.

The chef beamed and, under the watchful gaze of his guests, placed his dessert in the centre of the table for them to admire before he sank in his knife with the care and precision of a heart surgeon.

'It smells divine and looks like a work of art, but only a very small piece for me, please, Marcus,' Kate said, patting her rounded stomach.

'Go as big as you think is decent for me,' Sam said, dodging a dig in the ribs from Kate—playful, this time. 'And if there's an extra piece, I could always fling it Jimmy's way in the morning.' He slapped his thigh, as though he'd just remembered an important fact. 'Ah, it's Monday. Might have to eat it myself for morning tea then.'

The chef served out their portions then looked around the table expectantly. The others applauded lightly. The chef dipped his head, the signal to begin eating.

'I've had a thought,' Kate murmured, before anyone could take a bite.

'Yes, love?' Ettie said, fork poised midway to her mouth.

'Assuming that finding a replacement would solve Brian's problem and prevent what could turn into a nasty situation . . .'

'Yes?' Ettie prompted.

'I think it might be worth talking to Lizzie about joining the GeriEcstasies' household.'

'Lizzie?!' Sam and Ettie shouted in unison.

'Lizzie? Who is Lizzie?' demanded a confused chef.

'You mean the recluse who lives with a few cows on a couple of hectares of what must be the last remaining piece of private land on the escarpment?' Sam said, incredulous.

Kate nodded.

'How do you know Lizzie?' Ettie asked, surprised. 'She hardly says a word when she comes into the café.'

Kate explained. 'She always looks so immaculate, so stylish. I told her I'd love to be like her when I'm her age. Since then, we've had a few chats. One day, I mentioned she looked a little tired and asked if I could do anything for her. She said she wasn't managing as easily as she used to, living alone and pretty much isolated. She made a joke about ageing—I forget what it was, but it exposed her vulnerability. If you had to guess, where would you put her age?'

Ettie shrugged. 'Not sure. Mid-sixties?'

'Nearly eighty,' Kate said.

'No! Really?' Ettie's eyes were round with disbelief.

'Come, come, the tart is at the perfect temperature,' Marcus said, trying to get his dinner back on track. 'In a few minutes the optimum experience for the tongue and tastebuds will dissolve. Poof!'

Ettie gave him an apologetic glance and again picked up her fork. The chef watched her closely as she took her first bite. 'Sublime,' she declared, her eyes closed.

Silence then ensued while they did justice to the chef's magnificent effort. It would have been unthinkably rude to break the spell woven by culinary perfection with a discussion about death.

After a while, Ettie sighed contentedly and put down her cutlery. 'Lizzie,' Ettie mused. 'Not such a crazy idea, Kate.'

'She was a playwright, back in the day. Quite famous.'

'Did she tell you that?' Ettie asked.

'Of course not. She's extremely private. I looked her up online. She had a couple of hit plays in the seventies, although probably no one remembers them now. Film scripts in the eighties, two of them blockbusters: *Portrait of an Affair*—'

'I remember that movie,' Ettie interjected. 'Brilliant. The bloke. What a shi—'

'And *Redemption*,' Kate finished quickly.

'Oh goodness. I remember that one, too. Bleak.' Ettie gave a little shiver. 'Who played the lead? She was fabulous . . .'

The chef cleared his throat. 'Forgive me, Ettie, but are we not wandering from the topic?'

'The point,' Kate said, picking up the thread, 'is that Lizzie's credentials are immaculate.' She attempted to rest her elbows on the table but, finding it too awkward, leaned back. A waft of cool air crept off the water and wound around their ankles. Sam grabbed a blanket from a pile Ettie had placed on a nearby stool and arranged it over Kate's lap. 'It occurs to me,' Kate added thoughtfully, 'that Brian had a great deal to lose—but perhaps even more to gain by Cameron's death.'

Ettie almost choked: 'What are you suggesting, Kate?'

Kate shrugged.

'Eh?' Sam said, eyeballing the group around the table in search of an explanation.

Marcus placed his hand on Ettie's forearm protectively, as if to guide her through uncharted terrain. 'It is extreme, this proposition that perhaps what took place was not an accident.'

'Eh?' Sam repeated. 'You're not suggesting Brian knocked him off, are you? He loved the bloke. Look at him. He's wrecked by grief.'

'And yet . . .' Ettie murmured. Three pairs of eyes instantly turned to her. 'When he told them he wanted to pull his equity out of the house, he gave the impression of a viper about to strike. Even though I wasn't in the room, I felt my blood run cold.'

The group sat in shocked silence for a minute or two at the thought of murder.

Marcus broke the spell, offering Ettie more wine, Sam another beer, suggesting he make Kate a cup of chamomile tea. Heads were shaken.

'Desperate people are capable of desperate actions, and Ettie heard him say he was against the plan from the start,' Kate said eventually.

Sam thought of Kate's mother, her criminal attempt to trick an innocent and married man into believing he'd fathered her child. The tragic fallout. Even the most unlikely people were capable of heinous acts. But in this case?

'You're damn near perfect in my eyes, Kate, but you sure can send a bloke's mind to the dark side without much to back it up.'

'I saw something dark in the man,' Ettie whispered, 'which is hardly an incriminating fact but . . .'

'Précisément,' said the chef. 'We are involved in the dangerous business of speculation without facts. This is unhealthy, yes? This is what makes trouble along the pathways ahead. Let us allow the chocolate we have recently consumed to ease our concerns and the ginger to settle our anxious stomachs.'

Jolted out of her thoughts, Ettie brought her hands together in a gentle clap. 'It's time for you two to make tracks. Jenny is on deck at the café tomorrow and Marcus has a few treats to finish preparing so he'll he there for a while, too. Have the day off, Kate. You and Sam should do something lovely together while you can. Once the baby is born, your time will never be your own again.'

⌒

Sam settled Kate in the tinnie and untied. He moved to the stern, balancing his weight to steady the boat, reaching for the starter cord from a standing position. Hesitated.

Kate looked at him. 'Something wrong?'

'Nah. It's just . . . Lizzie. Not sure where you're coming from.'

Kate shifted uneasily. 'She's finding it hard where she is now.'

'Yeah, but she has a million options. Why choose GeriEcstasy? She doesn't even know the inmates.'

Kate grimaced. 'Inmates. Bit harsh, aren't you?'

Sam reached for the cord again. 'It's just that I'm wondering if you're more interested in an inside source than Lizzie's wellbeing.'

For once, the engine caught on the first yank. He dropped the revs to give Kate a chance to reply but she'd turned her head sideways, was staring towards the black expanse of the national park on the eastern side of the bay. He sighed and set off at a slow pace. A greasy sludge of sea water sloshed at his feet. He looked up at the sky, awash with stars, and let go of his fear that Kate, whom he knew to be single-minded and ruthless in the pursuit of justice, might jeopardise an innocent woman in order to nail the truth. A tragic accident, that's all it was, he told himself. When a bloke's number was up, it was up. He settled into the voyage home, keeping outside the shallow water markers and alert for tinnies travelling without navigation lights. He had precious cargo on board.

CHAPTER SEVEN

UNABLE TO SLEEP, HER MIND spinning with thoughts of Lizzie, the dead man, the future of the GeriEcstasies, Kate checked the luminous dials on her watch. Nearly midnight. Outside, the night sounds of the bush ramped up a notch. Powerful owls, the thump of wallabies, the chitter-chatter of bandicoots. She found herself fighting back tears, pressing down a sadness she hadn't been aware existed.

She rolled out of bed, careful not to disturb Sam, and tiptoed through the silent house, checking doors were firmly closed. Once, she'd woken to find a diamond python curled at the foot of the bed. Lain paralysed with fear for half a morning, until the snake opened a basilisk eye and, unfussed, slithered down the hallway through the door she'd forgotten to close. A lifetime ago.

She felt the baby kick. Fought down an illogical desire to run. Stepped onto the verandah and into the soft, moist air. The community had thought her mad when she'd bought the derelict house. Once south-facing, mouldy from neglect and a leaking roof, tucked into an isolated nook and locked in at low tide, the place was now transformed into a dry, comfortable home. She knew Sam found the bright white palette harsh, daunting; he was afraid, he said, that he'd leave great splodges all over the place. He'd suggested they live in his house on Cutter Island, where the winter sun warmed the rooms and every surface had *plenty of character,* said he'd renovate the bathroom to suit a woman—even the kitchen, if that's what she wanted. She'd insisted any blemishes in her house could easily be removed with a clean cloth, a little vinegar mixed with bicarb and warm water, some elbow grease. He'd understood immediately. She would never cross his threshold with a suitcase full of clothes. Most days, she loved her home. Some days, when her tinnie sat stranded on the sandbank at low tide, she felt trapped, felt the bush was closing in on her. But she would never trade the privacy of Oyster Bay for the crowded shores of Cutter Island, not even for deepwater access.

Another kick. Harder. In an unguarded moment a few days ago, she'd blurted her ambivalence about motherhood to Ettie, who had laughed. Once the baby was born, she'd said in a tone rich with reassurance, the desire to protect and nurture would be overpowering. Kate wasn't so sure. There were days when she felt smothered by Ettie's care, Sam's unconditional adoration. Until now, she'd been a loner, the kind of woman who'd politely declined offers of friendship, hastily stepped back from the casual kiss of an acquaintance met in the street. Protective, always, of her privacy and space. And here she was, not long out of the grind of journalism, heavily pregnant and surrounded by a tribe of well-meaning individuals with her best interests at heart. The situation was outside her experience. She had no idea what was expected of her in return. Even now, returning to a bed occupied by another person felt like a violation of all her carefully constructed boundaries. She no longer had the option of grabbing an assignment in the far corner of the world to escape the pressure of co-workers and office politics. In fact, the Kate Jackson book of options had been stitched closed for the foreseeable future. She was anchored to Sam, the Briny Café, Cook's Basin and a baby.

She gave herself a mental shake to stop her mood from spiralling further into a black hole, shot an imaginary kick in the direction of the black dog lurking near her feet, stared into the black night and thought about Cameron's death, Brian's future. Why would a man who couldn't swim venture so close to the water's edge? she wondered, mystified.

Suppressing a shiver, she pushed the question aside and struggled stiffly to her feet. Made a determined effort, as the chef had instructed, to count her blessings, remind herself she'd always been an intensely practical, self-sufficient woman who dealt sensibly and efficiently with problems as they arose.

Back inside, she rubbed the chill from her arms and decided to spend what was left of the night on the sofa, where she could read a book without the light disturbing Sam. She dragged a woollen throw over her feet, plumped a cushion to support her head and fell instantly asleep.

∽

Sam woke not long after dawn, panicked when he couldn't hear Kate's steady breathing beside him. Stark naked, he tore into the kitchen. Through the doorway into the sitting room, he caught the sight of a twisted blue blanket and a crown of shiny black hair. He crept across the floorboards, less anxious but needing assurance that all was well. Her chest rose and fell in a delicate rhythm. Her pale skin shone with health. The freckles dusted across her nose were in their customary positions.

His whole life rested there before him. He resisted straightening the blanket and walked backwards out of the room, softly pulling the door closed behind him.

In the bedroom, he pulled on shorts and a T-shirt and hurried down the sandstone steps from Kate's house to Frankie's boatshed. It was early, but Frankie was contemptuous of what he called *gentlemen's hours*. From dawn to dusk, he repaired boats with the devotion of a master craftsman who understood that sloppy work could result in catastrophe. Sam would find a cuppa there and, if he was lucky, a bacon-and-egg roll. Frankie, who boasted he owned one plate, one knife, one fork and two spoons, did all his cooking in a small frying pan over a gas bottle in a corner free from chisels, scrapers and a hardware store's collection of tools. He washed the crockery and cutlery in the same sink as his paintbrushes. So far, so good.

Sam smelled frying bacon before he reached the waterfront.

'Kicked out, eh?' said Frankie, a renowned pessimist.

'Nah, she's deep in dreamland. Didn't want to disturb her. The kid's been keeping her awake most nights.'

Frankie, a round-shouldered man in paint-splotched overalls and a Greek fisherman's cap no one had ever seen him remove from his head, tilted his head towards the frying pan. 'There's leftover bacon, eggs in the carton—help yourself.' The tea's stewed. You like tomato or barbecue?'

The mention of barbecue sauce made Sam's stomach flip flop in a bad way. In the days before Ettie became the proprietor, the Briny's burgers were awash in the stuff. Bertie, who'd had the sense to sell the café to Ettie at a knockdown price when he was handed a death sentence by a lung specialist, believed it killed whatever dangerous bacteria lurked in green-frilled beef patties, rendering them safe to eat. A jury would have sent him straight to prison after a single, gut-cramping bite.

'Tomato,' Sam said, nevertheless feeling a tide of nostalgia for a bygone era wash over him.

'In the fridge,' Frankie said, pointing to it as though Sam hadn't withdrawn enough frigidly cold beers to find his way blindfolded. B.K., he thought. Before Kate. Before she gathered up the after-hours slack and filled it with promise.

'That bloke?' Frankie said, raising his eyebrows so they touched the rim of his cap.

Sam broke an egg into a frying pan sticky with the detritus of former meals. He turned up the heat to kill any lingering salmonella.

'What bloke?'

'The one that no longer lives in the fairytale house with the country's longest jetty,' Frankie replied, as though it were obvious.

'Yeah. Cameron.' Sam flipped the egg, cut a hamburger bun in half and found space in the pan to fry one side. 'Got any butter?'

'No. They say he drowned.'

'Yeah. Sad as.'

Frankie tugged an empty plastic crate into a spot of warm sunlight and plonked himself down. Swore, and stood to fetch his mug.

'Here, give me that,' Sam said. 'I've got a fresh pot on the go and, second only to Kate, I am the world's greatest brewer of tea.' He took Frankie's mug and walked to the water's edge to tip out the dregs.

'Odd.'

'That I can brew a great cuppa?'

'The water is so shallow where they live.'

'Night-time and a king tide—maybe he lost his bearings.' Sam sniffed a carton of milk, deemed it safe, sloshed some in the mugs. 'Couldn't swim either, poor bastard. Helluva place for someone like him to choose to live.'

Frankie took his fresh cuppa from Sam without a word. Sam caught the unspoken question. 'What are you getting at? You reckon something dodgy went on?'

Frankie shrugged, took a deep slurp, smacked his lips noisily. 'I know nothing, of course.' He paused thoughtfully, his mug held between both hands, steam rising lazily. 'Odd, though,' he repeated.

Sam assembled his breakfast and dragged forward another empty crate, arranging it at a discreet distance. He anchored his tea between the steel tracks of the slipway, bit into the roll and wiped a trickle of grease from his chin with the back of his wrist. 'Bloody delicious. Here's to you, Frankie.' They stretched towards each other to clink mugs.

'You arrived at Stringybark Bay at the peak of high tide, right?' Frankie asked, unwilling to drop the subject.

Sam nodded, took another bite of his roll.

'The man was floating in the water for how long, would you say?'

'Jeez, Frankie, you're putting me off my brekkie.'

'Make a guess,' Frankie insisted.

'Well, I don't know. Maybe a couple of hours. More.'

'So not such a high tide that a man who stumbled from the seawall couldn't stand with his head and shoulders above the water-line? Whichever way you look at it, it's odd.'

Sam took a moment to reply. 'Maybe. This bacon is first rate. Where'd you get it?'

'Boat owner. He brings it from the country when his boat goes in the slip for an anti-foul.'

'Bloody delicious.' Sam finished the roll, raised his forearm to wipe his chin. Realised it was too big a job and waded ankle-deep into the water, where he rinsed his face. Turning he said, 'How is business then, mate?' he asked. 'Everyone in a rush for an anti-foul and paint job before summer fires up?'

Frankie said: 'Don't see much of Ettie's old tin can now she's landed on her feet with the café and the chef.'

'Trust me, it's the chef who's landed on his feet.'

'I miss those chocolate cakes she settled her bill with, though. That woman sure can cook.'

სთ

When Sam returned to the house, he heard movement. 'Kate?'

'In the bathroom. Won't be long,' she called out.

He drifted into the kitchen to make her a cuppa and saw she'd beaten him to it. He cleared the dishes, wiped crumbs off the counter. Straightened the bed, grabbed the laundry basket and started a load of washing, carefully avoiding Kate's whites. Afraid he'd stain them even with hands he'd scrubbed like a surgeon.

He found a sunny corner on the verandah and sank into a wicker chair, mulling over Frankie's words and wishing at the same time he could dismiss them as the kind of scuttlebutt for which Cook's Basin was renowned.

After a while, Kate joined him, towelling her wet hair.

'Fancy another cuppa? Or can I tempt you with a cruise on the *Mary Kay* to a magical bay known only to me and one or two others? We could take a picnic.'

'Just the tea, thanks,' she said, still towelling.

He watched her for a moment, swallowing his disappointment and pushing aside an uncomfortable little niggle that Kate deliberately avoided situations where she couldn't easily escape his company. Feeling a pang when he thought of Ettie and the chef—their palpable joy in being together, whether it was bent over a hot stove or fishing from the end of the jetty.

He stood up from the chair, determined to resist making comparisons, briefly rested a hand on Kate's shoulder. She passed him the damp towel. 'Marco Polo, please. No milk.'

'Your wish is my command.'

'Before you go . . .'

'Yeah?' he asked, hoping she might have changed her mind about the picnic.

'About Cameron. I was thinking . . .'

Sam let out a sigh. 'Marco Polo. No milk.'

As he disappeared into the cool well of the kitchen, Kate flopped into the recently vacated chair, twisting a strand of hair between her thumb and forefinger. On the north-facing side of Oyster Bay, she saw Jimmy and his mother cutting through the water in Jimmy's banged-up tinnie. Sunday was clean-up day on Artie's yacht. Amelia stripped Artie's bed, cleaned out his icebox—tossing anything on the verge of becoming an intelligent life form—and gathered up his dirty laundry in a pillow slip to take home to wash, iron and return. Jimmy scrubbed the decks, washed the portholes, checked the anchor was holding firm and tightened any lifelines that might have loosened. By the end of every Sunday, Artie's shabby old boat, where he'd lived since a stroke took away the use of his legs more than a decade ago, gleamed in the setting sun.

When Sam returned with Kate's tea, he found her laughing out loud. 'Check it out,' she spluttered, pointing to where Jimmy had his hands under his mother's backside to boost her from the tinnie while Artie tried to yank her from above.

'That's not going to end well,' Sam said. Dumping the tea, he headed for his tinnie at a run, shouting to Jimmy and Amelia to stay put till he got there. As though they could hear him on the other side of the bay. The sound of a belly flop cannoned across the bay, followed by loud laughter as Amelia's wet head appeared above the water's surface. Two seconds later, Jimmy's head popped up beside her. Sam exhaled in relief. Artie and his useless legs were still safely on board. No more drownings; not today.

When he reached Artie's boat, he tied on to the stern and climbed aboard. 'For an old man, Artie, you don't seem to have much common sense,' he said.

'We're having fun,' shouted Amelia, waving her arms to stay afloat. 'It's a perfect day for a swim. Water's cold, though.'

'I saw a stingray, Sam, bigger 'n any before. Took off like a spaceship when I locked eyes,' Jimmy said, treading water. Before Sam could say a word, he duck-dived. Came up shaking his hair like a wet dog. 'Nope. It's gone. You're gunna have to take me word for it.'

'Most boring thing in the world,' Artie said.

'What is?' asked Sam.

'Common sense.'

'Might keep you breathing a bit longer, old man.'

'Doesn't matter much at this stage of me life,' Artie muttered.

'It's me you're talking to, mate.'

Artie dropped the fake pathos and grinned. 'Worth a try, eh . . .'

Sam chucked a rope to Jimmy, who scrambled up it like a monkey, then the pair of them worked together to heave Amelia onboard.

Artie dug out some dry clothes from under a seat in the cabin, and a few minutes later, Amelia emerged wearing trackie daks and a windcheater that announced the Cutter Island dog race of 1963.

'Forgot I had that top,' Artie said nostalgically. 'Brings back memories . . .'

At the prospect of Artie reminiscing, Sam made a quick exit.

Back home, Sam found Kate dozing in the cane chair on the verandah, head at an awkward angle, her hands resting on her belly.

'Sam?' she murmured sleepily. 'That you?' She stretched her arms above her head, rubbed her neck, moving her head back and forth to ease the stiffness. 'I can't stop falling asleep. Sometimes, I wake up and I have no idea what day it is and only twenty minutes have gone by.'

'Building your strength for the bub.'

'Turning into a vegetable, I suspect.'

'Can I get you anything?'

Kate shook her head. 'I can't stop thinking about the way that man—Cameron?—died.'

'Not a cheery subject for a—'

'Pregnant woman?' She snorted. 'Everyone's an expert on pregnancy. The café's been assaulted by classical music for months because Ettie believes it soothes unborn babies. Even the politest customers have had enough of "Für Elise" and being stirred beyond their emotional capacity by Beethoven's Ninth.'

'She means well.'

'I know. It's just . . .' She shook her head. 'It doesn't matter. I was wondering, though: Richard Baines, the policeman—he's a mate, isn't he?'

'Yeah,' Sam said cautiously. 'He's a mate.'

Kate flicked off the blanket and came to stand alongside him at the railing, staring at the fissured face of the escarpment. 'If you found yourself having a beer with him at the Square, it would be perfectly natural to ask a few questions, wouldn't it? Normal curiosity. After all, you and Jimmy found the body.'

'What sort of questions?'

Kate sat down again. 'Think about it, Sam. First, why would a man who can't swim venture close to the water at night?'

'Could've lost his way . . .'

'Second, the tide wasn't high enough for the water to come over his head for another couple of hours.'

'Have you been talking to Frankie?'

'What? No. I checked the tide chart. Third, he could've held on to the seawall and yelled for help. Nobody heard a cry for help, did they?'

'Jeez, Kate, I don't know.'

'But Richard Baines must know.'

'Exactly—we should leave it for the cops to sort out.'

Kate grimaced. 'I suppose. It's just . . . I'd hate to steer Lizzie in the direction of a house harbouring a murderer.'

'Jumping ahead a bit, aren't you? Why don't we wait and see what happens before getting involved?'

Kate said nothing.

'Jeez, Kate, you're about to have a baby!'

She looked up at him with her sea-green eyes and said, 'Please? Couldn't you just talk to Richard?' Her hopeful expression cut straight through his heart.

He sighed. 'Okay, leave it with me. But I'm not making any promises.'

'Is there any cake left? I could slaughter a slice of orange and almond cake right now,' Kate said, radiating the sweetness of victory. 'Thank you,' she called as Sam, defeated, stomped into the kitchen.

∽

Later, Kate settled herself in her study with a stack of invoices and Sam found himself pacing the verandah, pressure to escape the confines of domesticity building like a head of steam. Spending time indoors when the sun was shining, the water sparkled and the fish could well be feeling suicidal was a serious waste of an opportunity.

'Anything need fixing?' he asked, interrupting Kate's work.

She shook her head.

'What about the tap in the laundry? Leaking, isn't it?'

'Nope,' she replied, a pencil poised over a figure on an invoice to indicate where she was up to.

'How's the oven, then? Thermostat working?'

'Never use it, remember?'

'Right. I could scrub the floors, if you like.'

Exasperated, she laid down her pencil and turned to face him. 'If you want to go fishing, Sam, just say so. You don't need my permission.'

'With the baby so close . . .'

'Weeks to go. Make the most of your freedom. That's what everyone keeps telling me.'

'Are you sure?'

'Sam!'

'Might grab some bait. I could see if Bainesy's on duty, too.' This got her attention. Capitulating absolutely, he went on: 'I could sidle up to the police launch, just for a polite yarn. That'd make any questions about Cameron's death seem less of an interrogation and more like idle curiosity.'

'Great strategy.' She grabbed a blank sheet of paper and began writing, folded it into a square and handed it over. 'Some questions that need to be answered.'

'Jeez, Kate . . .' But he shoved it in his pocket.

Once a journo always a journo, I suppose, he thought, as he fled before she could issue further instructions.

At the dock, he jumped in the tinnie and yanked the starter cord. After a couple of coughs, the engine caught and, twisting the throttle to a sedate speed, he set off towards the *Mary Kay*, the wind in his face, his lungs breathing in the brine and the clean scent of eucalypts, the life-affirming oxygen of the outdoors. He nosed up to the stern, grabbed the leader and jumped onboard, realising as he did that he'd forgotten the bait. Well, he'd never really intended to throw out a line anyway. He tied the tinnie so it would trail the *Mary Kay* and, humming tunelessly, started the engine, released the mooring and headed in the direction of Cat Island, a wildlife sanctuary at the mouth of the bays with a couple of hidden sandy coves. Top spots for the police boat to anchor while on the lookout for drunks at the helm of large yachts in dangerous winds or kids skimming the water in small crafts with monster engines, blind to whatever lurked in their path—all of them hyped by speed and testosterone and the belief that youth guaranteed immortality.

Fast Freddy, dressed once more in his rainbow clothing, sped past in his water taxi with a small wave and a big smile. Sam leaned out of the wheelhouse to return a salute. Nearer the shore, a flock of seagulls floated like toy dinghies, squawking in angry debate. Cormorants popped up from the water with heads like periscopes, the most skilful with a wriggling fish in their hooked beaks.

Reaching the entrance to Stringybark Bay, he made a snap decision to leave Cat Island for another day. He couldn't be sure he'd find Bainesy hiding out to catch miscreants and he couldn't call ahead to check without tipping him off there might be a hidden agenda behind what was meant to be a casual encounter when they were both out on the water. So instead, he turned left into Stringybark Bay and pointed the nose of the *Mary Kay* towards the elegant but (he couldn't help thinking) soulless house on the edge of the tidal lagoon. He wasn't being nosy, he told himself. He was just following the ethos held dear by every Cook's Basin resident: good communities took care of people in bad times. As far as he knew, no one had called on the Ancients to offer help and sympathy. The omission was unthinkable. Yeah, the Ancients. Sounded like a suitable collective name to him. If he kept his wits about him, he might even be able to suss out the agreement that held the house-hold together. If there was one. That'd give Kate something to think about.

He slipped into a higher gear, whistling happily—and felt happier still. 'You're a genius, mate,' he told himself. 'Without a shadow of doubt.' He felt a tickle on his lower leg. Leaned down, expecting to find a tick searching for a comfy spot to burrow. Instead, a tiny spider scrambled towards his knees. He brushed it off violently. 'Sorry, mate,' he said. 'No offence but I'd feel more comfortable if you were a shark.' He felt a throb where a funnel web nestled in a boot had sunk fangs into his foot when he was a kid. His imagination? Or the body's subconscious warning system at the sight of a former foe? The question kept him thinking until he spied the spiffy navy, black and white police launch tied at the end of the world's longest jetty. Some days, he thought smugly, all the pieces fall into place. He scanned the water, looking for a vacant mooring. If the cops had to leave for an emergency and found the *Mary Kay* rafted alongside, his name would be added to a file of selfish dingbats. He saw a red buoy bobbing on the water without a purpose, swung the barge until her beam faced into the breeze and let the current float her close enough for him to grab the mooring's rope with a boat hook. He wrapped it around a giant cleat on the bow then, at the stern, hauled up the tinnie and jumped in, congratulating himself for having the foresight to tow it along.

He reached the jetty in time to see Abe Smith and Richard Baines leaving the house. With Kate's questions burning a hole in the rear pocket of his shorts, he held up his hand in greeting. 'How's it going?' he asked.

Smith, a gnarly man who'd retrieved too many dead bodies from the water in his thirty-year career, rolled his eyes. 'No death is a good death,' he said. 'Never seen a smiling corpse in my life.'

'Er, right,' Sam said, not sure where the conversation was headed.

'Just informed them the body has been released, so they can get on with organising the funeral. Thought they'd be relieved, but the whole lot of them, barring the woman in the wheelchair, looked at me as though I'd grown horns. Funeral had nothing to do with them, they said. Cameron was Brian's problem. Whatever happened to all that touchy-feely communal living shit they banged on about when they got here?'

'Yeah, all for one and one for all,' Sam murmured.

'Bollocks. The atmosphere in there was poisonous enough to bring a buffalo to its knees.' Abe brushed past Baines and kept walking towards the launch.

Sam reached out to delay his friend: 'Nothing suspicious, eh?'

'Given the time of death and the tide, there's a bit of a smell about it, for sure. Nothing substantial, though. Coroner will have the final say.'

'But he drowned, right?'

'Yep. Right after his heart gave way.'

Sam felt a wave of relief. 'Heart attack?'

'The cracked skull had us guessing. The doc reckons the poor bastard must have keeled over, hit the bottom and found a rock there. Strike three, right? Heart attack, rock and drowned. He didn't stand a chance.'

'The rock . . .'

'Yeah. Something not quite right there.'

From the end of the jetty, Abe called to Richard impatiently.

'Gotta go, Sam. And you didn't hear any of this from me, okay? The old folks in the house will fill you in anyway. Brace your-self. That woman, Donna, she's a one-woman cyclone and the others are still in deep shock.'

As Richard hurried down the jetty to join his boss, Sam considered his options. Head home to Kate with enough details to keep her riveted, or carry on as planned? Anticipating embellishing his account with even more colourful details, he forged ahead to the glossy white front door, studied the antique ship's bell for a moment, and opted to knock firmly with his fist instead. He didn't want to be the first to leave fingerprints on the brass.

Mike Melrose opened the door with an uncharacteristic scowl. 'This is not a good time for us, Sam, as I'm sure you understand,' he said.

''Course, mate. Just wanted you to know that we're all happy to help if we can.' Stymied, and struggling to come up with a compelling but neutral reason to get a foot inside the door, he blurted: 'Kate's been working on your, er, accommodation logistics, given you're down a couple of residents, and might have the answer.'

Melrose pressed his fingers to his lips in indecision, then stepped back to allow Sam to enter. 'Everyone's upset, of course, so I hope you'll make allowances.'

'Terrible time. Doesn't bear thinking about.' Sam followed like a lamb with his hands behind his back and his fingers crossed in anticipation of offering one or two factual exaggerations that could later be construed as white lies.

The group in the kitchen, oddly dishevelled in comparison to their fashionable first appearance at the Square, nursed glasses of wine in groups of two. Sally and David Kinane held hands where they sat at the table, talking quietly to each other. Sheila Flowerdale, still clinging to killer heels but wearing a long red floral shirt that hadn't felt the hot fist of an iron, perched on a stool at the kitchen bench, swinging one foot nervously, yabbering incessantly in a tone that could be mistaken as accusing. Her husband Gavin, alongside her in shorts and a stained white T-shirt, looked at the ceiling while her words washed over him. Daisy and Rob, who'd chosen to look out the window to where the rainforest carpeted the cliffside, had their backs to the room. Their heads were bent close and they, too, held hands. Donna, feet bare but wearing a pink floral dress with a full skirt and nipped waist, emerged from the fridge holding up a fresh bottle of white wine. She noticed Sam immediately. 'Hey, barge boy! Come and join the party,' she shouted.

More drunk than drugged this time, thought Sam. He wondered if Kate really would be doing Lizzie a favour by suggesting GeriEcstasy as a new home. But a bit of odd behaviour now was perfectly understandable under the circumstances. People handled death in peculiar ways. It was the ones who never let their emotions show—generally speaking, of course—who warranted attention. In which case, Donna had nothing to worry about.

'Get the barge boy a drink,' she shouted to no one in particular, flinging her arm so white wine shot across the room. 'Oops,' she giggled. 'Anyone hurt?'

Melrose went to the kitchen sink for a cloth. Daisy wheeled her chair towards Sam, her hand extended in welcome. 'Not at our finest at the moment,' she said as Donna topped up her own glass and then everyone else's.

'At least we know it was almost certainly an accident,' Sheila Flowerdale said.

Her words were greeted with a hushed silence.

Sheila seemed to shrink lower on the stool. 'Well, it's a relief, isn't it?'

'Absolutely,' Melrose said. He began wiping the spilt wine with a dishcloth.

Donna lurched towards Sam. 'Have you heard? Our sandcastle—or is it our castle in the sand?—is about to come tumbling down. All for one and one for all? Pig's arse. Always thought so.'

'In a way,' Sam said, partly to fill the embarrassed silence that greeted her words, 'that's why I've called at a time when I suspect you'd rather be nursing your grief alone.'

'Grief?' cried Donna. 'I, for one, am celebrating the fact that the slimy, bad-tempered, selfish little bastard has stuffed his suitcase full of his tasteless clothes and done a bunk.'

Melrose intervened, patiently explaining to his wife that Sam was referring to the death of Cameron, not Brian's rushed exit.

'Whatever,' Donna said, waving her now empty glass and searching for someone to fill it.

No one moved.

'Don't mind me,' she said, heading to the fridge. 'I'll just help myself.' She paused, pirouetted unsteadily. 'Hey, I've got an idea—let's play a murder mystery game. Guess who killed Cameron.' She beamed at the group.

'That's in very poor taste, Donna,' Daisy said.

'Party pooper.' She opened the fridge and emerged empty-handed. 'We're out of wine, hubby dear. Bad management. Very bad.' She snatched the old bottle from the kitchen counter, held it up to the light to check if there was any left. Tipped the dregs into her glass, drained them in one gulp. 'I know!' she said, slamming her glass on the counter so hard there was a collective wince. 'Let's kill off Brian. That would solve everything.'

Melrose strode to his wife and took her elbow firmly. 'How about an afternoon nap, darling?' He dragged Donna towards the door.

She looked over her shoulder, pouting. 'You'll all just have to manage without me. Daddy says it's time to go to bed.' Fingers were waggled in the general direction of the kitchen. 'Ta-ta.'

'Phew,' Sally Kinane said. 'Even for Donna, that was a staggeringly hideous performance.'

She must have been a goddess once, thought Sam, or why would anyone put up with the current version?

Daisy, her smile threaded with apology, said: 'I think we're all still dealing with the aftershock.' She looked and sounded exhausted.

Rob, protective, rallied: 'If we were still farming, we'd be calling it time for smoko. Can I tempt you with a cuppa, Sam? No cake, I'm afraid, but I'm sure I can find a biscuit somewhere.'

Sam shook his head. 'Nah, it's all good.' He wasn't up to this, he thought. 'It's just . . . Kate was wondering whether, if you found the right person, he or she could buy into GeriEcstasy, fill the gap?'

Melrose, who'd slipped quietly back into the room, moved to Sam's side and took his arm. 'Why don't you sit down? Rob, the tea is a great idea—or would you prefer a beer, Sam?'

Right now, Sam thought, he'd prefer a sixpack. 'Tea's good. If it's no trouble.' He took a seat.

Daisy wheeled her chair towards the kitchen bench. Rob opened a door to reveal a large walk-in pantry heavily stocked with canned and dry goods. He found an unopened packet of biscuits.

Donna burst back into the room wearing a sky-blue silk dressing-gown. The hem was filthy.

There was a collective groan.

Without missing a beat, Melrose guided his wife towards a stool. 'Sam has something to say, darling, something that might solve our problems. Why don't we listen?' To Sam he said, 'You were saying you might know someone who could buy out Brian's share? At the risk of sounding mercenary, money speaks.' He explained: 'None of us has the means to pay for Brian's freedom. We set out the terms of agreement covering death—the deceased's share becomes communal property—but we failed to factor in a, er, live departure. In hindsight, that wasn't very smart, but you have to understand that, except for Brian, we've all known each other for decades. It was inconceivable that any of us would even contemplate breaking the trust. Brian met Cameron about ten years ago and he is a latecomer to the group. Clearly, he doesn't have the same sense of loyalty.'

Sam chewed his bottom lip, wondering how far he should go in revealing Kate's idea and figured it couldn't do any harm. 'Kate knows a woman in her late seventies who is finding it difficult to manage on her own, but who is heartbroken at the thought of leaving the area. Not saying she'll think living here is a good idea, but with your permission, Kate could sound her out.'

Daisy tilted her head sideways. 'A woman on her own, you say?'

Sam nodded. 'Lived alone for the past fifty years or so.'

Donna butted in: 'And Kate—she's the pregnant one, isn't she?— believes this solitary woman will suddenly think it's a good idea to share a house with eight other people, all strangers?' She snorted. 'Well, good luck with that one!'

Melrose stepped in to soften the atmosphere: 'No harm in asking, is there?'

Donna shrugged. 'Go for it, my darling. But if I were you, Mr Chancellor of the Exchequer and genius who never saw this freight train hurtling towards us, I'd work on a plan B.' She was sounding oddly sober and clear-headed all of a sudden. 'Now, if nobody minds,

I have developed a splitting headache and it feels like the right moment to have that nap after all.'

As before, the tension in the room dissipated the moment Donna disappeared. Sally and David Kinane, who had been standing silently in the corner, pulled chairs up to the table. Sheila went to help Daisy with the tea. Gavin collected the empty wineglasses, stacked them in the dishwasher and found a plate for the biscuits, set up mugs on a tray. Daisy passed him a large mint green enamel teapot, big enough to fill the mugs of a posse of cattlemen. One by one, the group convened around the table, ready to listen.

'I hope you understand,' Daisy said, laying a hand on Sam's arm, 'that Donna wasn't always . . . Well, once, she was the glamorous nucleus around which we all swarmed. Beautiful, funny, generous . . .'

Sheila coughed. 'Not always kind and tactful, Daisy, you'd have to admit.'

'No. Not always. But never mean, not until the last few years. Ageing affects us all in different ways.'

'As long as I don't end up doolally,' Sally said with feeling.

'Not a chance, love,' her husband responded heartily. 'Not that it would matter. Tolerance and forgiveness. Mandatory at this time of our lives.' He looked around the table. 'Frontal lobe deterioration and all that.'

'Or maybe,' Daisy said pointedly, 'we say what's on our minds because we don't want to waste time.'

'Ah, right,' David said, taking the hint. 'Sorry. Going off track. Blame age.'

Melrose barked a laugh. The others smiled.

Daisy, seated lower at the table in her wheelchair, managed to command the room with her authority. She tapped a finger on the table like a gavel, calling the group to order.

Sam took a deep breath and hoped Kate would forgive him for plunging in without consultation.

'Her name is Lizzie,' he began, squirming a little under the steady gaze of seven pairs of curious eyes. 'Back in the day, she wrote plays and film scripts. Always been a loner, according to local lore. I don't know her well myself . . .' He paused, aware he was about to give a character reference based on hope instead of facts. 'But I'm told she's tough, razor-sharp, independent, outspoken and a wee bit stubborn. She's also wise and very, very funny when she wants to be.'

Heads nodded.

'A loner, you say?'

'Yeah, not unfriendly, though. Kate talks to her when she comes into the café. Says she's a gem. Nah. That wasn't the word.' He searched his memory; grinned. 'Inspirational. That was it. Carries her age like a film star. Always beautifully turned out. And fit. Walks a lot.'

When no one spoke, Sam grabbed his tea and accepted a Scotch Finger biscuit.

Melrose said: 'Of course we'd prefer to stay here; that goes without saying. But there are always other options. If we sold the house, I'm quite sure we would all recoup our investments and perhaps even make a small profit.' He gave a rueful grin. 'There's nothing to stop us finding a well-equipped retirement facility on the Central Coast and leaving the practicalities of everyday life to skilled aged care workers. Much more sensible when you stop to think about it.'

'And incredibly boring, debilitating and depressing,' Daisy chimed in. 'Nothing makes you feel older than being surrounded by people your own age.'

Sheila swept her red hair into a makeshift bun. 'And yet here we are, Daisy.'

'Perhaps it's a trick of the mind, but to me you all look the same as the day we met. Us, this group, this is our youth reincarnated.'

Sally Kinane stood and placed her hand on Daisy's shoulder. 'Yes,' she said warmly. 'That's how I feel, Daisy dear.'

Melrose said to Sam: 'You'll understand we need to discuss the proposition among ourselves?'

Sam nodded. 'Floating the idea, that's all.'

'But I think I can speak for all of us when I say that if Lizzie is suitable, and if she found us so—well, we'd think seriously about inviting her into our home.'

'Hear, hear,' the others chorused. The conversation turned to funeral plans for Cameron. Melrose cleared his throat. 'It's my understanding there's to be a private cremation.'

Sam jumped to his feet. 'I'll leave you to it,' he said. 'If you don't mind me sticking my nose in your business, though, I'd suggest you cover every possibility in the new terms of agreement—including a bomb dropping on the house!'

↝

On his return from GeriEcstasy, Sam removed his boat shoes and stepped into a house echoing with an unmistakable air of abandonment. His stomach clenched as he moved swiftly to the kitchen, looking for a note. He scanned the table, the benchtops. Nothing.

He felt the first pangs of panic. Surely she would have called him in an emergency.

He pulled out a chair and sat at the kitchen table, his eyes closed as he tried to figure out where she might have gone.

'Penny for them,' Kate whispered in his ear, giving Sam such a fright he tipped his chair over as he jumped to his feet.

'Oh, love,' he murmured, gathering her into his arms and holding her close until he felt a slight stiffening in her body. 'Do me a favour, will you? Leave a note if you go off somewhere.'

She moved away from him. 'How did you go with the Water Police?' she asked, filling the kettle.

'Good, yeah,' he said. 'Had a long chat.'

'And?'

'Looks like it was Cameron's time to depart this mortal soil.'

'Coil.'

'Eh?'

'And?'

'Poor bastard must've slipped and fallen in.'

'Yes, yes,' Kate interrupted impatiently. 'But the time of death, the tides . . .'

'Hold your horses. Give me time to unroll the story in the right order.'

Kate squashed a bunch of fresh mint, star anise and a cinnamon stick into a teapot then filled it with boiling water. Swirled a teaspoon of honey around the sides of a delicate porcelain mug. 'Take your time.'

'So,' Sam continued. 'Time of death was approximately one hour into a rising tide. It wouldn't have reached much higher than Cameron's thighs and he should have escaped with nothing more serious than a dunking. But the back of his head was a pulpy mess. The cops reckon he must have hit a rock when he fell, which knocked him out. He drowned as a result. He had a heart attack, too, though they can't tell whether that came first or last in the sequence of events.'

Kate poured her tea. 'Sounds plausible,' she said thoughtfully. 'It's also possible he was assaulted first, then fell in and drowned.'

'Jeez, Kate, why do you want to turn an accident into a murder?'

Kate smiled. 'I don't. Just playing a mind game with myself. Helps fill in the time and takes my mind off . . . I'm sure nothing untoward went on.'

'Anyway, we'll have to wait for the coroner's findings for the final verdict.'

'Of course. The coroner. I'd forgotten.'

Relieved, Sam continued: 'I took it upon myself to call in to GeriEcstasy to check how everyone was coping, see if the do-gooders among us could help the old folks in any way.'

Kate's eyes lit with interest. 'How were they?'

'Surprisingly okay—well, apart from Donna, who seems to have venom instead of blood running through her veins. They were all sitting around with glasses of wine, trying to come up with a plan for the future. Oh, and there's to be no funeral once the body is finally released. Brian is insisting on a private cremation, date and time at his discretion and undisclosed. Bit rude, really.'

'Rude? In what way?'

'Cameron has been part of the GeriEcstasy group from the beginning. Brian has only been involved for about ten years. To deny friends the chance to say goodbye seems a bit rough. Remember Bertie's funeral? What a send-off. The old bloke would have been proud.'

Kate grimaced at the mention of the Briny's cantankerous former owner. 'All I remember is the green faces the following morning. It seems such a long time ago . . .'

'You were hard to get along with in the early days.'

'You were an arrogant know-it-all.'

'Really? Helpful is the word I would have used.'

Kate smiled. 'Up to a point.' She sipped her tea, the two of them comfortably silent.

'When did you recognise my stellar qualities?' Sam asked, breaking the spell. He went to the fridge and grabbed a beer.

'Fishing for compliments, Sam. Very uncool.'

'When you spruced up the top deck like a penthouse for Ettie— that's one of the things that did it for me.'

'Well, we all know it wasn't my cooking.'

They laughed.

'Remember when Ettie and the chef fell in love?' Kate said.

'The fire shed fundraiser dinner,' Sam recalled. 'There was no space for his berry jellies in the fridge because it was filled with beer, and Ettie took him for a walk along the waterfront to calm him down.'

Kate smiled. 'They were made for each other.'

'Like us,' Sam said.

'Yeah, well, there's no point holding a funeral for Cameron here. None of us really knew him.'

Sam, hurt at Kate's quick change of subject, took a long pull on his drink. 'It's just—ah, I dunno. It's like Brian's rushing to close the book on Cameron before anyone looks at their affairs too closely.'

'Now who's suspicious?'

Sam shrugged. 'Nah. I'm being ridiculous.'

'Maybe, maybe not,' Kate said.

Sam cursed himself for letting a sliver of light shine on Kate's shadier inclinations. 'Anyway, as I was saying, I stuck around for a cuppa and I mentioned your idea about Lizzie . . .'

Kate leaned across the table: 'And?'

'They reckon it's a great idea. In fact, it's the only option bar selling the whole shebang, and none of them is keen to ditch the dream.'

'Maybe I should give Lizzie a call, arrange a meeting at the café to sound her out. No harm in that, is there?'

'Go ahead. By the way, where'd you get to while I was out?' he asked, trying for a casual tone.

'Jimmy came by with Longfellow. He'd left Amelia on Artie's yacht to finish the cleaning and was on his way to pick her up. Said the old man was asking how I was doing, so he thought it would be nice if I called in to say hello.'

Sam stared at her, appalled. 'How'd you climb on Artie's boat? Amelia barely managed this morning and she isn't about to have a baby.'

'You know the worst thing about being pregnant? People treat you like a . . . a . . .'

'People are protective, that's all.'

'Busybodies, that's what they are. Interfering busybodies.'

And with that, the rare, gentle intimacy of the afternoon dissolved. Sam, desperate to restore the atmosphere, said, 'Word for you. Dunduckety.'

'It's a colour, Sam. Dull, usually brown.'

She rose and claiming she still had accounts to work on, retreated to her study.

Later, over a dinner of the last of the beef stew, Sam said: 'There's such a rhythm to that word.' He tapped a long beat, followed by three short ones, on his thigh.

'What word?' Kate asked.

CHAPTER EIGHT

OVER BREAKFAST THE NEXT MORNING, Sam checked his list of jobs and shuffled the order to suit the tides to the deliveries. Outside, he studied the lines of the *Mary Kay* where she was bedded on her mooring. Noted the water level along the hull, the angle of the hook on the crane, the lean of the wheelhouse. All good, he thought. He ambled down the steps to the pontoon, paused to chew the fat with Frankie for a few minutes.

'Bloody magnificent, isn't it?' he said to Frankie, indicating the early morning light corkscrewing off the water, sending the reflections of yacht masts into a wobbly dance.

Frankie pulled his cap lower over his eyes to shade them from the glare. 'Shaping up to be a scorcher and summer not even close,' he muttered. 'There'll be bushfires this year. Big ones, too. Mark my words.'

'You wake up on the wrong side of the bed this morning?' Sam asked.

'Just callin' it the way I see it.'

'Lucky we've got a big, beautiful bay filled with water then, eh? A place to run if we have to.' His words were flippant, but as soon as he uttered them, Sam felt a familiar twist of the gut. Bushfires and babies. 'Might clean up the grounds around the house anyway,' he said, tone more sombre now.

Frankie nodded, as though it had been his intention all along to spur Sam into action.

Before he boarded the *Mary Kay*, Sam swung the tinnie past Artie's yacht, as he did at least once or twice a week, to check the old man with his useless legs had woken up and was still breathing. He banged on the hull, got a thump in acknowledgement.

'Hang on, will ya?' Artie shouted from within.

A minute later a long pole was extended through a porthole with a piece of paper clipped to the end. 'Supplies are low—here's me shoppin' list.' Sam had been sharing shopping duties with Amelia and Jimmy since Kate's growing girth made clambering into a yacht with laden bags too much of a challenge.

Sam plucked the list from the rod and stuck it in his pocket. The rod was withdrawn, replaced with Artie's face. The old man cleared his throat. 'I've been thinkin' about the dead man in Stringybark Bay . . .'

Sam shook his head in exasperation. 'Not you too, Artie. Tell me this isn't going to be another cock-eyed theory about what happened.'

'I'd stake what's left of my puny life on the fact that foul play was involved.'

'Witnessed it, did you?'

'No need to get narky.'

'Let me lay it out straight for you, Artie,' Sam said. 'The cops reckon the bloke slipped, hit his head, knocked himself out, fell in the bay and drowned. The poor bastard had also had a heart attack, which is probably what caused him to slip in the first place. His time was up, Artie, and you and every other scandalmonger in Cook's Basin should leave the topic alone.'

'But—'

'I'll see you later with the shopping.'

Sam continued on to the *Mary Kay*, and from there to Cutter Island to fetch his first mate.

Jimmy and his dog were waiting at the end of the jetty, the former wearing knee-length yellow shorts splattered with a galaxy of exploding planets and an oversized purple singlet spangled with silver stars. Sam reached for his sunglasses. Was he imagining the mutt also had his paws over his eyes?

'What's on today, Sam?' the kid asked eagerly. 'We got a lotta jobs? Anythin' in Stringybark Bay? Ya know, there's somethin' not right about that poor fella what died.'

Sam rolled his eyes. Apparently there was nothing he could do to halt the rumour mill. He just had to be let the gossip roar straight past until the meddlesome locals lost interest. Then he looked sharply at Jimmy. 'Still carrying any awful memories on those bony shoulders of yours?'

'Me mum says everything that is born must die. Fact of life. Amen. Still—'

Sam broke in, changing the subject. 'A couple of moorings in Kingfish Bay, not far from the chef's home. Then we're picking up a load of building material for delivery to Eamon's on the east side of Cutter.'

The kid, the dog and the barge man settled into their routines. The *Mary Kay* gathered her skirts under the hum of a well-oiled engine and ploughed steadily across a calm sea. The sun felt like a warm flannel draped across the back of Sam's neck. Some days were cruisy, Sam thought, and this was one of them.

As they approached Moonlight Cove, a sandy nook in Kingfish Bay, Sam picked up a pair of binoculars from the dash and scanned a cluster of public moorings, looking for number eight.

'Plain as day,' Jimmy said, pointing. 'Me mum says you need specs after you turn forty, Sam. You might wanna think about that.' Then he skedaddled out of Sam's range, laughing with delight.

'Your mum's full of good advice, mate, but think about keeping most of it to yourself for the time being, eh?' Sam called after him.

Sam picked out the orange buoy, was about to set the binoculars aside when he noticed some floating rubbish. Cursing the lazy layabouts who thought nothing of desecrating the sanctity of Cook's Basin, he instructed Jimmy to find the net and get ready for a clean-up job on the port side.

The kid hit the target with his first sweep, withdrew a brown pulpy mass, and held it with a puzzled look on his face. Frowning, he handed it to Sam. 'A wallet,' he said. 'Someone must've lost it leanin' overboard.'

Sam looked inside. The plastic credit cards and a driver's licence were intact. Sam pulled the licence out and read the name: Cameron Smith. It took a moment or two for Sam to connect the wallet with the dead man from Stringybark Bay. As soon as it hit him, he expelled a single word: 'Bugger!'

'You wanna watch your language when the baby's born,' Jimmy said, with a sly look.

Then he looked at the licence Sam was holding and his eyes grew round. 'How'd that get here? We're a million miles from Stringybark.'

Sam pulled out his phone, found Richard Baines in his contacts. The call went to voicemail. He'd try again later.

⁓

By lunchtime, the *Mary Kay* was secured to the deck of the Briny Café, where a large number of people were enjoying the warm weather.

Sam shooed a colony of greedy-eyed seagulls from the railing and weaved through the throng, his eyes skimming plates. Most of them featured Ettie's Monday special of pumpkin, sage and goat's cheese risotto, with sautéed chicken on the side as an extra for committed carnivores. But he had a hankering for one of the Briny's more decadent hamburgers, dished up with fried onion rings. Then, recalling Jimmy's crack about his eyesight, he thought again. A man looking down the barrel of middle age should be restrained—especially with a baby on the way who would need his love and guidance for eternity, if he had anything to do with it.

'One of your fabulous spinach salads,' he called to Ettie as he banged through the screen door. 'And a burger for the kid, plain with tomato sauce—but slip in some greens if you can.' He looked around for Kate.

'Told her to take the rest of the day off,' Ettie said, without having to be asked, deliberately neglecting to mention that she'd sent Kate on a cross-country journey. 'Look, Sam, it's none of my business . . .' she began.

Sam blanched; those words never boded well. 'But?'

124

She patted his arm reassuringly. 'Kate seems to be in denial about this baby. She acts as though it will arrive and then life will pick up where it left off. I can't help worrying she'll . . . I don't know, just get thrown badly by the whole business.' She reached into the fridge for a handful of beef mince mixed with chopped red onion, flavoured with crushed garlic and parsley and bound together with a fresh egg, slapped it on the grill. Reached for a spatula. 'Ah, don't mind me. Having Brian upstairs wallowing in grief one minute and manic the next is wearing me out. I never know which way to jump.'

'Is he paying rent, Ettie?'

Ettie avoided Sam's eyes. 'Let's see how long he stays, eh?'

'How about I get the chef to handle him?'

Ettie rounded on him furiously, raising the spatula as though about to swat a fly or bring it down on Sam's head.

'Not that I don't think you're capable of handling it yourself,' Sam added hastily. 'It's just with so much going on . . . and you being so worried about Kate and all . . .'

The fight went out of Ettie in an instant. 'Well, she's not the first woman to have a baby and she won't be the last. She'll find out what it involves soon enough. A spinach salad, you said? How about I throw in extra bacon, an extra poached egg and a whole avocado?'

'You, my love, are the answer to every man's dreams.'

Ettie laughed, back to her old self. 'Haven't heard that line for a while. Oh, I almost forgot—Richard Baines is waiting at a picnic table in the Square. Said he'd like a private word with you. He didn't say what about, but if I had to guess . . .'

'Perfect timing! Call me when the salad's ready and I'll come and get it,' Sam said, heading out the door. The thought of another rumour exploding through the bays made him feel queasy. Or maybe it was the idea of all that healthy spinach. He should have stuck with the burger.

ⱷ

'Mate,' Sam said. 'Something on your mind? Or are you going to try to wheedle a higher spot in the queue to have your mooring serviced?'

Richard shuffled along the bench to make space for Sam, sliding his mug of coffee with him. 'Doesn't do to ask for favours in this job, Sam. Too many folks with nothing to do are looking for something to pounce on.'

'It was a joke, mate. Lighten up. Tried to call you earlier.'

'Saw the missed call.'

'Fished something out of the water this morning.'

'Not another body . . .'

'Jeez, mate, poor taste. Nah. Found Cameron Smith's wallet floating out towards the Tasman Sea. Long way from Stringybark Bay.'

A kid stripped to his undies, jumped in the sea, screamed with the shock of cold water. Groups of tourists batted away ravenous seagulls looking for an easy feed while they scoffed hot chips from cardboard containers. The smell triggered Sam's tastebuds. He desperately regretted his salad order.

'Probably doesn't mean anything,' Sam added. 'I mean, it's all sorted, right? Just bad luck. Poor bastard must have run over a pilgrim in another life or something.'

Richard was silent for a few seconds, brooding. 'Abe's retiring in two weeks,' he said finally. 'Might have rushed the decision so he could quit with a clean slate.'

Sam frowned. 'But it's all there—the fall, the rock, the heart attack.'

'Come on, Sam, think about it. The bloke's head was smashed like a baseball bat had connected with it. How do you get that by toppling from a low seawall into the cushioning effect of three feet of water? And I found all of three rocks in the sand, none of them close enough to shore to fit the scenario, even allowing for the body to have floated a short distance.'

Sam stared at him, lost for words, until Richard cleared his throat. 'So where's that wallet?'

Sam blinked. 'Drying out on the dash of the *Mary Kay*. I'll go get it.'

CHAPTER NINE

WITH ETTIE'S MAP SCRIBBLED ON the back of an order form, Kate followed a barely visible bush track hewn through dense scrub. It was a dirty, lacerating, strenuous trek. Once, confused by wallaby tracks, she found herself facing an impenetrable clump of prickly Moses and sharp-edged burrawang and was forced to retrace her steps. At times, she felt overwhelmed by the isolation, the thrum of insects, the eerie feeling she'd stepped into prehistory and might never find her way back to civilisation. But she kept on. Deep in her core, she was thrilled by the challenge. Sweating, puffing and awkward with pregnancy, she hauled herself up steep steps chipped into rock more than a hundred years ago, when new settlers brought picnics and spent the day picking wildflowers until there were none left to drop seeds for the next season. At one point, she had to squeeze through a narrow opening between two massive boulders. From there the pathway seemed clear, and ten minutes later she found herself on a rocky plateau.

Using the trunks of scrappy trees, she hauled herself upwards until she reached a large, dark cave with a rotting timber table and bench seats carved with initials and dates going as far back as 1921. Sam had told her about this spot when they first started seeing each other. He'd wanted to pack a picnic—always a bloody picnic, she thought, unsure why the idea made her cranky—and bring her here for a view of Cook's Basin that he insisted would leave her— a wordsmith—speechless.

As she flopped down on the ground to rest, she felt the baby kick and tried to visualise an infant in her arms. Instead, her imagination veered towards dirty nappies, chaotic kitchens, endless washing and nothing ever white enough to satisfy. She reminded herself that she'd quit journalism because it had lost its thrill, reporting stories she knew were a spin on the truth at best, at worst straight-out lies. But somehow, her old life had begun to gleam freshly and her current existence felt quite shockingly lacklustre. She thought uncomfortably of her mother, a narcissistic thrill-seeker who left ruined lives in her wake. Kate was about ten years old when she understood it wasn't normal for a wife and mother to disappear for long periods of time. In Emily's absence, Kate and her father cobbled together an efficient daily routine that kept them functioning, without once referring to the empty seat at the dining table. When she returned—weeks, sometimes months later—Kate would simply set a third place for dinner. Neither she nor her father uttered a single question. Emily behaved as though she'd never been away, pouncing on Kate's table manners if they fell short of her expectations, finding fault with the household cleanliness, once getting on her knees with a hairclip to scratch at the dust in a corner of a room, to make her point.

Kate had always judged her mother's behaviour with the ruthlessness of untested youth. Now here she was, accidentally pregnant and one foot already half out the door. Shades of her mother. But hadn't she always known those instincts lurked just under the surface? Until now, she'd been able to conceal it with the chameleon lifestyle of a globe-trotting journalist. A financial journalist, that is; no messy human interest stories for Kate.

She checked her watch, checked the map. The next landmark was a large rock, pancake-flat, with a carving of a whale that dated back to time immemorial, according to Ettie. From there, it was easy going. She hauled herself to her feet, dusting dirt from her hands, the back of her jeans. New. With a loathsome expanding waistband.

Outside the cave, Kate blinked in the sudden light. A flock of sulphur-crested cockatoos eyed her suspiciously from a branch overhead. 'Hello, birds,' she said, reassured by the sound of her voice, relieved she wasn't dreaming her presence here.

The birds flew off noisily.

'See you,' she called after them, her mood yo-yoing so she suddenly felt inexplicably happy.

A few minutes later, she fought her way out of the scrub to find herself on top of the escarpment. The landscape spread before her in swathes of scraggly blue-grey bush sliced through with ribbons of deep green rainforest gullies and great slabs of tessellated rock. Way below, the tiny imprint of her home shone in the afternoon light. She counted the bays until her eyes rested on the point where turquoise waters merged with ghostly mangroves. Stringybark Bay. From her vantage point, the GeriEcstasies' house was stripped of its glamour, reduced to a lifeless flatpack. A golden opportunity for Lizzie? Or would she be flung into a viper pit if she chose to join the group?

Kate wiped beads of sweat from her forehead with a handker-chief. Flicked an ant off her canvas shoe. Noted they would need washing when she returned home. Consulting the map once more, she looked around for distinguishing landmarks. She noted the grove of apple gums, leaves almost blue, on her right and, up ahead, a wide, graded track of glaringly white sand. According to Ettie's map, it split in two. *Follow the left fork*, Ettie had written. The right fork, she'd explained, led to a bitumen road and a locked gate that prevented sightseers from bringing vehicles into the area. As far as she knew, only Lizzie, who had permission from the park rangers to use a car to access her property, had a key.

Kate pressed steadily on, passing a rusty car door propped against a tree, and then another, a short distance away, which Ettie had told her to ignore. She consulted the map again.

Look for a small arrow carved into the trunk of a scribbly gum, Ettie had written. *Follow it to a large clearing. Lizzie's shack is there, but well hidden. Look for a cow—maybe a calf as well. Clarabelle was due to give birth this month.*

Fifty meters further on, she came across a cow placidly chewing her cud. Clarabelle gazed at her curiously. A black calf with white splotches rested against its mother's flank, batting absurdly long eyelashes.

'Ahoy!'

Kate jumped at the voice.

A woman emerged from a copse of trees and strode towards her. 'Ahoy!' A hand waved.

Kate returned the gesture and walked forward to meet Lizzie.

'Saw you coming,' Lizzie said when they met in the middle of the pasture.

'Ah. Ettie called you.'

'A good woman, that one. Told me to send out a search party if you hadn't arrived by half past three. Been keeping an eye out. Follow me. You're almost there.'

Lizzie wore a crisp blue-and-yellow checked shirt under denim dungarees, and her work boots were shined to mirror cleanliness. Her hair, snowy white with smoky grey highlights that looked like they'd come out of a bottle in an expensive salon, was cut expertly into a sleek bob with a fringe.

'You look knackered,' Lizzie said, smiling. 'Would've met you at the café but Ettie said you needed some fresh air. By the way, the grapevine is ahead of you. I know why you're here.'

'Ah,' Kate murmured, out of breath, trying not to show it.

They pushed through a gate with squeaky hinges and walked towards a small shack made from weathered vertical timber slabs and surrounded by a deep verandah. Capped by a low-slung red corrugated-iron roof, it echoed the lean days of early settlement. A lazy wisp of smoke escaped from a stone chimney.

'Home sweet home,' Lizzie said.

Kate paused, scanning the surroundings as she tried to catch her breath. 'It's . . .'

'Not what you expected?'

'The lushness . . .'

'Volcanic soil from times long gone. Anything grows in it.'

'But clover? This looks like old farmland,' Kate said.

'Yep. Early settlers tried to grow fruit trees here. Oranges and lemons, I believe. The dream fell apart when transporting produce to the Sydney market meant abseiling down cliffs with a pack on your back or crossing a couple of temperamental rivers.'

'Tough times.'

'You ever heard of bandicooting?'

Kate shrugged. 'Not really.'

'It was a settler term for theft by the true landowners, who'd been robbed of their native food. Quite a bit of that went on, too.'

'What happened to the fruit trees?'

'They died. An old fella came along with a tractor and ripped out the stumps, planted clover and kikuyu. Wanted a lawn, he said. Ended up bringing in cattle to keep the grass down and the whole European-style, labour-intensive farming cycle began. Anyway . . . I'll get tea started.' She pulled a pair of floral gardening gloves from her back pocket, laid them neatly in a basket alongside secateurs, a ball of string and a large pair of scissors. 'Plump up those cushions, if you wouldn't mind. I'll bring out a tray and we'll have tea on the verandah. When's the baby due?'

'A few weeks.'

'Better make the most of your freedom.'

Kate made a funny little sound she hoped signified resigned agreement, but the statement infuriated her. As if she didn't know her future had shrivelled to a long-term stretch of what she considered to be a life sentence.

Lizzie disappeared through French doors with gleaming glass panes, leaving them wide open behind her.

Kate plumped up the cushions as directed, then, when Lizzie failed to appear after a decent length of time, she entered the house and walked down a dim hallway where every inch of wall space was covered by paintings of flowers, dogs, cats, birds and children.

'Are you the artist?' she called out, as a way of letting Lizzie know she'd ventured inside.

'Nope,' Lizzie responded from a room off to the left.

Kate waited for an explanation. None came.

Mystified, she went searching for Lizzie and found her in a space that was both kitchen and dining room, with two battered leather armchairs in front of a smouldering fireplace. A pine kitchen dresser housing an eclectic collection of colourful teapots and jugs hogged an entire wall.

Kate went over to the fire and, eyes closed, breathed deeply. 'The smell,' she said. 'It triggers such yearning. For what I don't know.'

'Earliest man. Campfires. It's embedded in our DNA,' Lizzie said promptly. She pulled a tray from a cupboard and plonked a sugar bowl on it along with two cups and saucers. 'Right, nearly there.' She fetched two side plates and scrabbled for cake forks in a drawer that took brute persuasion to open.

Kate indicated a row of mementoes placed on a carved timber mantelpiece above the fireplace. 'May I?'

Lizzie shrugged. 'Go ahead.' She took a cake tin from a high shelf, prised open the lid and sniffed the contents. 'Oh good, yes, quite good!' She cut two slices and slid them onto the plates.

Kate studied the items on the mantel: a candlestick holder, jug, a trio of intricately patterned plates, all silver. An antique clock. A brass bird; an ibis, perhaps. 'I bet everything in this house has a story,' she said. She looked towards Lizzie, inviting a response. When none was forthcoming, she continued with her tour, pausing in front of a small pencil portrait of an Aboriginal woman wearing a shell necklace. The style was completely different to the heavy, bold strokes of the paintings in the hallway.

'Beautiful. Who is she?' Kate asked.

'The woman in the portrait? She lived in this house before me.'

'Ah.' Kate moved on, lifted a silver cup on a timber stand, looked for an inscription.

'Tennis trophy,' Lizzie said. 'I was quite a good player in my day.' The kettle whistled. Lizzie threw three large pinches of loose tea into a pot and poured in the boiling water, replaced the lid. She added the pot to the tray. 'Ready? Let's head outside.'

'This urn?' Kate asked.

Lizzie smiled softly. 'Ah, that's where the artist now resides.'

'Oh, the paintings in the hallway. He's dead?'

'She.' Lizzie said, picking up the tray. 'Come on. Before the tea goes cold.'

When they were settled with a view across low bush as far as a thin blue line of sea, Lizzie looked at Kate. 'Give me the rundown on these people, and don't bother skipping any details or I'll come after you on my broomstick and make your life miserable.'

Kate burst out laughing. 'Ettie said you were direct.'

Lizzie blew across the top of her cup. 'Ettie and the chef? They still good?'

'Better than ever,' Kate replied.

'And you and Sam? . . . Oh, don't look so surprised. There are no secrets in Cook's Basin.'

'So far so good,' Kate said, after a slight hesitation. She quickly changed the subject. 'About GeriEcstasy. I don't know much. None of us do, really. Five couples, now four. They were at university together. The house was the culmination of a dream to have a grand

and glorious retirement. Sam says they'd say yes to a weasel moving in if it meant they could stay on.'

'What I want to know, Kate, is whether you think the idea of joining their household is worth investigating further,' Lizzie said. 'Ettie's well-meaning but you're sharp enough to see the underbelly.'

'Not sure about that,' Kate demurred. 'I've had almost nothing to do with the residents and have no idea about the financial details. I don't think anyone in Cook's Basin has the first clue how the house functions. It will have to be your call from beginning to end. But I'd get a lawyer to read through the fine print very carefully before signing anything.' She tried the cake and then turned to stare at Lizzie in awe. 'This cake is superb,' she said. 'Not even Ettie could top it.'

'It's the buttermilk and golden syrup glaze. What does Sam think about the residents?' Lizzie asked.

'I'm not really sure.'

Lizzie eyed her curiously but said nothing. She finished her cake and replaced her plate on the tray. 'Well, I've got nothing to lose. Might as well meet the group and then make up my mind.'

'Would you have to sell this place?' Kate asked, thinking it would break her heart in the same circumstances.

'Not mine to sell. The woman on the mantelpiece? She left me the lease on the house and land; it reverts to the National Parks and Wildlife Service when it runs out in about ten years or so. Haven't looked at the paperwork for decades. Should have abandoned the place a long time ago, but I love it, and my blood and sweat has been dug into every corner of the garden, spilled on every plank I've repaired. Stupid, really. People are only ever custodians. It's the land that calls the shots.'

'What was her name?' Kate asked. 'The woman in the drawing, I mean.' She was curious to know more about a relationship that must have been close for the woman to bequeath her shack to Lizzie.

'Dorothy.' Said in a tone that discouraged any more questions.

Kate swallowed the urge to probe deeper.

The two women sat silently for a few moments, each wrapped in her thoughts.

'Come on, let me show you around,' Lizzie said, standing abruptly. 'Know much about gardens?'

'Not really. Only that most native plants either scratch, sting or bite.'

'Yes, well, that's true up to a point, but the bush can be gentle, forgiving and even life-saving, if you know how to read it.'

Kate followed Lizzie along a winding stone pathway to the rear of the house, where drifts of dianella under apple gums drooped with cascades of what looked like purple pearls. In open spaces, flannel flowers were densely bedded with starry white wax flowers. A winding track through banksias covered in golden cones and eriostemons in shades of pink led to a massive bed of rock lilies in full bloom. The air was richly perfumed like honey, the low hum of bees provided a background song.

'It's quite beautiful,' Kate said. 'You're very lucky.'

'Lucky?' Lizzie murmured as she bent to pinch off the spent blooms of a spider lily. 'Well, maybe, in the sense that when the rain falls steadily and heavily, the garden flourishes. Mostly, it's hard work that makes luck. I've nursed every plant like a newborn for the last fifty years.'

Kate caught a look of sadness in her eyes. 'Are you sure that you want to give it up?'

'It's time,' Lizzie said briskly, walking on, so that Kate had no choice but to follow. 'For what it's worth, I have been agonising over what to do for a while now. Old age doesn't leave you with an inspiring range of choices.'

They wandered further into the garden, arrived at a vegetable patch with raised beds, enclosed in a wire frame with a latched gate. 'Had to do something to keep the birds and wallabies out.'

Kate pointed. 'Spinach?'

A nod.

'What's this?' She leaned over to stroke bold red and green leaves.

'Beetroot. I pickle it. Lasts for more than a year. There's basil coming on, although it's still too cold and I'll probably lose it. Chives. Sage. Rosemary. Tarragon. Lovage—so underrated as a herb. Tastes like celery.' She bent to pick a leaf. 'Go on. Try it. It's delicious.'

Kate nibbled the leaf then looked at Lizzie in amazement. 'Such a strong flavour.'

'A little olive oil and lemon juice is all it needs to lift it into a league of its own.'

For the next few moments, the two women stood together surveying the patch. 'Are you bored, or would you like to see more of the place?' Lizzie asked eventually.

'More, please.'

They ambled on in the red-gold light of afternoon. Every so often, Lizzie bent to pull a weed, move a dead branch that had fallen on a fragile plant. They rounded a bend and came face to face with half-a-dozen brown chooks, scratching away at the earth under a couple of lemon trees. 'My hard little workers,' Lizzie said. 'They're great housekeepers.'

'I thought there were foxes around. Signs go up when baits are laid in the national park.'

'See over there? That's where I lock them in every night. The walls of the enclosure go down eighteen inches into the earth. I still lose one or two occasionally. Mostly snakes.' She checked her watch. 'Might lock them up. Save coming back later.' She started towards the henhouse, stopped abruptly. 'Ah no, it's too early and the day is so gorgeous. Anyway, that's all there is to see, really. Shall we head back to the house?' And in what seemed like sudden urgency, Lizzie grabbed Kate's elbow and steered her back the way they had come.

'Here we are,' Lizzie opened a paned glass door, motioned Kate to go through. 'Help yourself to some water. I'll be back in a second.'

⟡

Lizzie's second turned into nearly half an hour. Sitting at the kitchen table, Kate felt her anxiety rising. When she heard footsteps coming closer, she jumped up with relief.

'Sorry,' Lizzie said. 'There was a brown snake in the chook pen. Didn't say anything because I didn't want to alarm you. Took a while to move him on. You've got to be patient with brown snakes. They have filthy tempers when they're riled.'

'What will happen to the hens if you leave here?' Kate asked.

'They're good layers. It shouldn't be hard to find them a home.'

'I'm sorry to keep pointing out the downsides, but it will take a fair whack of money to buy into GeriEcstasy, if that's what you want.'

'Well, I can always sell a couple of paintings if I get stuck.' Lizzie smiled at Kate's shock. 'My fortune is on the walls.'

Kate went into the hallway to take a closer look. 'I can't find a signature on any of the works. Who's the artist?' she asked, when Lizzie appeared beside her.

'My mother.'

Kate spun around, unable to hide her surprise. 'Really? That's amazing.'

Lizzie eyed the collection fondly. 'I always knew she was a great talent, but I didn't know how great until a modest still life of a single red geranium went to auction about twenty years ago and broke all Australian records for a modern artist. She didn't live to see it, of course.'

'The curse of the creative,' Kate said. 'No one values your work until you're dead.'

'Her style was revolutionary for her era. Naturally, that meant she was destined to die in poverty. I tried to help her financially when I started to earn a living, but she was a proud woman. I eventually bought her paintings through an intermediary. She never knew I was the buyer.'

'They're really wonderful.'

Lizzie led the way back to the kitchen.

Kate dropped into an armchair, suddenly breathless, the baby kicking against her ribs. 'Lizzie, you've lived here alone for . . . how long?'

Lizzie rinsed the tea dishes, placing the cups face down on the draining board, leaning the saucers against them. 'Longer than you've been alive,' she said, reaching for a towel to dry her hands.

'And now you're thinking of co-habiting with a group of people who have been close friends for years. You'll never have the kind of privacy and solitude you have here. Why gamble on the unknown?'

'I'm old, Kate. Nearly eighty. That's not *getting* old, that *is* old. It's when you realise a sharp pain might be the last pain you'll ever feel. Oh, I'm not afraid of dying. Can't imagine the nothingness of it. What I am afraid of is dying and being found weeks later by a friend or passerby. I wouldn't want to inflict that horror on friend or foe.'

Kate rose to her feet. 'Well, I guess by now you're a good judge of what's best for you. Just . . . I don't know. Make sure you tread carefully.'

Lizzie laughed. 'Ah, the murder theory. You don't subscribe to all those ridiculous rumours about foul play, do you?'

'Not really. No. It's just . . .'

'Just what?' Lizzie asked, serious now.

Kate shook her head. 'Nothing,' she said. 'Nothing at all.' The police had said as much, hadn't they? But she couldn't help remembering that it had been her idea in the first place that Lizzie should move to GeriEcstasy—and she was starting to wish she'd never suggested it.

CHAPTER TEN

BY THE TIME KATE ARRIVED home—the descent taking less than half the time of the ascent—the day was on the brink of evening and Oyster Bay was swathed in deep shadow.

Sam, who'd been pacing the verandah, bolted down the steps and met her as she reached Frankie's boatshed. 'Where were you?' he demanded. 'I've been sick with worry.'

'Hiya, Frankie,' Kate said, ignoring Sam. 'Beautiful evening.'

'That it is,' Frankie responded and quickly retreated into his workshop.

'Look at you,' Sam said, grabbing Kate's arm. 'You've hurt yourself.'

Kate pulled away. 'They're minor scratches, Sam.'

Too wound up with worry and fury to hold back, Sam's voice rose. 'I don't know what Ettie was thinking! It's a four-kilometre walk on an almost vertical ascent. You're about to have a baby! What if you fell, or the baby decided to come or—Jeez Kate, it's spring, the mating season for snakes. Interrupt a chase and a snake will strike without breaking stride. You'd be dead meat in minutes if a brown got you. What was Ettie thinking, letting you go?'

'I needed some exercise, okay? I'm sick of being cooped up in the house and the café. And snakes don't stride. They slither.'

But Sam wasn't done. 'Your phone was switched off and you didn't even call to say where you were. I had no idea what was going on. I thought you were dead!'

'Oh, for God's sake,' Kate snapped. 'That's enough.'

Sam knew he was pushing her too far, but he couldn't help himself. 'You could have phoned when it started to get late. Let me know you were okay.'

Kate glared at him. 'I'll make my own decisions. End of story.' She made her way up the sandstone steps, determined not to show an ounce of the exhaustion she felt.

Frightened he'd explode and say something he'd truly regret, Sam stormed off and jumped into his tinnie, yanking the starter cord with so much force the handle broke. But the engine caught and he made a beeline for Cutter Island, wondering how the evening had gone so pear-shaped.

As he passed Artie's boat, the old man yelled out loud enough to wake the dead. 'Me shoppin', Sam! Where's me shoppin'?'

Sam throttled back with a sigh of resignation. He circled and came alongside Artie's yacht. 'Clean forgot, mate. Can you give me a day's pass and I'll sort your stuff tomorrow?'

Artie looked wounded. 'Leave a man to starve, would ya?' He checked his watch. 'Well, lend me yer phone and I'll give Ettie a call. Me own phone has a dead battery.' He scrolled through Sam's contacts, found Ettie and hit the button. 'Ettie, love, are you still tidyin' up? That numbskull barge man with no more sense than his unborn baby forgot to bring me supplies.' He paused, listening. 'I'll take what you've got, but if there's any of last week's curry hangin' around . . . Thanks, love.'

'You are fair dinkum shameless,' Sam said, when Artie handed back his phone.

'A man's gotta live,' Artie responded happily.

'I'll go and pick it up myself, save Ettie the detour,' Sam said.

'Least you can do under the circumstances.'

⁓

Sam concentrated on fixing the starter cord handle and had calmed down by the time he dropped off Artie's dinner, but he lacked the nerve—or courage—to return to Kate's house, which he would never be able to think of as *their* home. He sent Kate a text message.

Won't finish work until late. Will stay on the island tonight. Back early in the morning. Call if you need me.

Her response came back a minute later. *Ok.*

Sam pointed his tinnie towards Cutter Island and gloomily considered the prospect of baked beans on toast. He tried to remember how his parents had lived so happily in a draughty and damp boatshed, his mum cooking on a stove his resourceful dad had made out of a kerosene tin. In a king tide, she rolled up their single floor rug and made sure she placed her knitting basket on a high shelf. Even though his memory was blurred by time, he recalled whole calendar years filled with love and affection. Adventure, too. A pod of dolphins passing. An elegant heron picking its way along the shore in a way that made you wonder if the bird didn't want to get his toenails wet. Goannas raiding the Sunday roast when your back was turned. Lyrebirds belting out spine-tingling sounds like a full-blown orchestra. The eruption of fresh green growth in the first downpour after a bushfire. The way waterfalls turned into raging torrents after a storm. Rockpools teeming with life. Miracles everywhere, if you cared to open your eyes to look beyond your belly button or those cursed phones every kid in Cook's Basin seemed to have glued to their hand. They had their place, those marvels of technology, but his child would also know the endless wonder of the physical world, if he had anything to do with it.

As a kid, he didn't know the meaning of boredom. Still didn't. He'd understood the gut-wrenching grief of loss, though, when his parents were wiped out in an accident while taking their first drive in their new car. He was sixteen years old, on that cusp between boyhood and manhood. He thought more than once about joining his mum and dad in the cemetery. Might have, too, if the Misses Skettle hadn't followed him out to sea in their bouncy little launch and kept watch until, worried for *their* safety, he'd turned his boat towards home. After that, the community stepped in with odd jobs for which he was overpaid but not embarrassingly so. He'd survived. But there wasn't a day he didn't mourn every joyous moment his parents had missed by dying so young. He wondered, then, whether his inability to find neutral ground with Kate hinged on his short experience of his parents' relationship. A relationship, he now realised, in which each partner put the other's happiness ahead of their own. As a kid, he'd taken it for granted; now he recognised the unthinking generosity of their behaviour and yearned to see it replicated in his own relationship. But he and Kate never seemed to be on the same page, he thought sadly, coming alongside his jetty.

Out of nowhere, Jimmy leaped in front of him.

'Jeez, mate. I nearly had a heart attack and toppled in the drink,' Sam said.

'Low tide, Sam, you might've choked on wet sand but you wouldn'a drowned.'

Sam headed for the steps to his house, Jimmy, his mutt on his heels, followed so closely the smell of his hair gel overpowered the aroma of sausages cooking on island barbecues.

'You head on home. Your mum will be cranky if you ruin her dinner.'

'Me mum sent me, said you should come with me if you're plannin' on spendin' a night on your tod sloan.'

'Thank Amelia for me, but I've got leftovers going to waste in the fridge. Now off you go, and take your mutt with you.'

'Longfella could spend the night if you're lookin' for company, Sam.'

'I'll enjoy the peace and quiet, mate. See you first thing tomorrow. It's a big day.'

Sam instantly wanted to cut out his tongue. He spent the next fifteen minutes explaining the work schedule before Jimmy finally agreed to leave.

∽

At home, Sam opened a beer out of habit and brushed the leaves off a deckchair. Night unfurled, plunging first the bays and then the open water into darkness. Lights came on in houses like great yellow eyes in the darkness. Sipping his beer without his normal pleasure, he considered opening a can of baked beans, finding some bread in the freezer and tucking into a dreary bachelor dinner. But he had no appetite. The chef could have offered him one of the signature dishes that had once earned his restaurant two stars and Sam would have choked on the first bite.

The briny, half rotting smell of an outgoing tide wafted onto the deck. Sam let his head fall on his chest and shuddered with the certainty that he and Kate were doomed as a couple. If it wasn't for the fact of the baby, they probably wouldn't have made it this far. The baby . . . and Kate so ambivalent not a crib, a bottle or even a bib had appeared in the house.

He drained his beer, skipped dinner. Took a long, hot shower— bugger the amount of water that ran down the drain—and then spent a sleepless night trying to decide whether remaining in a dysfunctional relationship for the sake of a child was a better or worse choice for that child. By the time he felt himself drifting into a light doze, the dawn was an orange line on the horizon and he'd admitted to himself that staying together would slowly drain the joy out of each of them. A thought that made him feel cracked wide open, started a dull ache in his heart, made him feel like the oxygen had been sucked from the room.

⁓

In her home in the darkest corner of Oyster Bay, Kate, still angry, abandoned the boiled egg dinner she'd been preparing and showered. She dried and moisturised her skin, avoided looking at her body in the bathroom mirror. Cleaned her teeth, stepped into fresh pyjamas and fell into bed, luxuriating in the space and her aloneness. She understood quite clearly that on some subliminal level she was deliberately trying to wreck her relationship with Sam. His simple-minded view of the world, his modest dreams and ambitions, his tenderness and consideration, made her want to scream. The steady routines that anchored him imprisoned her. To her, the repetitious work he took pleasure in doing to the best of his ability had the intellectual depth of a blade of grass. Not that she could talk. Her brain felt like mush most of the time, while her work at the café was a mindless round of paying bills, washing up, sweeping, mopping and dusting. The excruciating sameness of each day felt like a heavy load strapped to her back.

She lay awake for hours, listening to the night sounds of the bush: the tragic hoot of an owl; the scrabbling of bush rats or bandicoots; the gentle, breathing waters of the bay lapping against the shore with the same rigorous monotony as her life. In the end, every waking thought revolved around the inescapable fact that she was carrying a child that could lay claim to her forever. 'I am not good at commitment,' she told the black space of her bedroom. 'I have never been good at committing to anything beyond the next assignment.'

She rolled on her side, pulling the cream woollen blanket over her, feeling cold suddenly. Realising she'd automatically confined herself to one side of the bed, she wriggled into the centre. She began to think dying in childbirth might be an option, death a release, and wondered if she was quietly losing her sanity.

CHAPTER ELEVEN

THE NEXT MORNING, KATE ARRIVED early at the café to catch up on work after her day off. She checked drink stocks and wrote out an order for bottled water and orange juice. The bike riders, she guessed, had emptied the shelves. A woman in black jogging gear knocked at the door. 'We're not open yet,' Kate told her through the glass. The woman indicated that she might die of thirst and Kate pointed at an outside tap used to fill a water bowl for dogs. The woman made a rude gesture.

A few minutes later, Ettie came through the rear door in a swirl of colour, a red bandana holding her hair under control.

'You look like a gypsy,' Kate said.

'Is it too much?' Ettie asked.

'No. You look . . . delightful.'

Ettie plonked a leather satchel with Sunday and Monday's cash takings on Kate's desk. 'I was too tired to balance the till. Not sure of the total but we had a couple of decent days.' She handed Kate a slip of paper. 'New recipe. Might be a bit extravagant but . . . Could you do some costs?'

Kate read the list of ingredients. 'How do you feel about frozen prawns?' she asked.

'Them's fightin' words,' Ettie said, hands on hips.

'Fresh prawns, we're talking a dish with a price tag of thirty-five dollars minimum.'

'No way! Six prawns per dish, it can't be that much.'

'Factor in the labour, Ettie. Peeling prawns is time-consuming. Certain you don't want to think about frozen?'

'Nah. Can't go there. I'll come up with something else for the Friday special.'

Kate quickly counted the cash and slipped the correct denominations inside little plastic pouches supplied by the bank while Ettie threw the ingredients for a cake into a bowl, beating the batter distractedly while struggling to come up with a solution to prawn economics.

Jenny arrived in her uniform of navy trousers and a navy polo shirt, thick-soled sneakers. 'Morning one and all.' She tied an apron around her waist and switched on the coffee machine.

Kate gave her a quick nod. 'I need to stretch my legs for a minute,' she said.

Jenny waited until the flywire door shut behind her before she asked, 'Seen any baby supplies pass through yet?'

'Eh?' Ettie asked, her mind still on the prawns.

'Kate. Any sign of a crib? Bulk order of nappies being delivered?'

Ettie shook her head.

Jenny turned to press a few buttons on the coffee machine, cleaned pipes with the hiss of boiling water and steam. 'None of my business, but that girl has her head in the sand, and she might want to pull it out before too long. Speaking as a woman who's spawned a shoal and learned the hard way.'

'Make me a coffee, love, would you?'

Ettie took the brew onto the deck, holding it in both hands as if to warm them, thoughtful. Looking back, she realised there'd been none of the usual excitement around a pregnancy. Kate avoided small talk that drifted around the topic of colours for the nursery, the most practical strollers, the best crib and how long it would be useful until the baby grew big enough for a cot. If Kate found herself amid baby discussions, she seemed to dissolve from the group in a way no one noticed until they looked around for an opinion and realised she wasn't there. If Kate's hazy calculations were halfway correct, Ettie thought, the baby was due in a less than three months. The time for denial was over. She made a decision and strode back into the café.

'You look like you're on a mission,' Jenny said, noting the firm set of Ettie's mouth.

'Back in ten,' she responded.

She found Kate leaning on the sea wall, staring across the water. Ettie held back, suddenly unsure of what to say.

Fast Freddy's luminous water taxi skimmed over the water towards the ferry wharf. Ettie hesitated, then went back inside to prepare his breakfast order. Timing was everything, she thought. She had to pick the right moment.

'That was quick,' Jenny said.

'Freddy's on his way.'

Jenny nodded and cranked out a double-shot cappuccino, no sugar. Ettie wrapped a raspberry muffin in paper and placed it in a paper bag along with his regular order of toasted banana bread. A little treat now and then never hurt anyone.

❧

Kate watched Freddy tie up, leap onto the jetty, shake himself like a wet dog and raise his arms to the sky like a man invoking the gods. He bent to touch his toes, stretched from side to side with his hands on his hips, rotated his shoulders and gave a gnomish little jig of satisfaction.

Kate smiled. Freddy was one of nature's most gentle gentlemen. In his quiet way, he dealt with violent drunks, obstreperous passengers and unruly kids with patience and kindness.

'How you doing, Miss Kate?' Freddy asked softly when he saw her. 'You look as pretty as a picture standing there.' He gave Kate a sidelong glance. 'Not long to go. But by now, every day probably feels like a year.'

'A leap year, Freddy.'

'Any guesses on a boy or a girl?'

Kate smiled. 'Next you're going to tell me Jack the Bookie is taking bets.'

Freddy nodded. 'And just like the royal family, there's a board for names, too.'

'What's the frontrunner' Kate asked, curious.

'Can't say too much at this stage, but there's a fair number who reckon Sam's mum or dad will get a run, depending on whether you have a boy or a girl. Ettie—or Henrietta, as she's known on her birth certificate—is also a favourite.'

Kate shook her head. 'We haven't discussed names at all.'

Freddy looked surprised. 'I've never been a parent myself, you understand, but I've heard from reliable sources that choosing a name is the only fun part of pregnancy.' He blushed, as though he'd stepped into deeply personal territory.

'Ah well, we'll keep everyone guessing for a while yet. This baby doesn't feel in a hurry to arrive.'

'Lucky little mite, though, to have you and Sam for parents.'

'Yeah. Lucky.' Kate's tone was flat. She patted Freddy's shoulder. 'You ordered yet, or can I do it when I go inside?'

'Standing order. And here's Ettie now.'

Ettie smiled as she joined them. 'No dramas on the water last night?'

'Nah. Quiet as the falling snow.' Freddy ripped open the paper bag, gave Ettie a broad smile of thanks for the little extra. 'Kate? A taste?'

'No thanks, Freddy. I'd better get back to work.' She tapped the face of her watch.

Freddy's mobile rang. He looked at the caller ID and sighed. 'Excuse me for a minute,' he said, giving a little bow and stepping away.

Ettie looked closely at Kate. She noticed a small red stain near the neckline of her white T-shirt and wondered if it was a sign that, beneath her reserve, this ordinarily fastidious woman might be falling apart. 'Ordering up to date?' she asked.

Kate nodded.

'Invoices sorted?'

Kate nodded again.

'Why don't you take the rest of the day off? Go shopping. Buy a crib. Choose a colour for the nursery.'

Kate turned her back, gazing across the water once more. 'I don't know if I can do this, Ettie,' she said, so softly Ettie wasn't sure she'd heard correctly.

'Do what? The baby?'

Kate swallowed, unable to speak.

Ettie moved closer to the young woman who stood before her. 'Of course you can,' she said.

'I don't think so, Ettie. I really don't.' Her voice cracked. She stepped away from Ettie, crossed her arms on her chest, holding her shoulders tightly with her hands, as if afraid she might break apart.

Ettie floundered. 'But there's no choice, Kate. This baby is going to happen whether you're ready or not.'

'You don't understand, Ettie. You don't understand anything.'

'What? What don't I understand?'

Kate's expression became a blank mask. 'Nothing. Never mind.'

'We're all here for you, Kate. We're on your side. But we can't help if we don't know what the problem is.'

Kate smiled brightly, falsely, turned away to avoid Ettie's scrutiny. 'Sorry. I'm okay. It'll be okay.'

'Everyone fears parenthood. Fears failing. But you won't, Kate. You'll be fine. By the way, Amelia is organising a baby shower but she needs you to give her a date.'

'A baby shower? Why?'

'It's a gesture, Kate.'

'Signifying?'

'To refuse would be rude.'

Kate chewed her bottom lip. 'The thing is, Ettie, I'd rather not.' She felt a flush rise. Turning quickly, she walked back to the seawall and gazed across glassy water to where angophoras shone with blooms, creamy white against the rusted escarpment.

Ettie followed, anxious that Kate understand. 'It's a gesture of love and care, Kate. Nothing more, nothing less.'

'No baby shower. Not ever. Thanks anyway.'

Ettie shrugged, hurt. 'Suit yourself.' She walked back to the café. At the door she stopped, turned around. 'Go home, Kate. Have a warm bath, read a book, rest.' Then she disappeared into the Briny.

Feeling mixed up and edgy, Kate sat at the picnic table and stared at the cross-hatched carvings of generations of sweethearts who'd come before her and wondered how many had found everlasting love. If any.

Freddy, his call ended, returned to her side. 'All on an even keel between you and Ettie, is it?'

'Sweet as a nut, as Sam would say,' Kate responded, and then, remembering Freddy's finely tuned antenna for discord, she explained: 'Ettie thinks I should rest. It's not a concept I'm familiar with.'

Freddy's expression cleared. 'She has a point,' he said, with the sincerity of the genuinely good-hearted. 'It's advice well meant,' he added.

Finishing his food, he scrunched the paper bag into a ball and unwound from the cramped bench seat to place it in one of the big bins in the Square.

'It goes against the grain to see a grown man who should know better litter without a conscience,' he said, coming back to his seat.

'What man?'

'That debonair fellow from Stringybark Bay.'

'Mike Melrose?'

'That's him. Chucked it over the side of the boat when I was bringing them over after that fella died. He's a little cavalier about telling the truth, too,' Freddy said. 'Now, off you go and rest. Ettie's orders.'

Kate patted Freddy's shoulder and made her way back to the café. A couple of tradies who were about to enter stood aside, waved her in with a flourish. She smiled her thanks and resumed her seat under the stairs.

'What's up, ladies?' the tradies asked at the counter, without expecting an answer. 'Cracker day, eh?'

Jenny took their orders. Ettie fired up the hot plate. The young blokes argued over a crucial point in a weekend football game. Jenny rolled out a carton of eggs and a stack of bacon. The morning rush had begun.

Ettie caught sight of Kate and came out from behind the counter. 'Burying yourself in a pile of accounts isn't going to change the simple fact that you are having a baby. Now take some time off. I don't want to see you for at least a week, and then only if you feel up to filling the salt and pepper shakers.' She left to flip eggs, turn bacon. Called out over her shoulder: 'Set foot in the café, Kate and I'll chase you out with a wet tea towel.'

'Lucky you,' Jenny said, rolling her eyes.

స

On the deck, Kate ignored chairs that needed straightening and navigated a ramp leading to the pontoon where the stern of her boat was aground. She untied and dragged the tinnie into deeper water. Stepped in. Started up, propeller barely submerged, reversed into the waterway, dropped the engine and headed slowly for Oyster Bay. Her stomach rumbled. She wished she'd thought to grab an egg-and-bacon roll on her way out. A week, she thought, furious when she knew she should feel grateful, was a lot of time to fill.

She pulled her phone out of her pocket and dialled Lizzie. The call went through to voicemail.

'Hi, it's Kate. If you're planning to meet the GeriEcstasy group, I could take you there in my boat. I'm on enforced leave. Ettie's orders. But if I don't keep busy, I'll go stir crazy' She ended the call.

Within half a minute, her phone buzzed. 'I've arranged to meet them on their premises at one o'clock this afternoon,' Lizzie said. 'If I walk to your house, we could do the last leg by boat.'

'You know where to find me?'

'See you around noon.'

Kate roared home too fast, scooting through the moorings like a teenager on a joyride. The noise brought Artie out of his bolthole. He stuck his head through the hatch and waved a fist in Kate's direction. Filled with remorse, she swung around to come alongside his battered old yacht, festooned with algae and molluscs.

'Sorry, Artie,' she said. 'Got carried away with the beauty of the day.'

The old man shook his head sadly. 'Didn't expect it of you, Kate. Thought you had more sense.'

Kate, tempted to tell him that she'd apologised and that would have to do, settled for a quick nod. 'Blame baby brain,' she said.

Artie's face lit up. He hauled himself to the top step on his backside and leaned towards her. 'Gettin' close now. S'pose you know. Boy or a girl, eh?'

Kate laughed. 'Artie! You're not trying to get inside info to make a killing with Jack the Bookie, are you?'

The old man made a show of being offended. 'Let me remind you that cheats never prosper, young lady.' He hitched his trackie daks higher around his waist. 'Although a small indication of which way the wind's blowin' wouldn't go astray . . .' He looked at her, wide-eyed with hope.

She laughed again, feeling more like her old self. She pushed away from Artie's boat to head home at a pace he couldn't fault.

∽

Half an hour after Lizzie was due to arrive, Kate checked the time on the kitchen clock. Ten minutes later, she checked it again. In another ten minutes, she planned to go looking for the old woman, convinced she'd either had an accident or been bitten by a snake.

'Ahoy! Anyone home?'

Kate hurried to the door, dizzy with relief.

'You're okay?'

'Sorry I'm late. Track's more overgrown than it used to be.'

'I was beginning to think I'd have to send out a search party.'

'Why? I know those tracks like the back of my hand.'

'Yes, but . . .'

'I'm old, you mean?'

'I started this ball rolling. I'd feel responsible if anything happened.'

'I had a choice, Kate. My call, not yours. Long time since I've done that trek. Not many people use that track anymore, I guess.'

'See any snakes?'

'Not many. Anyway, snakes and me, we have an understanding.'
Lizzie grinned. Despite the hike through the bush, she looked
remarkably clean and fresh in khaki trousers, a pressed, white
button-up shirt, a pale blue kerchief tied at her throat.

In the kitchen, Kate pulled a jug of water from the fridge and set
it on the table. She fetched a tall glass and filled it with ice and
water. Cut a slice of lemon.

'Almost a cocktail,' Lizzie said.

'If you want, I could add whisky, gin, brandy.'

Lizzie laughed. 'Do I look that bad?'

'Of course not. Call it Dutch courage or something.'

'It's a big day. I need my wits about me.'

Kate slid onto a chair opposite her.

'Never thought I'd leave my old shack,' Lizzie said. 'Nobody
warns you about old age. And by the time you realise you're not
immune, the damage is done.' She rubbed a spot of blood from a
scratch on her hand. 'Paper-thin skin being one among many of
age's frustrating consequences.'

'What will happen to your home, that wonderful garden, if
you leave?'

'I'll miss the garden. The house is held together by sentimentality
and stubbornness. My fault. I put off repairs. Who'd have thought
I'd be old for such a long, long time? Shall we go?'

Kate gathered her phone, sunglasses, picked up a cake tin
from the counter. 'Homemade but no guarantees,' she said. They
made their way to the front door, where Lizzie had left a staff made
from a sturdy branch. Below them, in the tawny green waters of the
bay, a school of fish jumped, attracting a flock of hungry seagulls.
'Tailor, chasing baitfish,' Lizzie said, pointing at the churning water.

'There's a big feed down there for anyone keen enough to throw in a line.'

'Are you a fisherman?'

'More farmer that angler. We humans—why is it we value most what we're about to lose?' Lizzie asked wistfully.

'The deal isn't done yet,' Kate replied. 'You can always change your mind.'

'And go where?' Lizzie began to descend the steps to the pontoon.

'I have to tell you, Lizzie, I've heard that one inmate—as they're commonly known—is borderline unhinged . . . and that's from Ettie, which makes it doubly disturbing.'

Lizzie leaned on her staff. 'Unhinged? Or perhaps eccentric? Sometimes, Kate, those people can be the most interesting of all. Anyway, nothing's been settled. Let's wait and see how it goes. They may loathe me on sight.'

Kate's commuter boat, a solid little aluminium tinnie with a covered cabin, was tied alongside the pontoon. She'd bought it from a Cutter Island couple, at least a decade younger than Lizzie, who'd moved onshore when island life became too challenging for their rusty joints. She'd named it *Ghost* for reasons she'd forgotten. 'Need a hand?' she asked.

'Better if I go it alone.'

Kate crouched to grab the gunnel, holding it hard against the pontoon. Lizzie gripped the edge of the cabin and placed her right foot on the deck. Twisting slightly, she swung her left leg inside. She spun the passenger seat to face the stern and plonked down, giving a thumbs-up. 'Easy. There's a knack after a certain age. Hand me the cake tin. Is there a communal runabout at the house?'

'Not that I know of.'

'Pity. Nothing beats packing a picnic, jumping in a tinnie and heading for a secluded little beach to snooze away the afternoon.'

Kate threw her a curious sideways look.

'Ah, back in the day . . .' Lizzie's voice faded into silence, then she brightened. 'Maybe I'll invest in a tinnie, reveal the many offshore pleasures that exist beyond those four glamorous walls. What do you think?'

Kate stepped into the boat which tipped to one side with her extra weight. 'In your own words, Lizzie, one day at a time.' She used her sleeve to wipe the dust off the seat and sat down. Turned the key and exhaled with relief when the engine kicked over.

'I've heard none of them know much about boats,' Lizzie said. 'Makes me wonder why, with all the glorious areas to live in this vast country, they chose a difficult-to-access—and, for that matter, difficult-to-escape—waterfront property.'

'One member of the party couldn't even swim,' Kate added. 'And now he's dead.'

She checked the coast was clear, slipped into reverse. Made a U-turn towards the mouth of Oyster Bay, heading east past a finger spread of small bays to the north and Cutter Island to the south. She waved at Frankie, who looked up from scraping a reef of barnacles from the belly of a pretty little sea-green yacht nestled in the boat cradle. He touched the brim of his black cap in acknowledgement.

Out on the open water, Kate kept her speed slow and easy.

'You make your past sound so utterly mysterious,' Kate said, picking up the conversation. 'If I were still a journalist instead of a waitress, I'd grill you mercilessly.'

'We were all young once, Kate, as unbelievable as that seems to most people under the age of twenty. Then there's a moment, uninvited, shocking, when you reach into the crisper for a lettuce and find yourself falling forward, your body refusing to obey orders, your head suddenly spinning, and you wonder whether this is it. Emerging unscathed and not sure whether to feel relief or regret for what might have been a quick and merciful end.'

'If anyone asked me your age, I'd put it around sixty-something.'

'Flattering. The right clothes and make-up help, but on the inside, there's no holding back the years.'

The two women were silent for a while. The boat cut through a mirror-flat sea.

'Such a privilege, all this,' Lizzie remarked.

Kate nodded, pointed ahead. 'Stringybark Bay.' She made a wide turn, a white-fringed shawl of froth spreading in her wake.

Lizzie looked around. 'A few more houses and jetties than there used to be. But not much else has changed.' She closed her eyes. 'I've always felt it more strongly here than anywhere else,' she murmured.

Kate slid the boat into neutral and killed the engine to rock quietly on the water. 'Felt what?'

'Hard to explain. Impossible to explain.'

'Come on, Lizzie, you can't leave me hanging.'

The older woman breathed in deeply. 'All this,' she said, waving an arm around to indicate soaring ochre rockfaces, huge sandstone boulders, rainforest gullies where tree ferns spread like great umbrellas and, way ahead, silvery mangroves that twisted above clear blue water. 'The timelessness. As though the past is right here, right now, and at any moment Dorothy's spirit will appear to take me by the hand.' She made a self-deprecating gesture. 'Don't mind me. Too many memories colliding, I guess.'

'It's certainly one of the most beautiful of all the bays,' Kate said, knowing it sounded lame.

'The thought of being heaped into a gulag where the only exit was death, well, I'd curl up and die within a week.'

'My mother, Emily . . . she died recently.'

'Oh, I'm sorry to hear that.'

'No, no, it's fine. I only mentioned it because she lived in a retirement village. Quite enjoyed it, she told me. It was like having a large personal staff to cater to her whims.'

Lizzie straightened and opened her eyes. 'Staff? Do you mean nursing?'

'No. Gardeners and garbage collectors and cleaners. Said it was a wonderful change not to have to lift a finger.'

'She was ill, was she?'

'Well, no. Not really. At least, nothing diagnosed. But it turned out she had a dicky heart.'

Lizzie patted Kate's knee and pointed towards their destination. 'We're going to be late at this rate.'

'Oh, sorry—baby brain.' Kate restarted the engine and moved the throttle forward but kept their speed slow to give Lizzie a chance to absorb what might be her new neighbourhood.

A few minutes later, she nodded towards the sprawling building on the western side of the bay. 'There it is. GeriEcstasy.'

The house stood out from the rugged backdrop in crisp, white-trimmed orderliness and solid sandstone blocks.

'Bit different to my shack,' Lizzie said, trying to smooth her hair into place and giving up.

Kate laughed. 'You could say that. And yet, give me your old house any day. More heart and soul.'

'I expect the plumbing is more efficient.'

'Wouldn't count on it.'

Lizzie let rip with a belly laugh, then leaned forward to get a better look. 'Hang on, is that a welcoming committee?'

'Looks like they've have been watching for you.'

An assortment of straw hats, colourful dresses and white linen was visible on the jetty.

'They don't look too scary,' Lizzie said, squinting.

'Donna is the one to watch. Makes a viper look friendly, according to Ettie.'

'Can you point her out?'

Kate scanned the group, searching for a silver head on a stick-thin body. 'Nope. Can't see her.'

'Is that a woman in a wheelchair, for God's sake?'

'Daisy. Sam says she's the pick of the bunch and not to be fooled by the wheelchair. You forget her disability the second you meet her.'

Lizzie raised her eyebrows, took a deep breath, folded her hands in her lap. 'Right. Let's get on with it, shall we?'

'They'll love you, Lizzie.'

'Don't know about that. But thank you.'

Kate eased alongside the pontoon, reversing to bring the boat to a standstill, aware her skills were being assessed but not judged by curious eyes.

Mike Melrose, immaculate as always, stepped forward and Kate tossed him the stern line. He wound it expertly around the cleat. Either not such a novice or he was a quick learner, thought Kate.

'Welcome!' Melrose said, holding out a hand to help Lizzie from the boat. 'I'm Mike Melrose.'

Gavin Flowerdale stepped forward to take her other hand. He smiled charmingly. 'Gavin. How do you do?'

'Lizzie. Well, thank you.'

Together the two men hoisted Lizzie onto the jetty.

'My wife, Sheila,' Gavin said, pointing her out.

Sheila, in colours to rivals Jimmy's more flamboyant combinations, stumbled forward.

'After fifty years in stilettos, she is having trouble adjusting to flats,' Gavin confided.

Sheila gave him a filthy look. 'We were in the business of selling shoes,' she explained. 'If I didn't wear the latest fashions, we couldn't sell them. One of the endless sacrifices I made in the name of marriage. Not that I've ever been thanked for it.'

'You know I worshipped every stiletto-driven hole in our floorboards,' Gavin said, winking in Lizzie's direction. He slid an arm around his wife's waist and she gave him a friendly swat, looking pleased.

'David Kinane, cheesemaker, and my wife . . .' He searched the group, reached behind him for the hand of a woman wearing a shapeless aqua cotton dress and pulled her forward. 'This is Sally. My beautiful bride.'

'Hi,' she said, blushing. 'Take no notice of him; he's trying to make up for burning the toast this morning.'

'Poor you. You must feel like a prize beast at a cattle auction,' Daisy said, easing her wheelchair through the group and coming to a stop an arm's length from Lizzie and a few inches from the edge of the jetty.

Lizzie laughed. 'Not quite. More like a young girl at her first job interview. You must be Daisy.'

'Ah, the wheelchair. It gives me away every time.' Daisy smiled, no sting in the words. 'And my husband, Rob.' She indicated the ruddy-faced man behind her, his eyes glued to the spot where the planks stopped and the sea began. 'G'day,' he muttered. 'How about we move back a fraction, love? One bump and you'll be a goner.'

Daisy made a dismissive gesture. 'He worries too much.'

Melrose resumed control. 'Right then. Shall we head to the house? I believe Donna's preparing a little refreshment.' He shook his head as though he'd forgotten his manners. 'Donna is my wife—the last member of the group for you to meet. Well, there's Brian Callaghan, of course, whose place in the house is up for grabs, but he was unwilling to return. Bad memories.'

'Poor man,' Lizzie murmured. 'It must have been a hideous shock.'

'For all of us,' Melrose replied, shepherding the group towards the house.

'Speaking of refreshment,' Lizzie said, placing a hand on his arm to slow him down.

Kate held up the tin and Lizzie took it.

'An offering for the table, kindly made by Kate,' she said.

'Thank you!' Sally said, beaming. 'A lovely gesture. When's the baby due?'

Before Kate could answer, Daisy said, 'Pass it to me, please. I'm in charge of light haulage.'

'All done? Let's move along, shall we?' Melrose sounded mildly impatient but added a few comic herding gestures to indicate good humour.

Lizzie settled the basket on Daisy's lap, bent low to hear her whispered words. 'Take no notice of Mike. He's in director mode. He's only like this when he's nervous.'

'Nervous?' Lizzie replied, puzzled.

'He feels responsible for our situation.'

'Is he?' Lizzie asked bluntly, ditching the whisper and looking Daisy square in the eye.

Daisy shook her head. 'We seized on the idea of a shared home in a beautiful environment like a lifeline. Got lost in the dream and, as a result, we were a tad too casual about the details. Each one of us shares the responsibility.'

Melrose, who'd marched ahead, turned, visibly irritated now.

'Coming!' Daisy called, waving her hand.

'Do you need help?' Lizzie asked.

Daisy laughed. 'I won't even let even my husband mollycoddle me.' She spun the wheelchair towards the house and travelled smoothly over timber planks already losing their rawness and weathering to silver-grey. Lizzie turned to Kate. 'You're coming, too, aren't you?'

Kate hesitated, then shook her head. 'I don't want to interfere. You're the one who might be living here, not me.'

Kate settled comfortably in the boat, tilting her seat backwards as far as she felt was safe. She stared into the mangrove forest, thinking about Lizzie's talk of spirits and imagining she could see human forms in the way the branches fanned out like arms, the trunks sturdy as legs. On a moonlit night, the whiteness of the bark could easily give the illusion of a ghostly world at play. She closed her eyes, rested her hands on her stomach and crossed her fingers for Lizzie. Under the hull, water rose and fell. Within a minute, she was sound asleep.

෴

A pair of noisy miners and a couple of ferocious magpies chasing off a sea eagle woke her. She stretched to ease the stiffness in her body, and saw the sun was much lower in the sky. Needing the bathroom urgently, but unwilling to disturb the household, who might be in the midst of a delicate negotiation, she decided to find a secluded spot beyond the mangroves. The tide had dropped significantly, and the sandflats were golden in the afternoon light. She disembarked and walked along the jetty to the shoreline, removed her shoes where the jetty met the seawall, taking care not to slip on the slimy bottom step leading to the beach. She stayed close to the shore, where the sand was yellow and soft under her feet, steering clear of mangrove roots poking sharply through muddy sand. Ahead, where a freshwater creek trickled into the lagoon, she saw a dune to hide behind. She hurried. Her bladder felt like it might burst. Around her, armies of blue-uniformed soldier crabs kept tight formations as they scuttled out of her way. She crested the dune, saw a young couple locked in an embrace that looked barely decent, their tent nearby. She staggered backwards, embarrassed, and dropped to the ground. Losing control, she wet her trousers. Teary with helplessness and frustration, she walked into the clear blue water of the lagoon fully clothed and sat in the shallows until the sun dropped behind the escarpment and she could no longer bear the cold.

Shivering, she walked back to the boat, her wet jeans chafing her thighs. There was still no sign of Lizzie. Realising she had no option but to swallow her pride, she knocked on the door, then rang the shiny brass bell.

'I was wondering how much longer Lizzie would be,' she said, when Melrose appeared.

'You're wet,' he observed.

'Went for a swim to cool down,' she lied. 'A mistake, in hindsight.'

'Come in and dry off,' he said, standing back to let her pass.

'If you're all done, we should get going, or it'll be dark by the time Lizzie gets home.'

'I see. Give me a minute and I'll extract her from the celebrations.'

'She's moving in, then?'

'She's a delight, Kate. Donna adores her already. And we owe it to you.'

'I'll wait in the boat,' Kate said.

As she set off down the jetty, an image of Lizzie's treasured house, abandoned to the elements and gradually collapsing, came into her head. She fought the urge to cry a second time. Then she asked herself if all human endeavour was pointless, including the act of procreation. It was a question, she knew from experience, that would allow entrance to the black dog. She checked her watch just as she heard voices coming towards her. Realised she was ravenous.

Lizzie's face was radiant. 'I'm so sorry, Kate,' she said. Her cheeks were suffused with pink, her eyes gave off a glassy sparkle. 'Donna insisted on serving sherry and I lost track of the time.'

Donna, in skin-tight white trousers, a rose-pink cotton knit sweater that matched her rope-soled shoes, piped up: 'We were having such a good time, I didn't want the afternoon to end. Imagine! A famous playwright. Living out here in the wild bush. It's a miracle!'

Lizzie rolled her eyes. Donna, unsteady on her feet, extended a bony, limp-wristed hand with pale pink nails and a large turquoise ring on the middle finger. 'Hello—I'm Donna,' she breathed, tilting her head in a feigned display of shyness.

'Hate to be a party pooper, but if we don't get going it'll be too dark for Lizzie to walk home,' Kate said, pretending not to see Donna's outstretched hand.

Melrose, who'd hung back, took his wife's elbow to draw her out of the way and cover the snub. 'There'll be plenty of time to talk when Lizzie moves in,' he reminded her.

'But when will that be?' Donna whined. 'We have so much to discuss. Work to do.'

Lizzie grabbed hold of the cabin and stepped into the boat, sure-footed this time; perhaps the sherry had made her more relaxed. 'I need time to come up with a theme anyway,' Lizzie said.

'This is *so* exciting,' Donna gushed. 'Hurry, hurry, okay?'

Lizzie gave a salute of assent.

'I will play the lead role, of course?'

'Wouldn't have it any other way,' Lizzie said. Kate caught the irony in her tone but Donna, oblivious, beamed.

Mike Melrose untied as Kate fired the engine. 'I'll get the legals started,' he said, directing his words at Lizzie.

'Good. Let's not have any grey areas. Then we can all relax.'

'Bye bye, darling Lizzie,' Donna called, blowing a kiss.

As the boat rounded the point, Kate dropped speed and swivelled to face Lizzie. 'Surely you're not seriously thinking of moving in?' she said. 'That woman will drive you insane within a week. And what work? What lead? You're not going to write the woman a play, are you?'

'The house is beautiful, Kate. Separate spaces designed for optimum privacy. Easy to be alone if that's what one wants. As for Donna, she's clearly unwell. Mentally, I mean, although she's barely got enough flesh on her to keep that ring from slipping off.

The others treat her with great tolerance and kindness, as far as I can tell. And she was charming today. Witty, interesting, kept us entertained with stories about her days in the sun—her words, not mine. She's an actress, of course, so who knows if what I experienced was genuine or Donna playing her favourite role? And does it really matter in the long run? I don't think so. I'll write her a little play. Why not? Apparently she gives performances every Friday night. You never know—it might be fun. As for the others, well, there may be dark and turbulent emotion simmering under all that geniality, but I didn't sense it.'

Kate picked up speed, shaking her head. 'Better you than me. According to everyone who's met the group, Donna is a borderline psychopath.'

Lizzie turned to stare at the wake as twilight embraced Stringybark Bay. 'It will be like living in an Ibsen play. All those heightened feelings underscoring every dull moment. I'm quite looking forward to it! Oh God, I left your cake tin behind. And Kate, you're soaking wet!'

'Went for a stroll while I was waiting and fell in,' Kate lied.

'You must be cold,' Lizzie said.

'Just a little. I'm okay. What did you think of Mike Melrose?'

'Bossy but harmless. Did you notice Donna's ring?'

'The turquoise?'

'Yes.'

'Beautiful.'

'Native American. Very old. Worth a fortune.'

'I just don't understand it. The whole place oozes wealth. Why did they have to pool their resources in their retirement?'

'There's nothing sinister going on,' Lizzie said. 'I'd stake my life on it.'

'Unfortunate choice of words, if you don't mind me saying so.'

They reached the mouth of Stringybark Bay, and Kate turned towards home. 'It's too late and too dangerous to tackle the trek to your house,' Kate said. 'Would you like to stay overnight?'

Lizzie placed a hand on Kate's shoulder. 'Thanks, but I have chooks to feed and plants to water. And I could navigate my way blindfolded.'

'Text when you arrive. Okay?'

⁓

Lizzie disappeared through the cabbage palm tunnel that led to the walking track and Kate, exhausted, climbed the steps to her front door, a hand on the small of her aching back. Inside, she stripped off her damp clothes and threw them in the washing machine then stood under a shower until the chill seeped out of her bones and the mirrors were fogged with steam. The heat made her drowsy. She dried off, stepped into her pyjamas and fought the urge to go to bed, knowing she needed to eat. In the kitchen, she boiled the kettle for tea and foraged in the fridge. Roast chicken, potatoes and green beans in a plastic container, the remnants of a loose Briny Café version of salade niçoise. She set a place at the kitchen table, then changed her mind, picked up the plate and went through the door to the verandah. The bay shone silver. She nibbled at her food.

A short while later, her phone pinged with a message from Lizzie: *All good. No snakes. Or none that I noticed in the dark.* Kate sent back a thumbs-up.

A chill rolled down from the escarpment to sit on the water like a cold compress. She shivered and went inside to finish her dinner.

After a while, she made her way to bed and lay down on top of the cover. Suddenly aware that Sam had made no effort to contact her.

CHAPTER TWELVE

KATE WOKE TO THE SOUND of running water. She rolled onto her side to take the pressure off a full bladder, reluctant to get up. 'Sam?' she called.

He appeared in the bedroom doorway, holding a cup in a mute question.

She nodded and swung her feet to the floor. Checked the time. Almost nine o'clock. A record sleep-in since the new tenant had taken up residence in her womb.

In the bathroom, she stripped and showered quickly, then pulled a white cotton shift over her head.

Sam handed her the tea, grabbed a mug and filled it with instant coffee for himself, even though he knew Kate would turn up her nose. 'I meant to tell you, Cameron's wallet was picked up a long way from where it should have been,' he said.

'Really? Who found it?'

Sam looked into the depths of his mug. 'Jimmy and me.'

'When?'

'Couple of days ago. Planned to mention it the other night but the timing was off.'

'I see. Battery flat on the phone was it?'

'Jeez, Kate, it's a bloody wallet. No big deal. And you're not that flash in the phone department yourself.'

'You know I'm interested. You know I have my doubts about the death. You know I have nothing better to think about right now!' She glared at him.

He let out a long sigh. 'I've been thinking, Kate. Long and hard. All night, every night. About the two of us. I care about you more than anyone else in the world.'

'Even Jimmy?' she asked lightly.

'Only by a short half-head.' He managed a grin.

'Where are you going with this, Sam?'

He took a deep breath. 'We don't work. You know it. I know it. The sooner we face the fact the better.'

Kate swallowed. She turned away, refilled the kettle, emptied the teapot ready for a fresh brew, her movements automatic, the ritual its own comfort.

Sam remained silent.

'If you're hoping I'll disagree, it's not going to happen,' she said tersely. Sam opened his mouth to speak, but she held up a hand to silence him. 'So we're breaking up? It's your call.' A faint flush rose from her chest and Sam knew he'd caught her in a lie.

'It's never been my call, Kate, as you well know,' he said softly.

With a half-smile, she dipped her head in agreement. 'Caught red-handed. You know me too well.'

'What I see when I look at you, Kate, is a woman who finds the responsibility of relationships—even friendships—too much to bear. Maybe because it takes all your energy to keep yourself on track. I wouldn't know; I'm not a shrink. All I know is, when a man walks through the door of his home, he's meant to feel relief, not anxiety. I feel like I'm stepping through landmines here. One wrong move and—poof! Nothing but dust and ruins. I thought I was the one at fault. But all along, whether you're aware of it or not, you've been manoeuvring me into untenable situations so that, eventually, I would be the one to pull the plug. Your conscience would be clear. Well, plug pulled. Doesn't mean I won't support you and the baby. That goes without saying. Just means you'll have your space free and clear. No more Solvol in the bathroom or greasy marks in the sink.' For a second, Sam's blue eyes went hard and flat: 'But just to be absolutely clear, if you try to do a runner with our kid, I will hunt you to the ends of the earth.'

He heard Kate's quick little sip of breath. 'Don't hold back,' she said.

'I've been holding back from the beginning. Didn't do either of us much good.'

Sam stood, preparing to leave.

Kate tried a smile. Faltered. 'I warned you I was difficult.'

'Can't say you didn't. Truth is, without the baby we wouldn't have made it this far.'

'You deserve a good woman, Sam. And no matter how hard I try, it's just not in me.'

'Maybe not.'

Kate gasped as though he'd hit her. 'Well, I opened that trap-door all on my own.' When it appeared this time, the smile was genuine. 'About the wallet . . .' she said.

Sam couldn't help it. He laughed. 'You are bloody incorrigible. No wonder you were a great journo. You never give up, do you?'

'Where did you find it?' she asked, and in a subtle segue that they both understood, they slipped into new roles as friends.

'In the open waters of the bay. Why?'

'Freddy was upset when Mike Melrose threw something overboard when he ferried the group to the café the day after Cameron's death. They were minutes away from the Square. Why wouldn't Melrose wait and use the bin?'

'Freddy get a close look?'

'I didn't ask. I didn't know about the wallet turning up.'

'In my defence, I was planning to tell you, but I got derailed when you took off to Lizzie's shack without a word.'

'That's us, Sam, good and derailed.'

'Yeah. I'd fight for you, Kate, if I thought that's what you wanted.'

'Nothing to do with you. It's just who I am. Thought I could change but there's something in me that runs deep, Sam, and it's not very noble. And about the baby?'

Sam stiffened, bracing himself.

'If I do a runner, I would never, ever saddle myself with a kid.' Kate grinned.

Sam wiped his brow in mock relief. 'Never fancied having to get on a plane. If God wanted us to fly, he'd have given us wings.'

'Cliché, Sam.'

'Yep. Got plenty more of them up my sleeve, too. By the way, those old folks in Stringybark Bay, there's the smell of ackamarackus about them.'

Kate wrinkled her brow. 'Simon again?'

Sam gave an almost imperceptible nod.

'Okay, I give up.'

'Means bullshit. And if you want my unguarded opinion, that fancy house down by the mangroves is brimming with it. How'd it go with Lizzie yesterday?'

'Good. Yeah, good. Looks like she's going to join the household.'

Sam rubbed his forehead with his hand like he felt a headache coming on. 'I hope she knows what she's doing.'

CHAPTER THIRTEEN

KNOWING HE COULDN'T KEEP HIS bust-up with Kate secret for long in a place like Cook's Basin where a single day watching tinnies come and go revealed who was doing it tough, who was doing it easily and who wasn't doing anything at all, Sam called in at the café and asked if Ettie could spare him a moment.

Ettie leaned on the counter and smiled. 'I'm all yours, young man.'

Sam shuffled his feet and looked at the floorboards.

Ettie gave him a look, immediately on alert. 'How about the back deck?'

'Perfect,' Sam said.

Turning to Jenny, Ettie said, 'Two coffees, please . . . And chocolate cake.'

'One slice or two?' Jenny asked.

'One for Sam,' Ettie replied, with genuine regret.

Ettie directed Sam to an isolated table in the furthest corner from the kitchen, where a potato vine screened the café from the Square and prying eyes.

'I'd prefer to stand,' Sam said.

'Now I'm really worried,' Ettie said, dropping heavily into a slatted chair. 'You're not ill, are you? Oh! Is it Kate?'

'Nah, nothing like that,' Sam said. And, realising things could be a lot worse, he let go of his worry and took a seat near Ettie. He reached for her hand and held it lightly.

Jenny appeared with a tray. 'You two look like lovebirds,' she teased. 'Might start a rumour, eh? We're short of scuttlebutt at the moment.' Then, noticing their expressions, she plonked the tray down in front of Ettie and did a runner back to the counter.

Sam struggled for a way to lead into a conversation he'd hoped he'd never have. In the end, at a loss for any fancy way to dress up the end of his relationship, he came straight to the point. 'Kate and I are done.'

'What? Don't be ridiculous,' Ettie said, withdrawing her hand from Sam's grip and reaching automatically for the chocolate cake. She forked some into her mouth and chewed. 'A little dry and needs more orange peel,' she declared.

'Don't make this harder than it is, Ettie.' Sam pushed back his chair and stood, leaning on the rail, his back to her.

'Correct me if I'm wrong,' Ettie said, 'but there's a baby on the way. A baby that will need a mother and a father.'

'You think I'm unaware of that fact?' Sam demanded. 'Do you think I haven't turned myself inside out trying to be everything Kate wants in a partner? Well, I can't do it anymore, Ettie. Can't keep waking up every morning wondering whether today's the day the sky is going to crash down on my head.'

Ettie, softening, rose to stand beside her friend, sliding an arm around his waist. 'Pregnant women are at the mercy of their hormones, Sam,' she reminded him. 'Wait a while. Things will change.'

Sam shook his head. 'We're done, Ettie. Better to cut the cord now before we turn into two miserably unhappy human beings staying together for the wrong reasons.'

'Kate's . . . different from the rest of us,' Ettie said carefully. 'Maybe—'

'Even if I understood what she truly wants,' Sam interrupted, 'it would be more than I can ever give her. I'm a simple barge man, Ettie. What you see is what you get. Kate? What you see is never the whole picture. I'm not even sure she knows what that is herself.'

'Oh, my love,' Ettie murmured, resting her forehead on his broad chest. 'What a bloody mess.'

After a few minutes had passed, Sam muttered that he had work to do and Ettie agreed that she'd left Jenny to cope alone for long enough.

Sam headed back to the *Mary Kay*.

'Sam!' Ettie called.

He turned around, one foot on the gunnel.

'Dinner. Tonight. Kingfish Bay. No arguments.'

He nodded. 'You're on.'

Humming softly, looser in spirit but aware he'd be hurting for a long time, he fired the engine. He checked the list of jobs scribbled on a scrap of paper then swung into the waterway and made for Cargo Wharf, where he'd left Jimmy and the mutt to keep an eye on a delivery of six reverse-cycle air conditioners for a new home build on the south-facing side of Cutter Island. A house so huge locals were already referring to it as New Parliament House. Sam reckoned he'd transported more marble slabs destined for kitchen benchtops in the past two years than in the two previous decades of offshore living. Not to mention enough stainless steel to build a warship. The shabby old hand-built holiday shacks with outdoor showers and bedrooms stacked with enough bunk beds for an army of kids were disappearing. He slowed the barge, thinking about his own home and wondering if it was time to install a few mod cons, such as reverse-cycle aircon and a marble kitchen with shiny black cupboards that opened and shut with the press of a finger. 'Ah, bugger,' he said out loud. 'A man needs to stretch his legs in front of an open fire on a cold winter's night and no amount of marble is going to improve my cooking.' He gunned the *Mary Kay* and covered the last hundred yards at the cracking pace of eight knots.

On the wharf, Jimmy jumped around like a lunatic, slapping his arms, legs and neck like he was under attack by a swarm of bees. As it turned out, it was wasps.

'Where ya bin, Sam?' the kid yelled. 'I'm gettin' bitten to blazes and there you are takin' your time like Lord Muck.'

'Give up that hair gel, mate,' Sam advised. 'It's enough to bring wasps from miles around.'

The kid froze and frowned. 'You reckon?'

'Lay-down misère. Now get on board and let me look at you.'

'Aw, it's nothing much, Sam. I swung a few punches and sorted the lot.'

His right eye had swelled almost shut, Sam noted, and the welts on his left arm resembled a strange tattoo. 'You breathing okay?' Sam asked.

'Yeah. I'm good.'

'Just the same, mate, we might run you home so your mum can keep an eye on you.'

The kid drew himself up to his full height and said indignantly, 'I keep an eye on me mum, these days, Sam. I'm good to keep goin', and I'll let you know if anythin' changes.'

Sam hesitated and decided it might be wiser to keep Jimmy in sight. 'Alright then. Check the first-aid kit for some ointment and let's get this overdue show on the road.'

'Overdue alright. You and Ettie, first-class yabberers. Even Artie couldn't compete.'

The kid scuttled off. Sam placed slings around the aircon units and slowly craned them onto the barge with a light touch and not a single rough jolt.

Jimmy emerged from the wheelhouse with yellow spots of iodine all over his body. He looked like he'd been struck by a rare disease. Sam swallowed his laughter, rearranged his expression into approval and stepped behind the helm. Longfellow whined, spun his compulsory three times and settled in his bed. Sam wondered what was so magical about the number three.

⌒

At 6 pm, after a working day free of problems and with the welts on Jimmy's body subsiding, Sam chugged alongside the chef's pontoon in his tinnie. Scrubbed, his wiry hair slicked flat with damp, he'd dressed in his best khaki shorts and a pale blue cotton shirt. His boat shoes gleamed. His fingernails were free from dirt, and he was clean-shaven. He wanted to look his best tonight. He wasn't sure why it was so important, but it was.

The front door was open. 'Permission to come aboard?' he yelled down the hallway.

Ettie flew from the kitchen wearing a colourful kaftan that billowed in her wake. The chef followed more sedately and handed Sam a beer encased in a cooler that was printed with a picture of the Briny Café and a phone number for bookings. One of Kate's marketing ideas.

'This is sad news,' murmured the chef, throwing an arm around Sam's shoulders. 'But why this has happened is none of our business, we want you to understand this. You are our friend. So is Kate. There are no sides in this sorry business for those of us who love you both. I am speaking correctly, am I not, Ettie?'

She nodded, the lump in her throat rendering her speechless.

'So tonight, we will eat and say whatever is on our minds without fear of judgement,' the chef concluded. 'Yes?'

This time, Sam nodded.

His speech delivered, the chef clapped his hands. 'Good. And now I must make a declaration which I hope will bring joy: dinner is served!'

'Hear, hear, Chef,' Sam said, thinking this was the best news he'd heard all day. 'What's on the menu?'

'Lamb shoulder, braised tenderly in a rich broth—of my own making, naturally. I have adorned it with anchovies, finely chopped rosemary and garlic, and added some butter to enrich the sauce. It will cut like velvet. I, myself, have never cut velvet, but—'

'And dessert, Chef? What spectacular dish have you created?' Sam interjected smoothly.

'You will not be disappointed, my friend, but it must remain a secret to be a surprise. Food is performance. A scene in a play. A magician's role is to make magic, yes?' Then, sensing a hint of impatience in his guest, he instructed: 'To the table.'

Over dinner, Sam gave an account of the pressures in his relationship with Kate without, he hoped, betraying trust or failing to
be fair. Ettie and Marcus listened intently while he pushed his
lamb around his plate, suddenly unable to eat and consumed by
a nagging worry that leaving Kate at this time was a risk, even
dangerous.

'What do you think?' he asked his friends when he had revealed
the depth of his concern. 'Should I have put up and shut up?'

Ettie leaned forward, anxious to comfort. The chef put a
restraining hand on her thigh. 'These issues are impossible upon
which to comment,' Marcus said. He enfolded Ettie's workworn
hand in his own where calluses from holding carving knives and,
in his retirement, fishing rods, formed hard lumps under the skin.
'But my dear friend, we know, my love and I, that you are a good
man, a man—as a great philosopher whose name I cannot recall
once said—a man for all seasons.'

Sam smiled: 'Think it was a movie title, chef.'

'Yes, yes, but about a man who recognised that to lose his moral
compass—this is correct, yes?' He looked to Sam for confirmation.
Sam nodded. '. . . to lose his moral compass would make a mockery
of all that he stood for in life.'

'Sir Thomas More. My dad's favourite movie. The bloke died
for his beliefs, Chef, if I remember correctly.'

Marcus hastened to explain. 'Your moral compass, my friend,
is unbroken by this current situation which saddens our hearts but
will not break them.'

Ettie's eyes shone with tears. 'It's about the baby now. You and

Kate are about to become custodians of a new life. Neither of you has it in you to put your ego ahead of the baby.'

'And yet here I am, back on the island in my old house.'

'Because this is what Kate wanted, if I am correct, and you are a man who puts others first,' Marcus said. 'This is what your moral compass told you to do. Yes?'

Sam nodded, relieved the chef understood and forgave motives he'd struggled to fully defend to himself. He found himself able to pick up his knife and fork and pull away tender portions of meat, swirling them in the sauce, inhaling the strong scent of rosemary, believing for a moment that the chef and Ettie were correct—good food could erase for a while the sharp edges of sadness and inadequacy. While his hosts watched approvingly, he ate heartily, leaving not a single scrap on his plate. A moment after Sam had placed his cutlery neatly together in the centre of the plate in a manner that would please Kate, Marcus announced he would serve dessert on the deck.

'A simple mandarin cake which we will eat from our hands while the stars shine above us. It will lift our fallen spirits, will it not?'

A man used to his own way, he suggested that while he and Ettie cleared the table Sam should find a comfortable spot. One where he could study the night sky and the wonders of the universe which—if the chef wasn't being impolite or unfeeling—reduced humankind and their eternal problems to infinitesimal specks without importance beyond a single lifespan. 'Sometimes, it must be said, even a day or two,' he added, to make his point.

Seated alone at the end of the jetty, Sam studied the moon, which was surrounded by a misty ring. 'It will rain tomorrow,' he said, hearing Ettie come up behind him.

'Farmers reckon a crescent moon positioned like a bowl means no rain. If it's flipped upside down, look out for floods,' Ettie said.

'Never heard that one before.'

He gave Ettie a hand to sit down. She took off her shoes and passed them to him and splashed her feet about in the water like a child. 'Still cold. Feels like heaven on my tired feet.'

'You and Marcus seem to have it sorted,' Sam said.

'We're much older than you and Kate. For us, every moment counts. Better to focus on contentment instead of nursing niggles that don't amount to much.'

'I knew Kate had issues. But I thought love and care, finding a place to belong, would steady her. Every time she finds an even keel, though, she devises a new way to blow up her current existence.'

Ettie, abiding by Marcus's instructions at great cost, said nothing.

'Remember how right at the beginning, when you started out together in the café, she did a runner? Took off a second time, too. No warning. No explanation. Oh, you coped, Ettie, you always do, and you forgave—as usual. But Kate's lack of concern for the consequences . . . well, it's unsettling. It's like there're two personalities operating in her head at the same time: Miss Kind and Compassionate, and Miss Self-indulgent and Indifferent. But somehow, it's always about Kate's needs. There's a pattern there.' He turned so he could look Ettie in the eye. 'Kate and I? We don't matter much. But soon there'll be a child. And I don't trust Kate, that's what I'm saying. I don't trust her for a moment.' He stood abruptly and paced the deck. 'It almost kills me to say it, but it's true. I don't trust her.'

Ettie, unable to keep silent any longer, was drawn to defend her friend: 'Kate has issues, big issues, but her instincts are good.'

'Rubbish. She's terrified of responsibility. Being tied down.' He stopped pacing and spun to face Ettie. 'Why is it that falling in love inevitably leads to handing someone the power to rip out your heart at a moment's notice? Tell me, Ettie, why? Explain . . .' Sam broke off as the chef appeared with a towering plate of cupcakes dusted with icing sugar. A sweet citrus scent cut through the dank, briny smell of the mudflats on the far side of the bay. Sam resumed his seat. Ettie whispered in his ear, 'This conversation is not over. Just so you know.'

Sam and Ettie wriggled along to make room for the chef to sit at the end of jetty. 'Choose, my friend,' Marcus said, presenting the plate.

Sam patted his stomach. 'Full as, mate.'

The disappointment on Marcus's face was so pronounced it was almost comic.

'Er, I'll take one home to have later, though.'

'But I cannot resist, my darling,' Ettie said. She held the cake between her thumb and forefinger and bit into it. After a moment, she said, 'Light but dense. Sweet but not sickly. The taste of orange with a perfumed overtone.'

'Yes!' Marcus responded, elated. 'It is the small teaspoon of orange blossom water that lifts this simple little mandarin cake to a higher level.'

'We will add them to the menu of the café immediately!' Ettie declared.

'Hurrah!' Marcus noticed, then, Sam's worried face. He sighed theatrically. 'My dessert has failed to bring you joy, so instead you must absorb the serenity and beauty of the night surroundings.' The low hoot of an owl carried across the water from the far side of the bay. 'This owl, it feels your sorrow, my friend. But sorrow can be borne after the passing of time—although, if you want the truth from my heart, this sorrow finds a small corner where it resides eternally. You may be thinking this is a terrible fact, but perhaps it is good to recall sorrows, if only to truly value sparkling moments as they rise.'

'You're quite a philosopher, Chef. Up there with Thomas More.'

'I am a man with the worn toes of his shoes now pointing in the direction of fading prospects, who has learned that creating a perfect dessert—which, naturally, I have done many times beyond counting—is poof! Nothing. It is true love that sustains.'

He put an arm around Ettie and she leaned into him.

Sam found a handkerchief in his pocket and blew his nose loudly. 'Pollen,' he said.

Ettie patted his knee.

'Did I give up too easily?' Sam asked.

'But it is never over—if you will permit me the indulgence of a cliché—until the fat lady sings.'

'Politically incorrect,' Ettie murmured.

'Never over? I'm not so sure, Chef,' Sam said.

'I remember in my youth there was a woman who could bring together cream, sugar and vanilla in a way that melted my heart.'

Ettie struggled out of his arms and stared at him. 'What woman?'

'Hush, Ettie. This woman, she was . . . impossible. This word is not too strong. To please her, I bended, I spun, I knotted my body into strange shapes. This woman, she looked me in the eye with sadness and disappointment when I declared myself no longer able to bend and spin according to her wishes. She said: "All along, I was testing your commitment—and you have failed."'

'Testing you?' Sam asked, struggling to follow the chef's meaning.

'This is what I am telling you now. Years later, we met once again at the opening of a new restaurant, where she was queen of a kitchen filled with the mouth-watering fragrance of burnt sugar and vanilla. She explained that her trust had been broken by others in the past and she no longer had faith in her judgement. Therefore, she devised tests for others. Which is no doubt why, I must add, she was still alone all those years later. Forgiveness is the bedfellow of compassion, after all.'

Sam frowned. 'Are you saying, Chef, that Kate's complicatedness is her way of assessing whether I'm a sprinter or a stayer?'

'I am saying nothing. Merely telling a story.'

'What woman?' Ettie demanded.

CHAPTER FOURTEEN

THE FOLLOWING MORNING, WITH THE bays glowing and spring growth so luminous and fresh it looked spit-polished, Sam woke with the dull thud of a headache and the sight of Jimmy standing at the foot of his bed, holding a cup of tea.

'Reckon you and Kate are done for, eh?' Jimmy said, his face creased with worry. 'Me mum says one night on your tod sloan doesn't count for much, but when it gets to be a habit, the writin' is on the wall.'

Sam sat up in bed, scratched his chest. 'Are you going to pass me that very welcome cuppa or stand there holding it until it gets cold?' he asked.

The kid lunged forward with the mug.

Sam took a large gulp. 'Perfect,' he said. 'Now scram while I get dressed.'

Jimmy looked down at his twitching feet. He rubbed his hands together like an old man contemplating the choice between two fine whiskies. 'I missed me compost pick-up yesterday and Ettie says if I don't get there first thing this morning, she'll garter me guts.' Jimmy looked anxious. 'I dunno what that means, Sam, but I reckon it doesn't sound too flash.'

Sam, relieved the kid wasn't about to grill him about love, threw back the bedclothes. 'First call for the *Mary Kay*, mate. I promise.'

The kid grinned and skedaddled.

Fifteen minutes later, the man, the boy and the dog cast off from the mooring. All around, the heart of Cook's Basin beat as steadily as ever, helping to ease the fracture in Sam's heart. His decision to walk away from his relationship with Kate, he reminded himself, was based on one premise: acting in the best interests of his child. He'd seen enough island kids hammered emotionally by warring parents. But still, worry gnawed away in the background. Had he deserted the ship at the first sign of a leak? Did his heart have no more resolve than a split pea? None of these thoughts helped his headache, which refused to budge.

The *Mary Kay* pulled alongside the Briny Café, and Jimmy leaped off to collect two blue garbage bags near the rear door.

Ettie emerged from the café, wiping her hands on her apron. 'Heard the news?' she called, walking towards the barge. 'Lizzie got the go ahead to join the GeriAncients.'

'Yeah. Kate told me a couple of days ago.'

'Can't help thinking they're a doubtful lot, though.'

Brian Callaghan, who'd come up behind her, said: 'Couldn't agree more.'

Ettie went crimson and stammered an apology. 'Not all of them, of course . . .'

Brian sat down with his coffee and opened a newspaper to the crossword page. 'Oh, it's all of them, Ettie, I can assure you.'

Embarrassed, Ettie fled inside.

Jimmy passed Sam the garbage bags, then stepped aboard to stow them safely for the short trip to Cutter Island where he'd drag them up steps set into the hillside, to the house his mother, Amelia, had swathed with embroidered cushions, knitted afghans, macrame wall hangings and anything else with which she could employ her nimble fingers. Sam had jokingly suggested a clearing sale one day when he'd popped in after helping Jimmy with a heavy weekend load of scraps, or she and Jimmy would have to move into a tent. He'd been rewarded with a look so fierce it still made his teeth ache. 'I'm off to order a heart-starter,' Sam called to the kid. 'Back in a minute.'

Jimmy dropped the bags and raced to his side. 'Has your heart stopped, Sam?' he asked anxiously. 'Will ya be alright?'

'A figure of speech, mate, for the effect of caffeine.'

The kid's face cleared. 'D'you reckon I could use one, too?'

Sam shook his head. 'You already operate on rocket fuel, my friend.'

On his return to the café, Sam debated whether he should stop to have a friendly word with Brian, to glean a little more intelligence about the goings-on in Stringybark Bay.

The decision was taken out of his hands: 'Six letters? Any idea?' Brian was tapping a blank space in his crossword.

'Nah. Simon's the crossword expert. Not me.' He leaned over the man's shoulder. 'Looks complicated, mate. Must help to take your mind off the sad stuff, though.'

'What? Oh, yes, of course.' Brian folded the paper neatly, set the pencil alongside it.

'How are you faring in Ettie's penthouse?'

'She's a gem, that woman. Never met anyone so kind in my life.'

'Salt of the earth.' Sam smiled inwardly at his newfound freedom to indulge in clichés.

'Lizzie and I are signing the sale and handover documents this morning. I'll be leaving for Melbourne as soon as I can. Thus endeth GeriEcstasy for me. Stupid bloody name. Always thought so. Stupid bloody idea from day one. I told Cam. Said it was insane. He wouldn't listen.'

'It's a good outcome for everyone, especially Lizzie,' Sam said.

'They must have kept Donna locked in the attic during the interview,' Brian said. 'No one in her right mind would sign up to live within a mile of the woman. Poisonous, she is. And not just from all the pills and booze she shoves down her throat day and night.'

'Lizzie can handle herself. Lived up on the escarpment alone for nearly fifty years. That takes courage.'

'I hope so. For her sake.' Brian stood abruptly.

'What about all your gear, mate?' Sam asked. 'Are taking it with you or would you like Jimmy to organise a dock sale? Offshore relocations can add up when they're stacked close together. Might save you money in the long run.'

'Lizzie's bought most of it and agreed to let me leave a few favourite pieces behind until I find a place to live. An offshore tradition, apparently, due to the whim of wind and weather.' He checked his watch. 'Better head off or I'll be late. The sooner this is all over the better.'

'Cameron's ashes, mate. Do you have a plan? I could scatter them from the *Mary Kay*, if you like. Have a small ceremony out to sea. Just say the word.'

Brian turned tear-filled eyes on Sam. 'What? And drown him twice? Cam stays with me. Forever.' He picked a path through the tables and chairs and disappeared inside the café to pay his bill.

Jeez, Sam thought, he'd handled that little encounter like a fully-fledged bird brain.

Brian's voice carried across the deck from the doorway. 'Mike's organising a boat trip to cheer the household and celebrate Lizzie's arrival. Disastrous idea. On a par with the whole stupid GeriEcstasy plan. Another accident waiting to happen.' He stood, looking undecided for a minute, then added, 'Tell Lizzie to be careful. Something or someone lured Cam to the water's edge. He wasn't a stupid man. Too kind, perhaps, but never stupid. And if it was *someone*, that person is still in the house. She might want to give that some thought.'

Before Sam could think of an answer the door closed behind him. He scratched his head. Diverted from the question of Lizzie's safety by the thought of a boatload of GeriAncients heading out to sea. Melrose must be mad, he thought.

～

Back at Cutter Island, Sam stayed on the *Mary Kay* while Jimmy lugged the compost bags up the steep incline to his home. While he waited Sam called Kate. 'Never let it be said again that I have withheld information,' he began.

Kate laughed. 'Out with it.'

'Before I reveal all, Simon texted a doozy. You want to hear it?'

Kate sighed. 'If I must.'

'Ophiolatry. Pronounced correctly, in case you're wondering.'

'Well, there's a hint of idolatry in there, so I'm guessing it's the worship of something.'

'Close, but no cigar.'

Kate laughed again.

'Okay, I give up.'

'The worship of . . . wait for it. Snakes!'

'Not bad. Now tell me why you called.'

For a reckless moment, Sam considered flirting but lost his nerve. 'Lizzie signs the dotted line to become a fully-fledged member of the GeriAncients today.'

'When's she moving in?'

'I didn't think to ask. Oh—here comes Jimmy. I gotta go.' He killed the call.

Jimmy, wiping the sweat from his brow, stepped on board. 'I'm gunna have to expand me worm business again, Sam. Café's goin' so good me worms are havin' trouble keepin' up with the scraps.'

Sam watched as the mutt lifted a leg against a patch of crofton weed. 'When we've finished the day's jobs, we're going to rip up those weeds before they spread all over the island.'

'Aw, Sam.'

'Our civic duty, son, and as usual, it looks like no other bastard is going to do it.'

'You know I'd walk through a burning bush for you, Sam, but I bloody hate gardening.'

'That's enough swearing for one day. Is that mutt on board yet? Right. Let's get to work.' He whistled tunelessly, unable to wipe the grin off his face. To Sam, Kate's laughter had sounded like music.

CHAPTER FIFTEEN

OVERNIGHT, AND WITHOUT WARNING, THE lazy feel of an early summer gave way to the lingering petulance of spring. A storm, filthy and black, roared in from the nor'east, catching the residents of Cook's Basin by surprise. Woken by wind and thunder, the sight of trees bent double and a roiling sea, they pleaded for celestial help in whispered prayers. While teeth rattled on bedside tables and the sound of pontoons groaning and bucking and boats being hammered against jetties filled them with dread, they lay in bed, waiting until it was safe to venture outside.

At dawn, like the flick of a switch, the wind dropped. The sky emptied of growling turmoil and the sea turned glassy in the orange light of early morning. People emerged from their homes like sleepwalkers, afraid to look around and even more afraid to look away. 'Could've been worse,' they murmured. A few tinnies lying on the seabed. A few trees uprooted. A couple of pontoons drifting aimlessly. A foamy khaki residue frilling the foreshore and water cascading from the escarpment to spread in brown stains in the bays that looked like a blight but would clear in a day.

Sam's phone rang. 'Tree down,' Simon said. 'It's taken the corner of the house.'

'You hurt?'

'Nah. Didn't even wake up.'

'Let me know when you're ready for help with the clean-up.'

'Er, I might need a place to sleep for a few days. I've got no electricity.'

'Hang on.' Sam reached for his bedside light and turned on the switch. 'Must be out all over the island.'

'Shit.'

'That's one way of describing it.'

'Might stay here then, if it's no better at yours.'

Sam called Kate. She picked up on the first ring.

'I'm fine,' she assured him. 'Nothing to worry about. You should see the waterfall. It's ferocious.'

'Artie?'

'Hang on, I'll check.' She carried the phone outside. 'All good as far as I can tell. But I'll give him a call anyway.'

'Catch you later,' he said.

Sam considered hauling Jimmy out of bed but decided to go it alone until a decent hour. He pulled on his clothes, grabbed an apple and made his way to the dock.

Longfellow bounded along the jetty to greet him and an eager voice came from Sam's tinnie. 'What took you so long, Sam? We've been waitin' all mornin.'

'You're a legend, mate. No doubt about it.'

'Been bailin' for a while now,' Jimmy said, pointing to the water in the hull. 'Your bilge pump must've carked it. Could've sunk to the bottom and been wrecked for good. You had a lucky break, Sam.'

'All okay at home?' Sam asked, sidestepping the issue of proper tinnie maintenance.

'Yeah. Me mum had a conniption and ducked under the bed. She can handle the lightning but the thunder scares her rigid. Longfella went with her to keep her company.'

'Good-o. Speed it up then, Jimmy. While you're yabbering the work's piling up.'

In response, the kid handed him a second bucket. 'Me mum says many hands . . .'

'Yeah, I know. Light work.'

Together the man and boy bailed until Jimmy pulled the starter cord hard and fast a few times and, grudgingly, the old engine caught. Longfellow jumped aboard and they wheezed towards the *Mary Kay* at a snail's pace. 'Not a mark on her,' Sam said, his tone a mix of awe and relief.

'Ah, Sam, you shouldn't've worried. She's a tough old girl. Not like me mum in a storm . . .'

They readied the barge, checking equipment, coiling ropes unravelled by the winds and removing stray debris from the deck. Sam's phone pinged constantly. He ignored it until he was satisfied there'd been no damage, then scrolled down a list of messages, all headed: *Urgent*.

'Get ready to cast off, Jimmy,' he said.

The kid dashed to the bow. Sam took a last look around then gave a thumbs-up and slid into gear. Jimmy released the mooring buoy and swiftly tied on the tinnie.

Sam's phone rang. Glenn, the removalist. 'That biscuit tin of a barge finally sink, did it?' he said, getting in first.

'No need for that,' Glenn replied. 'And for your information, it didn't sink. It's washed ashore among the mangroves in Stringy Bark Bay. Any chance of a quick rescue? I've got a few transport orders today.'

Sam sighed as he considered all the other jobs waiting, but he figured Glenn's need was greatest. He barely made rent money each week, Sam knew, and couldn't afford to lose any work. 'You want to be picked up at Triangle Wharf or is your tinnie still afloat?' he asked.

'How do you think I found the barge in the first place? I'm standing next to it right now with a foot on it to keep it from floating away, seeing as how the tide is comin' in but not fast enough so I can get to me first job for the day and avoid payin' your bill.'

'Take your foot off, mate, we both know it's full of water and going nowhere. And for your information, sarcasm is acknowledged by people in the know as the lowest form of wit. See you in fifteen minutes.'

'Good on ya.'

Sam cut the call and pushed forward the throttle. Jimmy headed to his lookout on the bow. Longfellow watched the kid take up position then jumped in his basket, spun three times, closed his eyes. 'Smart move,' Sam told the dog.

Turning into Stringybark Bay, Sam could see the locals picking their way along the foreshore in their pyjamas, cleaning up the storm's wreckage. Georgie stood on the end of her jetty staring into the depths. Looked up when she heard the *Mary Kay*'s diesel thrum, waved frantically and yelled. Sam stuck his head out of the wheelhouse and pointed towards Glenn, who was gesticulating madly in the distance. His phone rang instantly. 'You're next on the list,' he said firmly then ended the call.

'What did you do? Stop for a picnic on the way?' shouted Glenn when the barge was in earshot.

Sam rolled his eyes and positioned the *Mary Kay*, her bow in shallow water, the stern where it was deeper. With a yip, Longfellow leaped off the deck and swam towards the shore, where he lifted his leg against a pile holding up GeriEcstasy's jetty, looking back towards his master with a look of relief and apology.

Then he and Jimmy worked together to secure Glenn's barge in wide slings which they hooked to the crane, ready to be drained and dragged into deep water. By some miracle, the hull was intact. 'But she has about as much strength as a tea-leaf,' Sam told Glenn, shaking his head. 'She's liable to break apart when I haul her off the sand.'

Glenn thrust out his chest defiantly. 'She's a strong old girl and capable of outlasting the *Mary Kay*.'

'It's your call. No need to shoot the messenger.' Sam moved to the controls. Slowly, he raised the barge. Water poured out of gaping holes in the sides. Glenn backed out of the way. As the load lightened, Sam raised the pockmarked barge a little higher then reversed the *Mary Kay*. Glenn watched, chewing his fingernails. In deeper water, Sam leaned out of the wheelhouse and held his thumb up, then down, waiting for Glenn to decide.

Glenn hesitated, then gave him the thumbs-up. He closed his eyes and his lips moved in what Sam guessed to be fervent prayer. When he opened them moments later, the barge was floating serenely on the placid waters of Stringybark Bay.

Sam exhaled.

'Ya doubter,' Glenn shouted, vindicated.

'Leave you to it, then,' Sam called out.

Glenn gave a one-fingered salute in reply and released the ties.

Onshore, Longfellow barked and kept at it, his pitch rising. Jimmy leaped over the side and ploughed through the water towards him. Sam shook his head. The day had barely begun and the kid and his mutt were going off-grid. He wound in the ropes and packed them away, steered the *Mary Kay* alongside the GeriEcstasy pontoon. A voice drifted up from under the jetty at the shallow end. 'We're comin', Sam. Longfella's just diggin' somethin' up first. Hey, Sam, he's found a big silver ball!'

The kid, beaming with the thrill of discovery, popped out from under the planks. 'Sam, look!' he yelled, holding aloft a glinting sphere. The boy, followed closely by the dog, clambered onto the jetty and hurtled towards the *Mary Kay*. 'Take a look, Sam. It's bloody beautiful. Heavy as. Solid silver, maybe?' His words billowing with hope.

Sam, who'd been about to rip into the kid for breaching safety rules, studied the object through narrowed eyes. 'Not sure about that.' He looked at Longfellow, who was giving himself an almighty shake. 'Where did the mutt find it?'

'Bottom of the jetty steps goin' to the beach.' Jimmy pointed. 'He did a good job, didn't he? It wasn't buried too deep, but. Just sittin' there with a bit of sand on top. If it's silver, I reckon I might stick it on me mum's shelf where she keeps her treasures,' he said. Then he paused. ''Course, it might belong to the GeriEcstasies, eh? Reckon I should knock on the door and ask?'

'Hop on board and bring your mutt and the ball,' Sam said. 'We'll call it salvage rights for the time being. And Jimmy?'

The kid looked at him, wide-eyed.

'Next time, fill me in before you launch. Okay?'

'Oh jeez, Sam, I'm hopin' there isn't a next time. Not sure me heart could take it.'

∽

Sam steered the *Mary Kay* towards the jetty where Georgie stood in a smouldering rage, her dressing-gown clutched at her throat. 'Scuttling Glenn's barge would do the bays a favour,' she hissed, 'whereas my almost-new boat engine might have been salvageable if it had been hauled out fast enough.'

Sam took the tirade in his stride, turning his back on Georgie when he felt he'd been polite for long enough. He asked Jimmy if he wanted to do the dive to secure the hook, seeing as he was already dripping wet.

Jimmy went over the side, gasping as he hit the water, which was deeper and colder than the shallows. 'Jeez, Sam, this water is makin' me gonads shrivel.'

'All set, mate?'

'Ready as . . .'

Sam tossed the sling ropes. Jimmy, treading water, caught them one-handed. He duck-dived, secured the tinnie with clips and stayed under so long checking his work, Sam thought he might have to plunge in to drag the boy to the surface.

Finally, Jimmy's head broke through the surface. 'One breath, Sam,' he boasted, his lips blue with cold.

'Like I always say, you're a legend.' Sam hauled the kid on board, wrapped him in a towel and waited while he put on dry clothes.

'Better stand back,' Sam told Georgie. 'The boat will swing once the water drains and the load lightens.'

'I know how to get out of the way if I have to,' Georgie snapped.

Sam folded his arms. 'Either move or we'll leave your boat on the seabed. Your call.'

George bit back a rude retort and took a short step back.

'Further,' Sam ordered.

When she was safely out of the way, he craned the tinnie until it swung freely above the water.

'You want me to set her on the jetty or put her back in the water?' Sam called.

'Water. Let's see if she floats.' There was a new note in her tone, relief bordering on politeness.

Sam lowered the tinnie, setting it down gently. 'No damage to the hull then,' he called to Georgie, who came forward at a run. 'Give Frankie a call about the engine. He might be able to save it. You're the first boat we've lifted so, with a bit of luck, you'll be first in the queue.'

Without bothering to thank Sam, she dialled Frankie on the spot, using her free hand to wind ropes around the cleats to hold the tinnie fast.

'He might have an old bilge pump you can use, too,' Sam said.

Ignored, he shrugged and reversed.

As the *Mary Kay* slid smoothly out of Stringybark Bay, the boy stood on the bow with a boat hook and skilfully skimmed floating rubbish from the water, hoisting it high like a prize catch before dropping it on the deck. Two petrol tanks. A funnel. A yellow plastic torch. Plastic bags. A couple of buckets. Three boat hooks. An icebox. Ropes and rags. A few items of clothing, mostly life jackets. One high-heeled shoe, which Jimmy looked at disdainfully.

In the wheelhouse, with the kid out of earshot, Sam called the Water Police and asked for Richard.

'I'm flat out, mate,' Richard said when he came on the line. 'Is it important?'

'Nothing that can't wait. How about late this arvo? Drop by my house.'

'You're on. Gotta go. A yacht is down. No one on board, thank God, but the rumour is arson. Storm went over the top of the marina where she was berthed.'

Sam's phone rang halfway to the eastern side of Cutter Island, where there were eleven tinnies waiting to be hauled to the surface. Tempted to let it go to voicemail, he saw the caller was Mike Melrose.

'Mate,' he answered.

Melrose cleared his throat. 'Caught sight of you leaving our jetty. All well?'

'Good as gold, mate. Picked up Jimmy after we raised Glenn's barge. Your jetty was the closest. Hope you don't mind.'

Melrose gave a small laugh. 'Not at all. Of course not. Would have offered you a coffee if I'd caught you earlier. Most of us spent the night wide awake, wondering if the whole house was going to be swept out to sea. Slept in this morning.'

'Oh, that reminds me. Heard on the grapevine that you're planning a cruise.'

Melrose laughed again. 'No secrets around here, are there?'

'None that I know of. I just wanted to say, I'd be happy to take you around the bays myself on the *Mary Kay*. We could have a picnic in a secret cove I know. Could round up a few locals to come along, too—it's time you met some of the good folks from around here.' Sam heard the hesitation, a quick response swallowed. 'No pressure,' he added.

'Give me time to run it past the household,' Melrose said. 'There's a lot happening right now. Lizzie's moving in . . .'

'We could make it a welcome party for her,' Sam suggested. 'All for one and one for all, eh?'

Melrose's laughter had a tinny ring. 'Yes. Good idea. I'll get back to you.'

Jimmy stood in the doorway to the wheelhouse, frowning. 'You didn't tell him about the big silver ball that Longfella found. Me mum would reckon that was the same as stealin'.' He sounded disappointed.

Sam throttled back to an idle. 'You have to trust me on this, Jimmy—trust I'll do the right thing.' He looked the kid in the eyes. 'And, Jimmy, not a word to anyone about the silver ball. Okay?'

The kid nodded, though he still looked unsure. Then he grinned. 'You're on to somethin', aren't ya? That's what this is all about.' He danced excitedly in the doorway. 'Me lips are zipped, Sam. Honest. No crook could torture the info outta me.'

'Well, let's hope it doesn't come to that, but good to know you're on my side.'

'You know I am, Sam,' the boy said earnestly. Jimmy lined himself up in the wheelhouse alongside his captain, reeking of mud, mangroves and seaweed.

Sam pushed forward the throttle. 'Alright,' he said. 'Who's next on the list?'

∽

Late in the day, the electricity restored to island residents, Sam handed Richard Baines a cold beer and told him to take a seat on the deck while he heated up some of the sausage rolls for which he was justifiably famous. Both men were falling-down tired after a chaotic day of search and rescue.

Sam reappeared a few minutes later with a plate of sausage rolls: buttery pastry, herb, pear and pork stuffing. Apple chutney on the side.

Richard reached for one, sniffed appreciatively, took a bite.

Sam sank into the other chair and the two men sat side by side, legs outstretched, the food on a slatted timber table between them.

Richard shifted uncomfortably. 'Er, not sure what this is all about, but if it's relationship advice you're after, I am definitely not your man.'

'Nah. Too late for all that.' Sam drew in a deep breath, let it out noisily. 'S'pose the rumours about Kate and me are flying thick and fast?'

'People talk. Haven't heard a nasty word, though.'

Sam nodded. 'Yeah, well.' He ate another sausage roll. Flakes of puff pastry drifted onto his shirt front. He brushed them away. 'Did a job this morning in Stringybark Bay.'

'Yeah, Glenn's barely seaworthy barge. Heard about it.'

'Thing is, Longfellow took off for a run and a sniff along the beach. Didn't think much about it till he wouldn't come back.'

Richard sat forward, resting his elbows on his knees, dangling his almost-empty beer bottle by a forefinger. 'Yeah?'

'Jimmy had to go after him. Hang on a sec.'

Sam disappeared inside, re-emerged a moment later.

'See this?' Sam held the silver ball in the palm of his hand. 'A boule, I reckon. Part of a set, maybe? Buried, not deep, where the GeriEcstasy jetty is bolted to the shore.' He paused. 'Thing is, Longfellow must've smelled something on it to go after it.'

Richard locked eyes with Sam. 'You think?'

Sam shrugged. 'No way to know, but it's bloody weird. The oldies might have had a game at low tide. Lost a boule. Could've been dropped overboard by a pleasure cruiser—although why you'd have a boule on a boat is hard to fathom. There are probably a thousand reasons why it could be there. It's just . . .'

'Yeah. A coincidence.'

Satisfied enough had been said, Richard and Sam polished off the sausage rolls, washed down by a second beer. Light faded. A sea mist drifted in, settling like heavy dew on their shoulders. Eventually, Richard stood. 'Take this with me, if you don't mind,' he said, reaching for the boule.

'All yours, mate.'

'Might have forensics take a look. You never know . . .'

Sam cleared the table, carried the mess indoors. 'Being buried, something might have stuck.' His phone rang. He picked it up off the kitchen counter to check caller ID. Sighed heavily. 'See yourself out, if you don't mind.' He returned to the deck. 'Georgie. What can I do for you?'

CHAPTER SIXTEEN

LYING IN BED THE NEXT morning, Sam debated the pros and cons of informing Kate about the latest development in the Stringybark Bay tragedy, worried she'd feel compelled to delve more deeply into a situation that was starting to smell increasingly strongly of death by violence. He had an inkling he might be using the information as an excuse to chat, judge from the tone of her voice whether all was well or teetering on the edge of collapse. He mulled the issue over in the shower and kept mulling while he washed down two slices of Vegemite toast with a strong cup of tea. Eventually, he reached for the phone on the kitchen bench. It boiled down to a duty of care to Lizzie, he'd decided.

'Thought you'd want to know . . .' he said, when she answered his call.

'What?' she demanded.

'Bearing in mind we don't yet know the facts, it is just possible Cameron's death might—let me repeat: *might*—have been suspicious.'

He heard a quick intake of breath.

'Yesterday, Jimmy found a boule half-buried under the jetty at GeriEcstasy. I've handed it to Bainesy and he's going to get forensics on to it.'

'A *boule*?' Kate repeated, surprised.

'The thing is, nothing can help Cameron. The poor bloke's gone. But if there *is* something sinister going on in that fancy house, Lizzie should stay away until it's sorted.'

'You want me to say something to her?'

'Reckon you're up to another trek to the plateau?'

'Easy. Should I mention the boule?'

'It mightn't be anything.'

'I'll have to give her a reason to delay, Sam, or she'll think I'm nutty.'

'Play it by ear. If there's no other way, fill her in. Make sure she knows not to say a word to anyone, especially the GeriEcstasies.'

∽

Kate dressed in an old pair of cotton trousers with an elastic waistband that allowed for her expanding belly and a long-sleeved shirt. She filled a water bottle, grabbed her phone and, with Ettie's tattered map as reference if she lost her way, she set off. Underfoot, the ground was soft and sodden after the rain. Around her, the bush glowed with the bright red tips of new growth and the air was loaded with rich, clean smells. She breathed deeply, humming. Up ahead, a bedraggled wallaby with a joey in her pouch eyed Kate watchfully while two galahs, impossibly chic in shades of pink and grey, hung upside down on a cabbage palm frond, shaking loose drops of water

210

into their mouths. As she came closer, the joey ducked into hiding. Kate smiled, abruptly aware she desired the baby nestled in her womb and feared its arrival in equal measure.

Closer to the escarpment, she squeezed through the cleft between the giant boulders and knew that in another week she wouldn't make it.

She reached Lizzie's shack at around ten o'clock and called out before opening the gate. Lizzie came to the door wearing rubber gloves and a bandana around her forehead. 'Kate,' she said, surprised. 'I wasn't expecting you.'

'I thought you might need some help. I'm an expert packer and cleaner.'

'That's kind of you. I'll put the kettle on, shall I? It's time for smoko anyway.'

Not sure whether to follow her inside, Kate decided to sit for a while on the verandah, recover from her hike.

Like a ghost, an old man, with a shock of white hair sticking up like a cockscomb and wearing faded blue overalls, appeared out of the scrub. 'I'm Cliffy,' he said, walking towards Kate with his hand outstretched. 'A neighbour.' He waved vaguely into the bush. 'Lizzie called. Said there's a leak needs attention. Same one as always needs attention. Told her until she puts on a new roof, there's no way to track where the leak is coming from, and it'll only get worse. Won't have a bar of it, though. S'pose it doesn't matter if she's moving out. Someone else's problem before too long, I imagine.'

Kate opened her mouth to speak but didn't get the chance.

'If you're the new tenant, I'd recommend callin' an expert to have a look. I'll patch it, like I always do, but as I said, it's a bandaid on an amputation.' He paused to draw breath.

Kate dived in: 'I'm sure Lizzie will be pleased to see you. She's in the kitchen making a cuppa.'

'A cuppa tea wouldn't go astray. And if there's a slice of something sweet tucked away somewhere that wouldn't go astray either.'

'All I've got is toast, Cliffy,' Lizzie said, emerging from the kitchen with a tray.

'Wonderful!' he said. 'The apricot jam, as I recall, is on the top shelf of the pantry. Unless it's already packed?'

Lizzie laughed. 'Toast without apricot jam. Wouldn't dream of it.' She put down the tray and embraced Cliffy, then stood back to check him out. 'You look well for an old fella,' she said.

'I'm gunna miss you, Lizzie. Can't say that I won't.'

'I'm not going far and the door's always open. You know that.'

'Hear you're movin' in with a bunch of celebrities with dubious credentials,' he said, winking at Kate.

'Scraping the bottom of the barrel, that's me,' she said, laughing. 'I'll get your toast. No, stay where you are, Kate, I don't need help. Have a quick look at the leak, Cliffy, while you're waiting.'

Cliffy wandered off to the shed, returning minutes later with a stepladder. 'Seein' as you're sittin' there without a job,' he said to Kate, 'you might as well hold it steady for me. Old men and ladders. Lethal.'

Kate jumped up, alarmed.

His eyes widened in surprise. 'That's a baby you've got tucked in there. Hadn't noticed. You sit back down. I can manage on me own.'

'Don't be silly,' Kate said. 'I'm strong as an ox.'

'Nah, might as well have smoko while it's hot. Rushin' isn't gunna change a thing.' He carried the ladder inside then came back and sank into a chair.

Lizzie followed soon after and handed him a steaming mug and a plate of heavily buttered toast topped with glugs of golden apricot jam.

'Perfect,' Cliffy said, his face breaking into a smile. He took a noisy gulp of tea, set the mug on the floor at his feet and hoed into the toast.

'Top up?' Lizzie asked, holding up the teapot.

'A fresh pot, if you've the time. Got a thirst today. Bacon for breakfast.'

'Too much salt, eh?' Lizzie patted Cliffy's shoulder and went inside.

To fill in the silence, Kate said: 'Tell me about yourself, Cliffy. I'm guessing you live along the track signposted by that very artfully painted car door.'

Cliffy grinned. 'Gets up people's noses, that door. Turnin' the bush into a rubbish dump, they reckon. Serves its purpose though. Scares off nosy bastards who think they own the moral high ground just 'cause they have a recycling bin on their back porch.'

Kate frowned. 'What do you mean? Scare?'

'A bloke who puts up a sign like that, well, at the very least, he's a renegade, could even be dangerous. And a dead body out here? Wouldn't be found for years, if ever.'

'Cheery thought,' Kate said.

'I like me peace and quiet. That's the simple truth. Anyone who comes along thinkin' they can lecture me on environmental vandalism can skedaddle, takin' their fancy footwear, shiny backpacks and beeping thingumajigs with 'em. Planet's sinking under the weight of those annoyin' bloomin' interruptions to daily chores, but I'll bet me life if I gave a punter half a chance, I'd still get a lecture about an old car door servin' a useful purpose instead of clutterin' up a filthy rubbish tip.' He bit into his last piece of toast forcefully. Chewed with his mouth politely closed. Licked his jammy fingers one by one, making a popping noise. Sculled the last of his tea.

When he was done, he heaved himself out of the chair with a grunt. 'The lass can hold the ladder while I give the ceiling in the parlour a squiz.'

'You're a gentleman,' Lizzie said as Kate struggled out of soft cushions.

'If it's too much for you, you only have to say,' Cliffy told her.

'I'll manage,' Kate assured him.

In the parlour, Cliffy deemed the ceiling on the point of collapse. 'I've been tellin' her for years this was gunna happen,' he said, coming down the ladder. 'Stubborn as a mule when she wants to be.' He closed the ladder, tipped it sideways and tucked it under his arm. Kate tried to grab one end. 'Leave it, lass. I've got me balance and wouldn't want to chip Lizzie's pristine paintwork. Heh heh.'

Kate followed him outside.

'I'll check the roof, but I'm not steppin' on it unless it's bone-dry. I love Lizzie like a sister, but I'm not breakin' me neck for her. 'Specially as she's leavin' anyways.'

Squinting at the roof on the eastern side of the house, he chose a spot for the ladder and jiggled until it was stable. Kate grabbed both sides and put her foot on the lowest rung.

'Careful, Cliffy,' Lizzie said, coming out to watch.

'Go on inside, love. You're in me way.'

Lizzie threw him a grateful look and bolted.

'Scared of heights, she is,' Cliffy told Kate. 'Steady as she goes, then.' He tested the stability one more time. Three rungs from the top, he reached out and ran his hand along the red-painted corrugated iron, shook his head. 'Damp and slippery. Rusted through with holes bigger 'n a fifty-cent piece. Miracle the house isn't a swamp. Still, it was worth havin' a look. Ya never know, eh?'

He made his way down and staggered backwards a little when he reached the ground. Kate grabbed his arm, steadied the old fellow.

He nodded his thanks. 'Me balance is gettin' a bit questionable that's for sure.'

'Should you be going up ladders?' Kate asked.

'What's the alternative? Sit in a chair an' wait for the grim reaper to tap me on the shoulder?' He dusted his hands on the sides of his trousers. 'Weather permitting, I'll be back tomorrow with a tarp, but it won't cure the ailment, which in my opinion is terminal.'

He carried the ladder across the grass to the shed to put it away, then the two of them went inside to give Lizzie the bad news.

'I'll miss the pictures almost as much as I'll miss Lizzie,' he said, pausing in the hallway in front of a study of a child. 'Caught the innocence in kids, dogs and even flowers. Helluva a gift.'

They found Lizzie staring at the drawing of Dorothy on the mantelpiece. 'She belongs in this house, but when the fire grate goes cold and the kettle dry, it amounts to abandonment. Sounds silly, I know. It's a drawing. But that's how I feel.'

She wandered around, touching odd bits and pieces. 'When my mother died, I brought the things that meant most. My father smoked his pipe in this chair. I sat on this stool as a child. A famous writer gave me this dictionary. The dresser belonged to my grandmother, who died before I was born. That cast-iron pot hanging over the fireplace? Dorothy concocted her healing brews in it.' She made a sweeping gesture. 'My backstory reaches right down to and through the floorboards. I can't take much with me, but at the same time we old people need our objects around us to remind us of who we once were.' She gently traced the lines of Dorothy's face with a finger. 'This flight to comfort and safety, I worry it's a betrayal of a good woman and her faith in me.'

Cliffy went to Lizzie and pulled her hard against him, his hand holding her head close to his chest. He stroked her back until the sobs subsided and she stepped away, wet-faced and red with embarrassment. 'Sorry. Too much change too quickly,' she said, attempting a smile. 'I hadn't fully understood how utterly gut-wrenching it would be to leave behind a lifetime of memories. I'll be right, though. I am always alright.'

Cliffy refilled the kettle at the kitchen sink. 'You are the toughest woman I know, Miss Lizzie, and you're gunna be fine—better than fine.' He put the kettle on the hob with more force than he needed. 'I'm gunna miss you, call me I liar if I say I won't. But you're doin' a smart thing. This is no place for you anymore.' He grinned. 'Not without fixin' that bloomin' roof once and for all.'

Kate said: 'There's no reason you can't hold on to the place, is there? Keep it as a bolthole until you're ready to cut the umbilical. Or, worst-case scenario, it's a fallback position if things don't work out.'

Cliffy stuck his fingers in his belt and rocked on his feet. 'Girl has a point. I'll drop by once a week. Make sure no freeloaders— two- or four-legged—have taken up residence. Might even have a real go at fixin' that bloomin' roof . . .'

'Clarabelle . . .' Lizzie began.

'I'll take her home with me, along with her little 'un, and keep an eye on her,' Cliffy said. 'The chooks, too. My old girls have gone off the lay anyway and I was thinkin' to replace them.' He looked from Lizzie to Kate. 'Right, that's sorted then,' he said. 'I'll be off.' He left the room, then called from the hallway, 'What about the pictures, Lizzie? You can't leave those.' He stuck his head through the kitchen doorway, a sly look on his face. 'I could store 'em for you . . .'

Lizzie found a laugh inside herself. 'Choose one,' she said. 'You can be custodian.'

With that, Cliffy, who found it impossible to accept anything beyond a cuppa and a snack, took on the look of a frightened animal and bolted.

After he'd gone, Lizzie wandered from room to room, picking up and putting down objects. Kate left her to it and did the washing-up. When she felt the moment was right, she asked Lizzie if they could go for a walk in the garden.

Without a word, Lizzie led the way, picking up broken branches and tossing them aside, even though there was little point since the garden would soon run wild without her care. They reached the curve in the pathway where the orchids were planted and Lizzie turned to Kate. 'You look furtive, Kate. Something on your mind? Whatever it is, spit it out. At my age, I'm unshockable.'

Kate struggled to find a way to warn Lizzie about what might be ahead without giving too much away, then decided subterfuge was dangerous: she'd best give it to Lizzie straight. 'Sam called this morning to say Jimmy found a boule buried in the sand near GeriEcstasy. It's being tested to see if it was a murder weapon.'

'I see.' Lizzie bent to tidy around a plant, removed a few twigs from its fleshy leaves.

'He thinks you should delay moving in.'

Lizzie didn't say anything.

'Right now, it's all speculation. But there's been a bad smell right from the start. Most of us thought so.'

'And if I go ahead?'

'It's a risk.'

Lizzie stopped at the chook pen, to collect a couple of eggs from the nest boxes. She passed them to Kate to hold while she topped up the feeder with pellets from a large bag. The chooks rushed her, making a racket, and pecked at her hands. She made soft clucking sounds until they squatted. 'That's my girls,' she said, stroking their backs.

'You're ignoring our advice then,' Kate said.

'When I think of all their faces, shiny with welcome, I cannot imagine any one of them capable of killing a person. And from what I have managed to glean, Cameron was a sweet, easy-going man without a mean bone in his body. There's just no motive. But I have always been a cautious woman. Well, almost always. In the end, we're all human. So the shack stays. Might even get the roof fixed.' She laughed. 'That would make Cliffy's year.'

∽

By late afternoon, Lizzie's car was packed with the bare essentials: the paintings, two suitcases and the pillows that were so perfectly moulded to her neck and head they were indispensable. She would return to pick up more items when she had a better idea of what she needed.

Kate declined a lift back to the Square. 'I discovered a tree fern forest hiding in a deep gully. Thought I'd check it out on the way back.'

The two women took leave of each other with a nod and a quick touch on the arm. Lizzie climbed behind the wheel of her ancient Land Rover and turned the key. At the last moment, Kate placed her hands on the car door and Lizzie wound down the window.

'Don't be seduced too easily by all that charm,' Kate warned.

Lizzie patted Kate's hand. Kate stepped away and watched the vehicle disappear along the dirt track. Alone, she took one last look around a homestead straight out of the colonial past and decided that, with Lizzie's permission, she too would return every now and then, if only to escape the claustrophobia of a good-hearted community that sometimes didn't know when to retreat.

CHAPTER SEVENTEEN

AT HOME IN OYSTER BAY the following morning, Kate called Sam to tell him she'd failed to convince Lizzie to hold off joining the GeriEcstasies in Stringybark Bay.

'Did you have a real go or waffle around the edges?' he asked.

'God, Sam, of course I had a real go.'

'She say why she wasn't worried?'

'She's backing her judgement. Says none of them look capable of murder.'

'Who does?' Sam said.

'I tried, okay? She agreed to keep her shack as a bolthole, though.'

'Well, that's something.'

'No matter what you think of me, Sam, I wouldn't put a life in jeopardy for the sake of an inside source.'

After the call ended, Kate tided her desk in the study, made a peppermint tea, and slipped her feet into a pair of ugg boots. She ran her fingers lightly over the computer keyboard, like a pianist limbering up. Felt her old skills rise to the surface. With a sense of purpose, she opened a new document. She listed the known circumstances of Cameron's death with the same forensic detail she'd once applied to a major financial exposé for a newspaper. Then she created five separate documents under the names of each couple, deciding she'd research Donna Harris and Mike Melrose last, on the grounds their celebrity would make them easier to investigate. Cattle farmers, antique dealers and shoe retailers would be more obscure, although the cheesemakers would have a strong online profile. She began tapping.

By lunchtime, she was utterly mystified.

The cheesemakers' business was a publicly listed company. Sally and David Kinane had sold a forty-nine per cent shareholding in a multi-million-dollar deal with an American company. Their two children, a son and daughter, still held the controlling interest and the business appeared to be highly successful.

Sheila and Gavin Flowerdale were a rags-to-riches story. As a young couple, they'd snapped up small retail outlets in marginalised areas close to the CBD until they'd built a retail empire. They'd sold the real estate and the business for a mind-boggling amount of money. No signs of poverty there for the next three generations of Flowerdales, if Kate had done the sums correctly.

Rob and Daisy James had ridden the rollercoaster of farming through droughts, floods and bushfires, ricocheting from debt to wealth and back again at the whim of Mother Nature. But when they eventually sold the thirty-thousand-hectare property in central New South Wales, they'd pocketed close to twenty million dollars. They had no children.

Brian Callaghan and Cameron Smith had the fewest assets. Their rented premises, in one of Melbourne's toffiest suburbs, specialised in expensive, highly gilded furniture from before the French Revolution, and Roman sculptures that seemed to escalate in value with every missing arm, leg or nose. But with price tags in the tens of thousands of dollars, sales were few and far between. They had a high profile but they struggled financially from one sale to the next, which explained Brian's cash grab now. In any case, Cameron appeared to be the force behind the business. Brian was the glamorous social butterfly who guided customers—Kate enlarged a photo of the shop on her screen—through their gilt-edged and ornate front door, flanked by a couple of white pots with greenery trimmed into giant pompoms.

If her calculations were correct, even without including the assets of Mike Melrose and Donna Harris, the Ancients had enough capital to buy the whole of Cutter Island.

She took a break and made a fresh pot of tea, carrying it out to the verandah. Across the bay, ironed flat by the midday light, she caught the sharp glint of sun bouncing off a lens. Artie had his binoculars trained in her direction. The old man would be wondering why she was home instead of at the café. For a moment, she considered calling him to explain she was having a 'rest' and then put aside the idea. Amelia would fill him in and she didn't have time to indulge in one of Artie's confabulations, which would no doubt drift quickly towards his firm opinion that there'd been foul play in Stringybark Bay. Artie and his gut feelings. People laughed, but he was rarely wrong. She wondered if losing his ability to get around had made him more observant, taught him to listen more intently, honed his skill in sniffing out the murkiest information.

She finished her tea but remained where she was, mulling over what she'd learned. Why would a group of (mostly) extremely wealthy people pretend to be too cash-strapped to enjoy a luxurious retirement without an injection of funds from other sources? Unless they were propping up Donna and Mike in a way that saved face for a once-famous couple that might have fallen on hard times. But Donna's ring? Melrose's expensive clothes?

She decided to research the turquoise ring before wading through half a century of fluff to weed out the facts in the celebrity background of Donna Harris and her not-so-famous but endlessly supportive husband.

She returned to her computer. An auction site in the US reported a sale of a strikingly similar piece of jewellery at close to a quarter of a million dollars, she discovered. So Donna Harris and Mike Melrose did not lack funds—and she was quite sure that, with a little more digging, she would find a healthy portfolio of assets.

In the past, when she began an investigation into skulduggery, she asked one critical question: *Cui bono?* Who profits? But aside from Brian, who was simply asking for his original investment to be repaid without any extra additions (according to Lizzie), no one was short of cash. So why—given the apparent net worth of the group— continue with the charade that the whole GeriEcstasy scheme was in danger of collapse unless someone could be found to step into Brian's shoes? Kate was baffled.

She pushed back her chair and stretched. Felt an instant response from her unborn child. Footballer, she guessed, feeling a rare light-heartedness about the pregnancy.

She went into the kitchen to make a sandwich and was surprised to see it was early evening. She took cheese and tomato from the fridge, found a loaf of sliced bread in the freezer. The resulting toastie may have lacked the finesse of Ettie's creations, but it did the job. She wondered what Sam might like for dinner, then remembered with a mixture of sadness and relief that they had gone their separate ways.

To fill in time before going to bed, she returned to the computer and began looking into the career of Donna Harris under the guidance and management of her husband, Mike Melrose. Expecting to be bombarded with information, she found very little. A cryptic biography of Donna, her roles and awards, an assessment of her net worth (less than a million dollars, which was clearly an underestimation if GeriEcstasy was any indication), and an out-of-date note saying the actress now lived in seclusion in an historic house on the outskirts of Ballarat, Victoria, battling health problems.

Kate did the sums on Donna's age and realised she was due to turn eighty in December. With a shock, she learned that her last major acting role was at the age of thirty-eight, long before the internet erupted into the universe and changed information gathering forever. If she wanted to discover more about the early life of the one-time soapie star, she needed to access women's magazine archives.

One of her former colleagues, she recalled, had ditched dry financial reporting for the glamour of show business. Kate remembered she had red hair, freckles, that she favoured the colour purple in her clothes, lipstick and even nail polish . . . but her name wouldn't come. Frustrated, she shut down the computer.

Outside, it was now fully dark, a few early stars in the night sky, rain clouds etched gold by an indecisive moon. Inside, Kate reached to turn out the light and saw a dirty mark on the switch, licked a finger and rubbed it away. She cleaned her teeth, washed her face, rubbed moisturiser all over her body and changed into pyjamas.

Grabbing a notebook and pencil from the bedside table, she propped herself up against a stack of soft pillows. The space around her felt both luxurious and empty. Raindrops plinked on the roof. By the time she turned out the light, it was falling noisily, drowning out the night sounds. 'Mary Stuart,' she almost shouted. 'Her name was Mary Stuart, as Scottish as the Queen herself.' She would track her down in the morning and request permission to search the questionable archives of celebrity gossip.

She resisted an impulse to call Sam, to wish him goodnight, remembering with only a small pang how the sound of his voice had once made her feel safe.

☙

Two days later, Kate passed through the café in the morning. 'Can't stop. In a rush,' she told Ettie.

Ettie hurried out from behind the counter. 'You have a notebook in one hand, your laptop bag over your shoulder and you're wearing slick office clobber. If you don't tell me what you're up to, I will burst.'

Kate sighed. 'Chasing a couple of leads, that's all.'

Ettie's eyes narrowed. 'Leads for what?'

'Nothing much.'

'When you get secretive, Kate, you scare the knickers off me.'

'If I find anything useful, I'll let you know when I get back.'

'Useful about what?' Ettie called after her.

Kate held up a hand in farewell.

Ettie consoled herself with the thought that the enforced rest was clearly just what the doctor had ordered.

She returned to the café, where Jenny looked up from piping icing on a dozen little cupcakes, a special order for the Misses Skettle, who were hosting a bush regeneration meeting that morning and had worried their homemade fruitcake, liberally dosed with rum, might be inappropriate for anyone trying to cut back her alcoholic intake in a bid to get fit before summer. 'Checking out the GeriEcstasies, is she?'

Ettie slapped her forehead. 'Of course. What else would she be doing?' She moved behind the counter to continue making a zucchini frittata, picked up a mixing spoon and pointed it directly at her colleague. 'In the unlikely event I miss Kate's return, you are to tackle her to the floor and call me immediately.'

Jenny pushed the spoon aside. 'Are we delivering these cakes or are the Misses Skettle calling in for them?'

'You'll have to check. I can't remember.'

Kate arrived in the heart of the CBD a little before lunch. She found a parking space easily but was staggered by the hourly meter cost. It occurred to her that she was seriously out of touch with her old way of life. Feeling hungry, she made her way to a nearby café for a sandwich, which she planned to eat while she did her research. She joined a long queue of men and women with their heads bent over their mobile phones. While she waited, she studied the menu, written in multi-coloured chalk and illustrated with pictures of buns, cakes and drinks. When it was her turn, confused by the detailed description of every ingredient, including condiments, she asked if she could have a simple cheese and salad sandwich.

'Brie, camembert, cheddar, gruyere or gouda?' The girl looked at Kate's stomach. 'No brie or camembert, I'm guessing.'

'Cheddar, thank you.'

'Bread?'

'Um . . . bread?'

'Wholemeal, rye, white, brown, baguette?'

Overwhelmed by too many choices, Kate pointed at a ready-made baguette with ham spilling out of the sides, in the display case. 'Actually, that will do. And a tea, please. Herbal. Any kind.'

'There's a long list, love. Give me a clue.'

'Chamomile.'

She suddenly felt exhausted. Her sandwich landed on the counter along with a mug of hot water and a lonely tea bag. She looked around for an empty table and sat down to eat without enjoyment. The tea tasted like old straw.

Half an hour later, she walked through the doors of what had once been a magazine empire, now reduced to bare bones by the impact of the internet. She gave her name to the security guard and waited while he called Mary Stuart to let her know she had a visitor. Given the okay, he wrote her name on a pass and asked Kate to wear it around her neck. Ms Stuart would meet her outside the elevators on the second floor.

Kate felt a fluttering of anticipation, a strong sense that the real hunt had begun. She pushed the button to call the elevator and waited, tapping her toe with impatience. A couple of minutes later, she stepped into the hallowed halls of a magazine that had throbbed at the heart of Australian women for generations. Mary Stuart waited, her gorgeous, flaming-red hair streaked with green and purple, eyelashes extended well beyond her cheeks. She wore heels that added four inches to her height.

'Kate! Good lord, you're preggers!' She kissed the air on either side of Kate's face. 'Follow me. By the way, if I'm going to give you access to all our precious files, you'll have to tell me what you're up to. I have picked up the scent of what I imagine will be a fabulously good story. So, where have you been keeping? I heard you left the industry a while ago?' She chattered on without waiting for a reply, bursting with brittle self-importance. At the door to the library, Mary hesitated. 'We have a deal, right? If there's a story, it's mine.'

Kate laughed. 'Do I look as though I'm still in the business?' she asked, indicating her pregnancy, adroitly avoiding a direct answer.

'You'll have to tell me all about it sometime. Right now, I've got to rush. We're on deadline—and as you know, deadlines don't wait. Call me before you leave the building.' She pushed open the door and called, 'Edith? Where are you hiding?'

Edith, a slight woman of indeterminate age with salt-and-pepper hair and the look of a timid mouse, stood up from her desk and came over.

Mary said, 'This is Kate. She's a freelancer, doing some research for the magazine. I'll leave you both to it.'

Mary departed in a waft of perfume, and Edith asked, 'What exactly are you looking for?' Her voice was thin and uninterested.

'A murderer,' Kate responded, without realising she was going to say it.

Edith's eyes flew open. 'That's a new one. Mostly it's birthdates or name spelling.' She straightened her back, her bored expression now avid, and hurried back to her computer. 'Where would you like to start?'

By the time Kate left the building, the city was a carnival of lights against a dark night. Across the street, a small park with an avenue of trees decorated with fairy lights shouted Christmas in the wrong season. It was pretty, she thought, but nothing equalled a starry, starry night. She heard echoes of Sam in her head and for once, she couldn't fault his sentiments.

The commuter rush was well and truly over and the smart-looking parade of people who strolled the sidewalks were probably heading to a bar or restaurant, as she had once done in the days when a silver-haired man owned her heart and she'd loved him far too much for it to last. She reached her car and clicked the lock, pausing to pluck a parking ticket anchored under the windscreen wiper. She'd overstayed her time limit by six hours, but even so, she blanched at the amount. In the past, she would have added the fine to her expenses. Going solo, all costs would come out of her own pocket. She'd be more cautious in future. She slid behind the wheel, checked for traffic then swung out into the street, already thinking of a shower, scrambled eggs on toast, an early night.

Up ahead, the ramp to the Sydney Harbour Bridge looked clear of traffic. But her boat was tied to the café pontoon and would be inaccessible by the time she reached there. She'd have to call Freddy to take her home. Another expense. As a woman who'd always watched her pennies, the costs of what might turn out to be a waste of time and effort were beginning to mount.

Her research had revealed a clear and rapid decline in Donna's career from the day she celebrated her thirty-fifth birthday. But if the veiled hints of gossip columnists of the day were accurate, her dependence on prescription drugs and alcohol had begun much earlier. Kate had searched but found nothing that would explain if there was a single trigger that had set Donna Harris on the path to addiction and self-destruction. Edith, as tenacious as a terrier on the hunt, said she would continue to search the files.

'There'll be a catalyst,' Edith had said. 'There always is. We'll find it buried in a throwaway quote in one of those random "whatever happened to" interviews much loved by mass-circulation magazines.'

Kate had encouraged her to keep looking, but privately she doubted Edith would have much luck.

Mike Melrose, who remained a shadowy figure in the background of Donna's career, had graduated in business and commerce and was clearly entrepreneurial in his investments, although she had been unable to track the source of his funds. It was unclear, too, when the couple had met—and, oddly, there wasn't a word about their marriage. Throughout Donna's career, he'd been referred to only as her manager, never her husband or partner. A sea of information, she thought, but very few facts. White noise, she would have called it, when she'd been a member of the media pack.

There was a wild goose somewhere, she thought, mentally apologising to Sam for her constant criticism of his use of clichés. And she planned to hunt it down.

She found a parking spot, miraculous by Cook's Basin standards, and checked her phone. A message from Ettie. *Brian leaves in the morning, and if you don't tell me what you were doing today I'll confiscate half your holiday pay!*

To distract her, Kate sent a text describing how city cafés did business. *In comparison, the Briny is gold standard.*

A message pinged back instantly: *Good to hear but there's always room for improvement.*

Kate smiled and called Fast Freddy. 'Need a pick-up at the ferry wharf, please. Then home to Oyster Bay.'

'It would be my pleasure, Miss Kate.'

CHAPTER EIGHTEEN

A WEEK AFTER THE STORM and three days after Lizzie became the newest resident in Stringybark Bay, Ettie consulted Marcus about the idea of inviting Lizzie to morning tea. Marcus, aware of Ettie's burning curiosity about the inner workings of GeriEcstasy, gallantly suggested he replace her in the café, which would leave her free to enjoy Lizzie's company for the entire day instead of an hour or two.

Ettie made a half-hearted protest, murmured about being short-staffed with Kate on what, at Ettie's insistence, was now extended leave.

'We are talking of one day only,' the chef said. 'You must ask those questions that will put your mind at ease about your friend and fill in the gaps of your knowledge about a house of aged people and how they live together in peace and harmony. I am correct in this, yes?'

Ettie gave a little laugh and looked sheepish. 'A few questions. Not too many. I feel responsible . . .'

Marcus snapped his fingers. 'This will be an opportunity for me to sharpen like a knife edge my old skills. I am becoming rusty, I am sure, without the pressure of demanding clients and volatile ingredients.' He placed a finger on his bottom lip. 'Or perhaps it is volatile clients and demanding ingredients. I cannot be sure.' He slapped his thigh, pleased with his joke.

Ettie smiled. 'Either works, my love—but rusty? I think not. The dinner you create for me each night is worthy of royalty.'

'Yes, I can only agree. But what are you, my darling Ettie, if not my queen?'

She threw her arms around him. 'I will make banana bread. It's her favourite. Served with lots of butter.'

Ettie extended the invitation the same day. 'At the house, not the café,' she explained, anxious for Lizzie to understand the invitation was personal and went beyond their casual café friendship.

'Thank you, Ettie, that would be lovely.'

'Oh, great. How about tomorrow? Around ten?'

And it was agreed.

⤸

The day of the morning tea, Ettie woke to find Marcus gone from her side and the sun shining in an empty blue sky. The early heat hinted it would ramp up to a scorcher. She stretched her arms and swung her legs out of bed. Flew into a mild panic when she saw the time.

She showered and dressed in a rush, wishing she'd had time to think about what to wear. Lizzie always looked cool and elegant. Ettie sometimes felt more Raggedy Ann than gypsy queen alongside her.

She quickly measured out the ingredients for the banana bread, mixed them together and shoved the tin in the oven. While it cooked, she put the chef's kitchen whites, which he wore each night to cook dinner, aside for soaking. In the beginning, he'd insisted he would, of course, take care of his own laundry, which he had done since he was a child. Of course, he said, he would be delighted to assume the duty of washing Ettie's café clothes too, and she'd almost fainted in joyous delirium.

When the loaf sprang back in response to a light touch, and the house was infused with the smell of baking, Ettie removed it from the oven and left it to cool on a rack on the bench. Not long afterwards, she saw Lizzie making her way down the perilous stone steps that led from the fire trail to the rear deck of the chef's house; she should have offered to pick her up in the boat, she thought.

'Didn't reckon on the heat,' Lizzie said as she propped her staff against a wall and brushed spiderwebs from her chest and trouser legs. Perspiration beaded her forehead. 'Much hotter than it should be at this time of the year.'

'Might be a sign we're in for a hot summer. What do you think?' Ettie asked, holding open the door and standing aside to let Lizzie pass.

'Could be. We'll have to wait and see.'

In the chef's shiny stainless-steel kitchen, Lizzie pulled a handkerchief from her pocket to pat her face.

'You still drinking triple shots?' Ettie asked, firing up the coffee machine.

'What a memory. Yes. Not often, though. Seems to make my heart thump a bit too loudly for comfort these days. I might freshen up, Ettie, if you'll direct me to the bathroom.'

'Of course. Through there, first door on the right.'

By the time Lizzie returned, looking tidy and cool, the coffee was ready. Ettie put cups, saucers and several slices of still-warm banana bread on a tray.

'How about we sit outside, enjoy the sun?' Ettie suggested. 'You go ahead. I'll heat the milk and follow in a minute or two.'

Lizzie lingered in the sitting room. 'The chef has great taste in literature,' Lizzie said, when Ettie appeared.

'He does. I'm sure he'd be happy to let you borrow anything.'

'I might do that,' Lizzie said, selecting a volume from a shelf and squinting at the title on the tattered spine before replacing it, taking care not to add to the damage. 'I was wondering, though, if there's more to this little get together than you let on.'

'Two birds with one throw of the rock, as Marcus would say.'

'I always meant to ask. Where did the chef learn his, er, unique way of speaking?'

'His parents were German immigrants who lived on an isolated farm in . . . where was it? South-west NSW, I think. According to Marcus, their English was "troubled".'

'It suits him, though. He always makes me smile.'

'Me too.'

On the deck, Lizzie chose to sit where she could look across the water to the rocky shore.

Ettie put down the tray and fussed a little, concerned the bread was still too warm to hold together. She handed Lizzie a plate and passed the butter separately. 'I like to stack it on but not everyone agrees,' she said.

'I've earned extra today,' Lizzie said, helping herself to a generous amount. 'I sometimes wonder if I'd rather have the butter than the bread.'

'So,' Ettie said brightly, painfully aware that subtlety was not her strong suit, 'how's it going in Stringybark Bay?'

Lizzie relaxed into the back of her chair, holding her cup delicately with the fingertips of both hands. 'Pretty good. Early days, but everyone is bending over backwards to make me feel welcome.' She inhaled Ettie's brew and took a small sip. 'Good,' she said, approvingly. 'As good as the café.'

Ettie tilted her head slightly in shy acknowledgement. 'I've been dying to look inside the house but the invitations to a housewarming don't seem to have gone out yet. Understandably, under the circumstances,' she hastened to add.

'Cam's death. Not a great start to the big dream, was it? But they're coping pretty well . . . under the circumstances.'

Ettie, unable to hide her curiosity, asked, 'Is it like living in a five-star hotel without the room service?'

Lizzie laughed. 'It's been so cleverly and thoughtfully laid out within the footprint of the building, it's difficult to see where old meets new. Impossible to guess it was an old people's home if you didn't go looking for the clues.'

'What clues?' Ettie asked, instantly alert.

Lizzie shrugged. 'Handrails in the showers. Ramps instead of steps. Non-slip tiles on the floors. Power points at waist height. The tallest windows can be cleaned without a ladder. That sort of stuff.'

'Oh,' Ettie said, sounding disappointed.

'What did you expect, Ettie?'

Ettie shrugged. 'I have no idea. Silly me.'

'I haven't seen the other suites but mine is spacious, light, has views over the bay towards the mangroves and the bath water is always hot—which is more than I can say for my old home. I had no idea I was living so rough.'

'But how does it function, Lizzie? I mean, do you eat together? Who cooks? Who washes up? What if there's an argument?'

Lizzie buttered her banana bread and cut it into small portions, dabbing her lips delicately after each bite with the napkin Ettie had provided. 'There are rules. Nothing set in concrete, but guidelines.'

Ettie leaned forward, more curious than ever. 'Such as?'

'We take it in turns to cook dinner, but the cheesemakers are inspired chefs and rule supreme. We share the washing-up, but Daisy stacks the dishwasher. It's a job she can manage from her wheelchair. Men do the heavy work—hauling the shopping, keeping the jetty clean, minor repairs, attacking spiderwebs. Can't remember a worse season for webs. Must be the rain . . . Delicious, Ettie. As usual.'

'More?' Ettie cut another slice of banana bread into four equal parts, dividing the pieces between the two of them and putting a generous dab of butter on each. 'What about Donna?' she asked.

'The others are protective, but it's an unobtrusive sort of protection. Unless you knew what to look for, it would pass as good manners or perhaps deference to someone less physically strong. Even Sheila Flowerdale, who has a redhead's temper, doesn't let Donna's . . . lack of tact get under her skin. Daisy is the only one who pulls her into line. Daisy can reduce Donna to tears in a few words. It's a fascinating dynamic. Haven't seen much of Donna, though. The others seem to herd her away if she comes too close.'

'Frightened she might scare you off, eh?' Ettie sipped her coffee. 'Somehow, I find it hard to visualise her contributing to the household in any way.'

Lizzie took a while to answer. 'You know, she's so . . . difficult, unpredictable, whatever, that I think she takes the sting out of inevitable small niggles. Stacked up against one of her tantrums, failing to do the dusting doesn't amount to much.' She finished the last of the banana bread on her plate and placed her hands on her stomach to indicate she couldn't fit in another morsel. 'She couldn't find a particular pair of shoes the other day. Turned on a performance that would have impressed Bette Davis.'

Ettie asked. 'Over a pair of shoes? Really?' She reached to stack the empty plates on the tray. 'Did you find them?'

'Searched high and low. Mike tried to tell her they hadn't made the cut when they packed for the move. She was adamant she'd brought them. When she began accusing one and all of theft, he led her back to bed, promising he'd call the police to file a report. She went off as meek as a lamb. Mind you, they were Manolo Blahnik. A single pair would have cost more than a banquet for two at the chef's former restaurant.'

Ettie looked down at her feet, encased in sneakers with arch supports and zippers instead of shoelaces. 'I've always adored beautiful shoes,' she said wistfully.

'No point around here,' Lizzie said consolingly. She pointed across the bay, where smoke twirled skywards from a towering orange glow. 'Good day for burning off,' she observed, noting the fire brigade's tiger-striped launch lurking offshore.

'She scares me, Lizzie,' Ettie said, refusing to be deflected. 'There's something so out of kilter in her, she makes the hairs on the back of my neck stand up.'

'Is that what this morning tea is about? Warning me to watch out?'

Ettie blushed. 'Caught in the act, eh? But seriously, Donna is . . . well, weird is the kindest way I can put it.'

Lizzie took her time before responding. 'She's certainly drug-dependent, and that makes her erratic.'

'I think she's dangerous,' Ettie said bluntly. 'She's cruel. Oblivious to anyone's needs except her own.'

'Narcissism is one thing, Ettie, but dangerous? That's a big accusation. Dangerous in what way? Do you have any evidence? Because if you do, you should share it.'

'You know me, Lizzie: all instinct and intuition.' Ettie smiled, backing away from an outburst she already regretted.

Lizzie brushed a crumb from her lap.

'If I'm not being too nosy,' Ettie ventured tentatively, 'how does the money side of the household work?'

'Ah. It's always about money in the end, isn't it?'

Ettie blushed. 'I don't mean what it all costs . . .'

Lizzie took pity: 'There's a significant monthly fee to cover insurance, any big jobs such as jetty repairs or, God forbid, a tree falling on the roof. A modest weekly amount covers food. Alcohol expenditure is personal. If any of us wants to spend more than a hundred dollars on a general household purchase, such as candles or flowers or any other little luxury, it turns into a group decision.' Lizzie hesitated, looking puzzled. 'Melrose is strict with the budget and yet . . .'

Ettie leaned forward.

'I'd expected frugality. There's no sign of it, though.'

'Maybe they've decided it's not worth saving for their old age, since they're in it,' Ettie suggested brightly.

'Kate's right—there's something NQR.'

'I'm sorry?'

'NQR. Not quite right.'

'Did she say that? Did she warn you to be careful?' Ettie asked, feeling justified. She slapped the table. 'I knew it. Always trust your instincts, that's what I say . . .'

Lizzie cut her short. 'Whatever it is—if indeed there is anything—it will surface. It always does. The boule should clear things up.'

'What boule?' Ettie asked.

Lizzie wanted to sew her lips together. 'Not boule—ball. It's how the household is referring to Sam's offer to take them on a cruise on the *Mary Kay*. They're calling it a ball.'

Ettie frowned. 'You mean like an old-time dance where everyone dresses up?'

Lizzie nodded, relieved to have covered her slip of the tongue so successfully.

'No one's mentioned it,' Ettie said.

'No set date yet,' Lizzie said briskly. 'But we thought we'd ask you to cater.' She made a mental note to propose the idea the moment she returned to GeriEcstasy.

Ettie brightened. 'I'll start planning. How many people, do you think? Is it a dress-up affair? A sunset cruise. Black tie. Oh, it will be wonderful.'

'Lots to think about then,' Lizzie said, standing to go.

'I'll run you home.'

Lizzie sighed, knowing she was trapped. 'I hope you'll understand if I don't invite you in,' she said. 'New girl on the block and all that.'

'Of course,' Ettie said, shrugging. 'A ball,' she repeated, to hide her disappointment at failing to get a foot in the door of GeriEcstasy. 'Oh, this is going to be fun.'

CHAPTER NINETEEN

THE FOLLOWING DAY, IN THE midst of beating a batter for a chocolate cake made with sweetened chestnut puree (the cost excused by substituting Dutch cocoa for the more expensive Valrhona cooking chocolate), Ettie was struck by a flu that felt like a blow to the head. Afraid she might fall flat on her face behind the counter, she told Jenny she would lie down in the penthouse for a short while until she felt better. Overcome by nausea, she hurried up the stairs. Jenny phoned Marcus and told him to come immediately.

Ettie had no idea how long she'd been kneeling on the floor with her head in the loo when she felt the gentle pressure of a hand on her back. 'My love,' the chef said, 'we must get you home.'

'Can't move,' Ettie moaned, unable to open her eyes in case the room spun out of control.

Marcus murmured soothing words and left her briefly. He found clean linen and made the bed, fluffed the pillows and found a hot-water bottle for when the chills hit, as he knew they would. He placed a bucket next to the bed and a towel within reach, a damp flannel on the bedside table. Outside, the sun shone in a clear blue sky and the tantalising smell of flowering eucalypts flirted on a warm sea breeze. Inside, it could have been the depths of winter. Marcus closed the curtains, turned a heater on full blast and returned to the bathroom to find Ettie with her back against the wall, her eyes tightly shut.

He slid an arm around her waist. 'Come, my love. The bed is ready for you. Three steps and you will be there. I will not leave your side, this I promise, until you are well.'

Ettie groaned as the chef helped her upright. She let him lead her to the bed and helped her to undress and slip between the sheets. Marcus took a seat by her side and blotted a spot of perspiration from her forehead with the flannel.

'Where did you learn to do all this?' Ettie murmured.

'My mother, she was ill for many years. As a boy, she gave me instructions until I could judge for myself what was needed.'

'Ah, yes, of course. I had forgotten.'

Marcus took her oven-scarred hand and held it until her breathing dropped to the steady rhythm of sleep. He tucked the blanket under her chin, placed his hand on her hot brow. Then he left the room and descended the staircase to the café, where he demanded Jenny provide him with a kilo of lean minced beef and a whole chicken. He then plucked ginger, garlic, chilli and onions from a tray of vegetables in the fridge, gathered them in his arms and climbed the stairs. He found a stockpot in a cupboard and began immediately to prepare his healing broths.

A short while later, Jenny appeared, looking flustered.

Marcus held a finger to his lips and tiptoed towards her.

'Chef, I'm snowed under and I need help,' Jenny whispered. 'Busload of pensioners on an outing who will return disappointed to the retirement village if I fail to deliver.'

The chef nodded. 'Yes, yes,' he murmured. 'I will be there. Let me first see that Ettie is comfortable and then I will be yours to command.'

Jenny swallowed a bark of laughter at the thought of anyone being able to 'command' Marcus Allenby, chef extraordinaire, a man with a stratospheric ego when it came to cooking. She rushed downstairs to start on decafs, flat whites, cappuccinos, long blacks, short blacks, single shots, double shots and one low tide with a triple shot (whatever that might mean). Her head reeled.

A minute or two later, Marcus, his mane of white hair brushed and flopping into his eyes, descended the stairs in a regal fashion. He strode through the flywire door to the rear deck and stood before a crowd of startled pensioners. 'I am Marcus Allenby,' he declared. 'Once I had a restaurant with two stars. Of course, as you can see, I am not young, and I retired to go fishing, but today my beloved Ettie is ill and cannot attend to your needs. So, in her stead, *I* will create for you the scones Jenny says will assist you to achieve happiness. We must all, yes, have happiness when it comes within our reach, and I would not deny you this.'

There was a stunned silence while the patrons struggled to grasp what was going on. The chef held up his hand. 'You must be patient. These scones will not appear until the clock indicates that twenty-five minutes have sped past, but they will be worth the wait. This is a promise.' He bowed his head and left them confused and bemused but content to sit for as long as it took to produce a memorable scone.

The cook, whoever he was, was the best entertainment they'd had all day. During a two-hour whale watch, not even a fish had jumped.

⚬

That evening, after the satisfied pensioners had departed with full bellies, the schoolkids were fed and watered and the last loiterers in the Square had been provided with hot chips to munch alongside their beers, Marcus called Sam. 'My beloved Ettie is ill, my friend, and I am afraid to take her from the café to our home without assistance and perhaps the comfort of the *Mary Kay*, where she may lie down for the journey.'

The phone went dead in his hand. He climbed the stairs to the penthouse knowing that Sam was already hurtling towards the café on a rescue mission. He tiptoed to Ettie's bedside and reached for her hand.

She opened her eyes and smiled. 'You are my rock,' she murmured.

'We must get you home, my darling. Sam is coming with the *Mary Kay*. Together, we will carry you so not even one of your toes must touch the ground.'

'I am feeling better,' Ettie insisted. She struggled to sit up but found the effort too much and subsided. The chef felt her burning forehead, noted her eyes glazed with fever.

'Or perhaps we will stay here together, as we did in the beginning—when I, a man too big for this bed, nonetheless slept so peacefully alongside you.' He noted Ettie's relief at this suggestion. 'Yes! We will stay here together. This is a practical solution. You may direct my labour in the café without stirring, and all day I will make teas and broths to bring the colour once more to your beautiful cheeks.' He beamed at his beloved, whose eyes were closed once again. In moments, she was asleep once more.

Marcus left her side when he heard the unmistakeable throb of the *Mary Kay* as she approached the café. He made his way downstairs as softly as possible for a big man and carefully closed the screen door behind him, making a mental note to oil the hinges so the squeak would not disturb Ettie in future.

Sam saluted the chef as he came alongside. Marcus helped him to tie up. 'There has been a change of plan,' he told Sam in a soft voice. 'Ettie is not well enough to move, so she and I, we will stay here until she is well.'

Sam looked concerned. 'How crook is she, mate? Maybe we should call a doctor or take her to hospital?'

The chef pulled a chair from a table and sat down heavily. 'It is a flu, in my opinion. It has taken a firm hold, but the frequent ministration of my homemade remedies should see it release its grip within a week.'

'No offence, but you don't reckon it might be worth getting a doctor's diagnosis and some antibiotics, just to be on the safe side?'

The chef shook his head. 'No, my friend. I know what of I speak. This is a virus, immune to antibiotics but susceptible to healing broths.' Then, because food had always been his gateway to comfort and contentment, he stood and threw an arm around Sam's shoulders. 'Come with me. We will ascend to the penthouse, where you may see for yourself how Ettie fares while I cook a dinner fit for a king. We will dine together at the table within hearing of my love and together take care of her.'

Sam, with nothing to object to, did as he was directed.

◦⌒◦

When Kate heard about Ettie's illness, she returned to the routine of café life without fuss. After the aimlessness of her enforced maternity leave, she relished the sense of purpose. There was unexpected pleasure, too, in noting the to-ing and fro-ing of Cook's Basin's citizens. She eavesdropped as they sat on the seawall to exchange information meaningful only to those who lived offshore.

Can I put down your name for fire shed dinner duty?

Artists are gearing up for a summer exhibition—can they use your boatshed as a gallery?

There's a fundraiser for the kindergarten—silent auction, if there's anything you'd like to get rid of.

That new woman in Blue Swimmer went overboard tying up her boat at the commuter dock. Les fished her out. Said she wouldn't qualify as a local until she'd racked up three unscheduled dips.

It was, Kate thought, the unexciting background hum of a functioning community. She acknowledged the generosity and kindness of so many big hearts but, unlike Sam, she remained mostly unmoved by them. Sam, she thought with a pang. Too trusting and good for someone like her, a woman skilled in the art of duplicity and capable of the same ruthlessness as her mother. She'd always been destined to break his heart.

The chef, more dictatorial than ever as he shouldered responsibility for Ettie's wellbeing and the running of the café, ordered Kate to deliver a mug of broth to his beloved, who remained tucked in bed on day two of his highly organised recovery program. 'Not one drop must be left,' he shouted after her as she ascended the stairs.

In the penthouse, Ettie wriggled into a sitting position. She managed a smile as Kate passed her the mug. 'Every drop, Ettie, or the chef will rip me apart joint by joint,' Kate said, smiling.

'How's business?' Ettie croaked.

'Booming,' Kate replied, 'but I am forbidden to discuss anything to do with work. Chef's orders and I'm not brave enough to disobey a man with a wooden spoon in his hands and a mad glint in his eye.'

'He's a lamb really . . .'

'The spoon, which I assume he has brought from his private collection at home, is *huge*, and he's downstairs waving it around like a mad conductor, pausing only to straighten his toque. Even Jenny is cowed.'

'He's a good man,' Ettie said, taking small sips of the broth.

After a few minutes, Ettie held out the empty mug. 'Mission accomplished,' she said. Already drowsy and worn out by the effort, she closed her eyes. 'I have never felt this terrible in my life,' she murmured, turning to face the wall.

'You'll be right,' Kate assured her.

Kate returned to her seat under the stairs where, against her better judgement, she'd agreed to cost the chef's prawn salad recipe. Four prawns per dish, she'd insisted, or she would not pick up the phone to place the order. The chef had agreed so meekly, she was deeply suspicious. Whatever he had planned, Ettie would still see her compliance as a betrayal. Personally, she wasn't a fan of prawns. Sam, on the other hand, believed nothing could beat eating them from a bucket while sitting at the end of a jetty on a hot summer night. 'Kings used to live like this,' he always said. By the end of last summer, the repeated assurance had made her teeth clench.

Later in the morning, while the chef continued to create havoc and brilliance behind the counter of the café and where Jenny wore a permanent look of apprehension, Richard Baines contacted Sam. 'Got time for a coffee at the Briny?' he asked.

'Lunch suit you?'

Sam heard rustling papers in the background. 'Can we make it early? I need to be back in the office for a staff meeting at one.'

'See you there shortly. I'll order a couple of burgers.'

'On my way now.'

Richard appeared on the rear deck at the same moment Jenny delivered two plates with a towering concoction of meat, a fried egg, pineapple, beetroot, cheese and lettuce and the chef's special mayonnaise. She placed them on the table with a roll of her eyes that indicated her patience was being sorely tested and the food she was about to put before them was not her responsibility. 'Mentioned an old-fashioned Aussie burger included pineapple. The chef has taken the idea on board. Don't tell Ettie. She'll have a fit.'

'Our lips are sealed,' Sam said. 'Pineapple, eh? Brings back memories.' He flattened the burger with the heel of his palm to reduce it to a manageable size but gave up and used his knife and fork. Alongside him, Jenny waited without moving a muscle. 'What do you think?' she asked, after watching him eat a mouthful or two. 'A permanent addition to the blackboard or should we kindly tell the chef it was dropped from milk bar menus all over the country for a reason?'

'Have a go, mate,' Sam said, indicating the burger in front of Richard. 'What do you reckon?'

Richard chewed and swallowed. 'Not bad. Not bad at all. There's a hint of chili that blindsides the sweetness of the pineapple and balances the whole act . . .'

Sam stared at him in astonishment. 'Didn't realise you were a genuine foodie,' he said.

Richard blushed. 'Well, you asked for an opinion and I gave it.'

'Poetically,' Jenny said, turning back to the café. 'I'll pass on your compliments to the chef. The chilli, eh?' She laughed uproariously. 'That'll settle Ettie's nerves when she hears about it.' She pushed through the recently oiled flywire door, letting it slam behind her, which earned her a hurt and disappointed look from the chef, who was whisking egg yolks and olive oil to make a fresh lime mayonnaise for the new lunchtime special of prawn salad.

'You want a coffee?' Sam asked, polishing off the last of his burger. Richard nodded and, replete, pushed his empty plate towards the centre of the table.

Kate would reel, Sam thought. His own knife and fork were pushed together, plate fixed in position until removed. He shook his head, sad and glad those emotionally wrought days were over. He went to order two mega brews, one in a takeaway container for Richard to carry back to his office.

Inside, the chef inflated his lungs until his chest expanded twofold, raised his shoulders and threw out his arms in a gesture of enquiry.

'Nice touch with the pineapple,' Sam said, correctly reading the chef's body language.

The chef waved his wooden spoon at a tempo to suit a bouncy movement in a symphony. *'Ja,* it is true and my opinion that I make music from the humble hamburger which, like Craig Claiborne, esteemed restaurant critic for the *New York Times*—who is now dead, I must explain, from old age—who insisted mincemeat held far more promise and potential than eye filet, I have always favoured the burger above all snacks.'

Sam made a pretence of staggering. 'And you, a three-star chef!' he exclaimed.

'No, no. I must say truth immediately. Two stars only.'

Jenny placed the coffees on the counter and Sam took them out to the deck. 'Now what's all this about?' he asked Richard.

'The boule.'

Sam raised his eyebrows.

The policeman nodded confirmation. 'A couple of hairs got snagged in one of the seams.'

'Anyone we know?'

Richard nodded. 'All we have to do now is work out who clonked the bloke with it.'

'You going to tell the GeriAncients?'

'Nope. Not a word. Early days and all that.' He picked up his coffee, ready to leave. 'Lunch is my treat. Just saying thanks, is all.'

'No need, mate. A thought . . .'

Richard paused. Waited.

'It had to be one of the inmates. Even cynics reckon they've seen spirits in the mangroves on moonless nights, so only a dead-set muggins would venture there alone unless there was no choice.'

'Yeah. Tricky, no matter which way you look at it.'

After Richard had left, Sam sat thinking for a while longer. A few punters meandered onto the deck to check out the view. He heard them talking about a famous chef working incognito behind the counter, wondered whether they'd be thrilled or appalled to find pineapple on a burger.

He went inside looking for Kate and found her bent over the accounts for the café. Tapped her lightly on the shoulder.

She flinched. 'Sorry. The accounts are in turmoil. And the chef is a bit casual about the bottom line. Adding a dollar to the price of a dish solves a cost blowout, but it risks upsetting our regulars and they're our bread and butter.'

'You'll figure it out,' Sam said. 'You always do.'

'He's also muttering about adding a percentage for table service. I reminded him there's already a built-in cost for food served on plates instead of in paper bags but he had a sudden case of deafness. Ettie will have a fit when she finds out. Sorry, not your problem.' She turned back to work.

Sam shuffled his feet, scratched the back of his neck, cleared his throat. 'The boule,' he said.

Kate instantly swung around. 'What about it?'

'Might be an idea for Lizzie to go back to her shack for a while.'

'Meet you in the Square in a minute. Voices carry,' she whispered, pointing upstairs.

A few minutes later, they were sitting together on the picnic table, their heads bent close together, talking softly.

'You're sure?' Kate asked.

Sam nodded.

She rubbed her stomach absently. Sam fought the urge to place his hand there, to feel the life growing inside her, had enough sense to stifle the impulse, aware she'd shy like a horse at a loud noise, and bolt.

'Have a word to Lizzie,' he said. 'It's important.'

'Kate!' The chef stood in the doorway, pointing at the face of his large wristwatch.

'He's a bloody slave driver,' she said, sliding off the bench. 'Who'd have guessed? If Ettie doesn't get better soon, there'll be a mutiny.'

Sam watched her cross the Square, filled with a yearning he couldn't put a name to. After a minute or two, he called Jimmy, who was off on his worm compost deliveries. 'Need a pick-up, mate.'

Not long after, the kid weaved at a gentle speed through yachts on their moorings. A year ago, he would have roared flat-out, slamming the water, bow pointed to the sky, risking his life with the short-sightedness of youth. He was growing up, he thought, with mixed emotions.

A short distance from the café, Jimmy stood up and waved madly, rocking the tinnie to the point of tipping. Sam grinned inwardly. Still a kid then. He strode to the end of the ferry wharf as Jimmy came alongside. Jumped into the boat.

He raised his face and closed his eyes, letting the sun beat down on his skin, the wind whip through his hair. 'Where's that mutt of yours?' Sam asked, registering the fact that there was more space in the boat than usual.

'Waitin' for us on the *Mary Kay*. Where else would he be?'

CHAPTER TWENTY

AFTER BEING TENDED FOR THREE days by a man who cooked her exquisitely tempting, calorie-rich treats in such tiny, mouth-watering portions she felt they could do no lasting damage, Ettie felt well enough to leave her sickbed. She showered, warding off a dizzy spell while she washed hair that felt lank and greasy even though Marcus changed the bed linen daily, insisting fresh sheets would speed her recovery.

When he saw her appear at the top of the stairs, the chef dropped a roasting dish with a clang, pushed Jenny aside roughly and raced forward as if to catch his beloved in a swan dive. Seeing him with his arms wide open and a look of such intense alarm and fear on his face, Ettie couldn't help but laugh.

'If I fall, I will squash you flat,' she called down to him.

'If it is my fate, to die in this worthy cause, I will do so without hesitation,' he replied heroically.

Ettie gripped the banister and began a slow descent, to fall into his arms in a mock swoon. Jenny, who'd paused in her chores to watch the show, applauded from behind the counter. 'A dramatic entrance, if ever I've seen one,' she commented, wondering if the chef had a brother.

'You look a lot better than you did a few days ago,' Kate said, scrutinising Ettie in the same way the chef would check a fish for freshness. 'Let me know when you're fit enough to go over the accounts.'

The chef looked stricken. 'Kate, it is too soon for discussion of café finances.' He seized Ettie's hand. 'I know you are a tough and independent woman, my love, but this flu you have had, you cannot open the door even a tiny crack or it will sneak in and land you once again on your sickbed.'

Seeing that his anxiety for her was genuine, Ettie asked Jenny to prepare the chef's favourite brew and a green tea for her. They would sit together in the Square and take in the beauty of Cook's Basin. 'I have missed the hustle and bustle of local life,' Ettie told the chef, as she led him outside. 'It feels like I have been away for a year instead of a few days.'

Outside, the chef removed a white linen handkerchief from his pocket and dusted a bench, before supporting Ettie while she sat down.

She pointed over the water to where the *Seagull* churned a path towards the ferry wharf, its hull so low in the water she feared it might sink. But while Ettie and the entire Cook's Basin community had been predicting such a disaster for more than ten years, somehow the old ferry driver had kept its reluctant motor thumping and the vessel afloat. 'Let's watch the ferry arrive,' she said. 'I want to see how people have aged in the months I've been away.'

The chef looked at her, puzzled, then his face cleared as he understood the sub-text of her words.

Jenny arrived with their drinks and dumped them on the picnic table unceremoniously. 'Need you back in the kitchen, Chef, when you have a moment,' she said, a little tight-lipped. 'Kate's trying to help but her stomach's getting in the way.' She took off.

The chef raised his eyebrows and looked at Ettie.

'Go, go,' she insisted, patting his leg. 'I am content here.'

She watched until he disappeared inside the café, then sipped her tea with pleasure. The ferry docked and people she'd known for a decade or two spilled onto the wharf while a soggy cormorant, perched on a pile with its wings spread to dry, observed the depths with keen eyes, alert to opportunity.

Amelia, clutching a colourful cloth bag, pushed through the last dawdlers off the ferry and plonked on the bench beside Ettie with a small grunt. 'Up and about, then?' she said.

'Fit as a flea,' Ettie responded.

'Yeah, well, the jury is still out given the fact your cheeks are the colour of alabaster and the circles under your eyes are blacker than that shag's feathers.' She pointed towards the bird moments before it folded its body into a spear and dived into the water.

'Cormorant. Not a shag. Thanks for the vote of confidence,' Ettie replied wryly.

'You want to be a bit careful with yourself for a few more days,' Amelia advised. 'Judy came down with the same bug and she's been crook for nearly a month.'

'Ah, if she'd had Marcus to care for her . . .' Seeing Amelia muscling up for another round of advice, Ettie pointed at the bag on her knee.

'Want to take a look?' Amelia asked.

'Of course!'

'Not a word to Kate, though. I want it to be a surprise.'

Amelia's lovingly crafted baby blanket was knitted in fine, soft yarn in the pearly colours of Oyster Bay at dawn. The knitting, even and flawless, had a subtle stitched edge and felt as light as the passing glance of a stranger. 'A work of art,' Ettie murmured. 'Truly beautiful.'

'I was going to give it to Sam to hand over the day the baby is born, but now there's a few . . . er . . . ripples between him and Kate, I'm holding on to it myself until the baby shower.' Amelia paused, letting the statement hang in the air between them, an invitation for Ettie to fill in the facts.

'Ah yes, the baby shower,' Ettie said, sidestepping the relationship issue. 'Kate's not keen.'

Amelia took the news without surprise. 'Yeah. I sat down to make a list of her close friends the other day and realised she didn't really have any. Not in Cook's Basin, anyway.'

Ettie bristled. 'There's me. You. Jenny. The Misses Skettle. And don't forget Lizzie. She's up there at the top of the list now.'

Amelia touched Ettie on the shoulder placatingly. 'They're our friends, Ettie, not hers. Don't get upset. It's not a criticism. Kate hasn't been here long enough to bond closely with anyone. She has no old friends, either. As far as Artie is aware, Kate's mother was the sole visitor. Anyway, I decided a baby shower for six people might seem a bit sad, so I've dropped the idea.'

Ettie nodded, a faraway look on her face as she ran the blanket through her hands. 'So light but so warm.'

'Alpaca wool. The best.'

'Lucky baby.'

Amelia sighed heavily. 'If the rumours are true, this baby's going to need a bit of luck.' Although Artie had favoured her with a long discourse on the subject of the two mismatched lovebirds—as he'd referred to Kate and Sam—based on the state of his infallible gut, she thought Ettie's info would be more reliable. But Ettie, who seemed lost in thought, didn't bite.

Amelia patted her knee and remained uncharacteristically silent until Chris, the ferry driver, planted himself in front of Ettie, his arms folded across his chest. 'Never thought I'd give a hamburger with a slice of pineapple a culinary tick, but by Christ, Ettie, that Marcus has come up with a recipe that's world class.'

'Eh?' Ettie said, frowning in puzzlement.

'I'd best be off,' Amelia said, snatching the blanket out of Ettie's hands.

'Pineapple?' Ettie said, still confused.

Chris kissed the tip of his fingers with a loud smacking sound and wriggled his hips in appreciation, almost dislodging his jeans. 'The verdict is in. A winner,' he said, before hauling his trousers up and setting off at a trot to move his vehicle from the short-term section before he copped a parking ticket.

Ettie remained seated, thoughtful, responding to greetings with an automatic smile, but her mind was freewheeling down rocky emotional pathways. She guarded her recipes and the café territory like a rottweiler. Nothing changed without her permission and culinary input. A sacrosanct rule. One the chef understood and had broken. She fought a rising sense of betrayal and reminded herself to feel grateful he'd stepped in while she'd been ill, reminded herself that he'd nursed her with love and tenderness, cleaned up after her without complaint. She straightened her shoulders and told herself to behave like an adult and let the chef's tweaking of recipes drift past her without comment. As the last stragglers from the ferry emptied from the Square, she drained her tea and made a vow that no matter how powerful the temptation to speak out, she would remain silent.

Her attention was caught by the appearance of three young women in flashy sportswear. One emerged from the water onto the little beach beyond the seawall like a sprite covered in bright red welts. 'Blue bottles,' she explained, panting when she reached Ettie. 'A flock or whatever a patch of stingers are called. Got me.' She pointed into the bay. 'Over there.'

The second limped in from the sand track with lacerated legs and bleeding knees. 'My feet will never recover,' she moaned, removing her footwear.

The third threw down her bike and raced over clutching her rear. 'My arse is on fire!' she declared. 'Those bloody bike seats are designed for blokes—no surprise there!'

Clearly friends, the battered, bruised and bitten women fell into each other's arms and laughed uproariously. 'Whose idea was it to compete in this triathlon?'

'Should we call a taxi?' asked the cyclist.

'How about an ambulance?' suggested the swimmer.

The runner pointed towards the café. 'A coffee before the final leg, okay?'

'Good idea,' Ettie agreed. I love this place, she said to herself. I love this place with a passion I cannot begin to express or even define. All I know is that, even with the chef by my side in some new and beautiful Eden, there would be a corner in my soul forever bereft at the loss of Cook's Basin. She shook off what she felt might be rising melancholy, attributing it to her illness. Swarm, she thought. A swarm of jellyfish.

Ettie looked up to see Sam coming towards her from the café.

'Chef sent me out to check on you,' he said, dropping down beside her. 'If I may say so, love, you might be up and about but you're still not looking crash hot. Chef reckons he'd be my eternal slave if I could persuade you onto the *Mary Kay* to take you home.'

Ettie battled with herself for a moment before deciding that her promise to avoid raising the pineapple issue with the chef did not preclude mentioning it to Sam. 'So. Your verdict on the pineapple?' she asked, getting to her feet, turning away so he couldn't read her expression.

'Yeah. Pretty good. Bloody good, actually. Bainesy reckons it's the hint of chilli that makes it stand out. Slightly Asian, the sweet and hot, he reckons.'

'And what's your take?' Ettie asked, trying hard not to snap.

Sam, oblivious, shrugged: 'Long as there's chippies on the side, it's all good. Now let's get you home, love.'

He held out his arm in a way Kate would approve and led Ettie towards the *Mary Kay*, which he'd tied up at the end of the ferry wharf at the chef's request.

'She must not come into the café,' Marcus had declared. 'Not for one second. It would bring all my efforts tumbling down like a house in an earthquake, as she would find herself unable to leave and, before you could say Mary Popsicle, she would have an apron around her waist and a mixing bowl resting on her hip . . .'

Sam had walked away from the rising crescendo of the chef's soliloquy with a wave of his hand. 'I ride to your orders, Chef. As always.'

Ettie stepped onto the barge and opted to sit in the open air, which felt like a blessing after being confined to a tiny, windowless bedroom.

Sam pulled away from the wharf, barely disturbing the surface of the water. A gentle trip, a safe delivery . . . or the chef would decapitate him.

Ettie drank in the landscape like a parched woman handed a glass of water. Seagulls bobbed where schools of fish cast grey shadows under the surface. In the distance, a sea eagle soared and where the trees were thick and tall, cockatoos flew about clumsily, like white laundry at the mercy of the wind. The wonder of it all, she thought. A flush of shame rose from her chest and put colour in her cheeks. She'd been guilty of pettiness and, if she were to be strictly truthful, a bout of competitiveness with the man she loved. She told herself firmly that the pineapple issue was dead and buried.

'Has a date been set for the GeriAncients' cruise yet?' she asked.

Sam slapped his forehead. 'Thanks, Ettie. I'd forgotten. I'll give Melrose a call to see what they've decided.'

'Sound out Lizzie first,' she advised. 'She's already mentioned the catering. I'm thinking lovely little smoked salmon canapés. Cucumber sandwiches cut into fingers. Asparagus is in season, too. Oh, it will be gorgeous.'

'Eh?'

'And it looks like the dress code will be black tie.'

'Eh?' he repeated, his anxiety levels ramping up by the second.

'Your sunset cruise,' Ettie said, a little impatiently. 'They're calling it a ball. You know, a dance where everyone wears long dresses and black ties. Lizzie says everyone is very excited.' She turned towards Sam. 'Do you think they've organised the band yet?'

Speechless, Sam increased his speed. He came alongside the chef's jetty and helped Ettie to disembark. Waited impatiently until he saw her go through the door and then grabbed his phone off the dash. 'Lizzie,' he almost shouted. 'What's this about a bloody ball on the *Mary Kay*?'

⁓

Five minutes later, and feeling much calmer, Sam had secured a date for the cruise and a promise that the dress code was casual and the catering should reflect a lazy early evening picnic consisting of plenty of prawns in a bucket, a few baguettes and some homemade aioli. Paper serviettes. BYO drinks. No band.

Still with an hour to spare before he and Jimmy were due to do their mid-morning pick-up from Cargo Wharf, he set off towards the café for an emotionally restorative coffee and to report to the chef that Ettie was safely at home. Before he reached the mouth of Kingfish Bay, his phone went off.

'Ya gunna pick me up for a nosh or head off and leave me here with me mum gone to town early and no one around to fix me lunch?' Jimmy asked.

Sam sighed and changed course. 'Be there in five.'

The kid hopped on board with his mutt and a shopping bag that looked heavy. He gave Sam a nod and raced to the stern, settled himself on a milk crate and withdrew a copy of *Great Expectations* from the bag. He found his place, rested his feet lightly on the dog's ribs and picked up the thread of the story, running his finger along each line as he read, enthralled.

'Jimmy!' Sam called on his approach to the café. 'Jimmy!'

The kid failed to materialise.

He stuck his head around the wheelhouse. 'Jimmy!'

The dog jumped. The kid looked around as though he had no idea where he was.

'You suddenly gone deaf, mate?' Sam asked. 'Stand by to tie up at the Briny.'

Jimmy dropped the book, scrambled to his feet. 'We there already?'

They docked safely and, curious, Sam went aft, picked up the book. 'Thought your mum was reading this to you?'

'Nah. Neighbour gave us his old telly when he upgraded, and she dumped the story halfway to catch up on the shows she's missed since ours carked it. If I don't read it meself, I'll never know if Pip ended up in debtor's prison or made a go of it. I could pass it on when I've finished, if you like. It'll keep you company. That Dickens fella, he sure could tell a story.'

'Appreciate the thought, mate.'

✂

Lunchtime business at the Briny was brisk. Dirty dishes were piled high in the sink and Sam could see the pressure building while Jenny and the chef tangoed behind the counter to fill orders strung up like bunting under the rangehood, the chef incredibly light on his feet for such a bulky man.

'Jimmy!'

The kid appeared at his side.

'Hop into those dishes, mate, and the chef will be so grateful he'll put aside a few choice titbits for that mutt of yours.'

'Aw, Sam . . .'

'Now, my friend. No arguments.'

The kid gave him a long-suffering look but did as he was told. Sam, deciding he'd wait for the rush to ease before he ordered lunch, sauntered into the Square. He pulled out his phone and checked his messages. Nothing urgent. Just the usual routine of carting building supplies and servicing moorings. An ad for a baby's crib flashed onto the screen. Was there no privacy left in this world, where technology was meant to make life cruisy but instead added layers of complications? Oddly, the thought cheered him. With a baby on the way, it wouldn't be long before he had a little techno guru of his own. He marched back inside the café, pleased to see the dishes done, the benches wiped down, and the chef and Jenny with their backsides propped against the rear bench while they slugged back glasses of water.

'The boy,' Marcus announced, 'he is a master of the dishcloth and has earned a bonus for seeing us through this stampede which we have finally quelled.'

'Aw, Chef, happy to help,' Jimmy said shyly. 'And me mum deserves the credit. She gives me plenty of practice at the kitchen sink.'

Marcus gave the boy a pat on the back so hearty it nearly sent him flying. 'A man must acknowledge and pay his debts in full. Kate! What should we pay this fine young man for his labours on our account?'

Kate, distracted, barely looked up from her desk. 'A free lunch, Chef—that should do it.'

Marcus almost reeled at her lack of appreciation. 'Yes. A fine idea and the best the house has to offer. But also, a small amount of cash in a young man's pocket is required. I will see to it myself.'

Jimmy shuffled his feet, embarrassed. 'Nah. No money, Chef. Without the café, me worm business would struggle. Reckon we're all fair and square.'

The chef gave Jimmy's words the proper amount of consideration, then he nodded. 'Very well. Now, what dish may I prepare for your joyful delectation?'

'The burger, chef—the one with pineapple,' Jimmy said. 'That sure is a winner. And a side of chippies, if that's not askin' for too much.'

'Make that two, chef,' Sam said.

Kate came over with an envelope in her hand. Sam took in the sight of her thirstily, his eyes dropping to the bulge under her loose shirt. He wished she would give him a rough date, at least. Last time he mentioned it, she'd given the impression he'd stepped way out of bounds and gave a response so vague he was still floundering.

'Did some research during my time off,' Kate said. 'Here's the background on all the GeriEcstasies. Have a read. Tell me what you think.'

He tucked the envelope under his arm and headed for the rear deck, where he could eat his lunch and indulge in a few minutes of pure relaxation before dealing with the entitled new owner of a waterfront property on Cutter Island who demanded his jobs be placed automatically at the top of Sam's queue. Sam gave him a year before he sold up in frustration and roared back to the city, where he would spin bitter tales about a bunch of layabouts who failed to understand the meaning of time and deadlines to a busy businessman. No loss. Same old. Except Kate had broken the pattern. Oh, she'd had a good slug of city ways about her when she first dipped a toe in offshore waters. But she wooed the local tradies in a manner that called those rackety young fellas to her like music. Rain, hail or shine, they plugged the draughty holes in walls and sealed the cracks in the roof. Plus, she paid them full rates at the end of each working day. No hanging around waiting for a cheque while the boss gorged and his workers starved. He'd always known she was smart, but the day he found himself searching for her whenever he entered the café he'd known he was a goner. The kid, he thought; *their* kid. He'd always have the proof his time with Kate had been real.

Jimmy, recognising that Sam was lost in the kind of thoughts that made a man's eyes glaze over like he'd drifted off to a place unreachable, cleared the plates. Sam boarded the *Mary Kay* with his mind still churning through the if-onlys of the past, both recent and further back. He started the engine, dragging his mind back to the present. Jimmy leaped on board, all skinny arms and legs he'd grow into one day, waving Kate's envelope. 'Ya forgot it, Sam. On the chair. I always check, 'cause me mum reckons the best way to lose a hat or brolly is to leave without checkin' behind you.'

'Good man. Now cast off, Jimmy. We're on a mission.' The words said loud, more to rouse himself than to make a point that didn't need making.

'Me hearin's okay, Sam, and so is me memory. Better than yours, anyways.' He skipped off, full of cheek, before Sam could think of a suitable response.

⚭

Mid-afternoon, Ettie woke, disorientated, in the chef's favourite armchair. She looked around guiltily and then told herself not to be silly. She'd been unwell. She was still recovering. She could allow herself to rest. She decided to shower, hoping it would cut through a somnolence she couldn't quite shake off. Unused to being ill, she was disturbed by her lack of energy, her mind taking her down dangerous paths—her mother's increasing tiredness, the diagnosis and, finally, after a short battle riddled with treatments that stole her hair and luminosity, her death. Ettie tried to remember the last time she'd had a medical check-up and figured it was about five years overdue. But she had the energy of three women, her life was filled with joy, she woke each day with a sense of wellbeing and purpose.

It's just a bout of the flu, she told herself.

She quickly stripped and stepped under a stream of hot water, letting it hit her back like a needle massage, feeling kinks and knots ease and unravel. Then, restored, she reached into her wardrobe for a skirt Marcus had once told her was very becoming. Had trouble fastening the button. She took a breath and held in her stomach. No deal. She stepped out of the skirt, braved the bathroom mirror and reeled in shock. A new roll of skin had positioned itself around her waist. Aghast, she hurried back to the wardrobe, wrenched an elastic-waisted skirt from a large collection of tie-dyed garments, found a loose, longline shirt to cover the bulge and then, exhausted by the effort, took to the sofa. Those little morsels of deliciousness, she thought. Such tiny bites. But so many of them. Impossible to hurt Marcus's feelings by refusing to indulge. 'Time for action, Ettie,' she said to the empty room. Getting up, she went and found a pair of walking shoes.

Halfway up the steep steps leading to the fire track, legs like lead, fighting off dizziness, she thought she might faint. She reminded herself firmly she'd once climbed two hundred steps from the shore to her cottage daily and, minutes later, stepped onto the hard clay track. Above her head and through the straggly arms of stringy eucalypts, the sky was all clean blueness and she reeled with the bigness of the outside world, one she'd forgotten since she'd anchored herself to the café and wound her after-hours life around Marcus, their happiness.

The bush was resplendent. Her eyes sought out celebrations of goodenia shining gold in the rich afternoon light. Under her feet, brachycomes—yes, she remembered the name!—peeped shyly. She stopped still, hardly daring to breathe, at the sound of cracking. Glossy black cockatoos feasting on casuarina nuts. A rare sight. A brush turkey, indignant, yellow gobble quivering, cast a beady eye over her. 'Shoo,' she said, clapping her hands.

Wondrous, Ettie thought, vowing to make more time for this. But still, the word 'pineapple' resonated loudly. Bloody pineapple. What was so desperately lacking in her special relish recipe that there was space for pineapple on a hamburger? The question buzzed in her brain like a trapped bee. One she was unable to swat into oblivion.

꩜

That night, after a simple dinner she'd insisted on preparing on the basis he had worked hard all day at the café, Ettie fixed her gaze on the chef. 'I want you to tell me the truth,' she said, in a no-nonsense tone.

Marcus, who had sunk into his favourite armchair, straightened in alarm. 'My love, what is it?' he asked, frowning. 'Have I offended you?'

Ettie's ferocity was extinguished immediately. 'Of course not. No. This is about me.'

Relieved, Marcus settled back comfortably, the cushion exhaling noisily under his shifting bulk, and waited for Ettie to explain.

'It's my waist,' she murmured, eyes downcast.

He was puzzled. 'I am not following you, Ettie.'

'It has . . . disappeared.'

Marcus, concerned the fever might have returned to affect her reason, smiled with what he hoped passed for understanding. 'No, my love, I do not believe so.'

'Do you think I am fat?'

Ah, he thought, understanding now what was afoot. He opened his mouth to respond diplomatically, hesitated, unable think of a way through the question to a benign and satisfying end.

'Perhaps,' he said eventually, 'I should ask if you think *I* am overweight? My waist, you see, it has not been apparent to me for many years.'

'Men don't have waists. Women do. But not fat women.'

'Tell me then what you think is the meaning of "fat"?'

'Marcus, I am asking a simple question. Am I fat? Yes or no.'

'But this is not a simple question, my love. However I respond, it will lead to a minefield of dangers. So, I ask this instead: do you feel well? Do you feel healthy? Do you have energy each day? Of course, you have been ill, but I am referring to a day in which our normal routines are followed . . .'

'I couldn't fasten the button on my skirt this morning.' The words flew from her mouth in a plaintive wail instead of the short, sharp statement of fact she'd intended.

The chef heard the anguish and rallied instantly. 'Once you have returned to your honoured position behind the counter of the booming Briny Café, my love, the skirt will fall from your hips to the ground. This I promise.'

'Really?'

'Yes. Yes. Believe me on this.'

Marcus patted the scaly leather arm of his chair in invitation. Ettie approached, trying to hold in her stomach. She nestled against the warmth of his body.

Marcus slid his arm around her waist. 'You see? All is well and as it should be. I have found this missing waist in an instant.'

She slid onto his lap and kissed him in a way he'd remember for the rest of his life. After a while, hand in hand, they stood to go to bed.

As Ettie lay tucked into the crook of his arm, her head resting on his broad chest, Marcus said: 'If I may be permitted, I must mention the word pineapple and beg forgiveness . . .'

Ettie's buzz was immediately silenced. 'I've been told it's a triumph,' she murmured sleepily. 'And we are partners in all, are we not?'

The chef kissed the top of his beloved's head and closed his eyes. For a moment he considered suggesting the inclusion of fresh tarragon in the frittatas but wisely decided to quit while he was ahead.

CHAPTER TWENTY-ONE

AT HOME THAT SAME NIGHT, Kate completed the café's book-keeping for the month. She'd come to savour the privacy the dark brought with it, aware that Artie and even Frankie, now she was closer to her due date, were spending too much time looking in her direction. She saved and closed the file. Enjoyed, for a moment, the satisfaction of a healthy bottom line.

The screen on her phone lit up. Sam. 'You've read the research?' she asked, not bothering to say hello.

Sam sighed. 'Not yet. And I'm well, thank you for asking.'

'Sorry. It's just you don't usually call this late without a good reason.' She paused, giving him an opportunity to share that reason, but Sam let the silence stretch out. Kate gave in. 'No, I haven't spoken to Lizzie yet. I'll call her now.'

Ending the call with Sam, she keyed in Lizzie's number.

'Did I wake you?' Kate asked when Lizzie answered the phone.

'Old people don't sleep much,' Lizzie replied. 'What can I do for you?'

'I thought I might have a day off tomorrow and wondered if we could go for a walk. You could teach me a little about the bush.'

'Ettie's better, is she?'

'Well, she's getting better. Another day and she'll be back behind the counter.'

'Can you be spared?'

'The chef's got the place under control. I just get in the way.'

'A bushwalk, you say.'

'Yes! I want to learn more.'

'What's this really about, Kate?'

Kate sighed. 'You're always way ahead of me, Lizzie. It's unnerving.' Kate hesitated then said, 'Best if we discuss it privately.'

'I see.'

'I could pick you up in the boat, if you'd like.'

'I'll walk. It sharpens my mind and keeps me fit. I'll see you at your house around mid-morning.'

⁓

Lizzie set off in the cool of the early morning after a restless night. She avoided the oyster-encrusted foreshore, where she knew she'd be the target for any resident interested in wheedling out scuttlebutt about the GeriAncients, and stuck to the overgrown tracks of the national park. Like all serious bushwalkers, she had navigation points. The copse of casuarinas. The massive boulder split clean down the middle. The spotted gum growing horizontally out of a crack in a rocky outcrop. Landmarks everywhere, she thought, and yet bushwalkers so often seemed to lose their way and even, occasionally, need rescuing.

As always, the cleansing smell of eucalyptus lifted her spirits and brought a smile to her lips, although if she'd been asked to explain why, she would be at a loss.

Despite Kate's misgivings, she felt comfortable in her new home. On her first night in her suite she'd watched moonlight strike the mangroves and turn their silver trunks into a crowd of restless souls. 'Our spirit people,' Dorothy had told her long ago when they sat with the damp sand creeping into their clothes, numbing their backsides, waiting for the 'show' to begin. Dorothy had found Lizzie sitting on a rock not far from the shack, crying her eyes out over a failed romance. Without a word, she had slipped an arm around Lizzie's shoulders. After a while, she'd said, 'You be right, daughter; you come with me.' She had taken Lizzie into her home and cared for her until the heat and sorrow leached out.

Dorothy had spent the next weeks, months, guiding Lizzie along twisted wallaby tracks, showing her rock carvings almost hidden by lichen or worn by time to a faint shadow. 'Look hard enough, you find 'em,' Dorothy said. She pointed out caves where the ochre hands of her ancestors graced the rough walls like a living presence. Told her that some plants healed, some killed. Her ancestors, she said, respectfully made way for the snakes, goannas and hairy-legged spiders. She always felt safe in the Quiet, she told Lizzie, gesturing to the bush around them. 'The Wilderness. That's where the bad stuff happens.'

'Wilderness?' Lizzie asked, not sure of Dorothy's meaning.

'The city,' Dorothy replied.

Back then, Lizzie had at first tried to disguise her sorrow as an indulgent bout of self-pity about nothing very important, but after Dorothy's kindness Lizzie felt she owed her the truth. She confessed her affair with a married man and an illegal abortion, and waited for Dorothy to respond with the scorn and judgement she believed she deserved. Instead, Dorothy just smiled. 'You let it go now,' she said. 'We send them bad times into the Quiet and learn from them. You listen to me. You a young woman. You got a life to live.'

And now here she was, heading into what she knew would be her end song, walking those same tracks, her mind increasingly awash with a past that seemed sharper in detail than ever, and every poor decision, casual cruelty and thoughtless deed, a noose of self-condemnation. They reared increasingly, those misdemeanours, leaping at her in odd moments, throwing her off balance. She wondered if, on a subliminal level, she might be preparing a defence upon arrival at the Pearly Gates. If she believed in them. Which she didn't.

By the time she reached the fork in the path that led to Kate's house, she felt hot and tired, her earlier exhilaration wiped out by the ache in her legs. Feeling the sting of a blister forming on her left heel, she asked herself why she'd been so pig-headed. A gentle cruise past her old haunts would have been lovely. Maybe she'd left her common sense back in the shack on the escarpment along with the fitness she'd taken for granted.

She came to the place where she'd thought she would find water, but the clean little spring of her memory had become a muddy pond, undrinkable. Two tawny frogmouths, like logs, watched while she rested again, took flight when she continued on her way, dodging ditches and deeply eroded channels, some slippery with moisture. She would mention the deterioration of the track to the head of the fire brigade at the next fundraiser dinner even though it had been more than thirty years since she'd sat down at a trestle table to a feast prepared by volunteers to raise money for firefighting equipment. The equipment was more sophisticated these days, she thought, recalling the fireboat, the controlled burn she'd witnessed from Ettie's deck. The fireys in bright yellow unforms, hard hats, boots. Stubbies and singlets and flip flops consigned to an era when people did the best they could with what little they had. What was it the fire chief told her when, as a young woman, she'd joined the volunteers the day the fire truck sank into mud flats and the training exercise was abandoned? 'No need to go looking for entertainment around here,' he said. 'It'll bite you on the bum where you stand.' It took a week to rescue the truck, which needed a complete over-haul to prevent saltwater damage. He'd be dead now, that fire chief. Well and truly. She walked a little faster, ignoring the burning pain in the back of her heel.

When she finally reached her destination, parched, exhausted and in considerable discomfort, Kate said, 'You look terrible, if you don't mind me saying so.'

'Next time, I'll accept the offer of a pick-up in the boat,' Lizzie said, meaning it.

In the kitchen, Kate pulled out a chair, fetched a glass of water. Lizzie drank thirstily and held up the glass for a refill. 'Better—much better,' she said, when the glass was empty again.

'Let's get you into a comfortable chair on the deck,' Kate said, 'and I'll make a cuppa.'

Lizzie sat on the deck, catching her breath, as inside the kettle sang to the accompaniment of cutlery clattering on plates. A few minutes later Kate stepped outside bearing a tray.

'Do you recall the big storm?' Kate asked, setting the tray on the table and pouring the tea. 'Milk?'

'Smells like something herbal, so no thanks.'

'Red zinger. A pick-me-up.'

'Just what the doctor ordered. Which storm?'

'The most recent one.'

'Well, of course I remember it. I'm not senile, Kate, as far as I know.'

Kate smiled an apology.

'This is about the boule, is it?'

Kate nodded. 'Cake?'

'In a while,' Lizzie said. 'What about the boule?'

Kate took a breath. 'There were hairs embedded in a seam that match Cameron's DNA.'

The sentence hung between them like unfinished business. Lizzie looked away, over the water and then up to the escarpment, sideways to the waterfall, only a dribble as far as she could tell from the distance.

'It wasn't an accident, then—is that what you're saying?'

'Sam thinks you should find an excuse to return to the shack until the police have investigated . . .'

'I see. Sam wants me to do a runner. What do you think, Kate?'

'It's not my decision to make, Lizzie.'

Kate told her then, about searching through the muddled resources of the internet, pulling together threads, uncovering hugely successful business histories—mystifying, given their dogged insistence on frugality, even meanness. 'They're loaded, Lizzie. Rich. Any one of them could have bought Brian's share. Split between the group, it would have amounted to peanuts. So why the charade? Why bring you into the fold?'

Lizzie held up her cup, indicating she'd like a refill.

Kate took the teapot and went inside to make a fresh brew. She had her theories, of course she did, but she couldn't see it would do any good to voice them, baseless as they were. Artie would call what she had a gut feel, Sam would call it his radar going off. But she, Kate Jackson, once a hard-nosed financial journalist covering the top end of town, liked facts that formed a pattern—and she couldn't uncover a solid one here. Which left her with theories which, voiced out loud in a newsroom, would invoke derision from her peers. No, she'd keep her theories to herself.

She returned to Lizzie with a fresh pot of tea.

The older woman, refilled cup in hand, said: 'I don't know what to think, Kate. I really don't.' She sounded frustrated. 'On the surface, we're a bunch of well-intentioned, good-hearted oldies trying to stave off the savage, incremental stealth of age for as long as possible.'

'About Donna . . .'

'Ah. It's always comes back to Donna.'

'Oddly, I couldn't find much background on her. The soapie that made her famous is regularly rerun on television. At the very least, I'd expect her to have done a few interviews over the years or to be sighted at television industry awards. But there's nothing. It's like she fell into a black hole. I mean, how does a former celebrity disappear so completely there's not even a small reference to her in a gossip column? It's bizarre.'

Lizzie shrugged, eased off her shoe and rolled down her sock to reveal a red-raw blister the size of a twenty-cent coin.

'Ouch, that looks nasty,' Kate said.

'Would you have a bandaid handy?'

Kate went off and came back with a first-aid kit, extracted a small pack of gauze pads.

'A bandaid is fine, no need for triage,' Lizzie said.

'Sit still. You're in no position to give orders.' Kate tended the blister with gentle hands, easing the sock over the tender area when she'd finished.

'You missed your calling,' Lizzie said, flattening the heel of the shoe with her foot so it wouldn't rub when she put it on again.

'You'll ruin that shoe,' Kate said. 'I'll find a spare pair of scuffs.'

'Sit down, Kate. The shoe, like me, is unbreakable.'

After that, neither woman spoke for a long while. A sea eagle soared, clean and elegant. They watched it circle, swoop, skimming the water, a fish hunted down, dropped a few seconds later.

'Too heavy,' Lizzie said.

'Poor fish,' Kate said.

'Uh-uh. Lucky fish.'

'Yeah. Lucky fish.'

In the distance, the ferry turned from the western shores of the island, churned doggedly towards the Square, engine wheezing. Kate cleared the tea things and offered Lizzie a glass of something stronger, which was declined.

'No one ever talks about Cameron,' Lizzie mused. 'Strange, don't you think?'

'Maybe it's still too raw,' Kate suggested.

Lizzie shook her head. 'No. It's a furtive silence.'

'Why don't you bring it up?' Kate asked. In a similar situation, she would have gnawed away like a terrier with a bone.

'Prying's not my style. Never has been. Not about to start. Nor am I going to up stakes. Too many ifs and buts to turn everything on its head. And that's my final word.'

At her request, Kate dropped Lizzie off at the Square so she could head to town to do some shopping.

On her return, Lizzie rushed to catch the last service before the *Seagull* was bedded down for the night, but by the time she arrived the old vessel was already pulling away from the wharf. She was on the verge of dialling the water taxi when she caught a shadowy movement inside the café, where the lights were dimmed and the door firmly closed with a *See You Tomorrow!* sign in plain view. It wouldn't hurt to ask if anyone was going her way, she reasoned. She knocked.

Ettie appeared, and the stern expression on her face broke into a smile when she saw Lizzie. 'Thought you might be another no-hoper looking for a bag of chippies to wash down a longneck,' she said, opening the door.

'Missed the ferry. I'm happy to give Freddy a call, but thought I'd check first if you were headed in that direction, just on the off chance.'

Ettie called over her shoulder, 'Lizzie needs a lift, okay?'

Marcus came in from the deck, where he'd been straightening tables and chairs.

'Of course, of course! Hello, Lizzie. It would be my greatest pleasure to deliver you home, but perhaps, if I could be so bold . . .' He looked towards Ettie. 'The evening is so beautiful, I would like to propose a cruise to a quiet cove where we could partake of a picnic. I could assemble a few tantalising leftovers, fetch a bottle of wine and some beer from the fridge upstairs. It would be a treat for my Ettie after her encounter with a flu of uncommon force.'

Ettie gave him one of those smiles that tipped his heart sideways. 'A picnic,' she said, as if thinking it over. 'If Lizzie agrees . . .'

'Impossible to resist,' Lizzie said, smiling.

The chef hurried to the kitchen and began withdrawing containers from the fridge.

Ettie noticed him limp a little as he crossed the floor. Marcus, she realised, was worn out, although he would never admit it; he had insisted that he would remain at the café until Ettie was fully recovered. 'He is a most remarkable man,' she said softly.

Lizzie nodded. 'You each found a treasure.'

Ettie weighed up the etiquette of asking Lizzie, a deeply private person, a deeply personal question. Curiosity won. 'Was there ever a treasure in your life?'

'I thought so once or twice. In the end, I realised I had an infallible instinct for bastards.'

Ettie spluttered.

'Have I shocked you?' Lizzie asked, smiling.

'No. Not at all. I was only thinking, we women, none of us are immune to men who make our legs go weak even though we know, with absolute certainty, we should be using them to run.' She glanced towards the chef. 'Not all men, it goes without saying.'

Ettie slipped an arm through Lizzie's, grateful the days of succumbing to empty words and practised charm to ward off loneliness were way behind her. Throwing a few words of encouragement over her shoulder, she guided the old woman outside while the chef waved his magic wand. They sat on the sea wall, the mucky business that had engulfed the house in Stringybark Bay deleted, for a while, from conversation. Around them, renegade Islanders dressed in ragged shorts and holey T-shirts, clutching a frigidly cold beer as though immortality awaited in the bottom of the bottle, untied tinnies illegally tethered to the seawall and set off across a quiet sea while the sky shone pink and purple and a high silver-white moon declared night was only briefly detained.

'Your cruise ship awaits,' Marcus called from the café.

The sun was dropping fast. Ettie snatched a couple of blankets from the café and then the trio made their way to the chef's snazzy runabout.

They cruised at a pace that suited the end of a working day, the chef keeping his speed to an idyllic eight knots. Suddenly, he slapped his hand against his forehead. '*Gott in Himmel*,' he blurted.

'What?' Ettie asked, looking left and right anxiously.

Up ahead, the *Mary Kay* chugged towards the chef's house, where Sam had been invited to dine to celebrate Ettie's return to health. 'Oh, my love, I look inside my old head and find only a sea of mush. I did not inform Sam of our change of plans. My noodle, carried away in the moment, must take this blame. We will call our outing a party, which will explain my forgettery. It will soon be summer, after all, which must be celebrated. There is always a solution, is there not?'

The chef ratcheted up his speed. Alongside the *Mary Kay*, he leaned over the gunnel and shouted the change of plans. Sam gave a thumbs-up, waited for Marcus to get out of the way, then swung the barge around, and cruised steadily back the way he'd come before turning east at the mouth of the bay.

He picked up a vacant mooring in a sheltered cove a small distance east of Stringybark Bay. A mecca for noisy holidaymakers at the weekends, the pretty beach, shaped like a horseshoe, was peacefully deserted on a weekday. He threw fenders over the side to protect the chef's immaculate paintwork, and Marcus motored up beside him, tying his runabout to the *Mary Kay*.

'Come aboard, Sam,' Ettie called, waving her arm in welcome.

'With pleasure.'

Sam stepped into the hull to join the party. Ettie shifted from her seat next to Marcus to join Lizzie on the upholstered white banquette in the stern, leaving the men to their gossip: Where the fish were running. The best bait for kingfish. Sam mentioned sightings of a seal in Oyster Bay and, later in the day, closer to the café.

The chef produced treats from his picnic basket and Sam poured the wine, which was, according to the chef, thrillingly crisp. He chose a beer for himself, relieved to feel it was only two degrees off freezing point.

The chef passed around small plates of chargrilled octopus in a chilli sauce with a slice of lime on the side. The talk turned to café business for a short while. Then Ettie raised the subject of the forthcoming cruise on the *Mary Kay*.

Sam and Lizzie stiffened. The chef, oblivious to the undercurrents, fussed with his food. A smoked trout salad with dill and a golden frittata filled with baby potatoes and freshly shelled peas, raised up by the addition of mint.

'I haven't been given a firm date for the catering yet,' Ettie said with a smidgin of petulance.

Sam looked to Lizzie for support. Lizzie stared at the shoreline.

Marcus beamed. 'This cruise is to be the social extravaganza of the year, my darling Ettie tells me.'

Lizzie, snookered, took a deep breath. 'The thing is, the household has a strict budget and it doesn't stretch to anything fancy. They're embarrassed, naturally. No one wanted to be the one to put the brakes on Sam's wonderful offer, but it would suit them best if it was a simple affair. Sam mentioned the joy of a bucket of prawns and it instantly appealed to the group.'

Sam, out on a limb and unsure where Lizzie was headed, nodded his agreement.

'Prawns are expensive,' Ettie responded, beginning to smell a conspiracy.

'Well, we are old people, remember,' Lizzie replied. 'We don't eat much. Two prawns each at the most. That won't break the bank.'

Ettie sat back and sipped her wine. 'No black-tie ball, then,' she said. 'No dressing up. No music.'

Lizzie shook her head.

'This is their first outing, Ettie,' Sam said. 'They've had a tough time with Cameron's death and barely seen anything beyond their home. Anything too extravagant might seem to be in poor taste— and besides, it would distract from the beauty of the surroundings.'

Ettie, resigned, said, 'Well, a heap of geriatrics—I don't mean you, Lizzie, you're ageless—dancing on a barge was always going to be fraught with danger. A lovely, safe cruise with some simple food sounds perfect.'

Marcus asked: 'And what is the date of this conversion of *Mary Kay* into a pleasure craft?'

Sam pulled out his phone and scrolled down his calendar. 'Weather permitting, next Monday. Which puts it about three or four weeks before the baby is due. Kate is unsure.'

'Chicken sandwiches,' Ettie murmured. 'Not everyone loves prawns, and if the women dress up a little, they won't want to get their hands dirty. That's not a step too far, is it, Lizzie?'

'Not at all,' she replied, knowing when to give in graciously.

The light turned pewter-soft and lustrous as moonlight dusted the tips of small waves and then dissolved in the evening air. They ate the chef's victuals with groaning contentment. He reached for the wine bottle and shared out the last few drops between himself and the two women.

Sam shifted slightly so he faced Lizzie. 'What was the name of the show Donna appeared in?'

'*Sanctuary*,' Ettie replied immediately. 'She played a rather nasty character. I wonder . . . Do you think if you play a role for long enough, you become that person?'

'It's usually fame that corrupts, not the part you play,' Lizzie said. 'Mike told me Donna had a breakdown when the spotlight was turned off. He said she hasn't been quite right since.'

The group went on to discuss, in general terms, degrees of madness. Eventually, Lizzie was persuaded to give an example of Donna's behaviour. 'The other night, Mike refused to refill her wineglass and she threw it against the wall. Mike apologised and hurried her off to her room.'

'What did everyone else do?'

'Well, Sheila swept up the mess. Gavin said he'd open another bottle of wine now they didn't have to worry about Donna drinking too much and falling flat on her face. Rob asked Daisy if she'd like a cuppa or a whisky. And so on. We were back to five o'clock happy hour—or five o'clock follies, as they're called. It was as though nothing untoward had occurred. For a moment I wondered if we'd all been in the same room. Then the penny dropped. They'd witnessed scenes like this so often, it had become normal.'

Ettie would have liked more detail, but before she could speak a snore erupted from the captain's chair. 'Marcus?'

The chef sat bolt upright. 'Yes, yes, my love, I agree.'

'You were sound asleep,' Ettie accused.

'Perhaps slightly less than soundly. Now you must tell me, what is it I have agreed to? My soul, I hope, has not been on the auction block while I have been resting my eyes.'

'Nah, you're good, Chef,' Sam assured him.

Ettie signalled that it was time to head home, and the chef looked grateful. She tidied away the remnants of the picnic, placing leftovers in a container for Sam and Jimmy to have for lunch the following day. It was much cooler now, with a dampness coming off the sea to settle on their shoulders. Kookaburras, late to bed, made a sudden racket that cut through the peace, but it only lasted a minute. No one said much: just a few murmurings about the beautiful food, the wondrous night, the pleasure of being among friends.

Eventually, when the sky was awash with moonlight, Sam boarded the *Mary Kay*, hauled in the fenders, untied the chef's boat and gave it a push with his foot.

Kings never lived this well, he said to himself as he set off with a wave.

GeriEcstasy was lit up like a fancy hotel when Marcus came along-side the pontoon. As Lizzie disembarked, using Marcus's arm for balance, the front door burst open and six pairs of feet pounded down the jetty. 'We were about to send out a search party,' Mike Melrose said furiously. 'We thought you were lost in the bush, or drowned, or something awful had happened to you.'

'As you can see, I'm perfectly fine,' Lizzie replied, turning her back to Melrose to take her shopping bag from Marcus.

'Next time, let us know if you're going to be late.' From Sheila, this time.

'It's just . . .' Sally began.

'After Cameron,' Daisy said, pushing through to the front with her wheelchair.

'Ah,' Lizzie said, understanding. 'I'm so sorry. It never crossed my mind you'd be worried. Marcus offered me a lift and then Ettie came up with the idea of a picnic in the boat.'

'Call us next time, okay?' Daisy repeated sternly.

She spun her chair around and headed back to the house, followed closely by the faithful Rob. The others fell in behind. Lizzie felt like a child being punished for bad behaviour.

CHAPTER TWENTY-TWO

THE MORNING AFTER THE PICNIC, Lizzie woke feeling uneasy about what she considered to be an overreaction to her late return. They were, after all, a group of independent adults capable of making rational decisions without consensus. She felt their disapproval was an invasion of her privacy, which she'd always guarded fiercely, even during the heyday of her playwriting career. She needed to make the group understand that within the walls of the house, she would abide by the rules, but outside them, she was her own boss.

Rising from her bed, she showered and dressed, put a fresh bandaid on her blister and decided a brisk walk would stretch her body and improve her mood. She wasn't ready to face anyone.

Outside, she climbed the rough steps to the fire track and stood to catch her breath. To go left would take her deeper into the bush. Turn right and she would descend to the mouth of the freshwater creek that spilled into the tangled arms of the mangroves. Choices, she thought, so many to be made in a long life, and no way of knowing whether they would lead to joy or sorrow or nothing much at all.

As always, the mangroves called. Holding on to tree trunks for support, she picked her way down a crumbly wallaby path to the shore. She was about to step onto the sand when she heard voices, caught the unmistakable body language of two people arguing. Too far away to catch more than a random word or two, she approached Donna Harris and Mike Melrose slowly, listening intently as she drew closer, waving innocently when they saw her. 'Fabulous front yard isn't it?' she said, indicating the surroundings.

'Is there something we can help you with?' Melrose asked, frowning.

'Oh. Well, yes.' She scrabbled to think of something. 'Visitors. What's the protocol? I'd like to ask Kate to come by.'

Donna smiled sweetly at the man she just been shouting at. 'What do you think, darling? Shall we give an entry ticket to the snoring café bookkeeper-cum-dishwasher who is so delicately enceinte?'

Melrose threw his wife a warning look. 'She's a former journalist, isn't she?' he asked.

Lizzie nodded. 'That's right.'

'Always feel a bit unsure when they come sniffing around.'

Lizzie bit back a biting retort and managed a smile with a hint of complicity. 'Of course, I understand,' she said. 'Donna's fame. Such a difficult thing to handle.'

Donna, missing the irony and preening under the weight of flattery, stepped forward and linked her arm through Lizzie's. 'The play, Lizzie. How is it coming along? I've been doing my voice exercises every day. So excited about returning to the theatre after all this time.'

Lizzie looked to Melrose for support. He turned away.

'It takes time to write a play. Doubt you'll see anything for a while.'

Donna dropped Lizzie's arm like a burning stick. 'Why else do you think we let you come to live with us, you stupid woman?' Donna said, her face twisted and ugly.

Melrose swiftly stepped forward. 'I'm sure Lizzie will do her best.'

'Well, that's just not good enough, is it?' She prodded Lizzie in the chest. 'Not good enough at all. You better lift your game, girlie . . .' Again, the finger struck Lizzie's solar plexus. As Lizzie stumbled backwards, Donna swung at her wildly. Lizzie, dodging the blow, fell to the sand.

Melrose grabbed his wife's arms and held them behind her back, making an urgent gesture for Lizzie to leave.

She staggered to her feet and backed away clumsily.

Donna rounded on her husband, red-faced. 'She's a liar, my dear. Pulled a scam to get a foot in the door but she's a hanger-on, just like all the others.'

'See you back at the house, Lizzie,' Melrose said, keeping a tight grip on his wife.

In shock, Lizzie ploughed awkwardly through damp sand, and retreated to the house, making a beeline for her suite, closing the door firmly to discourage visitors. Solitary nights, months, years in her shack, an easy target if there was a madman looking for one, she'd never spent a sleepless night. Sleepless in Stringybark Bay? For the first time, she took a close look at the locks on the door. Overkill, she'd thought, when handed a set of keys. Now she wondered.

After dinner that night, Melrose took Lizzie aside and apologised for Donna's outburst.

Lizzie shrugged. 'Forgiven but not forgotten. It would be best if it didn't happen again.'

'If she bothers you, let me know. She can be . . .' He paused. 'It never lasts long. She forgets, and that's it.'

Lizzie nodded.

Later, she sat in Brian's glamorous blue velvet armchair near the window, gazing through the darkness to where the mangroves shone whitely. She hankered for the comfort of her old leather armchair, yearned for flames flickering lazily in a grate. Fifty years alone on an isolated escarpment and she had never felt fear. Here, among a crowd, she was deeply disturbed.

⟡

The next day, Lizzie trekked to the nearest public ferry wharf and hung out a red flag to alert the driver of a pick-up. Chris helped her board, holding out his great callused paw to haul her in safely, the ferry lurching under the pummelling of an irascible nor'easter. She took a seat on the rear deck, her hair unruly in the wind, rubbed the heel of her blistered foot, gazed out to sea, breathed in the salty spume. At the café, she waited while two people ordered coffee and cake and then asked Ettie where she might find Kate. Ettie, pink from exertion and looking much more like her old self, pointed at the ceiling. 'She and Marcus are upstairs going over the accounts. I've been ordered to stay away.'

'A coffee, then, a double shot, and banana bread on the deck while I wait for her,' Lizzie said, reaching for a newspaper.

'Coming right up.'

Five minutes later, the chef appeared at the top of the stairs with his hair all over the place. He looked like he'd been tumbled in a clothes dryer. Ettie smiled inwardly and felt justified in her choice of Kate as co-owner, despite many in the Cook's Basin community warning her she would regret inviting the quiet, stubborn, aloof young woman without any discernible sense of humour into the business. She greeted Marcus at the bottom of the stairs and kissed his cheek.

'Kate,' he said, his tone veering between forlorn and furious, 'she is relentless. Every cent she scrutinises with a magnifying glass until it gives up its secrets—such as six prawns in a dish when she allowed me money only for four. She is ferocious like a lion and I am an old man who cannot withstand such an inquisition on profit and loss.'

Ettie took his hand and led him to the deck to join Lizzie. 'I will bring you a herbal tea to soothe and perhaps a slice of chocolate cake to cheer,' she said sympathetically.

'You are a treasure,' murmured Marcus, falling theatrically into a chair opposite Lizzie. 'But I would find one of your orange and polenta muffins a little kinder on my ageing stomach at this hour of the morning.'

'Of course,' Ettie said, rushing inside to hide her laughter.

'Kate nailed the chef's prawn dish, eh?' Jenny said.

Ettie nodded, and both women doubled over with laughter.

By the time Kate appeared on the deck, the chef was restored to his customary good humour. He stood and seized Kate in a bear hug. 'You are impossible, but I wish you had been beside me in my restaurant. Nothing would have escaped your attention, which is the same as an eagle searching from high in the skies for a little mouse in the grass.' He turned towards the café and boomed through the door: 'Ettie, my heart's desire, I tender my resignation as of this moment in time. A kingfish awaits the gentle coaxing of my finger on a line, and tonight I will cook for you alone. We will return to normal, yes? This is my plan.' He turned on his heel and marched down the ramp to his boat.

After waving him off, Kate sat down with Lizzie. 'Ettie mentioned you were waiting for me,' she said. 'What can I do for you?'

'Yesterday morning,' Lizzie said, 'I stumbled across Mike and Donna on the beach. They were having an argument.'

'Did you hear what it was about?' Kate asked.

'Not much of it. She hates the house. Said she's a prisoner there. Hates the location. Too much water. Hates the bush. Too many spiders. Hates her fellow tenants. Too many people. That's when they saw me.' Lizzie drained her coffee. 'Donna turned on the charm as though someone had flipped a switch. It was quite unnerving. She asked about a ridiculous play I mentioned the day we all met, and when I told her it might take a very long time to write, she turned violent. I fear she would have punched me in the face if Mike hadn't grabbed her arm.'

'No!' Kate said appalled. 'Are you alright, Lizzie? Were you hurt?'

Lizzie shook her head. 'I'm fine. But deeply concerned.'

'Are you going to mention it to the others?'

'No. I think they know what she's capable of and Mike has probably told them what happened. They would feel forced to defend her out of loyalty.'

'Go back to the shack, Lizzie.'

'I'm not afraid.'

'You should be.'

'I'm only telling you because I wanted someone to know what happened, just in case . . .'

'Please, Lizzie, it's not too late. Walk away now.'

'Don't let me keep you,' Lizzie said, opening the newspaper.

She refused to be drawn by Kate's entreaties, and eventually Kate gave up and went back to work, bitterly regretting she'd ever suggested Lizzie move in with the GeriEcstasies.

CHAPTER TWENTY-THREE

SAM QUASHED THE IDEA OF a sunset cruise for the GeriEcstasies on the basis it might stretch into evening before anyone noticed and disembarking in the dark would be hazardous, especially during a low tide or if a strong onshore wind gusted in. 'Make it early afternoon, mate,' he insisted, when he called Mike Melrose to settle the final details. 'Trust me, it's the wisest way to go.'

Ettie and the chef handled the catering, with clear instructions to keep it simple and to contain their costs to an amount Mike Melrose paid in advance. When Kate heard the figure, she grimaced. Knowing the healthy financial position of each couple, the budget was miserly, without even a meagre profit for the café, given that Ettie and the chef, who had volunteered to help on the day, would silently add extra supplies because neither of them could bear the thought of anyone going hungry. Kate, who'd agreed to oversee the café in Ettie's absence, was baffled all over again by the GeriEcstasies' display of penury.

On a clear, sunny Monday, with a tender sea under the hull, Sam, Jimmy and Amelia set off to collect the guests. Jimmy's mother had insisted on coming along to help with the cruise—although everyone understood she was more intent on assuaging her curiosity—and she had brought with her two laden picnic baskets. Sam had filled an icebox with freshly cooked prawns. Mike Melrose, they had decided individually, would be given a lesson in Cook's Basin generosity. With a bit of luck, some of it might rub off on him. Didn't they always train newcomers in the generous ways of offshorers until it became second nature to them?

Jimmy, his face covered in fluorescent green sunblock, spun like a dervish to draw attention to his outfit, a lurid rainbow T-shirt and pink shorts dotted with pineapples. 'You reckon the oldies will like it?' he asked.

'They'll love it, mate.'

Amelia rolled her eyes. 'Hope they remember to bring their sunglasses,' she said. 'In full sunlight, he strobes like a rock concert.' Her own get-up was in stark contrast. White shirt, white shorts, white bandana on a straw hat, as though she was doing her best to tone down her son's impact.

They marched in single file down the steps to the jetty, then along the salt-stained boards to the pontoon where the spruced-up *Mary Kay* waited. Jimmy, who'd scrubbed the decks, polished every corner of the wheelhouse and primed the cleats so they shone brightly, leaped on board. Sam and Amelia passed him the supplies, which he stowed tidily in the wheelhouse. This done, he stood ready to help his dithering mother, who worried if she let go of her hat—for which she'd paid good money, as it came with a guarantee against sun damage from the Cancer Council—the sneaky little breeze that rounded the corner of Cutter Island even on a still day would whisk it away. 'Take me arm,' Jimmy said, offering a knobby elbow. 'And keep hold of your hat with your other mitt.'

'Thanks, love,' she said. 'You're a good boy.'

'What about you, Sam?' the kid asked, a cheeky grin on his face. 'You need any help?'

'Not yet, mate, but it won't be long.'

Sam made a final check and fired the engine. Jimmy untied and Sam eased the barge off the pontoon, negotiated a U-turn, and set forth for Kingfish Bay to collect Ettie and the chef. It was hotter now. The sun blazed down from a clear blue sky, merciless even though midday had come and gone and, by rights, with full-blown summer still around the corner, it should have been losing strength. For the umpteenth time, Sam checked the weather forecast on his phone, judged the temperature a few degrees above the expected maximum and rubbed his forehead, worried. Sunstroke had a nasty habit of taking out unwary old folks.

He let the breeze blow him hard against the chef's jetty and whistled.

'Just getting all the gear together,' Ettie called from the doorway. She disappeared inside and re-emerged, an icebox in each hand. Marcus appeared with two more. They both went back inside the house. Sam groaned inwardly.

'You want me to tie on or hold on?' Jimmy asked.

'Tie on, mate, and then give them a hand or we'll be here for the rest of the afternoon.'

The chef reappeared, barely visible among a tangle of beach umbrellas, fold-up chairs, a large hold-all with beach towels, sun lotion, cloth hats and picnic blankets. He handed Jimmy a heavy canvas bag that appeared to contain a pop-up gazebo. The kid shook his head in disbelief, not sure where he'd find space to stow the stuff.

As they lugged their provisions aboard the *Mary Kay*, Sam said, 'Jeez, Chef, any more and we might sink. We're not expecting the armed forces, as far as I'm aware.'

Marcus looked pleased with his efforts. 'We are prepared, of course, for every eventuality.'

'Including being lost at sea for a month,' Sam muttered under his breath. The wheelhouse was stacked to the ceiling.

'This madwoman from the big house in Stringybark Bay, it is to be hoped she will stay at home,' the chef said. 'Ettie is not a fan; therefore I am not inclined towards her either.'

'How about checking on your mum and Ettie,' Sam said, directing his words at Jimmy.

'Gettin' rid of me, are you?'

'Safety first, mate. You know the rules.'

The kid sighed. 'I know what's goin' on, Sam. And I'm with the chef. Reckon we'll all have a better time if the nutcase stays locked up.'

'Jimmy!'

'Yeah, yeah.'

When the kid was out of earshot, Marcus said: 'Today he is a rainbow in those clothes, but every day, he is sunshine. This is my understanding of Jimmy.'

'Can't fault you there, Chef,' Sam said.

While the *Mary Kay* cut through the water on her way to Stringybark Bay, Ettie and Amelia sat on a bench that Sam had installed hard up against the wheelhouse wall for the occasion. Jimmy found a couple of cushions to go behind their backs and then joined Longfellow on the bow. He threw his arm around the mutt and nuzzled his furry neck.

The two women talked about Cutter Island issues that remained unchanged from one year to the next. Overflowing septic tanks; the growing suspicion the ferry was genuinely on its last legs and would need replacing soon; the rising number of yachts crowding the bays; the influx of newbies who needed to learn a few manners on the water; a working bee to paint the kindergarten before the end of the summer holidays.

'Will Kate's baby be enrolled when she's old enough?' Amelia asked.

Ettie shrugged. 'Bit too early to speculate.'

'Hopefully, she'll have Sam's common sense and not Kate's flightiness.'

'Kate is smart, and practical,' Ettie said, immediately defensive.

'Maybe. But she's unreliable, too. You never know where she's headed.'

Ettie bristled. 'Everyone's entitled to an opinion, I suppose.'

'Going to be a scorcher by mid-afternoon, so they say,' Amelia said, backing off.

The barge began the swing into Stringybark Bay. Up ahead, the GeriAncients had gathered on the jetty. In their midst stood Donna Harris, wearing sunglasses twice the size of her face and a hat more suited to the races. The pontoon was strewn with baskets, iceboxes and enough beach paraphernalia to open a retail outlet.

Sam groaned. 'No good turn goes unpunished,' he muttered.

At the edge of the group, Lizzie indicated the mess with a sweep of her arm, then shrugged in apology, mouthing: 'Sorry.'

Sam dredged up a grin and gave her the thumbs-up.

'Looks like the Wicked Witch of the West is coming along for the festivities, Chef,' Sam said. 'Get ready for the floorshow.'

Jimmy flew to starboard, a vibrant streak, and grabbed a rope. Mike Melrose waited to catch Jimmy's throw. Sam spun the helm quickly to come about. Melrose caught the rope expertly and secured the stern. Jimmy chucked him another rope to hold fast the bow.

'Jimmy, secure the gangplank,' Sam yelled.

The kid hurried to the stern to fetch a piece of marine ply wide enough for a stroll then Sam and Jimmy stood on opposite sides, ready to help the guests on board.

'Ladies and gentlemen,' Jimmy said. 'Walk the plank . . .'

Sam caught his eye and Jimmy checked himself with a deep breath. 'I'll give you all a helping hand. Sam and me, we'll organise the wheelchair between us.' His voice held an unfamiliar note of authority.

Amelia heard it and smiled smugly. Her boy, a star.

Mike called names one by one, starting with Donna and leaving Daisy until the end.

'Me last, if you don't mind,' Rob said. 'I'll wait behind Daisy's chair until she's safely on board.'

The rest of the group, noisy and animated, lined up behind Donna like kids in a tuckshop queue.

'Sorry, love,' Sam said, pointing at Donna's shoes. 'No stilettos on board. They leave punctures in the deck.'

Donna instantly appealed to her husband, who shook his head. 'The instructions were quite clear, Donna. Rubber soles—no heels, for safety reasons. You'll have to go barefooted or stay behind.'

'Well, nobody bothered to tell me,' Donna said accusingly.

The group suddenly fell silent.

Daisy rolled forward. 'Take off the shoes, Donna, or stay here,' she said, her tone sharp. 'Your choice.' Donna opened her mouth to argue but Daisy held her ground, eyes flinty. 'We haven't got all day,' she added.

Donna grabbed Melrose's arm and slid first one shoe off her foot, then the other. He took them and placed them neatly at the junction of the jetty and the pontoon. 'Ready for your return,' he said, smiling.

Chat fired up easily again. The collective anxiety dissipated. Donna boarded demurely. Daisy returned to the rear of the queue and Sheila Flowerdale, resplendent in diamanté-studded sneakers and a flowing kaftan, boarded next. Sally Kinane, subdued but crisp in white, was followed by Lizzie, wearing sensible khaki. Gavin Flowerdale and David Kinane jostled jokily until Gavin bowed in mock deference to his 'elder by six days' and waved him ahead. Melrose touched Daisy's shoulder. She gave him a nod to precede her.

Sam and Jimmy lifted Daisy's chair over the gunnel and set her safely on the deck. 'Lucky last,' Rob said. He reached for Jimmy's arm. His balance, he explained, wasn't as good as it used to be. 'You've put the brake on, Daisy, haven't you?' Distracted, he stumbled.

'Watch out,' Daisy called, leaning forward, reaching out as if she could catch him.

Sam grabbed his arm in a steadying grip. 'You're no good to her dead, mate.'

White-faced, Rob nodded. 'Sorry. Sometimes she forgets, you see. I must be sure . . .'

'Our responsibility from now on. Okay?'

He nodded and went to his wife, who caught his hand in hers and held on tightly.

Sam called for attention. 'We're not getting underway until everyone is sitting down. Find a spot and don't move until you're given the green light.'

Donna scanned the spaces, stepping around the barge like a ballerina terrified of getting her feet dirty. She came to a stop in front of Ettie and Amelia. 'Room for one more, is there? Or would one, or preferably or both of you, be so kind as to sit somewhere else?'

Ettie and Amelia ignored her. Sam went to head off a confrontation, followed by the chef, who said he would deal with the rude woman, if necessary. 'Leave it to me,' Sam said, already wishing that he'd kept his mouth shut and let them all take their chances on a yacht. 'Let me assist,' he said smoothly, taking Donna's hand and leading her away. 'Your reserved seat is in the wheelhouse, the nerve centre of the barge. On the banquette. Best seat in the house.' He quickly shuffled the chef's paraphernalia around to make a space, wondering where the idea that the wheelhouse was a nerve centre had come from. Panic centre, more likely.

'Lovely theatrical turn of phrase,' she murmured, fluttering her eyelashes in a way that made Sam look away quickly. 'The wind out there would have ruined my hair, anyway.'

'Cast off, Jimmy,' Sam called. 'And, mate, you're tour guide. A running commentary as we pass each landmark so the good people of Stringybark Bay can learn a little about the new world they've chosen to make their own.'

'Aye, aye, cap'n.' Jimmy stood on the bow, the mutt at his feet. 'Cat Island.' He pointed with a finger. 'A penguin sanctuary and a top spot for cops to hide out and catch ya speedin'. The beach over there? That's where me mum and dad had a picnic once. Must've been pretty good, 'cause nine months later . . . well, here I am.'

The crowd laughed and Amelia covered her face with her hands. Sam grinned. The kid was a natural.

Donna rose to stand by Sam's side. She rested her hand flirtatiously on his forearm. 'Do you mind?' she asked. 'I'm feeling a little unsteady.'

Sam forced a smile and pushed the throttle forward. With the help of the wind, he might cut the length of the trip by five minutes.

By the time they anchored, the breeze from the nor'east had stiffened to a brisk wind, creating a chop outside the shelter of the cove that would gather momentum during the afternoon. Sam whispered to the chef to get the picnic underway as quickly as possible. 'A big sea all the way home if we don't hurry,' he said.

The chef, a dedicated fisherman, understood the risks immediately and called Ettie, Jimmy and Amelia to action. Ten minutes later, the gazebo was erected over a folding table set with cloth napkins, plastic glassware and platters of food. 'Lunch is served!' announced Marcus.

The GeriEcstasies remained seated.

At first, Ettie thought they were holding back out of politeness. Then she realised they were unsure of their balance on a rocking barge. She passed around the chicken sandwiches and indicated to Amelia that she should offer Sam's bucket of prawns. Jimmy, picking up the vibe, followed with the baguettes, breaking off pieces as required. The chef called Melrose to organise his beverages 'tout de suite, schnell schnell', to complement the wonderful but simple food which had been raised to a culinary pedestal with a little tweak here and there by himself, a master chef, and his beloved, Ettie, a cook of national renown.

Melrose spread his feet against the motion of the barge, testing his balance. Then, moving confidently, he took Ettie aside to ask, in an accusatory tone that she found offensive, by how much the budget had been blown.

'All the extras were contributed by Amelia, Marcus, Sam and the Briny Café,' she explained, smiling sweetly. 'We didn't want anyone going home with an empty stomach.'

The barb went straight over Melrose's head. He nodded as if the gesture was their rightful due.

Soon, a gentle contentment settled over the *Mary Kay* and her guests. 'I can taste lime in the chicken sandwiches, Ettie. Am I right?' asked Sally, with the well-developed palate of a former cheesemaker.

Ettie gave a little Marcus-like clap. 'Yes! There is finely grated zest in the mayonnaise.'

'Inspired,' Sally told her. 'May I have another?'

Jimmy filled a bucket with sea water, set it on the table. 'It's to wash your hands,' he explained, 'so you don't stink of prawns.' When no one moved, he added, 'Or I can bring it around to you, one by one . . .'

'Good man,' Gavin Flowerdale said heartily. 'One of many jobs you perform, I imagine. Why don't you tell us about them?'

'Yes, Jimmy,' Donna said icily, having slipped onto the bench vacated by Ettie and Amelia. 'Entertain us, why don't you?' She stretched out, placing a cushion under her head, and closed her eyes.

Daisy handed Melrose the blanket from her knees and he laid it over Donna. 'Have a rest for a while,' he said softly. 'It will refresh you for the journey home.' She gave a catlike wriggle.

The group leaned towards Jimmy. Sam, Ettie and Marcus began to clear up.

'It's pretty basic stuff,' Jimmy began. 'Servicin' moorings, loading buildin' materials, makin' heavy deliveries. 'Course, when there's a whopper storm like the other day, me routine gets thrown and me mum says I turn into Jack.'

'Of all trades,' Amelia quickly explained.

'Storms are pretty interestin'. Lotta stuff ends up in the water. Real treasure sometimes. The other day—'

'Jimmy!' Sam called out, realising where the kid was headed. 'Tell them about how you dived to put the slings around Georgie's boat. More interesting than picking up drifting petrol tanks, torches and life jackets.'

'Don't forget that crazy shoe, Sam—the one with the spiky heel and pointy toe. That would've given a whale stomach cramps if we hadn't pulled it up before it headed out to sea.'

Donna sat bolt upright. 'What shoe?'

Jimmy, who didn't hear, launched into an account of his epic dive.

Donna threw off the blanket, planted her legs on the deck, raised herself to her full height. She marched up to Jimmy and grabbed his shirtfront. 'What shoe, you thieving little brat?'

Amelia gasped. Lizzie, who'd been sitting next to Amelia, saw what was about to happen and stepped in front of Jimmy. Donna shoved her out of the way. Lizzie fell backwards, landing on the gunnel with the sickening sound of a bone breaking. Donna punched the kid's head and stomach like a boxer, left, right, left right. Amelia screamed. Jimmy staggered, toppling headfirst and backwards overboard.

Sam yanked off his boots and dived over the side. Longfellow locked his jaw around Donna's ankle. 'Thief, thief,' Donna screamed, batting at the dog, as Ettie ran to Lizzie. Amelia came alive and whacked Donna so hard she fell flat on her face and was mercifully silenced. The dog held on.

Sam dragged Jimmy to the surface. The kid was breathing but unconscious, blood pouring from a gash on his head. Amelia reached over the gunnel to take his weight, and together she and Marcus hauled him on board. Sam, dripping, hoisted himself back on the barge. Ettie abandoned Lizzie momentarily to fetch her phone, and dialled triple zero, babbling so badly the operator had to pull her into line with a few sharp words.

Sally and Sheila, legs wonky with the roll of the deck, crawled to kneel beside Amelia and the boy, ready to assist. Sam, drilling into memory, turned the kid on his side. Open airways. Check for blockages. Sea water ran out of the kid's mouth. Amelia ripped off her shirt and held it against the head wound, murmuring to her son, desperate for a response. The kid opened eyes fuzzy with incomprehension. Sam sat him up, thumped him lightly on the back. 'You all good, mate?'

Jimmy cracked a grin through swollen lips. Amelia, in her bra, pulled him back into her lap and called for a blanket. Sam fell on his haunches, tears running down his cheeks, the image of the boy lying lifeless below the sea engraved in his mind for all time.

'You're going to have a shiner, mate,' Sam said.

Amelia took Jimmy's hand and reached for one of Sam's. 'My best boys,' she said. 'My two best boys.'

'Could someone pull that bloody dog off Donna?' shouted Melrose.

Later, as dusk fell over Kingfish Bay and the noisy cockatoos were silenced by the kookaburras, Sam, Kate and Ettie sat on the end of the jetty while Marcus prepared a cocktail that he said would, for a short time, wipe out the awful memories of a quite terrible afternoon. He set three martini glasses the size of small swimming pools in a line and from a cocktail shaker strained what looked like liquid gold into each. Nobody had the energy to ask what they were drinking.

'Sounds like I missed a wingding of a picnic,' Kate said, sipping lemon verbena tea the chef had made from leaves plucked from a tree on his rear deck.

'Lizzie's ankle is broken,' Ettie said. 'Jimmy is in hospital with suspected concussion. Amelia is threatening legal action.'

'And the GeriEcstasies have withdrawn to their bunker to tend the punctures on Donna's ankle,' Sam said.

'At least nobody died,' Ettie said.

The shell-shocked trio, feet dangling in the water, raised their glasses and clinked. Then, in the silence of a darkened bay, a gurgle, a rumble began in Ettie's stomach, rose to her chest. She began to laugh, softly at first, then uproariously. 'It was horrendous,' Ettie said. 'It was absolutely horrendous. The worst picnic in history—which, given some past events in Cook's Basin, is quite a feat. So awful it defies description. And that paramedic, the one in charge, what was it he said?'

'For a bunch of geriatrics, it looked like they knew how to party pretty hard,' Sam said and, throwing his head back, he too roared with laughter.

'And who would have guessed that Mike Melrose, Mr Debonair and Chancellor of the Exchequer, was terrified of dogs?' Ettie said, bent double now, wiping tears from her eyes with her wrist.

Marcus guffawed. 'Yes, yes, I must agree. This was a day of the best intentions which will be remembered for all the wrong reasons. It is good to laugh—and if I may be so bold as to suggest my special cocktails may have helped—so we can set this terrible experience behind us with the side of humour foremost in our minds.'

Kate raised her innocent drink to acknowledge the chef's sensible advice.

After a minute or two of contemplative silence, Marcus asked if anyone was hungry.

'No!' they chorused.

'Perhaps another cocktail?

'Yes!' they shouted.

Marcus filled their glasses for a second time and became solemn.

'Correct me if I am wrong in this assumption, but it has occurred to me that the behaviour of the unpredictable woman is not unknown to the people with whom she shares her home. There was no sign of shock on their faces, and they waited without moving a single finger for that woman's poor husband to come forward to sort out the fracas which, thanks to Longfellow's enthusiastic participation, took too long.'

Kate cleared her throat. All eyes turned towards her. 'Donna had a go at Lizzie a couple of days ago. Lizzie reckons if Melrose hadn't stepped in, she would've been badly hurt.'

'And you didn't think to mention it before we set sail for Armageddon?' Sam asked, incredulous.

'I thought . . . it was Lizzie's call. I didn't want to interfere.' She turned her head away from the group. 'An error of judgement, as it turned out.'

'Poor Lizzie,' Ettie said, deflecting the focus from Kate. 'Six weeks on crutches.'

'We must look on the bright side,' Marcus insisted, determined that the results of his inspired alcoholic triage would remain beneficial. 'Her bones are strong for her age and the break was clean.'

'She can't stay in that house,' Sam said, holding up his glass and wondering how it had emptied so quickly. 'Donna's liable to go after her with a hatchet next time.' He put his glass down beside him with regret. 'That drink's a winner, Chef. Up there with your best dessert.'

'She can't go back to her shack on crutches either,' Ettie said, slurring her words a little, 'and the penthouse has too many stairs.'

'We have a spare room . . .' Marcus said.

'You are a wonderful man,' Ettie said, kissing his cheek, 'but Lizzie is far too independent to accept. There is only one solution.' She turned to Kate, her face glowing with the pleasure of having hit on a brilliant solution. 'A couple of weeks' holiday on the escarpment with Lizzie until she is more mobile will do you the world of good.'

Kate looked horrified. 'But . . .'

'You're due for maternity leave anyway,' Ettie said, swallowing a hiccup and wondering why the distant shore had begun to tilt. She put the phenomenon down to encroaching darkness.

'What about the bub?' Sam said, feeling a knot tighten in his stomach.

'Baby,' Kate interjected. 'Not bub: baby. Bub is a terrible word.'

'If the bub comes early, Kate'll be stranded with an old woman with a broken leg who'll be no use at all,' Sam said, trying not to shout his concern.

'First babies are always late,' Ettie said, with an airy indifference created by the chef's inspired cocktail.

Marcus laid a restraining hand on Ettie's leg. 'It has come to my attention, my love, that we have not consulted Kate on this issue, nor Lizzie.' He turned his gaze on Kate. 'You must tell us your thoughts in a truthful manner so there can be no misunderstandings.'

'I'll do it,' Kate said.

'Jeez, Kate . . .'

'Two weeks. Knowing Lizzie, she'll have worked out a system to cope before a week is up. I'll be back in no time.'

'Wonderful!' Ettie said happily. 'Is the cocktail shaker empty, Marcus?'

'Drained even to the last drop,' Marcus replied.

'Oh well.' She stared into the bottom of her glass and sighed. 'Time for bed. Tomorrow is another day.' She tried to stand. 'Marcus, I believe I have misplaced my legs.'

'This mix I concocted in an effort to dull the horror of the day, perhaps it was too strong.'

'Nah. Never felt better in my life,' Sam insisted, and promptly fell face forward into the bay.

∽

Fast Freddy delivered Sam home, advising him to drink a lot of water and take two aspirins if he wished to function in the morning. 'A hot shower, too,' he added. 'Sea's still cold enough for a chill to set in.'

'If I ever say yes to one of the chef's cocktails again you have permission to lash me to a mast and shove the boat out to sea.'

'Learned a lesson, I expect,' Fast Freddy replied equably. 'But if the grapevine is even half correct, I believe you've had a challenging day.'

'That doesn't begin to describe it,' Sam said, feeling a thumping headache take hold in his skull.

Freddy helped Sam off the water taxi like he was an invalid then waited until he saw a light come on in the house before setting off to pick up his next fare.

CHAPTER TWENTY-FOUR

THE FIRST THING SAM DID when he woke—late enough for the sun to be high in the sky—was to call Richard Baines to set up a meeting. Then he rang Amelia to ask how Jimmy was doing.

'He'll be home from the hospital by lunchtime. He's tough, my boy.'

'Tell him to rest up; the *Mary Kay* is having the day off.'

'Hangover that bad, is it?' Amelia asked.

⁓

By mid-afternoon, Sam felt he might live after all. He spent a few hours house-cleaning and made a fresh batch of sausage rolls using minced lamb mixed with kofta spices, red onion, garlic and chilli, replacing fresh breadcrumbs with panko—a trick revealed by the chef after Sam mentioned he was sometimes held back from making his famous sauso rolls due to a lack of fresh breadcrumbs. He added a couple of eggs, unable to bring himself to separate the yolks to use only the whites—another Marcus suggestion. Then he remembered the yolks were meant to glaze the pastry. In his weakened state, he felt overwhelmed by Marcus's overcomplication of a simple staple.

His phone buzzed.

'Kate,' he said, walking onto the deck where phone reception was clearer. 'All okay?'

'I was wondering about Jimmy's injuries.'

'He'll be home by now. No lasting damage but Amelia has been talking to her lawyer. She's caught the whiff of pay dirt.'

'She's right. Melrose is terrified of the media. Makes you think there's lots to hide. Did you read the file I gave you?'

Sam slapped his forehead. 'Forgot all about it. Tonight, I promise.'

There was a yell, followed by some loud thumping on the door.

'You've got visitors,' Kate said. 'I'll let you go.'

'When do you and Lizzie head to the shack?'

'Tomorrow.'

'There you are, mate,' Richard said, letting himself in. He saw the phone against Sam's ear. 'Sorry,' he whispered.

'You'll need help . . .' Sam said, but the call had been cut.

In the kitchen, Richard peered into the glass window of the oven: 'The sauso rolls are turning to charcoal. What do you want me to do?' he called out.

Sam sprinted to the rescue. Opened the oven door and waved away a plume of smoke. 'Sausage rolls brûlée. A new trend. You're the first to have a taste.'

'Burned, right?'

'Up to a point,' Sam replied, grinning.

He plated up and grabbed his beer. On the deck, the two men hoed into the food. Blackened pastry crumbs gathered around their mouths, in their laps. Sam felt more like his pre-cocktail self with every swallow.

'Heard the crazy old actress went berserk over a missing shoe,' Richard said, rubbing his chin clean. 'A bloodbath, according to the ambos.' He grinned. 'Reminded me of a few family picnics when I was a kid.'

'Considering the woman can barely stand upright in slippers, her reaction over a stiletto was extreme. Wouldn't have bothered you with a recap but thought you should know that Donna threw a punch at Lizzie a few days earlier.'

Richard sat up straighter. 'Know why?'

'You'd have to ask Lizzie. It's just . . . Donna looks like a puff of wind would blow her away, but she's bloody strong when she gets riled, and after the boule . . .'

'Yeah. Lizzie hanging around with that lot when she's out of hospital?'

'Nah. Moving back to her shack with Kate to look after her until she gets the hang of crutches. She won't admit it, but she's scared, and with a broken ankle she'd drop like a stone if Donna had another crack at her.'

'Might call in for a chat to discuss Amelia's charges with that bloke who gets around in the fancy pyjamas.'

'Mike Melrose.'

'That's him.'

'She could've killed Jimmy, you know,' Sam said. 'If we'd been anchored in deeper water, he could've drowned before I got to him to the surface. I reckon that lot knows exactly what happened the night of Cameron's murder, and Donna is at the heart of it.'

'Proof, Sam. Can't do anything without proof. A stoush at a party isn't enough to slap Donna with a murder charge.'

'Take your pepper spray when you call in, mate. Just to be on the safe side.'

'Some days, I wonder what I see in this job,' Richard said, getting up to leave.

Sam saw him to the door then went back to the deck to clear away the empty beer bottles. The neighbourhood possum hissed at him from a high branch and released a stream of piddle followed by the rat-a-tat-tat of poo pellets hitting the deck. Sam resisted the impulse to open another beer and fell into a chair. He suddenly felt exhausted.

∽

He woke feeling cold and damp, his neck stiff. Midnight. He stumbled into the bedroom and flopped on the bed, fully clothed. He had an early start to catch the tide for a delivery to Stringybark Bay, where a high-tech holiday house was being built to comply with new bushfire regulations that effectively doubled the cost of construction and involved enough steel to build a battleship. He was also due to pick up steel plates that would be used as shutters against flames. The house already looked like a posh bomb shelter. He despaired of the world in which his child would grow to an adult; a world where humans put up barriers against nature instead of working with her. Common sense trashed by a suicidal appetite for profit and the unshakeable belief humans would always out-manoeuvre catastrophe with bold creative thinking and enough ready cash. It occurred to him that he was sounding like an old fella who was set in his ways and wondered if his inflexibility lay at the core of his difficulties with Kate. He vowed to accept change with more grace than disapproval in the future but was consoled, nevertheless, by his firm conviction that kindness and compassion invariably trumped greed and that change should always be scrutinised instead of blindly accepted.

∽

The following morning, Jimmy appeared for work with a black eye and cut lip, bruises on his cheek and scratches on his hands where they'd scraped the seabed, but good as gold, he insisted, his tone verging on belligerent.

'You look trashed, mate,' Sam observed mildly, 'but if you want to come along you ride to my orders or I call your mum to come and get you.'

'Longfella'll look after me. Saved me life, he did. Me mum's off shoppin' to get him a hero-sized bone.'

Hearing his name, the mutt looked up, alert.

'Settle,' Jimmy told the dog soothingly. 'There's just me and Sam. The nutters have all gone home.'

The man and the boy loaded twenty slippery steel plates, each as large as a queen-size bed, onto the deck of the *Mary Kay*. Jimmy's feet throbbed with anxiety, and his young, freckled face was creased so deeply Sam got a hint of how the kid would look when he was old enough to apply for the pension. He followed Sam's orders to the letter as Sam watched him like a hawk. One wrong move, and the kid could be sliced down the middle by a sharp edge. One near-death experience in a lifetime was enough. By the end of the delivery, Sam felt wrung out.

'You did well today, Jimmy,' he said. 'Trickiest delivery I've ever made. Couldn't have done it without you.'

Jimmy's face shone with pride. He swiped his brow with his wrist and nodded in agreement. 'It was a bastard job, alright. Oops— sorry, Sam, me language . . .'

'A bastard,' Sam agreed.

They laughed and high-fived.

Sam steered the *Mary Kay* serenely through the open waterway towards the café, the sky flecked with clouds, a silver sheen coming through the blue so the morning looked buffed.

Onshore, the clock edged towards 7 am. Bleary-eyed young tradies, with shaved heads and hairless cheeks, their boyish legs awash with tatts, were lined up in the Square. Sam noticed trends were changing. Egg-and-bacon rolls nudged aside by avocado, tomato and feta wraps. Meat pies—even Ettie's famous chunky beef and mush-room—replaced by noodle salads. The one unchanging constant? Coffee, but with a jumbo size now in the line-up.

Sam narrowed his eyes. 'Up ahead, Jimmy, notice anything wrong?'

The kid squinted. 'The Briny's deck. Looks like it's gunna topple.'

'Some incompetent bastard in a gin palace has whanged it and scarpered without owning the responsibility.' He checked the time. Still too early for the grey brigade to flock onto the deck to read their newspapers over smoko. He dialled Ettie, who failed to pick up. He tried Marcus instead. 'Where are you, mate?'

'Once more I am helping at the café. My beloved is recovering still from the turmoil of recent unfortunate events.'

'Wouldn't have anything to do with that rocket fuel you mixed, would it?'

'For medicinal purposes only, but perhaps I was a little too anxious to see to the quick restoration of the good humour of one and all . . .'

'Anyway, Chef, the reason I'm calling is the western pylon of the deck has been bumped hard. I'm going to chuck a rope around it and pull it back in alignment with the might of the *Mary Kay*, but it's only a temporary fix, mate, until I have a closer look at what needs to be done.' As he spoke, he saw Marcus burst onto the deck with his phone held to his ear.

'*Ach mein gott*, this is not good,' Marcus said, wagging his head, disturbing the erectness of his toque. 'The deck, we will fence it off right now.' He disappeared inside.

Moments later, Ettie and Jenny appeared. They took a close look and went back inside. By the time the *Mary Kay* had done her best—though not enough to make it safe—a sign had been strung across the entrance to the deck forbidding entry.

Sam took his time inspecting the damage, testing the strength of the boards under his feet, the stability of the railing.

Jimmy followed as closely as a shadow, mimicking Sam's movements. 'Pretty bad, eh?' Jimmy said, his hands on his hips. For the second time, Sam was struck by an image of Jimmy in his old age.

'New pylon, a few supporting beams replaced. Could have been worse. Keep an eye on the *Mary Kay* while I go inside.'

He stepped over the sign. Ettie, the chef and Jenny were waiting for him. Jenny passed him a jumbo coffee. 'Thanks, love,' he said. He took a long sip and then explained: 'You need Mick and his men. They're doing a job in Blue Swimmer Bay but I'll tell them this is urgent.' He took another long sip. 'Might be an idea to close the café for the day.'

Marcus looked shocked. 'But why, when it is possible to keep people away from this dangerous area with this clever and informative sign Jenny has already made?'

'Ever heard a pylon being hammered into the seabed?' Sam asked.

'The noise is horrendous,' Ettie explained. 'It will drive people off anyway.'

'Ah, yes, of course, it is clear to me now.'

'Best get this fixed up as soon as possible.'

'Sooner the better,' Ettie said decisively. For once, she didn't sweat on the cost. The café was making money. Her credit at the bank was gold-plated. She'd never been in such a rosy financial condition in her life and she was aware she owed a good portion of her newfound security to Kate's clear-minded and tough frugality.

Sam called Mick and explained the problem. After he cut the call, he said there was no need to rush. Mick wouldn't be able to start work until noon.

'So. We will work to keep our customers happy with food and drinks which they will partake of in the Square,' Marcus said, sketching a little bow to indicate his satisfaction with this strategy.

Ettie cupped Jimmy's damaged cheek tenderly. 'A special breakfast for a brave young man. Name your pleasure.'

Jimmy dragged a toe across the floorboards and scrunched the ends of his T-shirt. 'Aw, anything'll do. It's gotta beat me mum's Weet-Bix.'

The crew behind the counter fell into their well-oiled routine, moving smoothly around each other in the small space, sidestepping, reversing, dipping and swaying, like dancers without music. The chef took orders for hot food, which Ettie cooked on the hotplate. He called coffee orders over his shoulder to Jenny. Her memory was infallible. He spread butter on rolls, mashed avocadoes tickled with garlic, chill, salt and pepper, and lemon juice. Sliced tomatoes and crumbled feta. Added a touch of glazed balsamic because he was, after all, a chef, and reputations were made with little creative flourishes that lifted the ordinary to the extraordinary.

Sam, putting aside the issue of health and longevity on the basis he'd burned off the downside of cholesterol for the day already, ordered two egg-and-bacon rolls, a banana smoothie for Jimmy, another coffee for himself (even though he knew it would make his hands shake) and an extra side of bacon for Longfellow. Then he retired to the *Mary Kay*, where he and the boy sat on the deck back-to-back like bookends, their knees raised, the dog's eyes following the progress of food to mouth, food to mouth, patient until Jimmy opened the little white paper bag soaked in grease and handed him his share. When they were done, Sam gathered the plates. Jimmy wiped his greasy hands on his shorts and stretched out, hands under his head, his eyes closed. The mutt wriggled closer, his snout on Jimmy's chest, clocking the boy's steady heartbeat.

After a while, the chef came out, with a short black in a tiny white cup. Ettie arrived moments later. 'We've decided that's it for the day,' she said. 'I'm off to collect Lizzie from hospital. Kate's packing. Marcus will provision the expedition. We'll all meet back here at lunchtime.'

'And I am reliably informed that the pylon which is leaning in the wrong direction will be corrected before opening time tomorrow morning,' Marcus said, looking at Sam for confirmation.

'All in order, but what a bloody mess when you put the last few days together,' Sam said, shaking his head. 'It'll go down in the history of the *Mary Kay* as a stellar conjunction of catastrophes.'

'You can say that again,' Jimmy chipped in. He sat up, drew his knees under his chin. 'Lucky we're all still upright and breathin', although every time I mention the party, me mum takes to her bed moanin' till I bring a wet face washer to put over her eyes. Reckons seein' me lyin' there, she wanted to die as well. Right after she kyboshed that Donna dame, she said, and tipped her over the side to feed the sharks. She's got a temper, me mum, though you'd never think it till now.'

'Your job for the foreseeable future, mate, is to slap your mitt over my mouth if you hear me even hint at another offer to host a bash on the *Mary Kay*,' Sam said with strong feeling.

'How hard, Sam?' the boy asked. 'How hard can I slap me mitt?'

CHAPTER TWENTY-FIVE

LIZZIE SUGGESTED HER LAND ROVER for the trip to her old shack, but Kate baulked at the idea. 'Too many gear shifts and no power steering,' she explained. Now she stood in the scant shade of a sad casuarina, eyeing four lanes of tightly parked vehicles ranging from sun-bleached bombs to urban tractors, her mind a blank as she struggled to remember where she last stowed her small city car. She wandered up and down and finally discovered it buried under a layer of casuarina needles with rivulets of bird shit running down the windscreen. Using her hand, she swiped at the dead leaves. In the car, she turned on the wipers and sprayed water which only smeared the glass. Squinting through the blur, she drove slowly to the Square, unable to recall what had drawn her to Cook's Basin in the first place.

Fast Freddy, dressed in his going-to-town clothes of jeans and a windcheater and on his way to do his weekly grocery shopping, sighed at the sight of the car and suggested it might be wise to avoid parking under trees given the increased airborne activity in the area.

'Seagulls,' Kate said, disgusted.

'Like all creatures, they have a role,' he replied. 'But I believe they are innocent in this case. It's bats making the mess, ably assisted by common mynas.'

'Not sure what role *they* play,' Kate said. She was not a fan of the aggressive little black-eyed birds that hung around the Square scavenging titbits and destroying the nests and eggs of native birds.

'It's true, they don't belong here,' Freddy said, which was as far as he would go when it came to wishing them away. He trotted off to the café to find a bucket of warm water and a rag to attack the offending windscreen.

On his return, Kate smiled at this man whom she both liked and respected. Taking the bucket from him, she said, 'Your clothes. Might be better if I do the job. But thank you.'

'A pleasure, Miss Kate.'

Marcus emerged from the café, followed by Jenny, both loaded with supplies. 'The café is closed for the day because of this wretched pylon business and this food would be on its way to Jimmy's worm farm, so it is good, yes, that now it has a purpose,' he said.

Kate popped open the boot. Just then, Ettie arrived in her car, tooting her horn, Lizzie strapped into the passenger seat. Marcus rushed forward to open the door and helped Lizzie struggle from the seat, her leg in a moon boot. Lizzie used his shoulder for support to hop over to Kate's car.

'We are prepared for two weeks away from home, although, of course, it is still your home, I understand this,' Marcus said. 'Naturally, as providore for this situation in which your find yourself through no fault of your own, I have considered breakfast, lunch and dinner with extra desserts and cakes for times spent recuperating when a small taste of sweetness is required to lift the spirit.'

'Such kindness, Chef. How can I ever repay you?' Lizzie said.

The chef waved away her thanks. 'This business of repayment is unnecessary among friends. This community takes care of its own. That is a fact.'

'In truth, though, I am a blow-in who hasn't been part of the community for thirty years.'

'Once a member, always a member,' Ettie said. 'And as we all know, most people who leave eventually find their way back.'

'All done?' Kate asked, feeling the leave-taking might descend into morbid sentimentality, which Lizzie would find embarrassing and she would find irksome.

Marcus stacked and closed the boot, brushing flakes of bird shit off his hands, his face a picture of horror. '*Mein gott*, this shit is good for growing vegetables, this I know, but even as a chef who loves vegetables this is too much for me. I must wash my hands this minute so right now this is goodbye.' He bolted across the Square to the café.

Ettie laughed and gave Kate a hug. Freddy, who'd hung around, said: 'Good health and happiness to you both.'

Kate felt a lump rise in her throat and inclined her head in thanks. She slid behind the wheel, adjusting the seat to allow for her increasing girth, threw the car into reverse, swung onto the sandy track that led away from the Square, changed gear and hit the accelerator with a heavy foot. Lizzie fell back in her seat.

'Sorry,' Kate said, horrified.

'I'll send you the physio's bill,' Lizzie responded wryly.

To make up for her carelessness, Kate drove with exaggerated care. At the point where sand met bitumen and a left turn headed to the crowded suburbs, right to the misty rainforests of the national park, she slowed to a stop. Lizzie smiled her thanks.

Two kilometres further on, the sealed road ended and a dirt track began. 'My turn-off is up ahead, hard to see unless you're looking for it,' Lizzie said. 'Hope this little car is stronger than it looks, because it's a rough road to the house. Potholes deep enough to swim after rain. Take it slowly. There! See!' She pointed at a chalky track squeezed by thick vegetation on both sides.

Kate changed to second gear to make the turn. Back wheels skidded in a soft spot.

'Keep going,' Lizzie urged, 'or we'll be bogged.'

Scrappy ti-trees and acacias scraped the sides of the car, a sound like fingernails on a blackboard. The car dipped into ruts, climbed out of them, a tyre spinning every so often. Kate clutched the wheel white-knuckled until the sand gave way to a hard, red clay surface for a while. Further along, they crossed a plateau of tessellated rocks, a wide track running off to the left. 'This it?' she asked, judging their position too far west of the shack, her inner compass telling her to go east.

'See that angophora, the tree with the pink trunk? It's less than twenty metres to the house from there.' And then a post-and-rail fence, hanging by a thread of timber to a crooked gate post. A wall of trees, shrubs and grasses, dense and prickly, a hostile barrier to Lizzie's sanctuary. A narrow cutting, barely a car's width. 'You wouldn't have seen this part when you were here last,' Lizzie said. 'I keep it looking feral to deter anyone who might want to call in without an invitation. Go left. The driveway, such as it is, runs around the perimeter. Stop at the back of the house. As close as you can to the porch.'

Kate's apprehension faded as she got her bearings. She reached the porch, switched off the engine, rested her head on the steering wheel. 'I knew you were tough,' she said, 'but I had no idea how tough until I made that drive.'

Lizzie sorted a set of keys she pulled from her bag. 'Blue dot fits the rear door. Red dot works on the front. The front door can be tricky. Heavy rain, the timber swells and the door sticks. Mostly I use the back door.'

Kate nodded. She got out of the car and dragged the crutches from the back seat, holding them ready. 'A few steps to negotiate,' she said. 'Think you can manage?'

Lizzie ignored the crutches and hopped to the steps. Artie-style, she dragged her way to the top on her backside, moon boot bumping all the way. 'A doddle,' she said, happy with herself.

Kate helped Lizzie settle in the kitchen, a stool to rest her broken ankle, a rug for her knees, a glass of water close at hand.

Lizzie began to laugh. 'Look at us,' she said. 'An old woman with a broken ankle and a young woman about to have a baby, hiding out on an isolated escarpment from a former soapie star with a bad temper and a powerful right hook. I should be upset but, really, it's hilarious.'

Kate raised her eyebrows and shrugged. 'Sort of.'

'The spiders have moved in,' Lizzie said, eyes directed at the ceiling. 'Place smells mouldy—more so than usual.'

Kate lit the fire: the only unfailing cure for damp, according to the old woman. Then she unpacked the car, stacked food in the fridge, filled an old kettle and hung it on the blackened hook that extended over the flames. By the time the water was boiling, Lizzie was slumped in sleep.

Leaving her to rest, Kate wandered around the house, inhaling the scent of char, the mustiness of an old house closed and unlived in. There were two bedrooms, the larger one facing north-west and catching the afternoon sun that cruelly highlighted dust motes and a light patina of grime. A cedar wardrobe, chest of drawers, a cane bedside table. Double bed. Lizzie's room. The other room a spare, filled with bits and pieces—embroidered footstool, empty baskets, a couple of chests Kate recognised as glory boxes, where once upon a time young women stored their precious linens to make a home when they married. Single bed. On top of a wardrobe, much smaller, a suitcase covered in ancient stickers for ocean liners long decommissioned and reduced to scrap. In the formal parlour, a floral couch, two matching armchairs, scratched coffee table, standard lamp with a skew-whiff shade and the old leak, resplendent like a great green bloom on the ceiling. Under her feet, the stink of damp wool. All of it on the brink of ruin. She guessed Cliffy had done his best but lost heart when Lizzie decamped.

At the back of the house, a bathroom with floor-to-ceiling windows. A deep, Japanese-style bathtub tucked elegantly in a corner with a view of the garden. Kate ran the hot water tap. Cold.

She found a duster, broom, a bucket and mop in a cupboard and went to work, taking pleasure from standing back, measuring the transformation.

Finally, with nothing more to do, she tiptoed back into the kitchen and, lowering herself into a chair smelling faintly of wood smoke and tobacco, she dozed. The clock ticked on the mantelpiece. Dorothy gazed out of her picture frame without judgement.

Flames leaped then dropped to a murmur, a dull glow by the time Lizzie stirred and Kate snapped awake.

'Tea?' Kate asked, shaking off drowsiness, getting to her feet. 'Chicken stew for dinner, okay?' She stirred the coals under the kettle. 'How's your ankle?'

'God bless painkillers.'

Kate made the tea. Lizzie inhaled the steam and tried to guess. 'Ginger? Lemon? Something else. I can't pick it.'

'Honey,' Kate said.

Lizzie sipped. 'Ah. Yes. If I'd tasted . . .'

The clock had barely struck six o'clock when Kate served dinner in a bowl to eat in front of the fire.

'Suppose I'll owe you a year of babysitting after this,' Lizzie said.

'Two years at least.' Kate took Lizzie's empty bowl, washed up.

The old woman requested a helping hand to the bathroom. 'Then bed,' she said.

Later, Kate sat in front of the fire, the achy half-alive smells a map of the past. Dorothy's healing brews. Lizzie's love of eucalyptus oil. Beneath the floorboards, the gamey scent of bush critters, disturbed earth. And soon, soft grunting, scratching, the click of toenails on the verandah, the rustle of leaves stirred by a breath of wind. She went outside, just to look, get a sense of the place. A wallaby bounced away and into the night. And there, on a fence post, an owl or frogmouth, still as a stone. Higher, wings flapping. A bat, perhaps. She shivered. Freddy insisted bats had their place but that didn't mean she had to like them. All around, heavy and rich, the herby smell of fresh grass, the underlying pungency of farm animals. She felt a lurch of happiness, wrapped her arms around

her chest, held tight to keep the feeling. Eventually, she went inside
to clean her teeth.

⟨⟨⟩⟩

Kate woke before sunrise with a sore back from a strange bed. She
made a cup of tea and took it to the verandah. Dawn crept forward
indecisively, first grey, followed by pale lemon, a moment later a
hint of pink. Then an explosion of burning orange. She stared into
the bush, the air whiffy with cow dung. A sound, not right. Kate
stiffened. Hairs on her neck rising, goosebumps breaking out on her
arms. Ear cocked, listening. Quiet footsteps. A stealthy approach.
She looked around for a weapon.

'It's you, lass!' Cliffy said, coming around the corner of the
verandah, brandishing a cattle prod like a sabre.

'Cliffy! You frightened the daylights out of me.' Hand on her
chest to steady her breathing.

'Saw a strange car arrive yesterday and figured a few squatters
might have thought they'd found a holiday house. Planned to
give them a hurry up with me cattle prod. All bluff. Me cattle do
as they're told, and the batteries have been flat for forty years.' He
rested the prod against the wall.

Kate made a shushing sound. 'Lizzie is still sleeping,' she said,
pointing towards the bedroom.

'The old girl couldn't stay away, eh?'

'It's a bit more . . . complicated than that.'

'Well, seeing as I'm here, a cuppa wouldn't go astray. Toast, too,
if you can manage. Bolted out of me house on a mission without
botherin' to fuel up.'

'I'll see if there's any apricot jam hanging around, too, shall I?'

The irony whizzed over Cliffy's head, and he gave Kate the thumbs-up.

Lizzie called out as Kate tiptoed past the bedroom. 'Visitors already, I hear.'

'Cliffy, checking us out.' Kate knocked and went in. 'Crutches or an arm to the bathroom?'

'Crutches. Might as well get used to them. Morning, Cliffy.'

Behind Kate, Cliffy frowned, taking in the scene. 'Let you outta my sight for a minute and look what you've done to yourself,' he said. 'Hold the tea for half an hour. I'll skedaddle home. Those crutches'll kill a woman your age—no offence intended, you understand—and Agnes's wheelchair is somewhere in the shed.' He scampered off, letting the door slam behind him.

Lizzie and Kate settled on the verandah, the morning sun warming their blood. Satin bowerbirds, a rare flock of them, fossicked in the grass, nervy at the slightest sound and dull until spooked, their wings flashing iridescent green as they fled. A couple of magpies strutted, circling the interlopers, plotting to steal back their turf.

They were on their second cuppas by the time Cliffy returned, a bulky folded wheelchair tucked uncomfortably under his arm, the sheen of effort on his weather-beaten phizzog. He dropped it in front of Lizzie with a grunt, opened it out, slapped the seat to shift the dust. 'A few cobwebs and a wonky wheel that won't take much to fix—it'll do you till you're back on both feet.'

Kate went to make a fresh pot of tea and cook a full breakfast: bacon, eggs, toast, the lot. Cliffy snaffled her vacated chair, gave Lizzie a sideways inspection he hoped she wouldn't notice. As if.

'I'm fine, Cliffy. Boating accident, nothing more.'

Cliffy harrumphed, not persuaded. Kate came back and placed a tray on his lap. The sight of it made him chortle with appreciation.

While Cliffy ate, Kate wiped upholstery, scoured spokes, dislodged a batch of redback spider eggs from under the wheelchair's seat. Cliffy patted his stomach when he was finished, and Kate took the tray inside. Cliffy made a beeline for the shed, where he found a screwdriver and a can of WD-40 and came back, tinkering with the wonky wheel until it spun freely. 'She'll run like a Rolls-Royce now.' He dragged an oily rag from a pocket to wipe his greasy hands. 'So, those celebrities not all they were cracked up to be, eh?'

'It's a long story, Cliffy, and right now, we're a little short of hot water. Would you mind showing Kate how the system works?'

Cliffy sighed, pushed to his feet. 'Story will wait, I expect.'

Lizzie turned to Kate. 'Hot water runs on solar energy. No sun, no hot showers.'

'Character-building, it is,' said Cliffy, regarding Kate's look of dismay with evident satisfaction.

Kate and Cliffy headed in the direction of the creek. A few grey clouds rose in the west, white and tight like cauliflowers. Cliffy gave the sky a thorough going-over then picked up the pace. 'It's gunna pelt down shortly. Better hoof it, lass, if it's not too much trouble for you and the bub.'

A splatter of rain fell on Kate's forearm, a drop on her nose. She hurried to keep up with the old man, almost jogging. The sky went dark. Then there was a metallic smell, the bush went silent, alert. Cliffy reached the creek bank, waited a minute for Kate to catch up then pointed down. 'There's your extra water source,' he said. 'Seeing as how Mother Nature is set to fill the tank today, you'll be right, but just in case . . . over there. Under the corrugated-iron shelter with the solar panels on top. That's the pump. Connected to an underground pipeline to the house. All perfectly legal, in case you're wondering. Creek's never run dry. Not in my lifetime, anyway.'

Raindrops plinked on leaves. Cliffy stuck out his tongue, held out a hand, to get a feel for what was coming. 'Full and fat. Best get back to the house to put out the pots and pans. That bloody roof. More holes than a sieve. Here, hold on to me hand. Five more minutes and we'll cop a drenching.'

On the veranda, Lizzie, Cliffy and Kate watched the storm roar over their heads. 'Fizzer,' Cliffy muttered. 'All bluster and no substance. Like politicians.' He got to his feet, taking a second while his knees unlocked with a click, and said he'd be back if they needed him, but he had cows to tend to, including Clarabelle and her calf, both doing very nicely, thank you, although with more bossy Jersey than laidback Holstein in her she'd bullied her way to the top of the pecking order and made a few enemies along the way. He also had a list of chores too long for toilet roll.

'Clarabelle was a terrible mother,' Lizzie said, watching Cliffy head into the bush.

'It's my greatest fear,' Kate said softly.

'What is?'

'Why was Clarabelle a lousy mother?' Kate asked, evading the question.

'Cows hide their calves, did you know that? It's to keep them safe while they graze, often quite a distance away. Clarabelle—ridiculous name but it was Cliffy's choice—would hide her calf and forget where she'd left her. Forgot she even had a calf half the time. Cliffy and I would go looking for the poor little thing at the end of the day when Clarabelle's bag was so full it looked ready to burst. It took her about three weeks to get the hang of motherhood. In the meantime, the calf learned to stick close to me until her mother turned up.'

'Not sure I'll ever get the hang of motherhood,' Kate said. She expected a quick, Ettie-style reassurance but Lizzie knitted her brows and moved her broken ankle into a more comfortable position.

'Not everyone is born with a strong maternal instinct,' she said. 'What was your mother like?'

'Narcissistic. Cruel. Mostly absent.'

'And yet you turned out alright. Clarabelle's calf turned out beautifully, too. Sweetest nature in the world.'

'I never asked. The water. I know where it comes from but how does it get hot?'

'Oh, there's a switch in a panel on the back porch. Cliffy didn't show you? Never touch it if the batteries are below eighty per cent. You'll drain the power in a jiffy, which buggers the batteries long term.'

'Glad we got that sorted.'

⁘

For the rest of the morning, Lizzie practised using the wheelchair, rolling up and down the hallway, turning into her bedroom, the kitchen. After lunch, she said she'd had enough exercise for the day and might have a lie-down for a while. 'I can manage on my own,' she told Kate, who'd risen to help.

While Lizzie rested, Kate—knowing she couldn't put it off any longer—went online and bought the deluxe newborn baby package which included everything from a bassinet to a remedy for nappy rash. Ettie would be thrilled, but the purchase made Kate feel slightly ill. She wasn't ready. She'd never be ready. She called Sam to ask if he could pick the package up from the café when it was delivered.

'How's it going?' he asked.

'Lizzie's already looking after herself with the help of an antique wheelchair her neighbour found in his shed.'

'So, you'll be back soon?'

'We'll see. It's quite lovely here. Peaceful.'

'No outboards, eh?'

'Something like that. How's Jimmy doing?'

'His bruises are turning yellow but he's fine.'

'Melrose apologised to anyone yet?'

'Nah. The silence out of that house is deafening. Hey! Got a word for you.'

'Go on,' Kate said, resigned, but in a good way.

'Antwacky.'

'I give up.'

'C'mon, Kate, you didn't even have a stab at it.'

'No idea, Sam.'

'Hang on a sec. I've forgotten myself.' He checked Simon's messages. 'Old-fashioned or out-of-date.'

'Good one. Simon's on a roll. I'd better go. Lizzie's stirring.'

Kate broke out one of the chef's more exotic treats—a soft meringue concoction perched above a lemon custard only slightly disturbed by the road trip and held in place by crisp pastry—and laid the tray for afternoon tea. Afterwards, she suggested, they could play cards. Or Scrabble. Dominoes. Draughts. Chess. Games she'd seen stacked on a shelf in the parlour.

'The garden,' said Lizzie. 'I'd like to take a tour.'

'In the wheelchair?' Kate said with disbelief.

'Why not? There are pathways. Not too rough for my chariot.'

Kate was doubtful but Lizzie insisted.

'Let's have a go, shall we? If it's too hard, we'll give up. Do you mind?'

How could she? It wouldn't take much, she thought, to rid the pathway of twigs and branches. The leaves wouldn't be a problem. A helpful push if the chair got stuck in a rut or the wheel jammed by a stone. 'Nothing ventured . . .'

Lizzie gave her a smile that would take the sting out of any mishaps, barring another broken limb. Kate shoved the thought aside before it took hold.

It was rough going, but they had both known it would be. The chair squealed and groaned in protest. Cliffy's repair job held off disaster but only just.

'Oh!' Lizzie said.

'What?' Kate asked, looking around for trouble.

'The boronia. It's dead.' Lizzie reached out and broke off a thin branch, snapped it between her fingers. 'Not enough water. I've nursed that bush like a needy child for years. Ever smelled boronia, Kate? It's so . . . extravagant.' She bent forward, scratched away the soil around the roots. 'Not a shoot anywhere. Done for, I'm afraid. Gardens don't wait for anyone, not even a woman who has spoken endless words of comfort.'

'You make plants sound human.'

'Watch them closely and they'll speak to you. *More water please. A dash of nitrogen, if you don't mind. No fruit without blood and bone, potash.* I give them all they demand but speak firmly if they refuse to behave and cut them down to size if they get arrogant or pushy.'

'My father . . .'

'Yes?'

'He liked to grow strawberries. As I recall, the birds were very well fed through summer.'

'A battle since time began.'

'Will you ever go back to Stringybark Bay?' Kate asked.

'Turns out I'm a solitary person by nature.' Lizzie smiled grimly. 'You'd think I'd have realised that by now. I thought I'd be able to fit in, but . . .'

'It wasn't your fault, Lizzie. Everyone in that house seems to be stuck in a web, with Donna like a black widow spider at the centre, ready to pounce and devour any transgressor.'

They made their way slowly back to the house. 'The GeriEcsastsies. They must be fully aware of Donna's . . .'

'Oh yes. There's no doubt about it.'

'Then why . . . ?'

Lizzie shrugged. 'There'll be a reason; there always is.'

⁓

After dinner, Lizzie asked Kate to find a bottle of cognac from a stash of emergency booze, hidden in the cupboard under the sink with the cleaning supplies. She'd forgotten it existed until now.

'Medicinal,' she said, taking a sip.

Kate stoked the fire.

'How do you feel?' Lizzie asked.

Kate looked surprised. 'Fine. Why?'

Lizzie smiled. 'You been uprooted from your home, there's a baby on the way, you're looking after an old woman with a broken ankle and you've spent the afternoon pushing a wheelchair over very rough terrain. I thought you might be tired.'

'Oh, right. No, I'm okay.' Changing the subject, she asked, 'Have you ever left here for long periods?'

'Oh, I've come and gone over the years. I travelled a fair bit when I was younger.'

'But you always returned.'

'Whenever the white noise got too loud,' Lizzie said. 'Humanity and its . . . demands. So many agendas. Nothing quite as simple as it first seems. Everyone stampeding towards . . . well, I don't know. Fame is ephemeral and wealth doesn't deter death. In many ways, this falling-down little shack has kept me sane.'

'I happen to love this falling-down little shack. But I'm curious: what's the longest time you've spent here without any human contact?'

'Three months. Would have been longer but I ran out of flour and Cliffy called to say there were a few water issues to discuss. He would have been so disappointed if I failed to provide a plate of hot scones with jam.'

Kate smiled. 'It's always about food, isn't it? Ettie believes providing pleasure for others is the solid foundation of a fulfilling life.'

'Pleasure? I guess so. For Cliffy, it's more about memories than comfort, I suspect. He told me his mother made the best scones in the district and his wife, Agnes, followed the same recipe and technique before she died. Each bite of a scone, he says, evokes a golden moment and memory from his past. Tell me, Kate, what is the most powerful food reminder of your childhood?'

'The strawberries. My father talked to them, urged them to sweetness. They tasted the way you hope and imagine. I've never found any to equal them.'

'If you look around near the chook pen, you'll find some runners.'

'Oh no. I'm not a gardener.'

'No one is until they start.'

'My mother used to say that gardening was a fool's hobby that consisted of ninety-nine per cent perspiration and one per cent success.'

'I'll bet she liked the strawberries, though.'

CHAPTER TWENTY-SIX

SAM TOOK THE MORNING OFF to read Kate's files on the GeriEcstasies.

He'd planned to tackle them on the privacy of his deck, but before he'd finished the first page, he realised only a strong brew would keep him awake. 'Too many zeros,' he muttered, flipping through page after page of financial columns printed spreadsheet-style. He gathered the paperwork, thinking that if anyone but Kate had asked him to read what came close to the way he imagined Swahili might look, he'd launch the *Mary Kay* on a circumnavigation of the world. He wasn't over her. Not yet. Possibly never, he conceded.

Sam regretted his decision the minute he stepped inside the café and Ettie descended on him in what felt like an assault.

'Spoken to Kate? How is she? How's she getting along with Lizzie? Have they run out of supplies? Marcus and I could deliver a food parcel after we close. Might be an idea to check on them both anyway.'

'They're both doing fine,' he reported when he could get a word in edgeways. 'And they've only been gone for two days, so I'm sure their supplies have barely been touched.'

'Yes, but . . .'

He searched for some way to reassure her and was hit by a brainwave. 'Kate did mention that a large carton of baby supplies will be delivered shortly.'

Ettie, instantly diverted, perked up. 'So, she's getting ready for the baby. Knew there was nothing to worry about. She's a deadline girl. Always falls over the finishing line. Typical journalist.'

Sam scratched his forehead, at a loss for words. In his experience, Kate organised everything with enough time to allow for a complete rework if necessary and kept a controlling finger on every stage of even the simplest project. 'Definitely a step in the right direction,' he said, settling for diplomacy. He ordered a jumbo coffee, suppressing a niggling suspicion he was becoming reliant on the caffeine fix, and held up the file. 'Kate's set me a bit of homework. A raspberry muffin might be in order, too.'

'What sort of homework?' Ettie asked suspiciously.

'Well, Ettie, if I knew, I wouldn't have to read the stuff, would I?'

'Give it to me when you've finished. I might be able to help.'

He craned his neck to see over Ettie's head. 'How's my smoko coming along?'

Jenny gave him the thumbs-up and put a large mug on the counter. His muffin was in a brown paper bag next to it. Sam grabbed the lot and bolted for the deck.

By the time he'd finished reading, the tide was dropping and a cool wind ripped across the surface of the water with a feverish urgency. Like Kate, he was baffled by a group of multi-millionaires choosing to reside in a tough location more suited to young, fit people with a knowledge of boats and a degree in the unreliability of winds, tides and weather. He couldn't see how the information could be of much use, but he invited Richard Baines to stop by his place after work on the basis that the policeman might have a better idea of what to do with it.

'Should I bring pizza?' Richard suggested.

'Good on you.'

'Ham and pineapple or the lot?'

'Your call. Just hold the anchovies, if you wouldn't mind.'

'Best part,' Richard grumbled before ending the call.

Sam looked at his watch, decided he'd better fetch Jimmy and try to knock over a few jobs in the hours left to him.

At the end of the day, Sam and Jimmy secured the *Mary Kay* on her mooring and steered the tinnie back to Sam's jetty. Sam reminded Jimmy he was due to fetch his scraps from the café and the kid set off for his own boat at a sprint, the dog at his heels barking excitably. Sam marvelled at the energy. He felt physically hammered which triggered a pang of sympathy for the GeriEcstasies with their ancient bodies and brittle bones.

He climbed the stairs then sat outside to wait for Richard. The smell of pizza arrived a few moments before the police officer. Sam met him at the door, then grabbed a couple of beers and led him to the deck.

'No anchovies, as requested,' Richard said, sounding sad. He placed the box on the table and opened the lid. 'Get into it while it's hot, mate, and tell me what this is all about.'

By the time Richard had heard Sam's account and read the file for himself, they were on their second beer and the moon was high in the sky.

Richard spoke first. 'It's interesting background, but I haven't got a clue what to make of it.'

'Kate reckons once you find out why they moved to Stringybark Bay, you'll solve the murder.'

'Don't want to sound rude or ungrateful, but Kate's not a cop and there's a bit more to it than that—like a small factor known as evidence. Seen any of them about lately?'

'The oldies? Nope. Fast Freddy delivered a stack of groceries to the end of their jetty yesterday. Stuff with a long shelf life.'

'Gone into hibernation, have they, until the dust settles?'

'Looks like it. Fair bit of heavy-duty medical stuff, too, according to Freddy. A drip pole among boxes of bandages and antiseptics. He didn't pry—well, Freddy would never pry—but when he called to say he was on his way, he asked if the community could be of any assistance. Melrose cut him off, told him to deliver and depart. Freddy only mentioned it to me because he felt a potential medical emergency was reason enough to override his moral responsibilities to his customers—his exact words.'

'Mystifying, eh?' Richard grabbed the empty pizza box. 'I'll drop this in the bin at the ferry wharf on my way out.'

'You're a scholar and a gentleman.'

CHAPTER TWENTY-SEVEN

BY THE THIRD DAY IN Lizzie's shack, Kate was satisfied with her routine. She cleaned the kitchen, made the beds, swept the floors and vacuumed the rugs. En route to collect the eggs, she tidied fallen branches to clear the way for Lizzie's late-afternoon tour of the garden, a ritual that lifted the old woman's spirit way beyond her new nightly habit of a small cognac.

'That weed, dear, it's about to go to seed—would you mind giving it a solid yank? Be sure to remove the roots or it will grow back stronger than ever . . . See that shrub? Dead bits need cutting off to bring it back to health. I have the secateurs here. Not too much for you, is it? . . . Those grevilleas. A few flowers in a vase on the kitchen table would look lovely. They like a regular prune anyway.'

Subtle lessons in gardening. Knowledge seeping into Kate's brain. Smoko at 9.30 am. A quick fossick among the chef's goodies for a little something to enliven the tastebuds. Tea sipped and savoured. No rush. An ear out for birdsong, quick repartee trying to identify obscure calls.

'No prize for magpies, Kate. But hear that? A chirrup. Where's it coming from? Can you see the bird?'

Before long, Simpson and Day's *Field Guide to the Birds of Australia* was a permanent fixture on the verandah.

As the days grew longer, the grass, green and lush with spring goodness, seemed to be growing before their eyes. Kate, her stomach tight as a drum, said: 'If a snake is headed towards us, best we see it coming. Where do you keep the mower?'

Under Lizzie's instructions, she checked the oil level, filled the tank and, after three solid yanks, yelped with triumph as the motor caught.

Later, during a lunch of cheese sandwiches embellished with the chef's crunchy gin-pickled cucumbers, Lizzie gave a lyrical account of compost-making. Kate, feigning interest at first, found herself drawn in. The secret was temperature, Lizzie explained. Sixty-five degrees. No hotter and only a degree or two cooler if you must.

'How do you measure the heat?' Kate asked.

'Shove a star picket in the centre of the pile. Should be just bearable to the touch when you pull it out.'

'Er, what's a star picket?'

∽

The following morning, Kate's mobile rang when she was in the middle of fixing breakfast. She briefly considered ignoring it when she didn't recognise the caller ID, but the instinctive curiosity of a journalist trumped making the toast.

'I've had more fun on this quest than I've had since my twenty-first birthday—which was a bit of a fizzer, if you want the truth.'

Kate scrambled to figure out who was on the line and came up blank. 'I'm sorry, I'm not sure who—'

'It's Edith. From the library. You came in a while ago wanting to know about Donna Harris and Mike Melrose.'

'Edith! Of course. How—'

'Sorry it's taken so long, but I had to fit in the research around my daily workload.'

'Yes, I understand. I—'

'There's a pattern. Took me ages to see it. But once I made the connection, it was clear as daylight.'

'I'm sorry, could you—'

'I'm babbling, aren't I? Excitement. I've been working late every night. Pulled out old files that haven't been opened for years. A dead mouse, dried skin hanging off tiny bones, dropped out of one. Gave me a heck of a fright.'

'Please, Edith,' Kate begged. 'Slow down. Start from the beginning.'

'There's too much to explain. I've put together a file. I'll flick it to you by email. Call me if you have any questions. I'm now an expert on the local television industry from the sixties and seventies. No political correctness in those days, I can tell you. What an eye-opener! All those women who have trailblazed in the entertainment industry since then deserve medals. Heroines, every one of them.'

'Thank you, Edith, I—'

'Or maybe I should refer to them as heroes. It's confusing. Oh well. Sending it now. Call me if there's anything else I can do.'

Wondering what had happened to the shy, colourless woman she remembered, Kate put bread in the toaster, set a tray with butter, marmalade, side plates and knives. She re-boiled the kettle, made the tea and carried the tray outside.

'I miss the paintings in the hallway,' she said, joining Lizzie on the verandah.

'Me too.'

'Those ghostly imprints where they've hung are so melancholic.'

As Lizzie poured the tea, Kate asked, 'Have you made a decision about what you want to do?'

'Follow your heart, isn't that what the experts say? I told Cliffy why I'd decided to give up the shack and he told me there was no fool like an old fool. If I dropped dead, he'd be the one who found me, and he's had a fair bit of experience with death and dying, being a farmer and all. There was more but you get the gist. To unravel what I've set in place, though? That's an issue. A big one.'

Kate handed her a plate of toast.

'Don't worry about the inmates,' she said. 'Each of those couples could buy your share without losing a zero from their bottom line. This is about your welfare, Lizzie, not theirs.' Kate gave a little start. 'I almost forgot.' She ran inside and fetched her phone. 'A file is on its way . . . yep, it's arrived.' She finished scrolling and looked up. 'I'll have to read this on a bigger screen. Anything else I can get you before I go to work? Another cuppa?'

'What kind of file?'

Kate looked at her blankly. 'Well, Donna Harris and Mike Melrose, of course. What else would I be interested in?'

cσ

Early in the afternoon, Cliffy returned with Clarabelle and her calf—now grown to a good size and chubby in the hindquarters. Lizzie saw them coming and waved.

'Me own herd was happy to see the back of her,' Cliffy said, after he put them in their paddock, closing the gate behind him securely. 'Likes to get her own way, Clarabelle does. Horace took a fancy to her, though; caught them cuddling up for a week or so. He would've sent flowers if he'd had a credit card handy.'

'He's always been a real smoothie,' Lizzie said.

'Reckon there might be a new young 'un, if you're plannin' on stickin' around for the foreseeable future.'

'Might not ever move from this chair.'

Cliffy nodded. 'Where's the lass?'

'Inside working on her computer.'

'Looks like I'll have to make me own cuppa, then.' He stomped down the hallway to alert Kate to his presence. 'How long you been sittin' there at the kitchen table?' he asked.

'A while,' she replied, without looking up.

He rested a callused hand on her shoulder. 'You're lookin' a bit pale, lass. How about stretchin' your limbs for the sake of the bub and brewin' a pot for the sake of an old man with tired legs and a parched throat? A bite of lunch wouldn't go astray, either.'

Kate looked at her watch, jumped up. 'God, poor Lizzie. She must be starving.'

Cliffy returned to the verandah and settled next to Lizzie, telling her not to worry about giving up her seat seeing as how her ankle was busted. He'd make himself at home on the less comfy one.

'Considerate of you,' Lizzie said with a smile.

Kate appeared in the doorway. 'Mustard with your ham?'

'Wouldn't have it any other way,' Cliffy said. 'Hot mustard. Not that stuff with bits that get stuck in your teeth.'

Kate put her hands on her hips. 'Tell me, Cliffy, what did your last slave die from?'

'That's easy, lass: backchat.'

Kate laughed and reappeared a few minutes later with a plate of sandwiches cut into halves. 'Hot mustard on this side, seeded on the other,' she said, pointing. She placed it on the table between them and went off to fetch the tea tray.

When everyone had helped themselves, Kate sat on the edge of the verandah with her back against a supporting column. She closed her eyes and relished the sun on her face. After a while, she stood. 'I'll leave you two to catch up. Haven't quite finished reading the files.'

After she'd gone inside, a scarred old goanna, his skin faded and hanging loose after the leanness of winter, ambled out of the scrub to cast a gimlet eye at the empty plate.

'Scrounger,' Lizzie said. 'Caught him in the kitchen last year looking for an easy feed, and when I went after him with the broom, he shat all over the place. Took hours to clean up, and the smell . . .' She rolled her eyes and fanned her face with her hand.

Cliffy dragged himself to his feet and Scrounger lumbered off disdainfully. 'I'll get the rake. Keep it handy when you're out here, 'cause he'll be back and bolder each time.'

'There's a brown snake hanging around, too. I haven't mentioned it to Kate in case she locks the doors to keep me inside.'

'What's she workin' on, back there in the kitchen?'

'She's looking for a murderer.'

'I'm hopin' that's a joke, young lady—and if I may say so, not a very funny one.'

'Nope. No joke.'

Without another word, Cliffy went off to fetch the rake. When he returned, he set it within reach of Lizzie and then plonked down in his chair again. 'You better fill me in, Lizzie, 'cause I thought I might have to deliver a baby if the lass was caught short, but catchin' a murderer who might come callin' is way outta my skill set.'

'Delivered many babies, Cliffy?'

'Heaps. Of the four-legged variety, naturally, but can't see as there'd be much difference. Now what's this about a fella that goes around with killin' on his mind?'

'A woman, Cliffy. We think it's a her.'

In what she had come to think of as an eyrie high on the escarpment, Kate considered the implications of Edith's information. Donna Harris was clearly mentally unstable and had been since childhood. Edith's research, which went back as far as Donna's grandparents, revealed a deeply disturbed child with a history of violence. Her parents, both schoolteachers, had been hurriedly transferred from one post to another after complaints about uncontrollable rages in the playground: a black eye for a boy who refused to give up his coloured pencil set; a girl shoved off a swing and her treasured pictures of the royal family grabbed and ripped to pieces; a first grader biffed on the nose when he demanded she return the apple she'd snatched from his lunchbox. These incidents and many more were meticulously recorded by the education department, along with a recommendation that Donna's parents seek psychological treatment for their daughter before she seriously injured another child. The advice was followed, and Donna lived in a psychiatric institution in

Victoria for two years before being released back into her parents' custody. They'd retired from teaching by then or perhaps realised it was no longer an option.

The next public reference to Donna Harris was a small column item in a television industry magazine. She was referred to as an up-and-coming sixteen-year-old actress of *incandescent beauty and enormous talent.* A rising star, according to the columnist, who went on to describe her *lustrous corn silk hair, sea-green eyes and luminosity onscreen.* Kate immediately guessed that Donna had flattered and flirted with the columnist, an overweight middle-aged man, if the picture at the top of the column was accurate. In a story in the same magazine dated a few years later, Donna revealed she'd been born in small country town in the remote south-west corner of Tasmania and had lived a solitary life. Home-schooled by parents who loved literature and the arts, she yearned to be an actress, to bring to life the words of great writers. Buried in the middle of the story was a brief mention of the fact that her parents had died tragically when a burning log fell out of the fireplace and their house caught alight. Donna had been staying with a girlfriend at the time or she, too, would have perished.

Kate knew most journalists would have focused on the tragic background of Donna Harris, by then a leading actress in a top-rating soap opera, using it as a peg on which to hang the rest of the interview. The fact that it was buried way down in the text was so odd it set off alarm bells.

She researched house fires in every town in south-west Tasmania and came up blank. Then she did a general search across the whole state. There were three in a five-year timeframe that might fit. In one, a family of five had died in a blaze caused by a faulty heater.

In another, an elderly man called Stan Greene had fallen asleep in bed with a burning cigarette. In the third, a couple who'd recently moved into the area, Mr and Mrs John Smith, had died due to a gas leak. Bingo, Kate thought—just substitute 'burning log' for 'gas leak'.

✺

Night fell on the escarpment, enclosing the shack in darkness. Lizzie switched on lights while Kate, oblivious to the time, sat in the lurid glow from her computer screen, pressing a key every so often to highlight text, another to cut and save information to a new file. Lizzie was tempted to read over Kate's shoulder but knew it would irritate the young woman. She found *Tinker Tailor Soldier Spy*, an early John le Carré novel, on the bookshelf in the parlour, placed it on her lap and wheeled into the kitchen, awkwardly transferring herself to her armchair to sit in front of the fire. She read a few pages, impressed, as always, by the writer's perfect pitch. Pleased, too, that the plot came back to her instantly. The old brain wasn't as doughy as she'd begun to think.

After a while, the fire dropped to a few hot coals. A chill crept into the room. She tucked a red tartan blanket over her knees.

At the table, Kate rubbed her bare arms and looked across at the fire. Jumped up. 'God, sorry.' She threw on a few dry twigs to bring the coals to life, then a couple of bigger pieces. 'Back in a minute. I need a sweater.'

When she returned, she busied herself in the kitchen, fridge door opening and shutting, the sound of scraping as she filled a saucepan with another of the chef's creations. The scent of lamb, with strong hints of cardamom and lashings of black pepper, shifted Lizzie's

349

senses into overdrive. 'Cloves, garlic, ginger,' she murmured, her tone almost dreamy.

'Rice or potatoes?' Kate asked.

'Potatoes, definitely potatoes.'

Kate shrugged, not sure why it made a difference. She set the table while the potatoes boiled and the curry whispered seductively. The room, bathed in firelight, a little steamy and highly fragrant, peaceful. The women, accustomed to each other by now, comfortably silent.

When dinner was ready, Kate helped Lizzie hop to the table, pushing her chair closer, letting a hand rest on a shoulder for a moment, a gesture that didn't need explaining. Lizzie bent her head, nose almost touching the food, and breathed deeply, her eyes closed, a smile on her lips. 'Something else. Coconut, I think.' She picked up her fork and dipped into the sauce, tasting. 'Definitely coconut. I must ask the chef if he will part with this recipe. It is sublime.'

Curious, Kate asked, 'Did you go to a lot of trouble with food when you lived here?'

'Lived alone, you mean? On and off. Less in the last few years. What do you think? A spoon for the sauce?'

Kate got up and fetched two from the dresser drawer.

After they finished eating, Kate got up from the table to clear the dishes. 'Dessert? There's some lemon tart or apple crumble.' Her back was turned to Lizzie as she neatly stacked the dirty dishes in the sink.

'I don't want to pull rank,' Lizzie said, careful to keep her tone light, 'but the woman nearly killed Jimmy and could have crippled me for life. If there's anything relevant in that file you've been reading for most of the day, I'd like to know. Lemon tart, please, no cream.'

Kate fossicked in the fridge. Found the container and carefully slid a slice onto a small dessert plate with a border of forget-me-nots.

'You're not having any?' Lizzie asked.

Kate shook her head. 'Indigestion. The curry might have been a step too far.'

She served Lizzie and then filled the kettle, throwing a few more small pieces of wood on the fire. Prepared the teapot, set out mugs, removed the cognac from the dresser cupboard ready for Lizzie's nightcap.

Then, sitting with both elbows on the table, her hands tucked under her chin, Kate said, 'Okay. From the top. Donna was a disturbingly violent child. The details are sketchy, but it's clear the violence escalated until her parents, both schoolteachers, had no choice but to place her in a psychiatric institution when she was a teenager. She spent two years there. Now, I'm making a leap here, and I could be wrong, but I'm fairly certain that when she was sixteen years old she murdered her parents.'

Lizzie gasped. 'But why? Why would she kill the people who loved her most?'

'They signed their daughter into an institution for the criminally insane.'

'Revenge,' Lizzie murmured, rubbing her forehead as though she'd developed a headache. 'Cross Donna and pay a price.'

'Her parents' death was buried in an interview at the beginning of her career, when she mentioned losing her parents in a housefire. It was so odd. Why would anyone bury information that would be a cover story under normal circumstances? There had to be a reason.

I had what Artie would call one of his gut feelings and checked the magazine's masthead. Michael Melrose was editor. A year later, he'd been replaced by someone called Colin Bibra and Actors Equity listed Melrose as Donna's agent.'

Lizzie pulled her tart towards herself and took a bite. 'Love at first sight, the desire to protect?'

'Maybe,' Kate said. 'Or maybe he saw her potential and realised she could be a goldmine.'

'I'd put my money on love: a deep and abiding affection that's kept him by her side. It can't have been easy.'

'Or all the assets are in her name.'

'It's not always about money, Kate.'

'Not always. But mostly.'

'Still,' Lizzie said briskly, 'the fact is we still have no evidence to suggest Donna is responsible for Cameron's death, and while we might know more about her background, we still have no idea what she's doing living with a group of friends at what must seem like the end of the earth.'

'Another hunch here—I reckon Daisy and Mike Melrose know exactly what happened the night Cameron died. And I don't believe they'll ever talk about it.'

CHAPTER TWENTY-EIGHT

AFTER A SHORT WORKING DAY, and with the sun still a long way off the horizon, Sam felt a churning of the insides of his stomach, a restlessness, like he'd had one caffeine hit too many. On a whim, he hiked along the potholed tracks to the peak of Cutter Island.

There, he gazed at the open sea, the mirror flatness, the clear blue sky and told himself he was probably worried about Kate and he would have to learn to live with his gnawing uneasiness until the baby was safely delivered into the world. About to turn towards home, he caught sight of a thin black line, way off. A pencil stroke where sky joined ocean. Not sure what he was looking at, he waited. In seconds, a big-bellied mass of brutish clouds rose and swiped the innocence from a sunny, late spring day. He checked the radar on his phone. A brewing storm with a gnarly twist in its centre that Sam didn't trust. He called Kate. 'Big storm on the horizon. Meant to track out to sea but I dunno, Kate—it has a look of malevolence . . .'

'Malevolence,' Kate said. 'Hostile. Evil. Not up to Simon's usual standard.'

'I'm serious, love. If a storm hits hard, you could be stuck for days. With the bub . . .'

'Baby. Not bub. And we're okay. Lizzie's little shack is rock-solid.'

Sam, tempted to ask a whole lot of questions about Kate's health, the baby, the looming due date, held back, knowing it would annoy her and break the thin thread of intimacy somehow created by distance. 'How's Lizzie's ankle coming along?' he asked instead.

'Stronger every day. She's amazing.'

'I delivered the stuff for the bub.' He wanted to snatch back the word.

'Gotta go. Lizzie needs her meds.'

Kate ended the call. Sam cursed himself for a fool.

ॐ

Kate dismissed Sam's worries, but Lizzie went outside to sniff the air, check the trees, see whether the leaves were folding in on themselves a little, as they did when the elements signalled apocalypse.

'Anything?' Kate asked.

Lizzie raised her eyes to the sky, carelessly blue. 'Doesn't look nasty yet but something's coming. You can smell it. As if the air is burning.'

'Maybe it will turn on itself and head out to sea.'

Lizzie frowned and gave a little shake of her head. 'All storms can be capricious. Big storms are totally amoral.'

They sat like sentries on the verandah, holding cups of tea that grew cold, eyes, ears and noses tuned to the slightest shift in the atmosphere. After a while, a frivolous wind flicked dead leaves, tickled trees, then silence dropped like a curtain. An unworldly stillness descended on the bush.

'Better get inside,' Lizzie said. 'Whatever it is, it'll hit in a few minutes.'

Kate felt it then: a pressure in her ears, her skull, a rush of adrenaline, heart-pumping fear. She pushed Lizzie's wheelchair inside the house. Pulled the door shut behind her, shooting the deadbolts home, hoping they'd hold.

A low grumbling, throaty, feral, and a giant explosion, short, sharp, ear-splitting. She screamed, jumped. In seconds, day turned to night—lit an instant later as sheet lightning broke through storm clouds, casting an eerie, throbbing glow. Then fork lightning, sizzling, zigzagging, lethal. Kate felt a sharp pain in her lower back and grimaced. It passed quickly. She settled Lizzie in the kitchen and hurried around the house closing windows and distributing buckets and saucepans to catch leaks. Lizzie filled kettles and stoked the fire. 'Fill the tubs in the bathroom and laundry with water,' she instructed. 'A storm like this could knock out the pump.'

They heard a roar, like an oncoming train. The little shack shook. Windows rattled. Outside, trees bent double in a gale that had the power to lift the roof. The sky pulsated, white light, blackness, white light. Rain pummelled the roof, rock concert loud.

Kate shouted to be heard: 'Should we keep the medicinal cognac handy?'

Lizzie found a smile and nodded. 'Did I ever tell you that, when I was a baby, my mother gave me sherry the moment I cried?' she yelled.

Kate screamed over the noise: 'Mine too!'

They grinned, comrades in battle.

Lizzie again: 'Hope we're not sitting in a pile of toothpicks by the end of this.' Not quite joking.

Kate crossed to the dresser to get the cognac. Pain struck like a stab and she grabbed the edge of the dresser to stay upright. Warm fluid trickled down her legs. 'Lizzie?' she whispered, white-faced.

The old woman turned towards her.

'I don't think the water on the floor is a leak from the roof.'

'Oh shit,' Lizzie said, closing her eyes against the sight of Kate's damp trousers, trying to shut out the reality that a baby was on the way. She reached for her phone. *No network connection.* 'Oh shit.'

Kate snatched the phone out of her hands and pressed buttons frantically. 'Nothing.' She threw the phone on the table. 'Perfect,' she said, in tears. 'That's just perfect.'

Outside, the storm raged. Inside, Kate walked around a house that felt dangerously flimsy, sucking in air, letting it go. She heard the gunshot crack and crash of a tree hitting a roof and ran to the kitchen, frightened for Lizzie.

'Must have come down on the shed,' Lizzie said, smiling in a way she hoped was reassuring. 'I'm sorry, Kate, I shouldn't have let you come here.'

'It was my choice,' Kate said. 'And the bays will be copping it, too.' She sank into the soft hold of the old leather chair for a moment of respite. Struggled to her feet again, the pain a punch in her gut.

'Should I boil water?' Lizzie asked, anchored by a broken ankle and blind ignorance, feeling utterly useless.

'How the hell would I know?' Kate almost yelled, fear getting the better of her.

Lizzie went off to empty buckets and saucepans, full to the brim with dirty water from the leaky roof.

The rain kept on, a herd of galloping horses on the tin roof.

An hour later, the contractions were coming closer together. Kate went into her room and lay down on the bed, her emotions swinging from fear to fury. A woman who'd built safety nets into every venture, stuck in a tatterdemalion shack with no easy way out. She began to laugh.

Lizzie looked at her in alarm.

'Tatterdemalion. It's a great word. This shack, Lizzie, it's tatterdemalion.'

'Yes, dear, of course it is,' Lizzie agreed, because what else could she do, with Kate on the verge of hysteria? She sat close by, holding the young woman's hand, trying not to wince when it was squeezed so hard she was certain not a bone remained unbroken. Every so often, she rinsed a washcloth in cold water and wiped Kate's face with it, something she had seen done in old black-and-white movies when the heroine was struck down by anything from a raging fever to childbirth. It seemed to do the trick on celluloid. 'Women have babies in the field in Africa all the time,' Lizzie said, trying to comfort. 'It's perfectly natural.'

'This isn't Africa,' Kate said, looking away to hide her tears, her terror.

Lizzie struggled to think of distractions. 'What makes you happy, Kate?' she asked.

Kate stared at her in disbelief. 'Happy . . .'

Just then, the lights went out. Kate groaned and curled into a fetal position, closed her eyes, clenched her fists to hold back sobs. Lizzie negotiated her way to the kitchen, where she found a candle and matches. She returned to Kate's bedside, lit the candle and placed it on the bedside table. A thousand words of comfort raced through her mind, but they would sound hollow if spoken aloud. She stroked Kate's back and fought the urge to hum softly. The candle flickered in draughts that found their way through gaps in the floorboards. Lizzie had never been more conscious of the precariousness of her life in this fragile little shack, suddenly and painfully aware of the encroaching decrepitude of both her body and her home. She had lived too long, she thought, with nostalgia but not sadness. She stared at the young woman about to give birth and couldn't imagine how they would manage. Outside, the storm was deafening, furious, uncompromising.

Kate managed to nap a little in between contractions and Lizzie relaxed back in her wheelchair, waiting but with very little idea of what she could do to make sure this baby would launch safely into the world. After a while, for no reason she could later pinpoint, she was flooded with a sense of calmness, and a certainty that Kate and the baby would be just fine. Her touch on Kate's body lightened like the touch of Dorothy all those years ago; Dorothy, who had made her see that her spirit was not broken but only bent out of shape.

When Kate turned towards her, catching her hand, Lizzie said: 'We can do this. I know we can do this.' She held Kate's gaze. 'We are strong, tough and competent, and one day you will laugh and tell your child how a woman with a broken ankle helped to deliver a healthy baby in a raging storm high on an escarpment where sea eagles nested and goannas called in for smoko.'

Kate squeezed Lizzie's hand, then gasped and rolled over to face the wall.

෴

At the height of the storm, Sam stepped onto the deck into driving rain and a wind that scoured his face. For the umpteenth time, he tried Kate's phone, Lizzie's. His call went straight to voicemail. It's always the waiting, he thought, that has the power to break your spirit. He thought he saw the *Mary Kay* bucking on her mooring but, blinded by the wind, water in his eyes, the darkness, he couldn't be sure. The spotted gum near the deck creaked and groaned in what sounded like agony.

'Take the deck, the house, the *Mary Kay*, weather gods, but leave Kate and the baby alone,' he pleaded, his words muzzled by the noise.

He squeezed through the sliding door and into the creaking shelter of the house. There was nothing to do but wait.

෴

It was almost midnight when the rain reduced to a gentle susurration, and the roar of the storm moderated to a whisper. The Misses Skettle were the first to call Sam, knowing he'd be on alert. 'There's no need to worry about us, we're fine,' Violet said. 'The side wall of the kitchen is missing, along with most of our pots and pans, but we were planning a renovation anyway.'

Sam called Amelia, who handed the phone to Jimmy.

'Me mum's still quiverin',' he explained. 'Her chin's going hell for leather and she's stumped tryin' to get a proper word out. Me and Longfella are good. Tree came down on the laundry but me mum had finished the washin'. She's cranky she hung it on the line, but. Line's gone, along with me undies. And hers.'

Sam told the kid to stay home so he knew where to find him. He called Artie. The phone went to voicemail. He tried a second time with the same result. The old man, he suspected with a pang, had got his wish, and would be found lying on the seabed at first light, in the boat he always said would be his coffin.

Marcus called before Sam reached him. 'We are in tiptop spirits, my friend, and also all is intact, although my little runabout appears to have a hole in her beautiful snout. But this is nothing. We do not sweat what can be mended with a little effort and dedication. Ettie's tinnie, well, it is travelling of its own accord we know not where. We are more concerned for Kate and Lizzie. Ettie has been trying to make contact for more than an hour.'

'They should be okay. Storm looks like it headed a wee bit south of them and petered out. They'll call us when they can,' he said, not believing a word of it.

Marcus harrumphed and cleared his throat. 'But you see, the love of my life is concerned. Her instincts have taken hold, and she is quite certain this baby of you and Kate is trying to enter the world on this stormy night.'

Sam laughed to hide his own worry. 'Ettie and her instincts, mate, are famous for being, er, slightly out of tune with reality.'

He heard a scrabbling noise and then:

'Sam, it's Ettie. For your information, my instincts aren't too different from your radar, and I have an instinct *and* a radar signal telling me that we should get up there now.'

'It's midnight, Ettie, and black as pitch. No point killing ourselves trying to reach them unless we're sure there's a good reason.'

Marcus came back on the line. 'These are wise words, my friend.

Lizzie is also wise and Kate is very smart. To panic is to do harm and this is to be avoided.'

Sam dropped his voice to a murmur. 'Can't raise them on the phone, Chef. Concerned about Artie, too. He's gone quiet.'

'The *Mary Kay*?'

'Not sure. Fingers crossed.'

❧

Kate, exhausted, her eyes black with fear, held on to the bedhead and groaned. 'I can't do this, Lizzie, I can't do this.'

'Darling girl, of course you can,' Lizzie said soothingly. 'Childbirth is the most natural thing in the world.'

'No. I can't do it. I definitely cannot do it.' Kate gritted her teeth against another contraction. 'I've had enough, Lizzie. I've really had enough.'

'Keep going. You're doing fine,' Lizzie said, hoping it was true. 'And listen! Hear the quiet? The storm is over. As soon as it's light—'

Kate screamed: 'NO! I CAN'T DO THIS.'

Later, Lizzie told Ettie that Cliffy stepped out of the gloom like an apparition. For a long moment, she thought she was dreaming, that her exhaustion, her desperate need for help and her anxiety for Kate had blurred the edges of reality.

'Arrived in the nick of time, did I? Good job I wore me cleanest clothes. Farmer's sixth sense. Never fails.' Cliffy bent to kiss the top of Lizzie's head.

Lizzie slumped into the wheelchair like the air had gone out of her. Tears rolled down her face. She wiped them away and pushed back from the bedside. 'I imagine a cuppa wouldn't go astray,' she said, reaching to take the hand of a brave man who put the welfare of others ahead of his own. She held it against her cheek, unwilling to let go.

'Thought I'd check on you after the storm. Just as well I didn't wait till mornin', eh?'

Kate squirmed, rolled from side to side. 'Cliffy, I can't do this. I really, really can't.'

'Yes, you can, lass. Look at it this way. You've only got two legs to deliver, not four. Now cows, they have a much bigger job . . .' He shooed Lizzie out of the room. 'Towels and hot water. Ride to orders, old girl, and together we'll bring this baby of Kate's into a beautiful world stripped clean by an almighty storm and ready for a new life to make its mark.'

∽

At first light, Sam ran down to his jetty. His pontoon was missing, along with his tinnie, but he could see the *Mary Kay* holding tight to her mooring. Relief was replaced with puzzlement. Something not quite right. It took him a minute to realise the wheelhouse roof was gone, the arm of the crane broken, smashed through the gunnel and dangling over the side. He took a deep breath and told himself that she was still floating, and the repairs would be relatively minor. He focused on Artie, and called him again. Nothing. He looked around for a boat, any boat, that he could borrow to check on the old man with the busted legs. The jetties to his north were stripped bare of boards and pontoons. Only the pylons remained, lined up like soldiers standing to attention. To the south, jetties remained but pontoons had been ripped away, along with the boats usually tied to them.

Standing there, unsure what to do next, he saw Jimmy, a vision in fluoro orange, emerging out of the gloom, his ancient outboard coughing and belching black smoke, Longfellow perched on the bow, his head swivelling as though he were looking for familiar landmarks in a reconstructed landscape. Sam took a deep breath to steady his emotions. 'Tipped me worms out of me old tinnie, Sam. Used me mum's bandages and a pack of glue to patch the holes. She's floatin' good as a duck. Worked on me engine while me mum ran around the house tryin' to stay calm, but it's a bit suss. Just so you know.'

'You're a legend, Jimmy,' Sam said, stepping into the boat, patting the kid and the dog one after the other. 'Let's check on Artie. The old man has gone quiet, which, as we both know, is a worry.'

Jimmy's eyes clouded with anxiety. Without a word, he turned the tinnie in the direction of Oyster Bay.

Sam looked towards the Briny Café and made out a new silhouette. The rear deck was gone but the pylons remained. Next door to the café, the ferry wharf pontoon stood vertically against the shelter. Nothing that couldn't be fixed, Sam thought as the sun etched clouds on the horizon with gold and a few rays broke through like a promise, making a lie of the night.

Jimmy turned into Oyster Bay. Sam held his breath.

'She's gone,' Jimmy said, a catch in his throat. 'Artie's old boat, she's gone.'

Sam squinted into the distance, hoping the kid was wrong. Normally choked with an armada of pleasure boats that rarely left their moorings, the bay was almost empty. None of the surviving yachts belonged to Artie.

'Keep going, mate,' Sam said, cursing Artie's stubbornness and understanding it at the same time.

As they drew closer, Sam searched the murky depths for the outline of Artie's yacht so he could direct the kid away in time to stop him from diving overboard to rescue an old fella who'd be well and truly dead by now.

The kid suddenly stood, rocking the boat, and pointed at the shore. 'There, Sam! There she is! Lyin' on her side on the beach.' He turned to Sam with a shining face. 'He's gunna have a few cuts and bruises, I'll bet, but Artie'll be okay. I can feel it in me bones.'

'Run up on the beach beside her, mate, but stay with the boat.'

The kid opened his mouth to protest but caught the hard look in Sam's eyes. 'Aye, aye, cap'n.' He thought for a minute. 'But I'm sendin' Longfella with ya. Probably needs a piddle anyway.'

Approaching the beached yacht, Sam knocked on the hull, called out.

Silence.

He crab-crawled up the sloping deck on his knees and removed the hatch cover. Peered inside. Not too catastrophic, he thought, remembering that once upon a time Artie's yacht had sailed the unpredictable seas in a race from Sydney to Hobart, and had been built with double-jointed fittings to compensate for vertical travel.

There was no sign of the old man.

He dropped into the cabin and made his way forward, using the walls for balance. 'Artie? Mate?'

He heard a groan. A grunt.

'Artie, you old bugger. Oh, mate . . .'

Artie lay on his side, squished hard up against the wall, an empty bottle of rum clutched to his chest. His face was swollen and covered with bruises, his trackie daks drenched in blood. 'Worst night of me life,' he mumbled, 'and that's sayin' something.'

'More lives than a cat, Artie, that's the truth,' Sam said, unable to hide the relief in his voice. 'Expected to find you snoozing the big sleep at the bottom of Oyster Bay.'

'I'll let you know when I'm ready for that,' Artie said.

Braced against the doorway, Sam dialled emergency services. He looked at Artie. 'You reckon anything's broken?'

'Seein' as how I haven't felt even a twinge in me legs for two decades, I've got no way of knowin'.'

'Any chest pains?'

A glimmer of understanding appeared on the old man's face. 'Ooh, yeah. Sharp and short.'

Sam gave Artie the thumbs-up and relayed the message, giving explicit directions as to where to find him and the logistics involved.

'You'll be out of here in no time,' he said to Artie when he'd ended the call.

'Don't suppose you brought a rum toddy along, did ya?'

Sam prised the empty bottle out of Artie's hands. 'Had a bit on my mind, mate. Next time.'

∽

Cliffy helped Kate to deliver a baby girl at ten past five in the morning, the time meticulously recorded in a spiral notebook by Lizzie. The birth went smoothly, Cliffy reassured both women. Afterwards, to give Kate her privacy, he went off to make his own cuppa.

Lizzie followed him a few moments later. In the kitchen, she looked at Cliffy, her eyes wide with query.

'Perfectly normal,' Cliffy said, without having to be asked. 'The lass is like a heifer, still a bit bemused by the process and not sure she wants to have anything to do with the calf. But she'll come good. Nearly all of 'em do.'

Lizzie noted the word *nearly* but didn't have anything to add. Cliffy handed her a steaming cuppa and stoked the fire to make toast.

'Must've been some damage to the solar system. I'll start up the generator when I'm refuelled,' he said. 'I'll take a good look around after I've checked me cows haven't run off in the storm. Has she mentioned a name for the bub?'

'No. She's barely said a word.'

Cliffy patted her shoulder and handed her the toasting fork. 'Might as well make yourself useful while you're sittin' there. Butter in the fridge, is it? And, if you've got some handy, a bit of—'

'Apricot jam!'

ᖰᕤ

By the end of the day, the storm damage added up to hundreds of millions. Outside the relative shelter of Cook's Basin, half the coastline had been rearranged. Cliffs where once there'd been dunes and beaches. Beaches where once there'd been cliffs. Ritzy water-side homes had partially collapsed into the sea, along with their swimming pools, cabanas and, in some cases, living rooms and kitchens. Yachts lay like beached whales on the rooftops of two marinas. Fishing boats were flung two blocks up the embankment to land upside down in the canopy of gum trees. A tan-and-white spaniel, sucked into the vortex when the roof came off the family home, was found wandering a kilometre away. When the media filmed his joyful reunion with his owner, there wasn't a dry eye in the country.

On Cutter Island, the community rolled up its sleeves with long-suffering sighs and stoically began the big clean-up. Chainsaws chewed out a hard rock refrain all day. Neighbours returned bits and pieces that didn't belong to them, kids competed to retrieve *treasure* from bays clogged with so much detritus a cruise ship might have sunk. There was a moment's silence on the island when it was learned that Glenn's indomitable barge had broken into small pieces and could not be resurrected. The news of Artie's miraculous survival took some of the sting out of Glenn's tragic loss.

When darkness descended, the island came alive, candlelight imbuing a sacred mood, some said, that triggered an urge to drop to their knees to give thanks for being spared. Romantic, insisted committed atheists, quickly dismissing what they felt was a maudlin reaction to a beautiful sight. Inconvenient, lamented the realists, who knew that in another twenty-four hours the beers in their fridges would be too warm to drink. Someone mentioned a recent delivery of red wine that had survived under the house and which, due to the uncommon circumstances, could be distributed to those bereft of supplies with only a minimum surcharge.

Some people called it a cyclone. Others insisted it had the characteristics of a tornado, never mind the fact that cyclones or tornados weren't natural to Cook's Basin. Whatever it was called, it was a wonder, everyone said, that no one had been killed. Even the most committed non-believers made a sketchy attempt to thank whoever oversaw the cosmos for their many blessings.

CHAPTER TWENTY-NINE

SAM LEARNED HE HAD A daughter when communications were restored late that night. He sat down on a kitchen chair and wept with relief and joy. Made plans to visit at first light the following day.

'Come on foot,' Lizzie told him. 'All the roads in the park are closed and half the trees on the escarpment are in a paddock somewhere out west.' She sketched a quick map, photographed and texted it.

Sam called Ettie, even though it was late, because he knew she would never forgive him if he withheld news of the birth for more than five minutes.

Marcus answered the phone, sounding sleepy but alarmed. 'Tell me this is good news,' he said, 'because I am too old for any more excitement.'

'I'd better tell Ettie first, Chef, or I'll be slapped with a lifetime ban from the café.'

'Ah,' Marcus said, understanding instantly from Sam's joyful tone that a baby had safely entered the world. He tiptoed into the bedroom and gently shook Ettie awake. 'Sam has news,' he said quietly, smiling widely so she would know it was of right kind. He went to the kitchen to make hot chocolate while Ettie and Sam talked. When he returned, she gave him a long look that spoke volumes. 'Yes, yes,' he said, 'your instinct has proved, as always, infallible.'

Ettie fell back against the pillows and accepted a mug of rich dark cocoa that held the subtle but definite tang of cardamom, cinnamon and vanilla. 'Once a chef, always a chef,' she murmured dreamily.

'Of course, my love. What else?'

At 4 am, Sam's phone buzzed. He sat bolt upright. Don't let it be about my daughter, he thought, knowing that any call outside normal waking hours rarely brought good news. He saw the caller ID and let his breath out with a hiss.

'Richard! Thought you'd be tucked up in bed and planning a well-earned sleep-in.'

'Had a call from paramedics who have just attended a death in Stringybark Bay. Circumstances a bit iffy, they said.'

'Who's dead?'

'No prizes for guessing. Thought you might want to come along, given your long and colourful history with the residents.'

Sam was already pulling on his clothes. 'The *Mary Kay* is out of action. Can you pick me up at the end of my jetty? Oh, and mate?'

'Yeah?'

'Bring a cigar if you can lay your hands on one.'

'Boy or a girl?'

'A girl. Born at dawn and delivered by a farmer in whose debt I will forever remain.'

'Good on you, mate. And congratulations. No cigar, though. Don't hold with dragging a whole lot of filthy muck into your lungs . . .'

'Yeah, yeah. Save the lecture. See you in a tick.'

ა

By the time the police boat slipped almost noiselessly into Stringybark Bay, a faint glow had appeared in the east. Morning mist rose lazily, like puffs of smoke from campfires in rainforest gullies. The dawn sky was crisp and clean, dotted with a few stubborn stars. The bush, where slivers of first light caught tips, looked like someone had taken a scrubbing brush to every leaf and added a spit and polish for good measure.

Stringybark Bay was eerily empty of yachts, and the shore, naked and stony at low tide, was littered with rags, clothing and ripped sails. A tree had smashed through Georgie's boatshed but missed her house. She'd been one of the lucky ones, though Sam wasn't sure she'd see it that way. Further along, rooftops were swathed in blue tarpaulins, while the trees that had fallen through them were now reduced to logs cut to size for next winter's fires.

When they reached the estuary where the freshwater creek spilled into the blue lagoon, Sam saw three commuter boats tangled in the treetops of the mangroves, way out of the reach of the *Mary Kay* when she was back in working order. It would take months, not weeks, to restore the area to its former glory, Sam thought, and even then, stuff would continue to surface for years.

'Six hours of mayhem and six years of recovery,' Richard Baines said, as though he could read Sam's mind.

He swung the boat towards the GeriEcstasy jetty, one of the few intact, although the fancy sign was missing, along with the chains that had held it to the rail.

'More misery for this mob,' Richard said grimly. 'Poor bastards.'

The house, tucked in a nook and somehow protected, looked unscathed. In the early dawn light, Gavin Flowerdale and David Kinane, wearing floral bermuda shorts, white T-shirts and waterproof sneakers, and carrying rubbish bags filled with flotsam and jetsam, waved from the seawall as they made their way back to the house. There was a lightness about them that Sam had never seen before. No death was a good death, he thought, but Donna's demise must have been like a release from purgatory. He checked his watch, anxious to finish with the GeriEcstasies as soon as decently possible and begin the trek to meet his daughter for the first time.

'Bet my life Donna died of natural causes,' Sam said quietly as the launch came alongside. 'It wasn't in any of them to knock her off. They protected her like a child.'

With the launch secured, they made their way towards the front door and were met by the two men. 'A sad day for you blokes,' Richard said, shaking their hands.

They both smiled and shrugged. 'Happens to us all in the end,' Gavin said.

They took off their shoes by the door and, barefoot, led the way to the kitchen. The remaining members of the household were gathered around the table, drinking cups of tea and eating toast, chatting as though it were just another ordinary day in paradise. They were still wearing pyjamas and dressing-gowns, except for

Mike Melrose, who was his usual picture of sartorial elegance in immaculate chinos, a pale blue shirt and tan boat shoes. He rose unsteadily and greeted Sam, laying a hand on his shoulder as if they were old comrades. 'Good of you to come,' he said. He turned to Richard. 'There'll be an autopsy, I expect.'

Richard nodded. 'Standard procedure under the circumstances.'

Daisy came forward in her wheelchair: 'Tea? Coffee? I doubt either of you has had any breakfast. Sally, perhaps you could do the honours.'

Richard looked at his watch. Daisy, noting the gesture, said: 'Before you get down to business, we have a story to tell. It might take a while. If you'd bear with me . . .'

'Coffee would be great,' Sam said, catching Richard's eye, signalling he could hang around for a while and knowing Kate would want details when she was up to hearing them.

'Yeah. Same for me,' Richard said, without meeting anyone's eyes.

David and Gavin fetched extra chairs from the dining room. Sally and Sheila bustled about, boiling the kettle, making a fresh pot of tea, coffee in a plunger. They heated milk in a glass jug in the microwave, placed it together with a bowl of sugar on the table. Sheila offered to make more toast but no one wanted any, so she filled a plate with shortbread biscuits that looked homemade and set it down next to the milk. When everything was done and all but Melrose, who stood by the rear window looking out at the cliff face, were seated around the table, Daisy cleared her throat.

'Once upon a time . . .' she began.

Later, Sam would say it felt like the edginess, the stiffness and rushed activity of the group, suddenly ceased on a long exhale. Shoulders relaxed, hands stilled. Anxious eyes and tight mouths became serene. As though they'd accepted their fate and if the guillotine were to fall, so be it. They had done their best. Melrose remained apart but he turned towards his friends, his head slightly tilted, with a small smile, more of gratitude than pleasure, on his lips. He rested against the window ledge, his legs crossed at the ankles, his hands held together loosely.

He's known this day would come for a long time, Sam thought, watching him. He's waiting for Daisy to bring an end to the heartache and effort of holding on to secrets, protecting the guilty. Then he will speak.

Richard studied his hands where they lay on his lap, picking at a fingernail. He hated confessions. Especially when they sought to condone the sin.

'Once upon a time,' Daisy repeated. 'I use the phrase in homage to Donna, who began all her stories this way.' She took a deep breath.

'Donna's early life has always been a mystery to us. Our understanding of her begins when she scored a minor role in a soap opera at the age of 18. At the time, Mike'—she nodded towards Melrose—'was the editor of a gossipy little magazine about the television industry. An interview with Donna landed on his desk; in it, she talked about losing her parents in a fire. He threw it back at the reporter. "This is attention-seeking bullshit," he said. "Tell her to either come up with the proof or invent something more believable if she wants to make the cover." Intending to kill the story, he took a quick look at the pictures, and he saw it at once. That extra little quirk of nature that sets one person apart from the rest. Indefinable, irresistible. Star quality. He called the reporter back. "Get her in here with her agent," he said. No agent, he was told. He asked for her telephone number and rang her the same day. They met for dinner. He fell in love. He quit his job, became her manager and enrolled in a business degree. University is where we all met and our friendship, which has endured for nearly six decades, began.'

Melrose came forward. 'Just so you know, I was scrupulous in my financial dealings. I took a modest commission out of her earnings, but I also set up a trust fund in her name. If anything happened to me, I wanted her to be secure. To my surprise, I turned out to be a pretty good investor. By the time Donna's . . . personality became a serious problem among her colleagues, she was worth a considerable amount of money. I'd also built a healthy portfolio of my own and continued as an investor after Donna's career ended.' His speech over, he returned to his perch on the windowsill.

Sally held up the teapot in a question. People shook their heads. Gavin reached for a shortbread biscuit. He bit into it noisily and smiled an apology. Daisy waited a polite moment and then resumed her story.

'Donna created problems on the set, but Mike handled them discreetly until an argument with a co-star escalated into a fistfight. The co-star was taken to hospital with concussion and a broken nose and later went public with the story. Donna's career ended abruptly. Mike had always understood Donna had behavioural issues, but he'd blamed the pressure of her work, her high profile. Grievous bodily harm was far more serious than a prod or a push, a strong verbal exchange. Donna needed psychiatric help, and he found the best doctors in the country. After a year of treatment, doctors told Mike that Donna had severe psychopathic tendencies and would always be a danger to the community. Mike and Donna had never married—she refused his offers—which made his care for her more difficult under the law of the day. To prevent her being institutionalised, Mike became her legal guardian and assumed responsibility for her wellbeing. Of course, Mike told us about her problems. He warned us she could be violent. But we were young, Mike was our friend, Donna was on heavy medication to control her mood swings and when we all got together—not often in those early days, when we were building careers and raising families—she was entertaining, fun and seemed quite normal. Her issues didn't seem real to us for a long time.'

Daisy paused, flagging. Her husband reached for her hand. She threw him a grateful look and, after a deep breath, continued.

'Rob and I were the first in the group to need financial help. Drought in the early eighties hit us hard. Without Donna and Mike's help, we would have gone bankrupt. When the stock market crashed in 1987, Sheila and Gavin were over-extended and the bank threatened to foreclose on their retail properties. Donna and Mike came to the rescue. Sally and Michael were in a different situation. Newly returned from France and Spain, where they'd studied cheesemaking, they had the passion but lacked the funds to set up their business. There's no need to spell out where the money came from. Cameron's business was rescued so many times, we lost count. The scale, compared to the rest of us, was quite small. A few thousand here and there.' Daisy looked over at Mike. 'As far as I'm aware, monies were never reimbursed.'

Mike nodded in agreement. 'It didn't matter. Cameron and Donna were soulmates. She adored him. I would have paid him for the time he spent with her, if he'd asked.'

Daisy added, 'The larger debts were repaid, but without interest.'

Again, Mike nodded.

'About ten years ago,' Daisy continued, 'Donna's episodes escalated dangerously and happened more frequently. Doctors increased her medication but warned she would get worse quickly. It was time for the rest of us to pay the interest on our debts. Mike came up with the idea of GeriEcstasy, a place where Donna felt free but where she could be contained. She could be with old friends whom she trusted and who were able to understand and forgive her . . . flaws. But Donna had to be convinced that, once more, we needed her financial help in order to retire comfortably, and so the charade of pooling our resources to make ends meet in our retirement began. Once begun, it had to continue. We never intended to bring Lizzie into the house, thought Donna would veto the idea, but she connected with her immediately. A playwright—who would have guessed? And we were trapped.'

Sam interrupted: 'Cameron . . . ?'

Mike moved closer to the table. 'It was late. I was reading in the sitting room. I didn't want to disturb Donna, who had gone to bed. Daisy stuck her head in the door and said she couldn't sleep and thought she'd make a hot chocolate; would I like a mug? Brian had mentioned going for a walk at dinner, so when Cameron appeared and said it was a beautiful night, a full moon rising, we figured they were going off together. He looked so young and boyish in his enthusiasm, Daisy and I were caught up in the idea. After she made us both a hot chocolate, we went out to see the moon from the jetty. We found Donna in her dressing-gown, wearing one idiotic stiletto—she thought high heels would make her tall enough to do some damage—standing over Cameron's body, that wretched boule at her feet, sobbing. She'd meant to strike Brian, whom she felt had replaced her in Cameron's affections.'

Daisy said, 'We made sure nobody else in the house guessed what had happened and, from that moment, neither of us let Donna out of our sight. When she showed signs of veering out of control, Mike upped her drugs—with medical consent, of course. But she started to catch on. On the day of the picnic, she only pretended to swallow her pills. We found them in the bathroom sink when we returned from that horrific picnic.' Daisy fixed her gaze on Sam. 'You must understand that we would never have intentionally put anyone at risk. Never. We have no words to ask forgiveness for what happened to Jimmy. Mike and I accept full responsibility and we will find ways to make amends. As for Lizzie, if she can ever forgive us, there will always be a place for her here, but we will return her money and pay all the costs of her move if she feels she can never return.'

Melrose took up the story. 'Donna was already on borrowed time when we came to Stringybark Bay. Skin and bone, her energy fuelled by prescription drugs and the mania that was part of her condition, it was always a matter of when, not if.'

'As it is for all of us, dearest,' Daisy said, to the soft murmur of, 'Hear, hear.'

'The dog bite caused an infection which we treated with antibiotics, but I think you'll find the level of drug toxicity in her system was the underlying cause of death,' Melrose said. 'Her body just couldn't take any more.'

Silence descended on the group and for a while no one spoke.

Finally, Richard cleared his throat and stood up. 'Donna's death. I don't mean to suggest foul play but, like I said, there'll be an autopsy. It's routine when someone dies at home in unknown circumstances.' And in a few words, he made it clear there would be no repercussions for the tragic death of Cameron Smith.

Melrose nodded, returned to his spot by the window and looked out at sunlight etching delicate tree ferns, highlighting the dance of insects, an early breeze rippling cabbage palm leaves like fingers on piano keys. 'On a good day,' he murmured, 'she had no equal.' A tear rolled down his cheek and dropped on his shirt, leaving a dark mark.

His friends knew to leave him to his grief.

∽

On the boat, Sam said, 'Nice touch, letting Daisy and Melrose off the hook.'

'If they were thirty years younger, I'd have had no choice but to charge them with withholding information. But look at them, Sam. Death is stalking the whole household; by the time the case got to court they could all be dead anyway.'

'Take the credit for a good deed, my friend. You don't often get the chance.'

CHAPTER THIRTY

A FEW HOURS LATER, SAM gave Kate and Lizzie an account of the resolution of the mystery of Cameron's death while he sat on the verandah of the battered shack with his newborn baby girl in his arms. In turn, Kate explained what she'd concluded from Edith's research although none of it could ever be proven in a court of law.

Halfway through the sorry tale, Cliffy emerged from the bush in his work overalls, holding a box that looked to be half a century old. He climbed the four steps to the landing, grunting a little, and lifted the lid to reveal four cigars that smelled surprisingly fresh. 'Been in me cellar for as long as I can remember,' he explained, 'where conditions are prime. Always meant to smoke 'em on special occasions, but I guess there weren't enough of those to finish the box.' He looked at the faces around him. 'Not sure if that doesn't sound a bit sad at this end of me life.'

'Agnes probably hid them. She hated the smell, remember?' Lizzie said.

The old man nodded. 'Or perhaps after Agnes died, nothing was ever special enough.'

Sam, who'd begun pacing the length of the verandah, patting his daughter gently on the back and making cooing sounds, shifted her tiny body into the crook of one arm to leave a hand free to shake Cliffy's. 'Owe you a debt that can never be repaid.'

'Nothing to it,' Cliffy said, shuffling his feet. 'Had me flummoxed for a second, when I could only find two legs . . .'

Sam laughed.

Kate looked away, a flush rising from her chest.

'Now lass,' Cliffy said, 'nothing to be embarrassed about. Natural as breathing, is birth.'

Kate struggled to her feet. 'If I know you, Cliffy, you'll be hanging out for a cuppa. How about I go inside and make one?'

The old man's face lit up. 'Milk and one sugar, in case it's slipped your mind,' he said.

'Lizzie's made scones for Sam, but there's a few left over.'

'Day just gets better and better,' Cliffy said.

When Kate was out of earshot, Cliffy filled Lizzie in on the news. 'Tracks'll be negotiable tomorrow, but not in that flimsy tin can of Kate's. I'll come by in me tractor and take her and the bub to the bitumen, where I'm assuming this young man will meet her in his chariot to take her to hospital for a thorough going-over.'

Sam halted abruptly and gazed at the child in his arms. He saw two eyes, ten fingers, two ears. Cliffy had already mentioned two legs. 'Kate's okay, right? No problems there?'

'None as far as I know, but heifers need a bit of extra attention with their first go.'

Sam frowned, at a loss.

Kate, returning with the tea tray, explained. 'Heifers are first time mothers,' she said.

Sam looked at her, still out of his depth.

'Cattle,' she elaborated.

'Ah. Gotcha.' He resumed his slow stroll along the verandah, his eyes glued to the tiny red-faced bundle in his arms. 'We'll have to find a name for you . . .'

'I was thinkin' Cliffy, meself,' Cliffy said, grinning. 'But since she's a girl, s'pose it's out of the question.'

Lizzie laughed. Sam grinned. Kate resumed her seat, lacing her fingers, her hands neatly in her lap.

Lizzie and Cliffy exchanged a look, then Cliffy gave a little shake like a dog and broke the spell. 'I've taken a gander at the shed, Lizzie. It's beyond saving. I've said me piece about the roof on the shack more times than I can count on both hands. Next strong breeze, it's gunna break apart. Wish I could soften the blow but that's a fact, plain and simple.'

Sam heard the exchange and broke the heavy stillness that had settled on the group. 'One working bee and it'll be good as new,' he said firmly.

Cliffy shook his head and made a hissing sound like he'd been pricked with a pin. 'Fixin' the roof would be same as flushin' good money down the drain. White ants in the roof struts, the floor joists. It's just about a rebuild from the ground up.' He reached out to take Lizzie's hand. 'Sorry, love.' He brightened. 'There's a spare room with me for as long as you like. Agnes would see the sense of it.'

The thought made Lizzie erupt in laughter. 'We wouldn't last half a day sharing a house and you know it. I'd rearrange your tools, iron your overalls and buy you colourful shirts and racy socks. You'd be dead from shock within a week.'

An expression of relief spread across Cliffy's face but, gentleman that he was, he held firm to his offer. 'Always there for you, Lizzie. Never forget that.'

Kate, who'd remained steadfastly quiet, almost otherworldly, with her eyes fixed far away on an invisible horizon, shifted in her chair. 'Donna is dead. You own a share of GeriEcstasy, Lizzie. This might be the true beginning.'

'From what was said during the big confession, you'd be welcomed back like a prodigal daughter,' Sam said. 'They love you, Lizzie, and they feel pretty awful about what happened.'

Kate rose to her feet, the black smudges under her eyes accentuating the blue in them. 'I might have a rest, if nobody minds.'

The men stood aside to let her pass. Sam felt a crackling, like his heart was short-circuiting, a fluttering of fear.

Lizzie chewed her bottom lip thoughtfully. 'My old armchair. It would fit nicely in front of the window looking onto the mangroves.'

'Could load me tractor with all your favourites,' Cliffy said. He reached for a second scone, smiling widely.

∽

Kate and her still nameless baby were kept in hospital overnight for observation but discharged the following morning with a clean bill of health. Sam borrowed Marcus's car, already festooned with child restraint hardware under Ettie's strict orders. Sam's banged-up, single-cab ute, she decreed, was not the way to bring home a new baby, if it was even legal. Bursting with pride and gratitude and happiness and relief and—well, everything—he collected his new family and returned to a noisy, joyful welcoming committee at the Square.

The Misses Skettle, wiry pinkish hair pulled into neat buns tied with pink ribbons, were turned out in their best day wear—pink shirts, rosy pink skirts, deep pink ballet slippers. Each carried a basket filled with their homemde preserves (from pink to deep red) and special fruitcake (wrapped in pink gingham fabric) laced with a tot of brandy which they felt would be permissible and perhaps even medicinal, now the baby was born. Jenny flung a quick salute in Kate's direction then rushed back to the café to serve the growing queue of caffeine addicts at the counter. Ettie flung open the rear door of the car before Sam turned off the engine and scooped the child into her arms, laughing and crying simultaneously. Marcus helped Kate from the seat with such tenderness, Kate also cried. Fast Freddy, who'd hung back, stepped forward with a clean handkerchief and offered it with a ceremonious little bow. Kate accepted it gratefully, leaving her hand on his wrist for a moment in appreciation and affection, and it was amazing, people said later, how the tired anxiety on her face dissolved into something close to contentment. Freddy often had that effect on people, they added.

A shout carried across the water and everyone turned to look. Jimmy stood in his barely resurrected tinnie, waving his arms madly. 'Me engine's just carked it,' he yelled. Amelia, wearing a cream silk dress festooned with crimson hibiscus, struggled to her feet, waved enthusiastically, lost her balance and tipped backwards, her legs flung in the air before she hit the water with an almighty splash.

Longfellow peered over the bow and gave a single yip. Jimmy lifted his shoulders expressively towards the onshore crowd and tossed his mum a rope. He slipped an oar into each rowlock and began rowing, hauling his mum behind until she caught up and swam ahead. In her day, she'd been a powerful force in the water. The dress would never be the same, she told people later.

Jack the Bookie materialised out of thin air and sidled up to Sam. 'A girl, is it?' he whispered, needing confirmation the grapevine was accurate before he paid out the punters. Then he asked slyly: 'And her name?'

Sam guffawed and slapped him on the back so hard he sent him flying. 'All in good time, mate.'

❦

A week after Sam delivered the most precious cargo of his life to her new home in Oyster Bay, Sam joined Ettie and the chef for dinner on their deck. Kate had declined their invitation. 'Still grappling with lack of sleep,' she said, yawning loudly over the phone to allay any doubts.

At the end of a dinner remarkable for its simplicity, Ettie asked, 'Does the baby have a name yet? Jack the Bookie is getting hounded by punters with money riding on it.'

'Nah. Kate can't decide.'

Ettie patted his arm and smiled encouragement. 'How about naming her after your mother?'

'Might be best to stay away from all close family references. Could ask Kate if she'd be happy to name her after you, Ettie, if you wouldn't mind?'

'Lovely thought, but no, love.'

The chef said, 'This child is her own person, yes? She needs not to be strung up by old ties. A new name without history—perhaps this would work?'

'Maybe,' Sam said, and they sat silently awhile. He shifted in his seat, straightened his back. 'Don't laugh, but my mum used to play a piece of music called "Clair de lune". Always loved it. She told me the name meant moonlight, not sure if that's right or not, but maybe Claire for the bub? I dunno . . .'

'That's inspired, Sam,' Ettie said, clapping her hands softly. 'A beautiful, gentle name. What do you think, Marcus?'

'Inspired, my love. Indeed.'

'I'll run it past Kate. If she agrees, Jack'll scoop the pool and old Artie won't speak to me for a year, even though I saved the old bugger's life, what with the tide coming in and him scrunched up tight as a crab in the shell of the bunk.'

∽

A month later, after closing time, Ettie and Marcus hosted a naming ceremony on the newly reconstructed rear deck of the Briny Café, spruced up for the occasion with a coat of paint and decorated with potted blue hydrangeas that picked up the colour of the sea at noon. At Kate's insistence, it was a quiet affair.

Artie, who was now a full-paying bed-and-board member of Amelia and Jimmy's household, travelled on the repaired *Mary Kay* in his new, battery-powered wheelchair. He wore freshly laundered trousers, a short-sleeved checked shirt, and grumbled to anyone who'd listen that Amelia had burned his trackie daks in the backyard while the neighbours watched over the fence and applauded. The stink of them, apparently, had crossed boundaries. Jimmy, afraid of scaring the baby with his assorted fluoro garments, wore a white T-shirt with navy shorts. His sneakers, which he considered out of Claire's eyeline, were luminous green with pulsating lights around the heels. Longfellow, a baby-blue bow tie around his neck, lay curled in a corner, as if ashamed.

Lizzie, managing well with a walking stick, although the moon boot remained, wore a simple black linen shift and a gold chain around her neck lent to her by Daisy. She handed over a parcel containing three sets of beautifully knitted bootees with matching jackets and beanies. Kate and Lizzie had together agreed that they would stay silent about what they'd found out about Donna's violent and chaotic early years, the suspicions surrounding her parents' deaths. Hearing the results of their research would only add to the guilt and grief of the GeriEcstasies. Nothing, they agreed, would *ever* be said.

Cliffy, who'd been persuaded to descend from his eyrie for the event, and who arrived with the earthy scent of cattle embedded in his overalls, took off his boots at the café door out of respect for the new timber deck. Lizzie offered to darn his socks later.

Ettie, who'd slipped upstairs to the penthouse to change out of her working clothes at the end of the day, was ethereal in a caftan that picked up the tawny green hues of the bay. Marcus, who'd forgotten to remove his toque after completing an afternoon shift in the café kitchen to prepare for the event, could not take his eyes off her.

Sam wore his best clobber, usually reserved for Christmas Day, while Kate, who had an empty look in her eyes that made Ettie feel uneasy until she put it down to the exhaustion of a new baby, was neat in navy trousers and a yellow silk shirt. No one had the heart to mention the blob of baby spit on her shoulder. Claire, whose features had lost their rubbery softness and who now looked more like her mother (to the relief of all concerned) held court from a cradle crafted by Fast Freddy, who could not attend the gathering as the timing clashed with his water taxi shift. Everyone guessed the shy man would have wilted under compliments about his handwork. Amelia's gossamer-soft blanket hung over the end of the cradle.

The food, which included a bucket of fresh prawns in homage to the baby's father, was matched with the finest champagne from the chef's cellar. It was spectacular. Of course. The prawns were garnished to the chef's exacting standards. Of course.

 birth and while the main night reflects a full year or more of novelty, providing for mating.

After the gathering, Sam ferried Kate and their daughter to Oyster Bay in his new tinnie, complete with a key start, clears and a bimini to hold back draughts and keep Claire dry if a squall should erupt without warning. They had a smooth ride over a plate-glass sea, twisted with silver in the late twilight. The outboard purred, and Sam steered from a side console that gave him an update on fuel usage, engine revs and boat speed. 'State-of-the-art,' Sam said, tapping the screen on the dash. Kate gave him a wan smile but didn't bother to look. Sam could sense exhaustion leaking from her skin and bones like brake fluid when the cable had been cut. He took his life in his hands: 'I could help with the midnight and four am feeds, if you like.'

A tear rolled down her cheek. Sam wiped it away with his thumb. Kate caught his hand in hers and held it against her face.

'We're in this together, Kate,' Sam said softly.

'You and me . . .'

'One step at a time. Right now, it's all about Claire.'

Kate let go of his hand. He reached to feel the silky texture of Claire's hair and skin, inhale the purity of new life. Her eyelids fluttered and Kate shifted the carrier on her chest just a little.

'The baby. Is that enough for you?' Kate asked, her head turned away.

Sam slipped the boat into neutral and let it rock on the rise and fall of a sleepy sea. He rested his eyes on his daughter, lashes fanning her cheeks, little fist in her mouth. 'More than enough,' he said, knowing even as the words were out of his mouth that he was still hurting and, while the pain might reduce to a dull ache in time, it would never entirely let go.

'Sam? Did Simon come up with *tatterdemalion*?' Kate asked.

Sam looked at her, puzzled. 'Tatter-what?'

'Tatterdemalion.' She pronounced it carefully, syllable by syllable.

'Nah. Not a word I'd forget. Why?'

'Lizzie says I yelled it out during labour. More than once. She thought I was referring to the state of her shack.'

'Are you going to tell me what it means?'

Kate smiled. 'Ramshackle. It means ramshackle. I wonder . . .'

'Yes, love?'

'Whether I was babbling about us. You and me. Our relationship.'

He felt hope flicker. 'Not completely wrecked, then, just ramshackle.'

'Yes.'

He restarted the engine and looked ahead. 'Tatterdemalion. Has a solid ring to it, doesn't it?'

Again, Kate smiled. A light shone in her eyes.

Sam reached over and encased her delicate hand in his. With his free hand, he slipped the boat into gear, and they continued on their tatterdemalion way.

ACKNOWLEDGEMENTS

NO BOOK HAPPENS WITHOUT THE golden input of committed publishers, editors and designers. My heartfelt thanks to everyone who worked on *Sleepless in Stringybark Bay*, but particularly Ali Lavau, whose steel trap mind saved me from more than one dastardly sink hole and who kept the story tightly on track.

Also, this book wouldn't have happened without the input of the kind people on Mitchell Island, New South Wales, who live in retired communal independence and on whom the premise (not the plot!) of GeriEcstasy is based. The rest is fiction and I own all mistakes, but there is homage, as always, to the kind and colourful offshore community of Pittwater that never ceases to inspire.